P9-DMG-865

VAGABOND

VAGABOND

Gerald Seymour

Thomas Dunne Books
St. Martin's Press New York

This is a work of fiction. All of the characters, organizations, and events portrayed in this novel are either products of the author's imagination or are used fictitiously.

THOMAS DUNNE BOOKS.
An imprint of St. Martin's Press.

Printed in the United States of America. For information, address St. Martin's Press, 175 Fifth Avenue, New York, N.Y. 10010.

www.thomasdunnebooks.com
www.stmartins.com

Library of Congress Cataloging-in-Publication Data

Names: Seymour, Gerald.
Title: Vagabond / Gerald Seymour.
Description: First U.S. edition. | New York : Thomas Dunne Books/St. Martin's Press, 2016.
Identifiers: LCCN 2015037442| ISBN 9781250075659 (hardcover) | ISBN 9781466887084 (e-book)
Subjects: LCSH: Great Britain. MI5—Officials and employees—Fiction. | Special operations (Military science)—Great Britain—Fiction. | Revenge—Fiction. | BISAC: FICTION / Espionage. | FICTION / War & Military. | GSAFD: Suspense fiction. | Spy stories.
Classification: LCC PR6069.E734 V34 2016 | DDC 823/.914—dc23
LC record available at http://lccn.loc.gov/2015037442

First published in Great Britain by Hodder & Stoughton, an Hachette UK company

First U.S. Edition: January 2016

10 9 8 7 6 5 4 3 2 1

For
Nicholas and James
and
Alfie

PROLOGUE

Behind them a smear of a softer grey crested the mountain and the forest's tree tops, but in front the rain, in usual obstinacy, refused to move on. They had been in the makeshift hide since an hour after dusk the previous evening, and had alternately slept and kept watch on the farmhouse. In front of them, way beyond Camaghy and Shanmaghry, and in line with the chambered grave of Neolithic times, was the building and the lit yard. Now, both were awake and alert. They watched and waited.

It was, of sorts, a reward for their patience. The flash, beyond the Pomeroy road, even in the low cloud, was brilliant.

'That's our baby,' Dusty murmured.

The sound of the explosion seemed slow to reach them, as if the cloud and the rain impeded it. Desperate – as he was known with some affection inside the only family he had – thought the noise, distant and muffled, sounded like a paper bag bursting after a kid had blown it up. 'Went off like a good one,' he whispered into Dusty's ear.

What Dusty had called 'our baby' and Desperate a 'good one' was likely to have been the blast of an eighth of a tonne of chemical fertiliser fired by a commercial detonator buried in the pliable putty of a pound and a half of Semtex. The flash was fast spent and the sound had dissipated against the higher slope of the mountain. The cloud was too dense for any smoke to force its way up against the rain.

They needed good hearing and the vantage-point in the hedgerow. Cattle had come close when they had first moved into the hide, dug two nights before. Cattle were always the worst. Sheep could be sent away, and most dogs could be quietened with biscuits and a tickle. Cattle lingered longest, but they had gone on before midnight and found shelter closer to the farm buildings. It was quiet around them and they could identify far-away gunfire.

Most on automatic. Few single shots. Men who didn't engage in a primitive form of warfare might have flinched at the barrage of bullets fired around the point where the light had flashed. At least two hundred shots. Out there, the ambush team would have been slapping on fresh magazines and keeping the belts fed through the machine-guns. The noise did not have the crisp tone of a drumbeat or a champagne cork's pop, but was a messy blur. It was the reward for waiting.

Both men – Desperate more so than Dusty – had imagination. It was easy enough for either to picture the scene close to the culvert drain that took rainwater off the fields above the lane. The culvert was of good-quality concrete and well built but had sufficient bramble and thorn growing around its mouth for it to be an ideal place to secrete an explosive device. It had, too, the necessary cover, with the reeds that grew in the field, for a command cable to be laid; would have been unwound until it reached a shed – the firing position for the bomb. The target, as they knew, was to be a Quick Reaction Force sent out from the barracks eight miles away where a fusilier unit was based. The troops would respond to a hoax call from an anonymous man, using a public phone box to report a rifle left on a verge close to the culvert. Both men, cold and soaked, would have known what had happened. In the darkness the 'bad guys' would have struggled to get the fertiliser, in sacks, clear of the Transit and manhandled it towards the ditch and culvert. Their last moments would have come as they slid to the concrete mouth. The night sights on the rifles and machine-guns would have locked on them. An electronic switch would have been thrown to detonate the bomb and the firing would have started. Maybe two had died in the blast, and the other two would have been cut down by the volume of bullets. All would have been mangled, body parts spread . . . Neither Dusty nor Desperate winced at what they imagined.

The rain was heavier and the shooting had stopped. They were probably too far from the culvert to hear the helicopter come in. If the shooting was over it would have been called for, and it would fly low, hugging the contours, from the barracks, and set down momentarily in the sodden field to take in the Special Forces men, the 'Hereford Gun Club', who had been the ambush team. Blacked up, weighed down with their kit, they would heave themselves past the helicopter's machine-gunner and flop onto the metal floor. Then it would lift, bank and disappear. Behind the helicopter there would be a scene of carnage. Dusty and Desperate were silent. Neither was a killer at first hand: both took more responsibility than the men who had slapped in the magazines and fed the belts.

They could imagine the scene where the culvert drain bored under the lane because Desperate had been told that was where the bomb would be laid, when it would be brought there, at what time the hoax call would be made, and which men would be settling into their firing positions to wait for the military response. He knew the features of those men and their histories in the war being fought out on the shallow slopes of the mountain, and where they lived in the Townlands between the Chambered Grave and the summit point called the Seat of Shane Bearnagh. His files carried their biographies and he could trace the tribal links that held them together: he had the names of the wives, girlfriends and kids. Desperate had furnished the information that had brought the special forces up from Ballykinler. He could have predicted each moment in the killing process. He had choreographed it.

The helicopter would have gone, and the guys inside the cabin would soon be showering away the stench of cordite, then heading for the canteen and breakfast. Not Desperate and Dusty.

The cows were on the move. They came across the open field into the teeth of the wind and rain. Through his glasses, an image intensifier built into the lenses, Desperate could see their steady progress, and hear the squelch of their feet. For a full minute they masked the farmhouse and the buildings where the man stored his agricultural plant livestock lorries, the weapons and bombs he dealt with. There were no lights on in the house. It was too close to the explosion, the firing and the ambush. Desperate felt no particular satisfaction at the part he had played in the matter and didn't imagine Dusty wanted a high-five. What both men would have liked was a cigarette – forbidden. The absence of a Marlboro Lite might have mattered more to Desperate and Dusty than their part in the deaths of four men.

They were good cows from a pedigree herd – not that they were milked by the man who owned – had owned – the farmhouse, the outbuildings and forty-nine acres of poor, if serviceable, land. They were led each morning and evening to a neighbour's parlour and milked there. When they had come back the previous evening, the man had been flitting from his back door to his buildings and had returned with heavy-duty navy overalls. He must have forgotten the balaclavas because he'd had to return to the big shed. They'd watched him.

Dusty had dug out the pit that was the basis of their hide. He had many skills and building hides was one. They were low in the hole – bracken and gorse grew around its edge. A man would almost have stepped on them before he realised they were there. Dusty and Desperate feared the cows. The animals had the habit of coming to the hide and forming a half-moon round it, obscuring any view. Both men now sat in a pool of water that had formed in the pit. The damp penetrated their trousers and underwear, and their thermals no longer kept out the cold. It was what they did, nothing exceptional. It wasn't exceptional either for Desperate to preside over the killing of four men. That was what he did.

Rescue came. A vixen strutted from the hedge to their right, threaded between the clumps of nettles and attracted the cattle's attention. They veered off in pursuit of her. The view of the farmhouse was restored.

Four men would have died. There could have been no survivors. The blast of the premature detonation would have killed some and the gunfire would have done for the others. There would be another killing on the shallow slope of Altmore mountain within a week or, at most, a month. Desperate would be as responsible for the final death in this sequence as he was for the others. The cold gripped him, the damp shrivelling his skin. His eyes ached from gazing through the image-intensified lenses. He had seen the man carry the gear between the farm buildings and the kitchen door, and later had watched as the lights went on upstairs – the child being put to bed.

Late in the evening, when the wife's television programmes were over, he had come out of the back door, then had turned, taken her in his arms and kissed her hard. A moment of seeming weakness and she had clung to him until he'd broken away and gone. They had watched him lope down the track leading from the farm to the lane and a car had come.

Later, the ground-floor lights went out and those in the principal bedroom came on. Desperate saw her for a moment as she stood at the window and gazed down the hill. They had no bug in the house so Desperate didn't know whether she knew about the culvert. Some talked to their women, most didn't. She was tall and straight-backed, with good bones and a clear complexion. Her expression, at the window through the lenses, was vacant. She would have been accustomed to her husband slipping away as night fell, and of him returning. She would have known what he did, but perhaps not the detail. She would have recognised the risks he ran because there were enough widows on the side of the mountain who had experienced what now confronted her.

'You all right, Desperate?'

'Grand, Dusty. Never better.'

There had been heavy talk in the small operations area at Gough. Inside that old heap of grey-stone misery, which the British Army had populated for more than a century, the issue had been thrashed out: no minutes taken, no written record. Could arrests be attempted? Could they be rounded up individually and linked to a murder conspiracy that stood a chance in the Central Criminal Court? The answer had been decisive: 'Blow the beggars away.' A last question had been put: 'Do we lose the source? Is he collateral?'

A response from Desperate: 'I think we can live with that if we're taking down four of that calibre.' Sergeant Daniel Curnow had spoken, and he was the oracle on matters concerning informers, agents, 'touts': a warrant officer, a major and a full-ranking colonel listened to him. He was called 'Desperate' because of his first name.

Two nights later, awake for hours, he gazed down at the farmhouse. He knew how he'd find out that the enemy were dead. They wouldn't send their own people, not yet. The priest would come. The light was growing from the east, beyond the Pomeroy road, and the rain fell. Wind rustled the hedgerow. A small car came along the lane, the headlights feeble in the weather. It turned onto the track, bouncing over the potholes, that ran between fields where more cattle were out and some sheep. Either the police or the fellow travellers supporting the Organisation would have called the man out.

The dog barked and ran from the buildings behind the house. A light came on upstairs.

The priest stood at the door and seemed to pause, as if reluctant to take a further step. Then he knocked. Desperate could see, with the magnification of the glasses, that she had thrown on a dressing-gown: as soon as she heard the vehicle progressing at snail's pace up the track she would have realised that the news was bad. She took the priest inside. As Desperate pictured it, she would lead him into the kitchen, sit him down, put on the kettle, then allow him to speak.

A child came outside in striped pyjamas, a size too small – he was well built, with a tousled mass of thick hair. The file back at Gough said Malachy was eight. Desperate had seen the child from that vantage-point in the hedgerow three days before, when the boy had ridden with his father on the back of the tractor as they took silage out to the cattle. Now he howled – not with misery but anger. It was an animal sound, primeval. Desperate blinked, then cleaned the lenses so he could see better. The child's face was twisted with hatred – the face of a fighter, he thought.

Dusty said quietly, 'He'll be a problem, he will. Remember his name.'

They covered the hide, picked up their rubbish and went on their stomachs along the hedge to the gap they could squeeze through. When they were clear, Dusty would summon the transport to the appointed rendezvous – using Desperate's call-sign, Vagabond – and they'd return to Gough.

He was responsible, not for the first time and not for the last. The face of that child seared in his mind as he began to trudge across the grass. He saw, too, the face of an older man who believed in him, had trusted him, pocketed money and thought himself Desperate's friend. He was despised as a traitor, the source of the information that had killed four men. A victory in a war now in its third decade had been won – and had taken the life of the child's father.

The informer, whose life might now be forfeit, was Damien. He did a bit of carpentry to eke out his unemployment benefit and the hundred pounds a month from his handler. He lived in a bungalow two miles to the east along the mountain, and was thought to be not the full shilling. He had been doing panelling in a man's home when he had heard the plan talked through in the open air. He had told Desperate, who had recruited him seven months before. His handler knew that the agent, Damien, was now vulnerable: the Organisation's security people would come from Belfast and check who had known of the plan, where the briefings had been given. Damien had been worth a few hundred pounds, but was not in line for a resettlement package in England, which involved heavy expense. He'd take his chance. If the Organisation identified him as a potential risk, he would be taken to a safe-house, interrogated, burned and beaten. Then he'd be hooded, stripped to his underpants, pinioned and driven to a lane close to the border where he'd be pushed to his knees and shot, one bullet, in the back of the head. The hood would be lifted and a twenty-pound note stuffed between his teeth.

His handler had manipulated him. That was the work Desperate did, and Dusty protected him while he did it.

He'd catch up on his sleep at Gough after the debrief. The kid, Malachy, had howled at the low clouds, but it was the hatred Desperate would remember, how it had creased a young face and made lines in the clear skin. The voice rang in his ears.

I

They'd killed him – not shot or strangled him, but when they'd sent him up the road.

The hut in which they had taken refuge from the weather was part collapsed. Three of the walls still stood and half of the tin roofing was there, but storms had taken down the rest; the floor creaked when any of them moved. Manure and a carpet of damp straw lay over the debris, and the place stank of cattle, and of the cigarettes smoked incessantly by the police who guarded them.

It was clear to Hugo Woolmer that he might as well have fired the bullet himself. His partner in the agent's death was Gaby Davies. Hugo was three years older, at a higher grade in the Service, so had nominal control of the operation. What else might he have done? He could have refused permission for the agent to drive off into the fog that hid the road that snaked up towards the mountain. He might have insisted that he would not allow his agent to be at the beck and call of those who had called him and go to them, without back-up, in the hire car.

The agent had worn no wire under his vest and no microphone in his watch. No bug had been fastened to the small car he had collected at the airport. It had been thought that a wire, a microphone, or a bug was too simple for 'them' to locate.

The agent had flown from London, had stayed the night in a modern hotel within a stone's throw of the police barracks. They had demanded a meeting with the agent. Two alternatives had faced Hugo Woolmer: he could allow his man to drive into the cloud and the labyrinth of narrow roads and farm tracks, which dictated vehicle pursuit was impossible, or he could accept that an agent who had worked with the Service for almost five and a half years should now be reined in, the contact with 'them' lost. The chance of replacing the agent was minimal. It had been his decision to make, and Gaby Davies's voice had been insistent that morning in the hotel when visibility across the car park was negligible.

At the heart of the decision was the agent's personal safety. He would be beyond reach, with no panic button because it was likely that he would be subjected to a search with detectors. To let him go forward, or not? A crushing weight had burdened Hugo Woolmer.

He was crouched against one of the hut's surviving walls. The wind came through the trees, whipping twigs against them. He sat on his heels. His head was down on his chest.

She had said, 'Of course he'll do the meeting with them. It's what we brought him over for. It's a tough old world out there. You should know that and so should he. If he's blown his cover, then that's a sound reason for them to summon him to their territory. Or maybe they have a different role for him and want to talk it through. He put himself into this situation. He should have known things might get tricky before he associated with them. To cancel his meeting with them and break the link would mean that any trust they had in him is gone. And they won't leave it at that. He'd be walking dead. He does the meeting, Hugo. You can't call MB and tell him you've lost your nerve. For God's sake!'

His chin was hard against the zip of his anorak. His arms encircled his shins. His fingers were locked together, and knuckles white, and he had begun to shake.

The hire car from the airport would have been driven by one of them into a farm gateway and torched. He wouldn't have seen the car burning. They would have picked him up and slipped him into the back of a van without windows. They might have trussed him, even hooded him, and gone to one of the little homes on the mountain. There, he would be sat on a hard chair and slapped around a bit, if they suspected anything. One would be the smooth talker and would tell the agent that confession would save his life. Or maybe he'd swear at him, put a lighted cigarette close to his eyes and tell him how bad the pain would be . . .

He heard whimpering and realised it was his. He had become fond of the agent, and reckoned Gaby Davies – for all her bluster about people making their own beds and having to lie on them – liked him too. He was one of those people who seemed to make the sun shine a little brighter, and had an infectious chuckle. He could have cancelled the business, and had not.

Hugo Woolmer was protected: he and Gaby Davies had four taciturn police watching their backs, with Heckler & Koch rifles. Their faces showed disapproval of the two young 'blow-ins' from the mainland: they reckoned that Service people from across the water were clever and had good kit but a negligible understanding of problems in the Province. The agent was without protection.

If 'they' broke him, which Hugo Woolmer believed was almost certain, they would forget about beating him and burning him with cigarettes. They would sit him at a table, give him pencil and paper and instruct him to write the names of his contacts, handler and the length of his association with the Service. Then they would extricate from him every detail on the extent of his betrayal. He'd be told that if he wrote it all down he would be driven back down the hill to pick up his hire car and drive away. That was what they would tell him, and it would be lies. Hugo Woolmer knew, of course, of the Second World War saboteurs and wireless operators who had been rounded up in the occupied territories, tortured and never broke: he didn't understand how that was possible. He had heard it said, by a Service veteran, that raw volunteers in the Organisation sometimes fought among each other for the privilege of killing an agent of the British occupation. He knew the agent's wife and daughter by sight. He could have stopped him going into the fog.

The police watched him, impassive. He wouldn't have said that Gaby Davies was pretty. From the corner of his eye, Hugo Woolmer could see her face. She was small and stocky, with short dark hair. She wore walking boots, faded jeans, a couple of T-shirts and a heavy anorak. She smoked with the police – kept pace with them. Her rucksack rested against her legs and held sandwiches, a flask of coffee, the communications equipment they'd use at the end of the day and her Glock pistol. Hugo was not armed. They had a correct relationship but when any issue needed closure she had the last word at the discussion stage, and he would make the decision. The agent had gone forward.

Rooks shrieked in the trees and the wind sang in the branches above them. His shoulders shook and tears came.

He was watched with a hawk's intensity.

It was Dermot and Dymphna Fahy's home. Daft, the pair of them. They had been sent in their car to the town with a twenty-pound note, which would last them the morning as they pushed a trolley up the aisles of the Spar, then the pound shop. They'd have enough left, maybe, after their shopping for a glass of Guinness each in O'Brien's. The bungalow was a good place, quiet, not overlooked by neighbours, the Fahys had no record with the police so there wouldn't be surveillance. The front garden was a wilderness – there was an old pram in it, and a bicycle frame; the paintwork on the window frames was flaking and the door knocker was askew. Nothing happened at that bungalow so it was the right place for him to have been brought to. There was a dog, a collie-cross, but the Fahy woman had shut it in the shed. It had barked when they'd arrived, but was quiet now.

He was watched closely and they looked for the signs – sweat on the neck and forehead, nervous blinking . . . Malachy stood beside Brendan Murphy and the two filled the doorway into the back bedroom. There was no bed – it had gone with the Fahys' boy to a room he rented in Lurgan town. A dressing-table with a mirror, cracked on the left side, was covered with old newspapers and some plastic bags from the Spar, and there was a pile of brown envelopes, unopened. Across them a cable, plugged to a wall socket, led to a well-used electric drill – not for heavy use, but big enough to make a hole in a wall for a Rawlplug or to damage a man's kneecap. Also under the cable there was a length of towel, folded into a strip, and a coil of baling twine from a farmer's yard. The man had his back to the dressing-table but would have seen what was on it, as was intended, when they'd led him in. He was sitting on a straight-backed wooden chair and kept his knees together – protection of sorts. He didn't make eye contact. Interesting that he hadn't complained at being bundled into the back of a van, or when he had been blindfolded at the end of the journey, or when he had stubbed his toe on a step between the collapsed gate and the front door. The curtain was drawn. He wouldn't know where he was. It was good that he didn't show fear: either he didn't feel it or he hid it well.

Brennie asked Malachy, 'Are you liking him or not liking him?'

A murmured response: 'We'd be putting a lot in his hands – maybe too much? I don't know.'

'And big money.' Brennie grimaced. He was the father figure. Brennie Murphy's reputation was different from Malachy's. He wasn't a soldier or a marksman; he was no good with a soldering iron and a circuit board. He seemed prematurely aged – his wrinkled, colourless skin and straggling hair gave the impression that he was older than the sixty-one from his birth certificate. He had judgement. From his teenage years, the younger man had listened to what Brennie Murphy said and hadn't contradicted his advice. If the man was a police or Five spy and a plant, Brennie Murphy would smell him. His nose seemed to slant towards the left side of his mouth – the result of a baton blow struck by a screw in the Maze during a protest. If Brennie reckoned he'd smelt a spy, the man wouldn't be alive in the morning. They needed this man and his contacts, but it was high risk. They hadn't seen him before; others had dealt with him, but only for cigarettes. An organisation resurrecting a war couldn't survive on cigarettes: it needed weapons. It was 'big money'. It would clear out bank accounts and strip away the limited funds that supported the dependants of the men in HMP Maghaberry. Brennie rolled a wooden toothpick between his teeth. 'He's not messed himself.'

The man gazed at the floor. His breathing was regular – he wasn't panting with panic. He hadn't demanded to know why he was there. He was sort of docile, which confused Malachy. He thought Brennie Murphy hadn't yet read the man – they knew his history, his address, his family, his circumstances. The link with the cigarette trade had run for years and the contacts were in the

Inchicore district of Dublin, across the border. They didn't know him, nor he them. What sort of Englishman would offer to facilitate, for a fee, the purchase of weapons for their organisation? He hadn't launched it, but had been propositioned by the cigarette people: he hadn't refused. Brennie Murphy wouldn't waste time looking for the answer. Malachy watched. He was the soldier, the marksman, and understood how to build a mercury tilt switch into a device, but he didn't have the nose for a spy.

'Would you stand up.'

He did.

'Would you take off your clothes.'

Brennie Murphy's voice was quiet, not aggressive, but it would have been a brave man who refused. The fingers were clumsy and the shirt buttons, the belt buckle and the shoe laces were awkward. If he was wearing a wire or his wrist watch was bugged, this was crisis time. Two at the door, two more closer to him, and one held the kit: it was the size of a cordless phone and was switched on. The shirt came off, the shoes, socks, trousers and vest. He paused, looked questioningly at Brennie Murphy. His underpants? Malachy understood. It wasn't necessary for the man to strip stark bollock naked. The detector could operate easily enough through flimsy cotton, but . . .

'Take them down.'

It was about domination. It wasn't like when he'd played Gaelic football and they were in the showers with nothing on: this man wasn't in their team. He was a stranger, and to be naked would humiliate him – the intention. The man was forty-one, they'd been told his age, and seemed in poor condition. He had a little spare flesh at his waist and his shoulders slumped. The detector was over his clothes and shoes, then his body, but the tone didn't alter. The little bleep was the only sound in the room, other than the wheeze of Brennie Murphy's breathing. It was switched off. Would intelligence people have allowed an agent to go forward without communications? They might have because they were hard, cold bastards, and Malachy knew it. He saw Brennie's head turn a little: his eyes were on the drill on the dressing-table and he nodded.

It was switched on.

It was carried round the chair and held in front of the man's stomach. Not a clean sound but searing, as if it needed fresh oil. The drill head, a blur of movement, was no more than a foot from his flesh. Malachy watched: the penis had shrivelled, the knees were closer and the hands were clasped. The eyes stared at the drill, but the man didn't flinch.

Brennie said, like it was conversation, 'If I get a bad smell about you, it goes into you. If I reckon you're a tout, it's the drill in you. At the first touch of it you'll be blathering to me the names of your handlers and where they are down the road. You'll have an hour to live, but you'll be telling me about your handlers or it comes into you again. You'll get the drill every time your tongue stops flapping. You with me?'

The man nodded.

'And if I'm liking what you say, you get to have your trousers. If I'm not liking it you get the drill and the cigarettes. . . . It stinks when skin melts from a cigarette burn. Why'll you do this?'

The man bent and reached for his clothes. 'Did I get it wrong? Seems I did. I thought you were in the market for assaults, launchers, commercial bang stuff and perhaps some mortars. If you want to go through this charade with me, forget the goodies.'

The man gazed into Brennie Murphy's face. Then he put on his vest, then his underpants, and picked up his shirt.

Brennie Murphy hissed, 'Don't get cheeky with me—'

'I'm talking of assault rifles, launchers, grenades, mortars, military explosive, and the groundwork's done.'

Malachy saw the flick of the fingers. Brennie Murphy's order was obeyed. The drill whined close to the man's ear. He kept his expression impassive. He didn't know of any stranger who had given lip to Brennie Murphy without a self-loading rifle in his hand and a section of paratroopers or Special Task Force police. The man didn't bother to button his shirt and slid into his shoes. He folded his arms across his chest. Time to talk business or to call it off.

Brennie Murphy took a step sideways, grasped the cable and

yanked it from the wall. The drill was off. 'Why would you do this for us?'

'There's a recession on where I live, and I've a family to keep. You pay me. Good enough? I need the money.'

His backside was lower, his shoulders had subsided further and he pulled his knees closer to his chest. He was still whimpering.

She was ashamed to be with him. Hugo Woolmer was superior to Gaby Davies in the Service hierarchy, and had outperformed her with a first-class honours degree at an Oxford college while she had a lower second from a provincial university. His family had connections and she was a 'token' from a sink school in the north-east. If it would have silenced him, she would have kicked him, hard, in the groin. When they were back at Toad Hall, as the local guys in Belfast called Thames House, home of the Service, she'd knife him. It was, she accepted, a unique moment for her: she had never before seen a man disintegrate in nervous collapse.

'We've killed him. He trusted us.'

She'd make certain he was dead in the water as far as his future went with the Service.

'He was paid peanuts, manipulated and compromised, and we betrayed him.'

She'd go down in a week's time, two maybe, and watch when he went through the barriers at the main entrance for the last time. His ID would be shredded.

'It should never have been allowed and we'll carry the burden of it to our graves.'

She liked the man who had driven away – without cover or back-up – into the cloud that had grounded the surveillance helicopters. He made her laugh. There was mischief in his humour and he was frank about the bullshit he peddled in his business dealings. Gaby Davies liked him – but he was an agent, a Joe. It wasn't for her or Hugo to call him off when a meeting was arranged. She'd thought him more remote the last week, vaguer in spitting out the detail of what these people wanted of him but . . . She thought, looking out of the hut and through the trees, that the rain had eased. There might even be a hint of sunshine in the west.

'They'll torture him, he'll talk, and then they'll kill him. I'll never forgive myself.'

Her phone stayed silent. She assumed her agent's would have been left switched off in the car. He would have been taken in one of their vehicles to the meeting place. If they had called him over it was not to discuss the next consignment of cigarettes shipped out of a Spanish or North African port and brought ashore on the wild south-west coast of Ireland. Gaby Davies had gone through in her mind, many times, every contact with her man to explore the chance of a show-out. She couldn't see the danger moment when suspicion might have arisen. Of course they couldn't have called him off.

The crying was louder.

A policeman spoke, a soft voice, faintly mocking: 'Makes a habit of it, does he?'

She said, brittle, 'It's brightening in the west. That was what my mum used to say when we were kids on the beach at Blyth and it rained. It always did the week we had the caravan – brighter in the west . . . but it was the bloody east coast.'

He was a big man, overweight, and his vest bulged. He held his weapon as though it were part of him – he most likely slept with it, was fonder of it than he was of his wife. The weapon entitled him to sneer. 'Not what you'd call suited to the work.'

'We'll save the inquest for later.' It was her way of telling him, a uniformed oaf, that it was none of his effing business how Hugo Woolmer behaved. 'Could be OK here by late morning.'

'And he's not suited for the place, miss . . . Mind if I say something?'

'If it's about the weather.'

The cloud remained locked on the mountain's slopes, still dense, but she could see a little gold on the summit ridge – watery sunshine on dead bracken.

'You've not been here before, miss. It's about as bad a part of the Province as you'll find, plenty of wicked wee boys here. There's communities that have bought into what we laughingly call the 'peace process', and there's communities that haven't. They keep going at it in these parts. It's tribal and the families don't know another life. Me, going off into that mist on my own, no panic kit, no one listening and watching out for me, I'd want to be in a main battle tank, hatches down. This part of the Province, they've not given up on the war.'

'I've had that briefing, thank you.'

'It's a hard place, the hardest. Lawless now and always has been . . . You were saying, miss, that the weather's clearing. You'll see the high point – that's Shane Bearnagh's Seat, a fine vantage-point on a better day. I'm talking of more than three hundred years ago and Bearnagh was what we call a 'rapparee', a thief, smuggler and killer. Before the military got him, he bedded the wife of a British officer while they were all out hunting him. It's a nasty place, miss, and has been for centuries. Has your man strong nerves?'

'I don't know.'

'Pity you didn't find that out before he went up there.'

'Have you got a cigarette?' He gave her one. 'Thanks.' Another man passed her a flask of coffee. She detected a trace of brandy in it. The cigarette and the drink warmed her. As an officer in the Security Service she wouldn't normally discuss an operational deployment with a police constable but asked: 'How long until we worry about him?'

'I heard there was a drone they were wanting to use, but it's broken. The helicopter can't deal with a low cloud base. What would you say, Baz?'

'I'd say, Henry, that if he's for the jump they'll have started on the heavy work. By now they'll have your name, miss, and his over there,' he nodded at Hugo Woolmer, 'and they won't hang about after that. They'll assume the mountain's crawling with security and that there's vehicle blocks. They'll want to nut him, then clear off home for a wash.'

'Too right. Might have done it by now, miss.'

'You know him well enough – how would he take a rough-and-tumble with them? Round here there was once a fist fight between two of the volunteers – the old days – about which of them should fire the bullet that killed a tout . . . How would he stand up to a beating, miss, burns and the full works? Another time, again in the old days but little's changed, they turned on the hob rings on a cooker and got the tout's trousers and pants off. When the rings were glowing, they sat him on them . . . Most don't last long. Might already be over.'

She nearly tripped over Hugo Woolmer's legs as she went outside. She threw away the barely smoked cigarette and was sick against a tree. He'd been staying in a hotel in London and had been with the cigarette people the night before. They'd needed to do the briefing early, and she'd knocked on his door. He'd unlocked it – must have come straight from the shower: a towel was knotted at his waist and she'd seen his skin. Nothing special – a few birthmarks, some straggly hair, no burns, no contusions from a club. His fingertips had been intact. The leaves at the base of the tree were saturated with her vomit.

Brennie Murphy didn't know. He should have known.

The men on the mountain looked to him for decisions on tactics and strategy, and for his guidance on targets in the mid-Ulster and Lurgan areas. He had good antennae and understood weakness in the enemy. Some had turned their back on the struggle, and the television each night carried clips of former fighters who now chuckled with the people they had tried to kill. It was as if the old colleagues of Brennie Murphy now pissed on him. He wouldn't compromise, take government grants, become a paid stooge and call himself a community officer: the armed struggle, for him, was alive. With so few engaged in – as they called it – 'keeping the fire lit', it was inevitable that the attention of the police and Five would be intense, worse than anything he had known when he was young. The attacks on what remained active of the Organisation were based on the technical excellence of the surveillance systems and also the infiltration of their cells by paid informers. Did he trust this man? Should he trust him?

The man sat on the chair. He did not quiz them, argue with

them or cringe. Men Brennie Murphy knew, who he might have believed were taking twenty, fifty, a hundred pounds a week would have come here and shown terror. The switching on of the drill would have brought a stain to their crotches, and they'd have pleaded their innocence too hard.

He and Malachy were in the hallway. They could see the man through the open door into the back bedroom. He asked, 'Do you believe him or not?'

'I don't know.'

'He's promised the shipment.'

'He's promised to bring it to a point in Europe. Then we get it home.'

'We need it.'

'The weapons bring the kids to us, not to the collaborators.'

'It's against every instinct in my body.'

'And mine.'

'But you must have the weapons.'

'Must have them, Brennie, or we're nothing.'

Brennie Murphy's nostrils flared. It wasn't strange, he told the kids, that a man of his age could harbour such hatred. More than anything in his life he dreaded abandoning the memory of the many who had died, old comrades. He prayed he would die before weakness pushed him towards compromise. The dead didn't deserve it. 'You'd have to go to test-fire – all of that,' he said. 'So's we're not skinned.'

'If I have to.'

Brennie took his arm. 'You do.'

They went back inside.

He sat on the chair, could have killed for a cigarette, but he wasn't offered one. Smoke came through from the hall where the two of them spoke in low voices.

He had realised that the room with the awful wallpaper would be easy to turn into a torture chamber. The makeover would be straightforward. He didn't doubt that in the kitchen or the main bedroom there was a roll of plastic sheeting, which would go over the carpet and a Stanley knife would cut it. The blood, if they used the drill, would be spread low but they might use more plastic sheeting to cover the walls, pinned up near the ceiling. How did he feel? Not great. What could he do? Not much. Who'd give a damn? Not many. The two main men, the older one and the younger – the minders were 'soldiers' and of no relevance – wore no face masks. So they didn't mind if he saw their faces. He studied them so that he could remember them and, in time, go through the books of activists' photographs and identify them. It meant, even to a man far less bright and without his survival instincts, that either he had passed their tests or failed. Failure meant death.

Quick? No.

Possible to appeal to their better natures? Inappropriate.

Time to front up.

They'd stand over him and look down into his face. The younger man would likely smack him and blood would spill from his nose. Then he'd hear the drill start up. Others would be tying him to the chair and he'd hear the plastic being unwound. Before they put the gag in he'd yell for paper and a pencil. Whatever they wanted they could have. He'd name them all, starting with Matthew, the recruiter: a sly, cold bastard and he'd never known his surname.

He knew the full name of the team leader. He shouldn't have, but a mobile had rung in the man's pocket during a meal one summer evening on the Thames – their treat. It had been answered, 'Hugo Woolmer.' They could have that name. A few revolutions of the drill tip and Hugo Woolmer was theirs.

The girl was Gabrielle Davies. Another time, she'd been rooting in a purse for a credit card to pay at Starbucks and he'd seen her Service card, just a glimpse of her name. She'd noticed him looking and had flushed at her lapse. Woolmer had called her Gaby when they'd walked in Windsor Great Park. She'd bailed out of a trattoria with a train to catch in Birmingham and the waiter had called that the taxi for 'Davies' was outside. They could have her too. She was nice, pretty, a striver, different from the tossers and their women, but she'd go on the paper if the drill started up.

Would he keep his mouth shut to protect Queen and country? Dream on. If the drill started up, he'd want the paper and the pencil. He hoped that, afterwards, they'd make it quick.

The one with the bent nose spoke. He met the man's eyes, as a prisoner did in the Central Criminal Court when the jury came back, and tried to read the verdict in the foreman's posture. The sweat was cold on his neck. He'd give them all the names they wanted if the drill started up.

'We want to get on with the business, get it moving and in place. A cup of tea would go down well. Milk and sugar?'

A call was made. The handset had not been used before. Numbers and seemingly random letters were routed off the island to a second mobile on the UK mainland. The code incorporated was sufficient to move it through a consulate in central Italy to a trade mission in the Danish capital, then to its destination. Its journey ended at a villa in a Croatian town close to the German border.

Such arrangements were in place only for a man of considerable importance to the regime ruling his country: only a long-standing, trusted friend of such a man could access the transfer of the signal. It was well disguised and would confuse the computers of a hostile intelligence organisation.

Theirs was a peculiar relationship. Timofey Simonov and Nikolai Denisov lived together in a hundred-year-old house built on three floors and covered attractively with variegated ivy. It was set back a few metres from the prestigious street, Krale Jiriho, and was halfway up the hill. It commanded majestic views over the spa town. The houses on that road were the most expensive in the town, which had the most inflated property prices within the Czech Republic. They were within easy walking distance of the town centre and its promenade, with the better boutiques. It was also near to the Orthodox church of St Peter and St Paul and that day the sun shone, making brilliant reflections on its gold-plated roof. Equally convenient were the dry cleaner's, the mini-mart and the restaurants, where the menus were in Cyrillic. It was a town of affluence, and the reputations of many who had arrived from St Petersburg, Moscow and Volgograd meant that the criminals who preyed on the wealthy had long ago realised that this town was best ignored. It was, anecdotally, the safest in the country, perhaps in the whole of central Europe. Big men, in their trade, lived securely 'under the radar', and walked securely at night on the pristine streets. Although the town was best known for its industry of health care, first publicised after a visit by Peter the Great, the most secretive residents bothered little with lymphatic drainage and hydro-colonotherapy. They ran empires producing vast revenues, and their assets were measured in hundreds of millions of American dollars or euros.

Kicking off his boots at the back entrance, shielded from public view by a high fence, Timofey Simonov crouched, grinning, to pet his dogs. He had walked his Weimaraner bitches on the wooded hillside behind the villa and now they licked his cheeks. He had been, far back, a captain in the GRU, military intelligence, with the motto 'Greatness of Motherland in Your Glorious Deeds'. A slip of paper was passed to him. The man who had brought the message was five years older; Nikolai Denisov had been promoted in his extreme youth to brigadier. Simonov had been little more than a clerk and paper-pusher in the section of the general's staff Denisov had headed. But the days when they had served the officer leading the Central Command of the Soviet forces confronting those of the North Atlantic Treaty were in the far past. The former captain now employed the former brigadier as driver, close-protection bodyguard, housekeeper and minder of secrets. The relationship was kept from public view, known only to a few.

He straightened. The message had been decoded. The smile spread. 'He's coming.'

'He has confirmed the list of items required.'

'It'll be good to see him.'

'He's your friend but . . .' He handed back the paper and began towelling the dogs. '. . . is it wise to help on a deal that's worth so little?'

'It's where they're going. I'd provide a bow and arrow if that was what they wanted. And he's my friend, however small the trade.'

Three days had slipped past since his friend had made his first approach. He had known the man for fourteen years when he himself had been at the bottom of the heap and hadn't known where his next meal would come from. An Englishman had helped him on his way. The friend's fortunes had now slipped, but the request had come with a list, and he knew where any consignment would be unpacked. A friend was a friend for life. Other concerns: a former bureaucrat who had worked in the finance ministry auditing tax and Customs revenues, had 'blown a whistle' and was talking to Swiss investigators, about confidential accounts in Swiss banks. The official was junior but his head and memory sticks were stuffed with detail. He had 'betrayed' his country, had embarrassed the ruling élite, and was all but dead: Timofey Simonov had been awarded the contract for the killing. Other concerns: Timofey still had 'commercial interests' in the city of Yekaterinburg; a hood there had climbed too high and had burned two kiosks by the river from which dealers operated and paid small sums that ended in Timofey's accounts. As with the official, death would send a message to others who contemplated similar actions. The smile split his face. 'It will be fantastic to see my friend.'

He hugged the dogs and sent them to their baskets, then slipped on his shoes. His man, who had been the brightest star on the general's staff, would take the boots outside and wash off the mud, then make coffee.

He was told who would travel and when they would fly. The bent nose, behind the front door, gave a final warning. 'We have your face, your wife's and your kid's. We have your home. If you scam on us, we'll come for you. You can't hide from us.'

In reply, Ralph Exton stretched out his hand. The bent nose took it and a close, cold grip crushed his fist. It surprised him that a man with so little meat on him was so strong. He gave a smile from his repertoire that indicated quiet confidence and trust. When his hand was freed, he offered it to the younger man. No response. He pocketed it and pretended not to notice the refusal. He said, as if it were a small matter, that a float for travel costs should be paid into the Guernsey account he used for cigarette dealings. Then the men who had brought him up the hill hurried him down the path, past the broken gate and across the road to the van. Some of the slope above him was clear, but the cloud was still low over the bungalow.

He was pushed, not violently but without ceremony, into the back of the van. He saw the shovel, the pickaxe and plastic bags. They would have stood over him and made him dig the pit, then pushed him aside and done it faster themselves. He had heard that they always took the shoes from a man they were about to kill – as if that mattered when the pistol was cocked beside his ear. They drove fast, swerving round the bends and potholes.

The driver braked. The door was opened and he crawled out. The damp mist seemed to cling to his cheeks and he blinked. The door behind him was slammed and the van was gone. He walked through the mud at the field's gate and fumbled for the key in his pocket. He tried many times to slot it into the lock but his hand was shaking. Eventually inside, he had the same problem with the ignition. His legs were rigid, the muscles cramped.

He drove out of the field, went into the fog and through it. He was panting and sweating. In the bungalow his confidence had been pure theatre and nerves now overwhelmed him. He went from one side of the lane to the other, past houses he barely registered. A girl swung her handlebars to avoid him and ended up sprawling. He didn't care. His heart was pounding.

He murmured, 'Fuck me. Just another day in the office. Fuck me.'

And he laughed.

'Fuck me. What a way to spend a Sunday morning.'

She was behind him. Gaby Davies jabbed her left knee into the back of Hugo Woolmer's lower thigh, propelling him down the aisle towards their allocated seats.

They went past the agent – white-faced, holding a small antique hip flask – and she didn't acknowledge him. When they came to their row, she grabbed Hugo Woolmer's collar, swivelled him and flung him into the seat beside the window. He seemed still in shock. She eased down beside him and leaned over him to fasten his seatbelt.

She hissed: 'You won't walk off this aircraft if you embarrass me again. You'll need to be carried.'

North of the bassin Saint-Pierre, where the wind rattled the masts and riggings of pleasure yachts and launches, and above the central streets of the city of Caen, a man used a sponge to clean a minibus. The logo on the side of the fifteen-seater vehicle was 'Sword Tours'. A thin, pale man, stubble on his cheeks, dungarees clinging to him, he worked with almost passionate commitment to get the paintwork glistening. A bell chimed from the church beside the Abbaye des Dames for the late Sunday-morning celebration of Mass. Worshippers hurried past but acknowledged him – he was, indeed, after so many years, almost one of them. His hair was spiky and grey-flecked, but his eyes were keen. When the bucket was empty, he turned towards an old house in a terrace, and shouted, 'Dusty! Bucket's empty. I need more water.'

He knew what *they*'d be doing – it was always the same on a Sunday morning.

They *were the clients. Clients always followed a routine on the eve of the trip. They'd be getting the computer's weather predictions for the Channel coast of France for the coming week, or filling in the baggage labels supplied by Sword Tours. The clothing would be laid out, and they'd ponder over their rainproof gear in case the forecasters were wrong. They would all have, in a travel pouch, the itinerary Sword Tours would follow: Dunkirk, Dieppe, the key places where the paratroopers had landed, and the gliders, Sword, Juno, Gold and Omaha beaches, and Falaise, with the closing of the Gap. Most of those clients would have had a friend's recommendation – 'Can't praise him highly enough. He knows his stuff. You won't find better than Danny Curnow. He lives those places, breathes them.' That Sunday, as every Sunday, clients would be preparing to head for a rendezvous in the morning. It was so difficult to decide what to take.*

Dusty brought the bucket. 'That the last, Danny?'

'Yes, thanks.'

'There's a sandwich in the kitchen.'

'I'll be there in a minute.'

Dusty watched him, lingered. Danny said softly, 'Problem, Dusty?'

'No.'

Dusty left him to finish. Danny Curnow understood. They had history together, almost thirty years now, from when he was Desperate. For the last sixteen they had been in an historic Normandy town. The moment that bound them was when he had walked out of Gough, a spent vessel, with his officer's shout in his ear for him to turn round, but he had kept on down Barrack Street and then had heard the footfall behind him. Dusty had followed him. They'd gone to the bus station and taken the coach together. Technically it was desertion, but they'd kept going and had finished up here. He knew that the older man was lonely when Danny was away. He had Lisette and Christine to look after him, good food and a warm bed, but he missed the company of his one-time sergeant, the man he'd shared ditches with.

Danny used the last of the water, paused to admire his work, then turned and walked down the hill, heading for his home. It was the right place for Danny Curnow to be because of his nerves and his memories.

2

A stalker? A sad little man who followed a woman and hid in shadows? Perhaps, but that would have been a view of himself that Daniel Curnow couldn't accept. He was a creature of routine, set patterns ingrained in him. It was Sunday, and the worshippers had cleared the abbaye, and the church of St Gilles – with the grave in the centre of the nave of Matilda, wife of William the Conqueror. Danny had eaten his sandwich in the kitchen, left the minibus parked on the kerb and gone to the bar he patronised. Routine governed him. In the Dickens bar he would drink, on a Sunday, one small glass of local beer, exchange a few inconsequential pleasantries with the *patron*, catch up on Caen news with a paper, smoke two cigarettes and be on his way. He wouldn't stalk a woman in the town where he lived, but as the afternoon drifted by he would be driving north-east on the fast road a little back from the coastline. The woman was at Honfleur, around halfway to his destination. It was what he did every Sunday, summer and winter.

Routine was important to him, and had shaped his character.

His acceptance of an ordered lifestyle had made him a near legend in his chosen military unit, the Intelligence Corps. He could, of course, innovate but routine made for safety. That was what he craved and why he had moved, with Dusty, to the French Atlantic coast, where the cliffs were, the wide open beaches and the killing grounds.

He stubbed out the second cigarette, drank the last of the beer, folded the paper he had been reading and pushed it back across the bar.

Some customers were in their best clothing, which they wore for Mass, others greasy from working under their cars. A few were sweaty and in tracksuits from football on the all-weather pitch. They nodded to him, touched his arm or shook his hand. They were nearly friends but not quite. The doorbell of the Dickens Bar would chime as he went out onto the street. He would take – as he did every Sunday – the narrow alley with steep steps that led from the street where his bar was to the one with his minibus and his home.

He let himself into the house and went into the kitchen. Dusty was having lunch, beef in a sauce. Christine fussed behind him. Lisette was at the sink. They lived on a sparrow's diet but cared devotedly for their long-time lodgers. All, in their way, were sad, but didn't recognise it. The house was Lisette's and Christine was her daughter. They had taken in the itinerant foreigners, and the arrangement suited them all.

He took bottled water from the fridge, smiled briefly at them and ducked his head. Dusty wished him a good trip. Lisette would have done his laundry when he returned next Saturday, and Christine would have tidied his room unnecessarily – he always left it pristine.

He was a gypsy, a traveller, as were they all.

He was an old soldier who needed routine. Dusty had long ago lost his parents, had a sister marooned in an urbanisation on a Spanish costa, a nineteen-year-old son living near Dortmund and another a year younger working in a Limassol hotel. Lisette's mother had been seventeen when a German officer billeted on the family farm – overlooking the Canadian beach – had taken her to the hay barn. The baby was born after the successful invasion and the death of the officer. Lisette's mother was dubbed a collaborator and her head had been publicly shaved. In response Lisette, sparky, aggressive and never one to compromise, had seduced a German tourist, come to visit the graves, and bedded him on three consecutive evenings. She had produced Christine, silkily blonde. The past governed all who lived in that house. It was worse for Danny Curnow than for the others: he lived with demons that had forced him to break away from his work and move on before it crushed him. He'd allowed no one to see him weaken.

He took his bag, packed with the little he would need for a week away, and carried it to the minibus.

His routine, on a Sunday afternoon, would take him to Honfleur within a couple of hours. There he would stalk a woman who refused to be sad. He walked around the vehicle and examined the tyres; he knew that Dusty would already have checked the engine. He climbed in, turned the key in the ignition, pulled away and slipped down the hill towards the great edifice of the castle.

It was the same for Danny Curnow that Sunday as every Sunday. In more than a dozen years nothing had altered for him. The disciplines of routine had made him a good soldier with a medal – long gone in a rubbish bin – and three mentioned-in-despatches commendations. He had shredded the certificates.

He drove out of the town towards Honfleur.

He lived a lie. Ralph Exton believed that if he ever lost its cover he would be dead. The likelihood was that his death would not be an easy release from suffering but would involve torture.

Part of the lie, a minor segment, had been to step out of the Heathrow terminal and avoid the stand for the coach service to Reading. Instead he had walked shakily to the taxi queue and waited his turn. When the driver had pulled up level with him he had given his address in Berkshire, more specifically in the nearly-royal residential road on the remoter outskirts of Bucklebury. It had been a bit of the lie to take the taxi because the Five woman wasn't picking up the tab and the Irish had not yet paid him. A whisky or three on the flight would have helped calm him, but he was sober and more than conscious of the debrief he would be put through. He would pay off the cab on his debit card, which would send his account further into the red but the fear still racked him. He might not have been able to hold a glass steady if he'd ordered a drink on the flight. He felt sick. Ralph Exton did not consider himself unnaturally brave. He wasn't a hero, would have grimaced at the idea. It was just that the 'little problems' of his life seemed disproportionably large. He existed alongside them, as if they were a constant but manageable head cold. He took the cab to the service station on the motorway going west. They, the bastards, would have had a chauffeured car from the airport. They would have watched him forgo the bus and get into a taxi. At that point his mobile had trilled and the location was given him. He could not have met them at Aldergrove or Heathrow, and certainly not at his home. It was thought the Irish might opt either for a surveillance run at him coming off the flight or stake out his home. The chance of them tailing him was almost negligible but nothing had been easy in his life, neither during the high-flying times nor later. He had survived, though, and there would be another deal around the corner.

There had been just coffee to drink.

The taxi's meter had been drumming in his mind, and his hip ached from when he had been in the closed van and they had driven him up the hillside. He had lain – too frightened to move – on the shovel's handle.

In the service station he'd sat across the table from them. The staff seemed to ignore that corner – the dirty plates and mugs had been left for them to gaze at. The man Ralph Exton knew as Hugo looked incapable of getting a tray to clear the debris, and the woman, Gaby, had brought the coffee and a muffin for him. The look on her face was thunderous, mostly for the hapless Hugo. Bugger it. Ralph had stood up and shouted at the nearest staff member in Polish, Romanian and then colloquial Russian. The guy had flushed, come over to their table and swept up the dirty crockery.

Gaby sent him a rueful smile. What had he said? 'Clear this table or you're on the next flight out tonight.'

They'd done the debrief.

Normally when they talked, he was close to her, and she had a small recorder in her bag. Hugo would play the man in charge and push the direction of the questioning. Sometimes Ralph would see her lips curl in exasperation because Hugo had interrupted the line they were following. It was important for Hugo, as Ralph Exton saw it, to be the man in charge, and he had the smart accent to go with it – like most people did in Bucklebury.

Not that day.

Ralph Exton was good at languages, a superior practitioner at selling high and buying low, and was moderately expert in staying a few steps ahead of the VAT or Revenue people, but he didn't claim expertise in mental health. He didn't need to. Hugo had clearly flipped, or whatever the word was for a full-blown nervous collapse. What was his problem? He hadn't been on his back in a dark van and lain on top of the spade that would dig a grave on the edge of a field in Tyrone. The man from Five hadn't had to listen to a drill being brought up to speed. The man from Five, good school and university, the type that inhabited the village further down the road from where Ralph Exton lived, had not been up close and personal, squeaking for his life with the two men who'd thrown the questions. Hugo was slumped, head on his arms, snivelling and sniffing.

She was all right, on good form, used his name when she spoke and sucked in what he told her, big stuff. Her expression was warm and he sensed admiration. It was confirmation of a trade. He knew now what was wanted, how much, and when delivery was required.

For Ralph Exton it made only a small difference if the commodity was furniture from a fire sale, cigarettes coming into Spain from North Africa, glass seconds from a middle-European factory, or rocket-propelled grenade launchers, machine-guns and military detonators. He was not big on moral dilemmas but took seriously the figures on the statements sent him each month by his banks. Money was his priority. Once it had brought him good things and Felicity, or 'Fliss' as everyone knew her, especially the dentist, had had the best, as had his daughter, Victoria – 'Toria Exton' on the loudspeakers at gymkhanas. Fliss and Toria hadn't realised that the good and moderate times were behind him or the bloody difficult times lay ahead. During the good times he had given a helping hand to a struggling Russian wannabe entrepreneur; during the moderate times he had facilitated the supply of duty-free fags to the Irish. Now, in bloody difficult times, any contract was manna from on high. Life was complex, frighteningly so. Ralph Exton was an agent. He was still breathing because he lived a lie – or several.

His changing landscape was where the fear lay. Perhaps the Five people frightened him most, or the Russian friend from the old days, but the Irish – the men he had met that morning – were currently on the rostrum. He played the fears against each other, let them compete, and clung to a series of lies. The vehicle was at the gate. The amount on the meter was extortionate. The Irish wouldn't pay it and Gaby from Five had shaken her head when he'd asked. He couldn't afford it but in his line of business he had to exude confidence and demonstrate success. He couldn't walk up the road from a bus stop.

He still felt the fear and seemed to hear the whine of the drill. He punched in his PIN and was given his card back. The man drove away fast because he hadn't rounded up a tip.

His daughter was coming out of the house, a semi that was one of twelve, a successful speculation, and dated from 1937. It had three bedrooms and was called The Cottage when the others in the row had numbers. She might have been attractive, if she hadn't been frowning. Her skirt was ridiculous and her eye makeup was carpet thick. If he'd asked her where she was going on a Sunday afternoon she would have said, 'Out.' She paused at the gate, a snapshot moment. The picture had come through the post six weeks earlier. It was in a brown-paper envelope, printed on cheap paper, and showed her in the same skirt, with the same amount of eye makeup and the same scowl. It was, of course, from the Irish – and there was no need to embellish the threat. They knew his home and his family. As did Five and the Russian.

Ralph Exton lived the lie. So, in their ignorance, did his family.

'Hi.'

A grunt.

'Where's Mum? At home or . . . ?'

A shrug.

He thought it indicated that his wife, Fliss Exton, married to him for sixteen years, was likely to be with her dentist. She had many appointments with him and a Sunday afternoon was as appropriate as any other.

'Have a nice time.'

He went past his daughter and walked up the gravel path, reached the front door and fished for his key. He lived the lie. He remembered, as he often did, a monochrome photograph of a man with a long pole doing the tightrope walk over Niagara. Ralph Exton thought, as he always did, Hey, man, you know nothing. I do it for real, no safety harness, each and every day. Wish me luck.

It would be good if there was some lunch for him in the fridge, but he wouldn't hold his breath.

He slammed the door, leaned against it and the shivering was back. He could barely stand. 'Fuck me,' he wheezed. 'Just another day at the office. Fuck me.'

Ralph Exton lived with the fear and the lie. Over his head he saw a cobweb that neither Fliss nor Toria had bothered to clear. A spider was lurking in the corner and a fly was wriggling, trapped. 'Know how you feel. Life's shit, isn't it?' He went into the kitchen in the hope that some instant coffee would kill the shivering.

Malachy Riordan did haulage work, cattle and sheep. The route would take him that afternoon through Dungannon, and he was hired to get over towards the Moy where a dozen bullocks awaited collection; the farm was a second cousin's. He had come down through Donaghmore and gone past the big stone Celtic cross, sculpted a thousand years before, and now he drove into the town through the modern housing estates.

Normally he would have regarded himself as safe at the wheel of a tractor or the heavy lorry and as good as any when bringing a getaway car clear of an ambush site: speed, distance – catastrophe if he spun off a road and ended up in a ditch, half concussed. Today, though, he had been within less than an inch of taking the side panels off a post-office van, and had missed the temporary traffic lights that the council had put up for roadworks on the Pomeroy road – he had gone through on red, and two cars had had to back up to clear a way for him.

The Englishman had confused him.

The man had said, *I've a family to keep. You pay me. Good enough? I need the money.* Where Malachy Riordan came from, men talked about the Cause, loyalty and martyrs. Their blood, they said, was in the soil. They knew each corner of their territory and could recite the atrocities that had been done to their people at which crossroads and whether it had happened a decade or a century before. The man had said he would do the deal for a slice of their cash. He seemed to think that money explained his actions. He was a funny little man. 'Funny' because he had been told of the smell of burned flesh, had heard the noise of the drill, and should have been wetting his trousers or blabbering. He hadn't pleaded for their trust, had seemed to suggest that Malachy and Brennie Murphy could take it or leave it: they could employ him as a source of weapons or walk away from him. A guy had gone to Lithuania four years before, had been stung and was banged up in a gaol in Vilnius. They needed the firepower.

Without trust there was a canker among them.

If the fight was to continue, they must have new weapons.

He had a good knowledge of target surveillance, had known since childhood of the techniques used by police, military and intelligence for bugs and cameras, but he was troubled because he couldn't judge that man. He knew his name, Ralph Exton, his home address, where his wife went most days and where his daughter went to school. He knew the man had organised cigarette shipments from southern Spain to Ireland and that their sale kept the Organisation financially afloat. If it was a sting, a cell door would close behind Malachy Riordan and he'd be off the mountain for ten or fifteen years, or he'd be shot and a weapon planted. Suspicion flooded him. Yet he couldn't say where the man had tripped. Brennie thought him clean.

He came up the hill that was Irish Street, skirted the town's sloping square and was below the ruins of the castle of the patriot O'Neill. He took the turning that would lead him to the Ranfurly road and towards the Moy. He saw Mikey Devine. He was difficult to miss: he wore a high-visibility orange jacket and held a lollipop sign warning of a school children's crossing point. He was smoking as he waited for them to come out of their afternoon classes. Mikey Devine was eleven years older than himself and had followed him like a dog. He was a good 'dicker' – message-carrier – and could play stupid well enough to linger outside a barracks and get the policemen's private car numbers when they came off shift. He and his ma, widowed, still lived on the mountain. He had been a volunteer, had moved weapons, tracked targets, had been a pall-bearer for one of those commemorated in the village of Cappagh where the names were done in gold on the stone . . . He had gone the other way. Most had. They had bought into the 'peace', and the reward for turning a back on the armed struggle was to wear the uniform needed to see kids across a street. 'Fuck you, Mikey Devine. You were bought cheap.' Everyone knew Malachy Riordan's stock lorry, as would Mikey Devine, but the bastard ducked his head and didn't peer up at the cab. There was enough puddle water close to the gutter from the morning's rain so Malachy edged the wheel over and let his near-side tyres splash through it as he accelerated, wetting the other man's legs. It was a brief moment of satisfaction.

The Sinn Féin people in the town paid small sums for a week of crap jobs and the money kept a sort of discipline among those who had copped out of the fight. Better weapons and better supplies of military explosive would draw back a few of the waverers and lessen the organisation's reliance on brave but untrained kids: like Pearse and Kevin.

He had been told by Brennie Murphy that he should take the Englishman on trust. That was why Malachy was driving badly. The Englishman claimed a Russian contact, a safe one.

The young man, mid-twenties, had dealt in heroin for four years. He prospered. Now he employed half a dozen enforcers and four sales people; he had targeted for his commercial expansion a district on the west side of the Iset river dividing the city of Yekaterinburg, and south of *ulitsa* Kuibysheva. The young man believed this city in the Sverdlovsk *oblast*, the capital of the Urals, offered a major business opportunity. Near to the wide river he had met with competition from men who used two kiosks, which had been torched; the people operating from them had been beaten. The young man had drunk local 'champagne' that evening in a nightclub on *ulitsa* Vosmogo Marta and had thought himself king of all he surveyed. A couple of months had passed since then and the young man was ignorant of certain factors that would affect what remained of his life.

The areas of ignorance stacked up. He did not know of a former captain in the old GRU named Timofey Simonov. He was unaware that, twenty-five years after leaving Military Intelligence, Timofey Simonov had made his first ventures in the new capitalism in Yekaterinburg, and provided a protective 'roof' for a network of kiosks. His limited contacts could not tell him that Timofey Simonov performed functions for several of the fringe élite, the *siloviki,* in Moscow and St Petersburg. The young man's knowledge of geography was limited to the supply routes running north from Afghanistan and through the Tajikistan city of Dushanbe into Russia, not of European maps and specifically not of the town of Karlovy Vary set in the hills of the western Czech Republic. There was no possibility he could have been warned that he was showing grave 'disrespect', or of the dangers in causing offence to an individual living a quiet life 3,800 kilometres away. Neither did he know that two sacks of cement dust and half of an oil drum had been delivered that afternoon to a lock-up garage on the east side of the Iset river, close to the weir where young lovers liked to leave padlocks on the railings. Men had followed him and learned his movement patterns, but he hadn't seen them. The young man's ignorance was perhaps a blessing because his awakening from it would be violent and cruel. He had lunch and drove now, in an Italian sports car, around his kingdom, checking his profit margins.

The bureaucrat once occupying a back office at the Finance Ministry in Moscow had slipped out on a spring afternoon five months before and none of those with whom he worked had noticed that his briefcase was in his hand. Why take a briefcase if the destination was a park, and the purpose to eat a sandwich? Memory sticks did not weigh heavily or bulge. It had not been noticed by those colleagues that this official had spent all of his previous lunch breaks in the last fortnight with sticks in the computers and passwords tapped into the machines. His absence had not been noticed on a warm, sunny afternoon. It was not until the next morning and his failure to arrive at his desk that security personnel were sent to his bachelor apartment. It had been wiped clean, the owner's personality deleted. He was gone – well gone. An evening flight had taken him from Domodedovo airport to Vienna. He had been airlifted on to Zürich and taken to a safe-house by Swiss financial authorities. Now he had moved on. The investigators had shifted him to a small gated estate just inside the M25 and to the south-west of London. At first, after arriving in the United Kingdom, he had been too scared to cough and had stayed inside the four-bedroom house with the handyman/housekeeper couple – both formerly with the anti-terrorist command – who were responsible for his safety. He had begun to relax. The secrecy around him had slackened. In the small hours of a morning in August, at first light, he had tiptoed downstairs and telephoned his mother's home, near to the aluminium smelter in Krasnoyarsk at the heart of Siberia. Where was he? his mother had demanded from her apartment in the Sovetsky district of the city. He had not answered her. He had repeated that he was well and would urge the authorities handling him to attempt to bring her out of Russia to him.

The conversation had been a disaster. Part of the disaster he had known of: she had refused to leave her motherland. The other part was the capability of Russian electronic intelligence to pick up the call to the Krasnoyarsk number, locate the caller and set a watch on the streets, lanes and bridle paths on that side of Weybridge. When he was found, Timofey Simonov was given a contract and turned to his considerable diary of contacts. A weapon had been made available to a Bosnian Serb marksman who had perfected the skill of using a precision rifle at long range while working from high ground, above the Jewish cemetery, during the siege of Sarajevo. It would be a deniable killing, and no trace could be laid at the feet of important men in the commercial banking world of the Russian state. The killing would send a message and whistle-blowers poring over files and computer screens in Moscow would hear of it.

The target, of course, knew nothing of plans being made to abbreviate his life. Now that the security regime had relaxed, he walked more often in the garden, seeing only a distant wall of trees on the south side of the property. It was another afternoon of rain so he did not go for his run, three circuits of the grounds. He had never heard of Timofey Simonov, and boredom had supplanted fear. That afternoon he played chess against himself on a laptop computer.

He woke with a start. The shadow moved in the room. He had been among the trees, the vandalised ruins and wilderness of the abandoned aircraft hangars. It was said to be the safest town in the Czech Republic and the police took great care of the residents of the street that ran up the hill. The evening had begun. Timofey Simonov had been asleep on the sofa in the first-floor room with the big windows that overlooked the town. The curtains had not been drawn and the dusk had crept up on him. The figure flitted across his eyeline.

The ghosts had been with him as he dozed. He had not been to Milovice for three weeks. It was almost home to him. He had nothing to fear, yet the breath had caught in his throat. He coughed. A light was switched on.

The brigadier came into the room most days at this time with a pot of coffee. It surprised Timofey Simonov that he had felt a frisson of apprehension when he had become aware of his man's presence. What had he to fear? Nothing that he knew of. And to look forward to? A concert that evening, and next week he had tickets for a Glenn Miller orchestra playing in the town. In his sleep he often walked on the old runways and aprons of Milovice, among the weapons arsenals and the side roads that went to the firing ranges where the battle tanks had performed. And, so many times in his sleep, he cringed at the engines of the Mig-29s of the 114th Regiment of Interceptors. They had been, to the NATO people in Germany, the fulcrum designation of Soviet air power . . . All gone, and weeds grew at Milovice. It was a scandal, a disgrace, an insult to the country of his birth and— The tray of tea was put down beside him.

He stretched and yawned, stood up and slipped on his shoes. 'Any calls?'

There had been none from Yekaterinburg or London, but his English friend had confirmed his arrival in Prague the next day. 'You're sure you want to see him?'

'Certain.'

'You knew him a long time ago – and his business is ridiculous, for someone like you to get involved in.'

'He helped me when it mattered.'

The brigadier gave a slight shrug. He had accepted that his advice was rejected. He said that 'necessary matters' were in hand.

Timofey Simonov hadn't shared with him the incentive to make available the weapons: they would be used against the government, the military and the authority of the United Kingdom . . . The memories were sharper each time he resurrected them. The meltdown of power in 1989, when he had been twenty-eight. The frantic efforts to clear the Milovice base of millions of dollars' worth of equipment; the accompanying triumphalism of the World Service from London and the Americans' Radio Free Europe. He had been at a humiliating conference in east Berlin, at the Ministry of Defence. They had discussed the practicalities of keeping the deployed nuclear arsenals safe while preparations were made to return them to a shrunken, shrivelled Russia. The Americans had been crisp, superior but practical. The French were indifferent. The British he had thought were simply patronising – they had offered an airlift to get the warheads home. He, only a captain in the GRU, had snapped at an RAF air vice marshal, 'We have, believe me, enough wheelbarrows to bring home our warheads.' The bastards had chuckled. He could see them now and still hated them. A suited official had remarked chirpily to the brigadier, Nikolai Denisov, 'Your problem is that you tried to match the big dollar's spending, failed big-time, and broke the bank. You didn't know when to stop so your country's in liquidation and your ideology is bankrupt. What a fuck-up.' He had watched the official and the RAF officer drift away across the salon.

And Moscow, where his 'roof' rested, had no love of the British, who harboured terrorists, fraudsters and enemies of the regime.

Weapons were wanted and would be supplied.

After a fashion, the war continued. Not at the same intensity as forty years before, but it was a 'clear and present danger'. In the Six Counties of Northern Ireland, policemen still patrolled in paramilitary uniforms and, in some areas, carried automatic assault weapons. They used cars and jeeps with armour plating, and state-of-the-art water cannon made regular appearances to soak rioters hurling Molotov cocktails.

Bombs of increasing sophistication appeared outside public buildings and were laid underneath policemen's cars. More calls were made to the police report lines about crimes being committed in the hope of drawing officers into a field of fire.

Most of the old men of the IRA's Provisional wing were bought off, given inflated wages as 'community officers', or were paid off by their former active-service-unit commanders, with government hand-outs to drive hospital cars or see kids across the road at the school gate. Others, though, rejected the ceasefire and kept a suspicion of war alive.

Security officials learned they were under surveillance. Their home addresses were watched, their families intimidated and nerves shredded. The political wings of the principal gaol, HMP Maghaberry, were full. A peace dividend seemed ever elusive.

There was a new and growing confidence among the activists and an increasing boldness. After each attack, politicians resurrected the old words: it had been an 'atrocity', the work of 'evil' men who had 'no care for democracy'. The killers were labelled 'cowards'.

It was as if, in parts of those Six Counties, a virulent disease had returned after the false dawn of remission. The need to prevent fresh supplies of weapons and explosives reaching the Province was of critical importance in the battle against the activists.

'Keep the fucking hardware out of their hands and we stand a chance of inching towards some sort of normality,' a departing intelligence officer had told his replacement. 'Let the hardware back into the Province and we go back to the dark days – fast.'

Gaby Davies took him into Thames House. More to spare herself than him, she brought him in through the side entrance, just up from the café and beyond the gardens in the square. She flicked her fingers irritably as he fumbled in an inner pocket for his wallet, then reached inside and took it out herself. She flashed her own ID and went through the gate, then swiped his and pulled him through. He might have been a truculent child wanting to skive off school for all the dignity she allowed him. The security team watched them.

They would have known Gabrielle Davies and might have reckoned her a little like girls from their own homes and streets, one who had done well and usually had time for a fast smile and a crack about one of the bloody awful football teams they might support. They'd have assumed that Hugo Woolmer, hangdog and cowed, had been out on the piss and was suffering. She took him up in the lift.

They were an unlikely couple spilling out on the second floor. His coat stank of old cowshit, and there were still oddments of straw caught in the pocket flaps. His shoes were mud caked and he was unshaven. Their driver had rewarded her with a baleful look that seemed to blame her for the filth her companion would dump on his upholstery. At the Belfast end she had cleaned her shoes in the toilet. On the shuttle, she'd washed her ankles, sponged the hems of her jeans and sluiced her face. In the services' toilets, she'd run a comb through her hair. The contrast between them was obvious, intended. She sat him down at his usual console.

She said to him, a clear voice, 'I suggest, Hugo, that you spend the next few minutes clearing your desk. After I've been in with Matthew I can't see you spending any more time here. Your performance was a disgrace to the Service. You were pathetic.'

She knew all about Hugo Woolmer from himself: father an accountant and mother a GP in the East Midlands, private school, Oxford, first-class honours, the family revelling in the 'hush-hush' and 'need to know', 'lips sealed, but it's important work he does – national security'. He'd seemed to regard her as 'staff', close to getting her to sort out his laundry. She was from a town on the North Sea coast, had the accent to prove it, and not many – if any – from her street had matched her.

She swept out and went down a wide corridor. Only the angels had individual offices. No name, but a number. She knocked. There were voices inside so she had interrupted a meeting. There was a sharp response: 'Enter.'

It was the lair of Matthew Bentinick. He was more the 'dominant wolf' or the 'alpha male' than an angel. She saw no expression on his face. Neither querulous nor irritated. He nodded to the two women with him. Laptops were switched off and files shuffled into bags. He would have expected, since she'd barged in, that her business was urgent. She had spoken to him only on the secure phone link from the base of the mountain, and again from the service station west of Heathrow. The door closed behind them.

Gaby Davies launched in. A story of a fog blanket and an agent going forward with no wire and no bug. The collapse of her superior and the return of the agent, pale and shaking but intact. He'd passed whatever tests they'd put him through, including waving a drill, power on, in his face. There had been new people at the meeting in the safe-house and it was hardware they wanted, a supposed opportunity in Prague to cosy up with Russians. He chewed gum while he listened.

'Did he learn the names of those who interrogated him, the principals?'

'One called Brennie did most of the talking. There was a younger one, less to say, seemed uncomfortable. He thought the name was Malachy, or Malchie, something like that. I reckon he did well.'

'Prague? When?'

'Within a couple of days.'

'So, our boy's best contact in the Czech Republic – who would that be?'

'Timofey Simonov. He's Russian. That's all. It's funny, Matthew, but the Joe talks his head off about the Irish and is economical with stuff about his pal who'll provide the hardware.'

'The relationship will go back a long way – not to worry. Thank you, Gaby. I'd like a few minutes.'

'Of course. Can I say one more thing?'

'Whatever.'

'Hugo Woolmer is complete crap, a waste of space. He needs a shrink. I can handle this, Matthew. I can lead the team that travels. The Joe likes and respects me. He'll jump when I tell him to. I just need a sidekick, but I'm up to running the show.'

There was a pencil in his hands and he twisted it, the motion constant with the movement of his jaws. He had shown neither interest in nor indifference to the names from the mountain, nor had seemed to register that of Timofey Simonov. She'd thought her play for taking charge was not to be argued with. Nothing wrong with ambition. It had taken her clear of her street, and driven her through American studies at Essex University, then into the Security Service. A girl with her accent and background had had hurdles in front of her and she'd cleared them. She was a little in awe of Matthew Bentinick, and it was his style to give away nothing of his feelings or inclinations. She had no partner at the moment. If Bentinick – double her age – had made a pass at her she was likely to have accepted: part of the 'ambition' package. It was hard enough to maintain a relationship outside Thames House and shagging guys on the inside often led to tears or gossip. An older man had his attractions – but no invitation had been forthcoming.

'Thank you, Gaby. As I said, a few minutes, please. Could you ask our Dragon to attend here? Persuade her.'

A man sat in a fourth-floor office. He let slip a small suspicion of emotion, but not for others to see. Memories were stirred and pain recalled. He thought an opportunity was paraded, unannounced, in front of him. There was a light knock at his door.

'You'd go for Vagabond.'

'It would be a powerful call.'

The Dragon was Jocelyn. She was a tall woman, flat-chested. From the creases in her dress it was possible she'd slept in it, and there were food stains by the buttons. She wore open leather sandals. Her hair was grey, her complexion ragged and wrinkled. She was at the top of the tree, and the ethos of the Service ran in her veins: her grandfather had interrogated senior German officers after the 1945 surrender while hunting for war criminals and a few, as a result of his diligence, had gone to the gallows. Her father had served in Cyprus, Aden and Ireland while her mother had filed expenses dockets in an admin department.

Jocelyn had been with them since 1973. It was said of her that she didn't suffer fools, also that her memory was elephantine. She had been an ally of Matthew Bentinick through all his days in the Province, knew his teams in Force Reconnaissance Unit and liaised between the FRU and the Service. He sought her guidance on any remotely contentious matter that crossed his desk. Half of the floor was quietly nervous of attracting one of her outbursts of fury at what she might consider incompetence or lack of commitment. She had never married, but had a large, lemon Persian cat and lived in a Barnes apartment. Bentinick rarely ignored her advice. She leaned against the wall and declined his offer of a chair.

'He was the best you ever had.'

'But ran out on me.'

'A long time ago. It was never categorised as "desertion". As I remember, it was "compassionate leave" to start with, then "disability", sorted out with decent discretion – as he bloody well deserved.'

'It wasn't the same at Gough after he'd gone. We never had the same control over our agents. He was wrecked when he went.'

'Yes, indeed, but he's had long enough to climb off the rocks and refloat himself.'

'I think I know this, but what does he bring to the party?'

She grimaced. 'He's ruthless, focused, committed to the cause. To hell with the Davies girl. You put in the best man.'

'The best man?'

'For what's at stake.'

'Malachy Riordan, son of the unlamented Padraig Riordan, a weapons shipment that would be the equivalent of scattering paraffin on old embers. It's attractive. I quite like your reasoning . . . and there are other agendas.'

'For God's sake, Matthew, get into the serious league. Hoist yourself up to high table.'

'Help me.'

The Dragon did. She was at his desk, pushed his wheeled chair aside, squatted in front of his screen and typed rapidly. He thought she used a password and digits that were beyond his security classification. The picture came up, and the name.

'That's high table.' Bentinick bent forward.

'I'd say so. I'd also say that you don't have a handler who isn't up to his chin in affairs that count. None of them, anyway, would match Vagabond.'

'But would he come?'

'Of course he would. Those people who think they've quit, they wait a year for the call to come back. The hallmark of the lonely ones is that the work is never out of their system. A bit of protest, which you ignore. They dream of being wanted. It won't be a problem.'

'Find him for me. Dig him out of wherever he ran for cover.'

She killed the screen, blew him a kiss and left him. He thought he'd brought 'fun' to her day, which she'd value.

Matthew Bentinick remembered the call-sign of Vagabond, could picture the face and recall the fury he'd felt when the man had walked out on him – the best man he'd ever had.

He drove steadily and well. Dusty had done the usual fine job of engine-tuning. There were no clouds on Danny Curnow's horizons, and he felt good. The next day he would walk again with heroes.

* * *

It was what they always did on the last evening before the journey to France. Their bags would be packed and the little padlocks fastened. They would have told the neighbours where they were going and been uncertain whether the visit to the battlefields and the graves was a holiday or a pilgrimage.

By now they'd have taken the dog to the kennels or to their daughter's.

And word would have been passed from those who had used Sword Tours before that the driver was excellent, reticent but knowledgeable and full of respect for the places he would take them to. Those who had been with Mr Curnow spoke of an inspirational experience with him.

Matthew Bentinick looked her in the eye. 'It won't be nailed down until tomorrow, Gaby. The position is this. Other sections answering to different priorities are unwilling at such short notice to proffer a replacement for Woolmer so I have to look elsewhere. There's a fellow we once used a bit, and—'

'He'll be my back-up?'

'A good job description. Back-up and general support.'

'It's my show.'

'How could it be otherwise, Gaby?'

Silly little cow, so naïve.

'Thank you, Matthew.'

'Good luck.'

She let herself out. He imagined that she would not have been five paces down the corridor before she'd punched the air. The message came onto his screen. The Dragon told him where he would find the man who had used the call-sign of Vagabond, but he'd be changed.

He chewed hard, then reached for the phone.

It was wet, which was usual for the little port and marina of Honfleur. There wasn't a cruise liner in and the streets were almost deserted, the cafés empty, rain dripping from chairs, tables and parasols. The floodlights had failed to illuminate the walls and turrets of the castle keep that guarded the harbour entrance. It was an expensive town and ripped off tourists, but in the galleries a few would produce credit cards and buy a painting of the wave crests and shores of the Baie de Somme.

Each Sunday evening Danny Curnow hung about a gallery, in a side-street close to the church of St Catherine. She worked there on a Sunday afternoon, helping to catalogue and clear the invoices into files, and the owner rewarded her with prominent window displays of her work. Danny knew what time she'd turn off the lights, lock the door and leave. She was Hanna.

He could have set his watch by her punctuality. She was thirty-five, tall, blonde, and had spent her childhood in the cod communities of the Lofoten islands. Rather than gut fish, marry a trawler owner and go to the funerals of suicides who hadn't been able to cope with Arctic Norwegian winters, she had gone south and ended up in the French town a few years before it had become popular – and painted.

He was drawn there each Sunday, and each Tuesday, when he came back to the town – sandwiched between the afternoon on the pebble beaches of Dieppe and the morning on the fields where the paratroops had landed at Merville – with his Sword Tours customers.

He followed her.

She was nearly beautiful, and maybe nearly talented. He accepted neither qualification. To a portrait photographer or an artist, her chin was too prominent and her hips too pronounced, while her work was at the lower end of collectible. To him, the woman who pocketed the key and set off down the pavement was both beautiful and talented. He was in doorways and shadows. From that gallery he had purchased all the pictures that covered his bedroom walls in Caen – the room was a shrine to her work. Dusty never remarked on it and neither did Lisette or Christine. His passion for the pictures and their painter was his own. Hanna had no idea that he bought her work and kept her stock moving.

Because of the rain, she walked briskly.

On a warmer, drier evening, she might have turned the other way and strolled along the esplanade, past the gardens, towards the open sea. It hurt Danny Curnow when she went that way. Off to the right from the main entrance to the gardens there was a small, secluded corner. It seemed guarded by twin sculpted lions, as high as Danny's waist. Past the lions there were old stone benches and an ornate fountain. That was where they had split. The tipping point had been his commitment to her. She had said, 'Would I have to share you, Danny, with the cemeteries? Would I be in second place to the dead?' He had not answered.

She didn't know of his past, or of his scars, or of men who now rotted in Irish graveyards because he, Danny Curnow, had played God with their lives. She didn't know that he had been a soldier in the front line of a dirty, cruel war fought without dignity. Survivors had crept in anonymity away from that conflict and didn't boast of what they had achieved. The war had eased back from the headlines, not through noble victory but mutual exhaustion. She knew nothing of it, but she had learned that a man whose company she enjoyed hid among the graves of the fallen. Why did he not 'move on'?

He would have had to give up the house in Caen, the friendship of Dusty Miller, the company of Lisette and Christine, and would have had to walk away from the minibus, Sword Tours and the small groups who stood every Monday to Friday on the sites of past battles. He needed them. He couldn't have explained it to her. She had turned and gone. He could have followed her but had not. He could have run and caught her by the castle or let her go as far as the rue de la République and the town's war memorial, almost to the little street where her home was, and had not.

She had said to him, 'You know what I see in you, Danny, what I value in you? It is what you do not share with me. The past weighs on you. A man must have sensitivity and humanity if he cares so greatly for the sacrifice of those who died here. I like that in you, and sometimes I think I love that in you. But you don't give me anything back, Danny – nothing. I wish you well.'

He could have come up behind her, stopped her, held her and dried her tears. Instead he had walked back to the hotel where the customers were and talked to them about the next day, what they would see, as if no skewer had turned in his gut. It was no problem for a man trained in surveillance to follow a woman who had no inkling that she was being tailed.

She went into a mini-mart. She came out with a plastic bag holding a litre of milk, maybe some tins, and a wine bottle. It was important that he should know what she bought and whether she was cooking that night just for herself or for someone else. He stayed behind her and she turned into the narrow street beloved of visitors for the hydrangeas in pots by the front doors and the prettily coloured window shutters. He worried that she wouldn't need to get out her key, that the door would be opened and a man would greet her. Now his breathing sagged in relief. She let herself in, and was alone because the lights went on.

Those years before, when Hanna had challenged him, Danny Curnow had stayed silent because he hadn't dared to do otherwise. He was tainted. To walk with the dead was the debt he paid. He drove out of the town and took the road that would bring him to Dunkirk. In the morning he would meet – as he did every Monday morning – his clients.

3

He parked the minibus in the secure yard at the back of the hotel. The rain had eased but the wind had strengthened. For the last week there had been gales with heavy showers, but this Sunday evening at the start of autumn it was blustery, leaves blowing around him, as he went into the wide square.

He felt at ease. Danny Curnow enjoyed his solitary meals on the evening before a trip began. He walked purposefully across the wide space, hair tugged, trousers flat against his legs and the tang of the sea in his face. He always went to the same place for his meal and the canvas covers over the outside seating rippled noisily. He glanced up – always did – at the high plinth in the centre of the square, topped by the statue of Jean Bart, a seventeen-century admiral, who'd scrapped with everybody who'd had a ship afloat in those times. In the town he was revered, but elsewhere he was regarded as coarse and ill-educated, if a skilled commander. He knew such men. His career in the Force Reconnaissance Unit had brought him face to face, in conflict terms, with guerrilla leaders of quality. They had been dedicated in a way that the salaried soldier rarely was. They had been targets for those operating out of Gough: it had been Danny's job to see them dead. Tough work, hard slog. And he had quit. He always thought, when he arrived in Dunkirk on a Sunday evening, that Jean Bart had been a peasant fighter, one who had employed unpredictable tactics, which were not taught in any lecture theatre. Before he had walked away, he had killed such men. Some said he had 'danced on the graves of brave men'. He had turned his back. His country was now populated by middle-aged counter-intelligence officers who had worked for myriad agencies across the Irish Sea, knee deep in the sewage of an undeclared war. They were alone, and he thought the isolation was cruel but unavoidable. And who cared? Nobody.

In front of him the bistro was brightly lit, the church behind it.

It was the right place to start. The walls of the church tower were pocked with artillery strikes, bomb shrapnel and bullet scars. Dunkirk would be the start, each week, of the journey he made. Danny Curnow, out of the regular military, could have been a 'soldier of fortune' or could have trained to be a teacher in an inner-city school for children with special needs; he could have gone into a factory to watch employees for signs of pilfering and 'shrinkage'. He could have gone on the courses and become an inspector enforcing building regulations and going after cowboys. He could have done anything. 'Anything' for him had been the ferry to France, then making himself available to Sword Tours. 'Anything' was being at the wheel of the minibus, knowing the routes and the parking places. 'Anything', most critically important, was keeping watch over the dead.

It was an obsession with him and some might have called it dangerous to his health. A solitary man, he lived alongside an old war but being close to it gave him a sort of comfort. Honfleur, for two more evenings, was behind him.

Across the road there was a second church, rebuilt after the bombing, then the town's memorial to the casualties of the Great War, and of those late-spring days seventy-four years previously. He was close to the bistro and seemed to hear the blast of shells, the scream of dive bombers and the whine of rifle bullets.

He was greeted. The staff knew him well. Because, the next day, he would bring the tour's clients there for lunch, he was favoured. A couple of times each year the patron offered a Sunday-night meal on the house, but he always declined politely. It was Danny Curnow's way. No one in the bar – the owner, his mother who guarded the till, his nephew, who led the kitchen staff, or his two daughters, who served the tables – knew anything of his past.

He greeted them with a cool smile and was led to a table that gave him a view of a football match on the TV. He would have soup, a thin-cut steak, a side salad, then local cheese and a beer. He did not have to order.

Dusty Miller had cursed all evening. And, rare for him, he had snapped at Christine. What time did he want his supper? How the hell should he know? Had he washing to go into the machine that night? No idea. When would he have finished retiling the shower cubicle on the second floor? When he was ready to finish it. He had sworn. He had not had his dinner but had stayed in his room. He had not brought washing down to the machine. He had not finished sticking tiles to the back of the shower unit. Christine, in her twenty-ninth year, was an attractive woman, with fair hair. Once a month or once a week, she slipped into Dusty's room, eased aside the bedclothes and slid in beside him. They would make clumsy love and she would be gone before dawn. They never expressed their affection for each other in the presence of her mother or Danny Curnow. It was, in the simple terms of Dusty Miller – a boy from the Lancashire town of Clitheroe, a soldier at sixteen, then a dogsbody at Gough with FRU, and protection for Desperate – about as good a life as he could have had. He didn't suffer from the wounds in the mind of the man he near-worshipped. His life was almost perfect, and what he had he owed to Danny Curnow. He expressed his gratitude often enough, not that it was acknowledged.

The mobile was always switched off when Danny was travelling. Dusty had lectured him about it. 'If your phone's off, you're out of contact. What happens if the trip gets cancelled?' Often enough, Dusty had fielded the look that almost, still, frightened him. The phone would stay switched off. Danny Curnow could be reached at his hotel.

It had been a good day and he'd intended to get the grouting done that afternoon. The minibus was gone and he could smell lunch cooking in the kitchen. The phone had rung and Lisette had brought it to him. She'd shrugged when he'd asked who it was and passed it to him. He had wiped the sealant from his hands and . . . it was like a great dark cloud had killed the light. He'd known the voice.

He'd damn near stood with his heels together and back straight to answer him.

The clock turned back. The pages restored to a rip-off calendar. No introduction, just the crisp voice.

'I'm assuming that's Dusty. Am I right?'

He had not shown deference to any man in more than a dozen years. 'Yes, sir, it is. Yes, Mr Bentinick, it's Dusty Miller.'

Where was Desperate?

'He won't be answering his mobile, Mr Bentinick. Later he'll be at his hotel, the Ibis in Dunkirk. Right now you won't get him because he'll be having his supper, on the place Jean Bart. In the morning, he's on the move with clients. Would you like me to tell him you called, Mr Bentinick?'

'Don't bother, Dusty. It'll be a nice surprise for him when I catch up with him.'

There was a pause on the line. Dusty could have sworn he heard gulls shrieking.

If Mr Bentinick had come into the Ready Room, Dusty had always gone to attention, as if at a drill sergeant's instruction. If Mr Bentinick had offered praise he'd always gone weak at the knees.

'Yes, sir. Right, sir.'

He thought the world had caved in.

The plane, twin-engine propeller, was at the Louis Blériot airport.

Matthew Bentinick told the pilot, pleasant young fellow – and he'd made a good fist of the cross winds coming in – how long he thought he would be. The tower had called for a taxi to take him into Dunkirk. He knew the pilot had the hours available and gave him a destination for when they took off again so that a routing could be prepared and the necessary fuel taken on.

A desolate place, and there was no cover as he waited outside the building for the car to pitch up. Birds screamed and flew low over the runway. He thought it would have taken any of the new intake who currently flooded Thames House around a week to locate his man, but the Dragon had warmed to the job. In three hours, she'd produced phone numbers and an address, a street view of a property in Caen, the names of the owners, and the cross reference to Sword Tours: closed for the evening, but their on-line brochure said the tour started the next day in Dunkirk. He drew euros and had authorisation for the aircraft hire, using a firm operating from Northolt to the west of London.

An idiot must have thrown some takeaway food onto the grass beside the step on which he waited. The gulls were like bats from hell, ferocious. He didn't think he faced a problem. Bentinick never anticipated failure, didn't countenance it – from himself or subordinates. Excitement flushed in him: he had set in motion a process that would draw in others, some he controlled, others who were allies and a few targets – some he knew and others he did not. It always bred in him a degree of exhilaration. The car came. He gave the address he wanted.

She could have turned heads but did not. She had been told by those who directed her that she should dress down and rarely be noticed. She wore jeans that were ragged at the ankles and knees, shapeless trainers, T-shirts that disguised the shape of her body, and her hair was dragged into a ponytail. The anorak could have come from a charity shop. No makeup, no jewellery. At her home, high up the Malone road, an artery coming into Belfast's centre, she was a source of frustration to her parents: her father managed a bank branch and her mother exercised influence in the Department of the Environment, specialising in Heritage. They would have liked their only child to demonstrate greater ambition and hunt harder for a meaningful career. Frances McKinney, aged twenty-four and with a degree in modern history from Queen's, should have challenged herself.

Her mobile trilled in her bag, which it shared with two MBA textbooks – *Legal Environments* and *Ethical Law* – a notepad and her laptop.

Frankie was with the four Enniskillen girls: Protestants by inherited faith. She would have called herself 'lapsed Catholic', and in the new Ireland – north and south – there were enough of them. Most nights they were out. It could be the Fly, the Sultan's Grill, the Elms or the subsidised bar at the union: the Elms did a plate of food and a pint for five pounds. One girl's father was an orthopaedic consultant and another's had a string of Mercedes showrooms in Belfast and up the north-east coast. There was money, and Frankie rarely had to dig deep in her purse. The other girls had sucked in a story of family poverty and her scholarship to a grammar school on the Ligoneil Road. They were good kids, liked to party and enjoyed her company – she made them laugh and could drink with them without falling over. They knew so little about her.

Frankie had been a good catch because she was a 'clean skin', had never featured in police files.

Her family knew nothing of their daughter's allegiance. They would have been classified by psephologists as in the catchment of moderate nationalists harbouring no sympathy for the Provisionals and the thirty-year war. They would have had, and shared with their social circles, a horror of violence, a refusal to consider that the 'gun' might influence the 'path of politics'. The bigotry in the city was an affront to decency, they'd chorus, and sectarianism as repellent as black-shirt Fascism.

Frankie fooled her parents, living in the big brick detached home high up the Malone road, her friends, with whom she shared a terrace house, and her lecturers, who thought her a fair prospect for a master's.

With her 'clean skin' she was confident, as were those who used her. Her contact messaged her.

She would finish her drink, then plead a headache and drift away. Her departure would not be noticed. Her contact was Maude, mother of three and supermarket check-out assistant, with no conviction for seventeen years. Maude had texted her and the code indicated urgency and a location. She felt warm under her anorak and her breathing came a little faster. She was on a road. At different stages she was tested and had not yet been found wanting. She had carried messages, minute writing on cigarette papers, and given them to men or women she had never seen before or since, passing them with brush contacts. She had done the difficult business of taking car-registration details from vehicles exiting Palace Barracks at Holywood, she had moved pistols from one side of the city to the other – west to east. She had switched money. Most recently she had been called up to the Sperrins, where she had met men and one woman, tramped in the bog while the rain had pelted them and fired four shots on single with an assault weapon. The impact of the recoil had been better, almost, than anything she'd experienced before. She had been lectured in the causes of blockages and the remedies, and afterwards had soothed the bruises on her shoulder with witch-hazel. Frankie had not failed at anything asked of her.

She knew that the next time they called her it would be for a mission of importance. 'Sorry, guys. My mother hasn't been well. I have to bug out. Don't drink the place dry – well, not without me.'

Frankie left them in the crowded bar to talk of lecture schedules, job fairs and men they fancied. She went into the night to meet her contact.

She would never have complained. Bridie Riordan was Brennie Murphy's niece. The relationships on the mountain slopes, in the small villages and among isolated farms, were tribal. Blood, and loyalty from fighting and suffering together, bound the families. She was the same age as Malachy and they had been married for nine years. In that time she had never argued with him over what he did. He would slip from the house when darkness had fallen and would sometimes drive away down the lane or head for the hedgerows and ditches in any direction from the farmhouse. She never reproached him when he returned – no explanation – in the small hours, smelling of strong soap and shampoo. She never took issue with him.

Explanations came with the dawn. Bridie Riordan, an uncomplicated woman with rich auburn hair and a solid frame from hard outdoors work, would hear the radio news at six thirty. A half-hour after the bulletin had announced an attack by gunfire or an explosion, the police would come: armoured Land Rovers from which they would spill with their guns. She'd the habit of opening the front door to remove their excuse for breaking it down. It happened each time, and Malachy was a principal target. She'd say quietly, at the door, to the first one in, 'One of your cars with a wheel punctured, and it's Malachy that did it?' or 'Angry, are you, that one of you's alarm didn't go off and that's Malachy's fault?' One day they'd smack her, but they hadn't yet.

The men from Serious Crime knew their way through the house, up the staircase and into the main bedroom, which had the view across the fields and down the slope towards the Pomeroy road, Donaghmore and Dungannon. He'd be out of bed by the time they came in, his hands would be on his head – no justification for them to belt him with their sticks. He'd be allowed to dress – taunted as 'Fenian vermin' – then cuffed, taken downstairs and out through the door. He never looked back at her, as if that might be seen as his weakness. He'd be driven to the crime suite at Antrim. Other officers would stay longer to bag up clothing and look for mobiles, pens and pads of paper, which they would check for the indentation of writing on the top blank sheets. She had to stay strong, and did. She had the impression that the detectives and the forensics teams harboured a degree of respect for her, maybe for Malachy too. They never abused Oisin, now seven, and she'd get him ready for school. They'd work around her and the boy as she dressed and fed him. A woman would search her before she was allowed to take him to the primary down the hill, but by then, each time, they'd seemed to know that – again – they would find no evidence. A year ago, Bridie had seen a big-built constable, sixteen stone or more, down on his knees in the boy's bedroom doing Lego with him. It didn't make her soften to them, never would, not while there was breath in her body. They'd only one question for her: had her husband been with her through that night? Her answer, each time: where else would he be?

They could hold him for seven days. He'd come home, flop in his chair, and the crime suite at Antrim was never mentioned, or what they'd asked him in interrogation. She was Brennie Murphy's niece and understood the struggle, that the Five people from the Palace Barracks at Holywood could put in people to do a close target recce, then a detailed target recce: every phone in the house, every power socket and every light fitting, every item such as a TV or a toaster or the power points in the barns where the haulage trucks were, might have been used as the source for an audio bug. They lived with it.

Bridie had known Malachy Riordan all her life. She knew him as shy and reserved, seldom messing about as other kids did, but deep and distant – and at thirteen he had killed a man: her uncle had told her. She knew about 'touts' – any thirteen-year-old did, boy or girl. Years before, Mossie Nugent had touted on the mountain and been nutted; his wife still lived there, alone and shunned. She knew, and everyone knew, that the Loughgall Eight had been fingered by a tout before their murder at the hands of special forces. She knew, and everyone knew, that Malachy's father, Padraig Riordan, had been killed because an informer had said where he would be and in which ditch the bomb was to be put. Her uncle, Brennie Murphy, had likely told thirteen-year-old Malachy who had given the information for cash. She knew: Aidan had driven a delivery van that took bread to the small stores in the villages either side of the Pomeroy road. He had been trusted and sometimes ferried weapons. It had been five years later that her uncle had told Malachy. He had gone to the buildings at the back, had taken a sledgehammer that had been his father's, had walked across the fields for at least an hour to the man's bungalow. He had waited in the shadows beyond the back door for Aidan to come out for a last cigarette, loosen his zip and piss in the grass, and had hit him with the sledgehammer in the back of the skull. Aidan had gone down and been hit again and again. He had been hit so often that his own wife had barely recognised him.

Malachy had gone home across the fields and along the trails in the bracken above the pastures that the cattle and sheep used. His mother had taken him in, stripped him bare, scrubbed him in hot water and burned his clothing in the incinerator. She had buried the killing weapon under several feet of rotting cattle manure.

They had come to the house, which was now her home, the next morning. The incinerator was cold and the teenager's body gave up no evidence. In the presence of an 'appropriate adult' he had claimed to the detectives questioning him that he had gone to bed early with a cold and had been there all night. They had known, of course, and he had been marked down as 'significant' and would be until he made the error that would convict him or laid himself open to the treachery of an informer or was shot dead.

She never criticised what he did.

The boy she had known had filled out. He had been a fair pupil in the classroom and promising at football, good enough for a trial as a seventeen-year-old with a youth side in Armagh City, and she'd watched him. He had given it all up. He had gone to war – fitness training replaced with learning the mechanism of weapons.

After two miscarriages, Bridie Riordan had given birth to Oisin, a warrior in Irish mythology, a great fighter. The child had a weak chest, was diffident and quiet, but he was what God had given her. From the kitchen, she could hear him wheezing in his bedroom. It was her life to wonder where her man was, and what he faced, and she knew no other.

'I don't know the place, and I don't know the people.'

'You have to go, Malachy.'

'I'll be off my patch. They're strangers.'

Better than most, Brennie Murphy – one-time strategist and one-time Maze cage leader – understood the nerves of fighting men. His arm was around Malachy Riordan's shoulders. They sat in the middle of a field on a plastic bag, which had contained cattle cake, to keep the damp from their trousers. The nearest hedgerow was more than forty yards away. The cattle tramped close to them and sniffed at the cake's scent. Brennie Murphy could soothe.

'Me go? How can I?'

'You have experience. You'd know the questions to ask.'

'I suppose so.'

The fingers, like claws, worked at Malachy's shoulders, at the tension there, easing it. 'We're busting our bank to pay for this. We're going to the edge and beyond of our finance. Hear me, Malachy. We're taking money from what we pay the prisoners' wives. We aren't doing organisers' fuel. It's all going in this pot. Malachy, tell me it's true. We need it.'

'We have to get better stuff.'

'And we're not paying for shit.'

'I don't trust any man I don't know.'

'Malachy, you have to test-fire it. You have to see each item. There'll be no going back if it's shit. It's different, not like it was. We don't have a Libya. We don't have those east-coast morons passing buckets round bars for dollars and sending us Armalites. It doesn't happen any more and we have to look for it. We haven't the explosives, the detonators or the firepower. We get a big shipment in, Malachy, or we could be looking at winding up the whole fuckin' business. Got me?'

A reluctant agreement.

'I can't ask boys to go out with stuff we can't guarantee. It has to be you.'

'But I've never been there.'

'Which of us has?'

Brennie Murphy, who had groomed his man from childhood, fed him the stories of war and trained him in the black art of low-intensity combat, reckoned he was close to the result he wanted. If the man stopped moaning, he might even get back to the village and into the pub before the lights went off.

'You'll be fine. Clever people are putting this together. I think I'd trust that Englishman. Why? Because he's a crazy bastard. And you'll have a good kid, streetwise and travelled, to look after you. It'll be a small team, and we're doing it fast because that's the secure way. You worry too much, Malachy.'

Brennie Murphy's joints creaked as he pushed himself up. It was like a bad dream that Malachy Riordan, the one man that all the volunteers would follow, was nervous of going abroad and doing business with people he didn't know. There was no one else he could have sent.

'When'll I go?'

'Tomorrow. Watch yourself and you'll be fine. A kid'll call by with your details, where to be and when. We're depending on you.'

They came down the field and split near the barns. The dogs came forward and nuzzled his hand, then Brennie Murphy was gone into the darkness, slipping in the mud. He had gone beyond his normal caution: *I think I'd trust that Englishman.* Not like Brennie to commit to his opinion but Malachy Riordan's spine had needed stiffening.

The BMW 5 series that Ralph Exton drove appeared, at a distance, to belong to a man of substance. It fitted in well in a village of almost royal connections. Two problems: it was seven years old, and had 189,000 miles on the clock – his skills didn't run to fiddling the figures. He was living a few hundred yards outside the famous community's parish boundary. The text had come through on his second, under-used mobile, the Samsung. He did business on the Nokia. The Samsung had been provided by his handlers. There was a code for meeting-place locations, in digits, then more digits telling him a time. Never a request, but an instruction. No recognition of how tired he was or what he had been through that day – but they tweaked him and he jumped.

Ralph Exton came out of the empty house. He had switched off all the lights, leaving it dark: he paid the bills. Usually Toria glared at him if he suggested that money didn't grow on trees, that wasted electricity cost money.

The fuel gauge showed the need for a refill. The handlers didn't pay more than basic expenses, the Irish were always late settling, a furniture deal with some Indonesian-manufactured bankruptcy stock had gone down the pan and there was a delay – bloody German form-filling – on fire-damaged Leica lenses out of a warehouse in Chemnitz. He was 'running fast to stand still', as he liked to say. And he could hear that drill, and smell the cigarettes that had been lit close to him. He pulled away and towards the road.

An oncoming car had an indicator flashing, then the headlights.

She was coming home. It had been a lengthy appointment at

the dentist – as good a fiction as any and he didn't argue with it. Not a bad chap, when Ralph was in the chair. He made small-talk while he was scratching around at Ralph's molars. He didn't mention Fliss, just prattled on about the stock market. He didn't know if they did it in the chair, set to horizontal, or in the back of his car – or in the high street in Reading in front of Marks & Spencer. He pulled out into the road and lowered his window – the system needed fixing, it was running slow, but that was an arm-and-a-leg job at the dealership. 'Sorry to miss you, sunshine. Off to a meeting . . .'

'How was your trip?'

'Not bad.'

'Anything concrete?'

Was her allowance going to increase or would she have to wheedle the dentist for some new clothes? And what about Toria's pocket-money hike?

'Early days. Anyway, I'll see you.'

'Did you find some supper?'

'Had something out of the fridge – thanks.'

He didn't know whether the dentist fed his wife first or afterwards, or whether he economised on that end of it. It had been good once, between Ralph and Fliss, when he had been starting out in the early nineties and had made his first million. She was a leggy secretary and he was a 'disappointment' to his skimping parents because he hadn't a real job with a career plan. He had lost that first million, gone to the edge of the crevasse but computers had lent a helping hand and another million had soon been in the biscuit tin. It hadn't lasted, but they'd been good times.

He accelerated up the road and saw her swing into the drive. Sometimes she had a shower afterwards and sometimes she didn't bother, but they still shared a bed.

Off the Pangbourne road, among the old gravel pits that had been filled with water and were leisure places for anglers, bird-watchers, sailors and dog-walkers, there was a turn-off to a car park. It was a regular meeting place – after dark it was a favourite for gays and doggers – a fifteen-minute drive from his house. He had long enough to reflect that life was not simple and that the people on each side of the fence he was astride had him by the short and curlies.

He was slowing and his headlights raked over a line of cars. Some occupants ducked their heads and others used their hands to cover their faces.

She was parked on the other side, near to the exit. It was a small car and she was in the back, two big bastards in front. He had first met her five years before when she would have been just off probation. She had been with a man Ralph Exton had met once – in a back room at Reading's main police station – and the situation had been explained. He'd had about five minutes to decide whether to co-operate or be taken to a custody desk, fingerprinted, photographed and swabbed for DNA. He'd have been charged under Customs and Excise counts and with a shedload of terrorism offences. It would have been a long one. He had bent under the pressure. Who wouldn't have done?

She slipped out of the car, with one of her minders. Cigarettes were lit. He thought she showed signs of tiredness.

'Just to bring you up to speed, Ralph.'

'Thank you, appreciated.'

'They want you in Prague tomorrow?'

'Yes.'

'My usual companion won't be with me. Sadly, he's not well enough.'

The minder's lighter was out, but enough traffic passed on the road above them, heading for the motorway, for him to see flickered moments of her expression. Triumph and satisfaction writ large. Ralph could do insincerity pretty well. 'I'm sorry to hear that.'

'I'll be there, and you'll answer to me. We rate it important, national security. It's imperative that we close down any possible upgrade in their capability of returning to widespread terrorism, and we need evidence. With evidence we can go before the courts. Ralph, my colleague might not have said this to you, but I will. You're a key player for us and we appreciate what you do.'

'Thanks.'

'And the risks you take.'

'Thanks again, and . . .' No, not the time or the place. Trouble was, it was seldom ever the right time or the right place to start hammering on about the exit strategy, identity change and relocation. Or to raise the business of cash up front. He shifted on his feet. A lorry came up the road slowly, probably pulling a trailer. Its lights caught her face, hit the left cheek at the right angle. She was good to look at. She had a pretty mouth, no lipstick, nice eyes, no makeup. Something attractive, too, about the trainers, the jeans, the fleece and the anorak with the brand name covered.

She said, 'I'll be in charge of the deal in Prague. We'll have discreet liaison, but it'll be my shout and I'll call the shots. Is that understood, Ralph?'

'Quite clear, Gaby.'

He thought she was rocked but he couldn't see her face now in the dark. He hardly ever used her name. She didn't slap him down and didn't kick his ankle. He wondered if she'd a home with a guy waiting for her, watching late-night TV. He thought she worked all the hours God sent.

'I'll have a bag-carrier with me. But I'll run it. He'll also do our basic protection, not that we need it. I'm very confident, Ralph, that we're going to do this really well.'

'Will the back-up know about me?'

'I'm not inside that loop but I'm sure he'll have been well briefed.'

She told him that his air ticket would be put through his letterbox before morning. Then she touched his upper arm and turned for the car. The minder was opening the door for her. He should have asked about a *per diem* allowance in cash because the Irish were slow – and should have raised the question of exit strategy, the size of the relocation allowance. He had to step back sharply because her car was into a three-point and skidded in the mud. There'd be another time. Did she fancy him?

The thrill of success was what she transmitted to him. He flashed his car and walked to it. He was annoyed that he hadn't mentioned the daily allowance he'd need and that he hadn't pressed for answers on the person joining them, how an outsider would fit. Her car had gone into the night. He wondered again who was waiting for her.

Timofey Simonov, a big man, was his best friend. He'd call him when he was away from this place and these people in their darkened cars. He'd call him from the car park on the station forecourt. He would be betraying his good, perhaps only friend . . .

His engine coughed and caught. Ralph Exton murmured, 'Fuck me. Another day at the office. Fuck me.'

It was an important evening in Timofey Simonov's social calendar. The seats in the nave of St Maria Magdalena were all taken. He could have been at the front where there were special places at special prices. This evening it was necessary for him to be seen but not to be prominent. The funds gathered by donation and from tickets would go towards the extension to the cultural centre that the Russian community in the town would promote. The ambassador had come from Prague, with the desk chief of the intelligence section at the embassy. Others had travelled from Moscow and were said to have influence with the personalities of the regime. And, he did not doubt it, there would also be people from the Americans' embassy – they had an office in Karlovy Vary, small but a presence – and from the Czech units that focused on what they called organised-crime groups. He waited for the choir to assemble. It was a warm evening and he would have liked to loosen his collar and shed his tie.

It was a fine building, he thought. The organising committee had tried to attract a wider audience than the Russian community in exile. The town dignitaries were present. Local officials did not bow and scrape to him, as they would have in the privacy of their office, and the ambassador did not envelop him in a hug. The desk chief acknowledged him only with a raised eyebrow.

His mobile rang. Voices stilled, chairs scraped and heads were twisted. Many eyes were on him. He looked behind and sideways but the phone rang persistently. A man in Yekaterinburg had shown no respect, and a man in a gated estate south-west of London had shown no restraint. He took the phone from his pocket. The caller introduced himself and told him when his visitor would arrive. He cut the call short and switched off the phone.

Early expectations had failed. Timofey Simonov had been near destitute. He had begun to wonder for how much longer he could support the deadweight of the former brigadier. He had no friends and nowhere to live. He was in a bad bar among the girls' streets in Amsterdam, nursing a beer. His brigadier was behind him and they had nothing. The chance to buy cannabis had slipped away and they had lost their money in a scam, caught out by a confidence trickster. Gloom and misery. Then he and the brigadier had been bought drinks. The conversation had begun and opportunities had been bounced. Timofey Simonov had explained the depth of his problem.

If the police had stopped Ralph Exton's Opel hire car that night, his licence would have gone and probably a fortnight of his liberty. The drive, drunken and meandering, had been across the Dutch frontier into Belgium and on to Ostende. There was an airport outside the town, filled with old Antonovs and Ilyushins, more battered and fragile even than when they had been at the core of the transport fleet at Milovice. Ralph Exton had marched him, swaying a little, to a complex of Portakabins, had found a man, Vladdy, and had done the big talk: he had brought his Russian friends, he said, men of talent and intelligence, whom Mr Vik could use; they were at Mr Vik's disposal.

To this day, years later, he could not have said what relationship existed between Ralph Exton and Mr Vik, who ran an airline of planes held together with sticking tape and glue. It had the protection of government and took crateloads of weapons from Burgas on Bulgaria's Black Sea coast to any of the small, but promising, bush wars of central Africa. Some chemistry had existed between the two men, and it had given Timofey Simonov the break he had craved. For years Timofey had been on the periphery of Mr Vik's operations, meeting intelligence people, who needed covert work done. When Mr Vik had gone down, stung by the Americans in

Asia and extradited to New York, Timofey Simonov had slipped back into the shadows.

Now he had an empire, founded on an alcohol-fuelled night and the generosity of Ralph Exton. Maybe the first true friend he had had. There was applause. The orchestra were in and so was the choir. The conductor beamed at his audience.

A year later, when he had been building a network of his own in weapons and the materials of war, well thought of by his new patron, Mr Vik, Timofey Simonov had met up with his benefactor. He had bought expensive champagne for Ralph Exton, and had thanked him for providing him with his first step up. He had asked how well Ralph Exton had known the Russian with the aircraft going in and out of Africa. 'Never met him, actually. Just thought, Timmy, from what I'd heard, that he might be right for you – and he was . . . You make your own luck, that's what I always say. You did. Glad I could be of assistance.'

As the lights dimmed, Timofey Simonov might have reflected that life had been kind to him. He had friendship and the security that residence in Karlovy Vary brought. He applauded. He was at peace and thought any danger points were well covered.

It was what they always did on the last night, Sunday, before setting off on a Sword Tours journey to the battlefields and beaches. He could imagine it. Bags were by the front door. A last phone call had been made to the taxi company to confirm a pick-up in the morning. Some would have put histories of the campaigns in their hand luggage and others would have iPads to second-guess the guide. A few were lonely and would look to form friendships. All were anxious to touch the awesome battles fought on that Channel coast. It was likely that all had heard of the driver who would be beside their guide, that his knowledge was encyclopedic. Last checks: papers cancelled, neighbours warned of absence.

He stood in the doorway. Curnow was at a table, alone, with an empty plate and glass in front of him. He studied the man's profile. The features were the same but he had seldom seen 'Call-sign

Vagabond' calm, untroubled.

'Hello, Vagabond. You're looking well. I never liked the "Desperate" tag – rather demeaning to a man of your qualities. How about, when you've paid, we go for a walk somewhere quiet, and I can tell you why I've come and why I'm taking you back? Come on, Vagabond. I've an aircraft out there, idling. Let's move.'

They walked on the open beach, the wind fierce. The moon showed the curl of the waves where they broke on the sand. There were lights on cargo ships out to sea, anchored while they waited for space under the cranes.

Bentinick had said, at the start, 'I don't want stories about the beach and what it was like, no statistics on how many drowned and how many were shot by their officers for discipline breakdown. I don't want anything about little boats ploughing up the Thames, then taking to the open sea either. Next week, or the week after, you'll be back in your zone. Now, though, I'm taking you back.'

'I quit.'

'You did, which was, to me, a severe embarrassment. I lost bets in the mess that night – said you'd be in the canteen next morning for breakfast and coming to the briefing group. You always were an obstinate beggar, never really an army man. But you, Vagabond, were the best agent handler we knew. Better than any before and any since.'

'I walked out on you.'

'Indeed you did, a long time ago. Made your point, water under the bridge. Remember Jocelyn?'

'Hard, brilliant, liaison with the Box.'

'You were her shout this afternoon. The best, she said, and I didn't argue. The Al Qaeda teams are sacrosanct and the Belfast crowd are running around in circles because there are new people to target and they don't have the toughness that you—'

'I quit.'

'Don't interrupt, Vagabond. We're running a Joe, speaks nicely and pretty plausible. The downside for him is that I can snap my fingers and he goes to gaol for ten years or more. The upside is that as long as he works for me he stays on the outside. Trouble is, like so many of them after they've cleared the first few hurdles, he's started to flex himself a bit and that breeds arrogance. Know what I mean, Vagabond?'

Bentinick had his arm locked into Danny Curnow's. Twice a pair of men sped past on sail craft with headlights spearing the sand, and a lone runner jogged at the surf line. Sometimes they wandered closer to the sea and the water slopped against his trainers.

'If I'd known you were coming, I'd have told you not to bother.'

'Vagabond, you should be down on bended knee thanking me for thinking of you.'

'You can go back with an empty seat beside you. You remember what we did. With hindsight, what did we achieve?'

'A poor argument, Vagabond. It was necessary, and we did it well. And, sometimes, like a wheel goes round, things have to be done again. I didn't come here for the sake of my health. Can we go?'

The sea was in his nose, and old memories stirred. He remembered how it had been and the guilt caught at him. The dead cried out, and the wind ripped at his clothes. It would be a turbulent flight back.

Danny Curnow wrenched free of Matthew Bentinick's grip on his arm and they went towards the dunes. He set a fierce pace. There had been no chance that he would refuse once he had heard the voice in the bistro, a siren calling.

4

The house did not seem to have been painted, but there were new window frames: plastic. The front door had changed, too; it had been green and was now blue. The fire had been lit and peat smoke issued from the back chimney. The garden was the same, except that the few trees were taller and the shrubs thicker. The beds were not a wilderness and the grass had been mown but the cuttings not picked up – they lay in yellowed lines.

Danny Curnow used small but effective binoculars from the vantage-point. The young man, Sebastian, was wedged close to him.

On that morning in spring, there had been no foliage on the trees and the view was unrestricted to the front, back and left side of the house. He could see the barns but now they were part obstructed by conifers – perhaps planted fifteen years ago – and a pair of oak trees. He remembered the green tractor, thought it had been a Massey, but now it stood abandoned, and rusted. A jungle of nettles grew round and through it. His eyes raked over the magnified images: a child's plastic pedal car, dumped on the lawn and broken, a kid's bicycle with stabilisers on the back wheels, a small football goal. There was a line beyond the back door, strung between an apple tree with fruit on it and an iron pole. A family's washing was pegged to it. A man's underwear and a woman's – functional – his shirts and her blouses, jeans for both of them, a boy's pants and vests, small socks, T-shirts, trousers and sports gear in the colours of a Gaelic club. There hadn't been washing twenty-five years before, when the dawn had come up and he had last been there.

There would have been rain the night before and prolonged showers through the morning, but in the afternoon it had cleared.

The night had been cold, no frost but a chill in the air and a wind. When they'd arrived in the hedgerow, it had blustered in the trees and had bent the nettles. The hole hadn't dried out. He had been in water then, and was now.

A God-awful journey, no sleep. Danny Curnow knew that a Joe had been up the hill less than twenty-four hours before, that fog had left him with no adequate protection and that he had passed a detailed interrogation. He knew, too, that an arms purchase was in the air, that the principals would be on the move before nightfall and that Matthew Bentinick had put the reaction in place. Danny doubted that others at Five could have moved so fast, avoiding a string of administrative committee meetings, assessments and delays. He knew, as well, that no one other than Matthew Bentinick could have pulled him out of the bistro on the square. A phone call had been made. Cash had been left in the glove box of the Sword Tours minibus. A hotel room had been cleared. The aircraft had taken them across the Channel to Northolt. There had been a brusque farewell from Bentinick, as if his mind was still locked in a time when he had held a commission and was addressing Sergeant Curnow, who was lucky enough to be attached to FRU. He was told when they would meet up. Another take-off, and another tossing flight across open sea. The pilot had been short of conversation and anxious to keep to the schedule. Daylight mattered, avoiding it.

Sheep could have used the hide that Dusty had dug out for Desperate all those years before. They had camouflaged it well when they'd slipped away, been gone before the priest had left and after the Riordan woman, newly widowed, had come out, gathered her boy into her arms and carried him inside, still howling. The sticks under the grass sods would have collapsed on a winter's day, when rain cascaded down from the upper field, and the indent would have been exposed. Sheep would have found it, or inquisitive cattle. It was a good place and gave them cover. He had led and Sebastian had followed. There had been a police team three-quarters of a mile back, probably using the same turn-off into a stand of trees that had hidden a close reaction force of Fusiliers a quarter of a century before. He had moved towards the hide with confidence.

The aircraft had landed at Aldergrove. It had been directed by the Tower to the old military area. In his day there would have been Hercules transports there, wing to wing, executive jets for ferrying generals, and helicopters in neat rows. Only a few helicopters remained under the floodlights. No formalities. Sebastian, from Five, had met him. He was based at the new complex out at the Palace Barracks north-east of the city: there was an orange glow to locate Belfast. Danny had been there so many times: had lived and breathed it and spoken its language. He was watched from the shadows by handling staff, as if a stranger coming under cover of darkness, not through Arrivals, heralded danger. The car was a Ford, with rust, dents and mud along its sides. He smiled coldly to himself when he stood beside it and waited for the doors to be unlocked. They could screw up the outside of a car but not the tyres: good tread and expensive rubber. He didn't doubt that the engine would be fine-tuned and that the car could shift if it had to. The young man had grinned, passed the fags, eased a Glock 9mm pistol from a rucksack on the back seat, checked the magazine and the safety, then laid it between his legs.

He had driven out of the airport and headed south towards Lurgan. Then they'd hit the motorway and gone towards Dungannon. It had not entered Danny Curnow's mind that he should refuse Matthew Bentinick. There had been alcoholics in the Green Slime ranks, who had drunk themselves half insensible in the Intelligence Corps' bars and in the 'safe' hotels: their commanders had sent them to shrinks. Most returned to duty as supposed new men. They had kept off the juice and been held up as warriors of will-power. Didn't matter how long they'd been dry, there was always one night – a Dear John letter or a bawling-out from a sergeant when they'd have 'just one . . .' and that was it. He had come back, hadn't fought it, and in the night they had seen the two unmarked cars, which would have been armoured, in the market square near to the library. They'd responded to the flash of headlights from the Ford, had tucked in behind and they'd all gone fast out of the centre of Dungannon. They'd headed for the high ground and Sebastian had used a sat-nav that took them to the trees and the track.

One of the police had said, 'Hope you don't fuck up like yesterday's man.'

Another had said, 'He was a pretty poor specimen.'

Danny Curnow hadn't answered. He was given overalls, too large, and wellingtons. The rucksack was hoisted onto Sebastian's shoulders. There was true darkness, no moon, and lights in the distance were pinpricks. There was only the wind in the trees for company. The dogs prowled, offspring probably of the ones he had been wary of years ago.

They had made good time, and first light would have been rising behind O'Neill's fortress. If the fire had been lit then the door would open soon. He could picture the boy as he had been, and seemed to hear him now: a child's voice, shrill with fury, which carried across the fields. Dusty had said to him, *He'll be a problem* . . . They waited for him to appear, for the target to show himself.

She met Bentinick at the coffee machine. He was senior enough to have a 'woman Friday' for paperwork, administration and hot drinks, but he preferred to do his own fetching and carrying. Gaby Davies had thought herself one of the first on the fourth floor to be in at that hour. She still had her coat on; he wore his suit trousers and waistcoat, his tie fractionally loose at the collar. She thought that more a statement than for comfort. It was difficult for Gaby to remember when she had been on that floor before him. She wondered how he would have been on a crowded commuter train, sardine tight, and how he would have been at his home – it was known that he had a wife but no one had met her. She managed a short smile. 'Morning, Matthew.'

'Good morning to you, Gabrielle.'

He did not have to look at his watch or allow an eyebrow to flicker. So obvious that he'd already achieved half a day's work: why did he have to lord it over the rest of them? She hadn't slept well: she'd gone to bed late and hungry because she'd been sorting out accommodation and liaison. Bentinick's light had still been on when she'd gone along the corridor with its dimmed lights: she'd remembered reading in a biography of Mussolini that the Duce had ensured bulbs burned late in the government offices at Piazza Veneto so the gullible public would believe in the sincerity of Fascist endeavours.

'We'll fly out on the last scheduled one, the Joe and me, Czech Air. I've booked BA for you and the hired hand. Right?'

'Thank you.'

'When do I have the pleasure of meeting him?

'A bit later – not sure.'

'Where is he? In the building with his head in a file? Not much he needs to know, other than to do what he's told. Sorry, when do I get him up to speed?'

'Soon.'

The dispenser had finished the last of its dribble. The coffee was a disgrace.

'Well, is he here?'

'Putting himself in the picture nearby. The mocha is tolerable.'

He turned away. The corridor was quiet.

She said, 'It'll be a good one, Matthew.'

'Of course it will. A big catch and a team led by a top player going for his throat.'

There was that brief smile again. He was one of those men who had iron tips on his shoes, and his footsteps echoed.

'You can learn to love me, Mr Exton, or you can hate me. Your choice.'

The clothes he needed were laid out on the bed, with a plain envelope that contained the airline ticket. Ralph Exton always packed carefully.

'You see, Mr Exton, because of what you've done – and the company you're keeping – I can either be friendly or I metaphorically break every bone in your body.'

He was less likely, these days, to find his shirts ironed and folded in the airing cupboard. More likely he would return home and they'd be on wire hangers over a radiator. Four should be enough. Money was the problem – or lack of it. The world of successful deals seemed to have slipped past him. He was down to cigarettes. Few commodities were lower in the food chain. Didn't everybody do it? Perhaps, but not everybody did it by the lorryload from the south of Spain to the Galician coast, and not everybody transhipped to a trawler at dead of night. He'd been down in Puerto Banús on the coast, and at the time he dealt in Transit-van loads. He'd had a drink with his local contact who dealt with the money and the transport, in an Irish bar, when the contact had introduced him to two Irishmen, decent enough fellows.

'I don't want any misunderstandings. You work for us, Mr Exton, or you rot in gaol. You can do yourself a favour or get to know the intricacies of prison life.'

Enough socks for a week, a pair of stout shoes, and some handkerchiefs . . . She was at a coffee party where plastic kitchen boxes, underwear or time shares were being flogged . . . It had gone rather well for a year. He had begun to believe that the sun shone on him, and there was a bit more money in his wallet, and Fliss's purse, and a bit more of the debt was paid off. Then he'd been summoned to a police station: he didn't recall going through a red light and was usually careful about speed limits. He hadn't connected it with the monthly runs of cigarettes to the south of Ireland, and hadn't been told to bring a solicitor. He had gone with a child's innocence to the enquiries desk and given his name.

'Ignorance, Mr Exton, is no defence in a court of law. You would find that both the judiciary and the public would have minimal sympathy for a cheap little crook who lines his pockets with a percentage of the profits used to subsidise terrorism. That is having blood on your hands.'

He had been left to cool his heels in a reception area, among vandals and wife-beaters, and was there long enough to become apprehensive. Then his name had been called. He'd been led through doors, most of them locked and needing punch codes, to an interview room. It stank – disinfectant, urine, vomit – and the windows were clouded glass in concrete fittings. The table was Formica-covered, and the light was protected with a grille. He had sat on a hard chair facing the table and another chair in front of him was empty. He was watched from the door. Eventually he'd heard the approach of steel-shod shoes. A mobile had rung. A crisp answer: *Yes, it's Matthew. Speak, please.* A half-minute later, the footsteps had reached the door and the constable watching him had stood aside.

The man who came in wore a suit, with a gold watch chain draped across the waistcoat. A young woman had followed him. When the man, Matthew, had realised they were short of a chair he had flicked his fingers in annoyance and the constable had reacted. They'd sat and faced him. The girl had rooted in a bag and produced the file with the pictures – guys he used to meet in Puerto Banús, others he did business with in London, in a pub north of the Emirates stadium, and some he hooked up with in a bar off Galway's Flood Street. She laid the police mug shots on top of the covert pictures, then a sheet detailing allegiances and criminal convictions. Matthew had let her outline their membership of Real IRA, and the time they'd done. Ralph Exton could remember to this day how the shabby little interview room had seemed cold and dark. Nothing to say, and there hadn't seemed much point in denying what was on the table.

'They pay you a percentage. With the rest they keep their murderous campaign from collapse. What's it to be, Mr Exton? Are you on board or jumping ship?'

His washbag went into the case. His pyjamas followed.

He had numbly nodded agreement. She had produced a sheet of paper with two lines committing him to co-operation: he had signed and dated it on 1 April 2009. He was the 'fool'. He'd said to Fliss he'd be in Reading for a meeting then might do some shopping – he needed a couple of shirts. She'd known he'd be out all afternoon. Next morning, when she'd gone early to the supermarket, he had been at home, still shaken from the previous afternoon's experience and twitching with tension. He had made their bed and a condom wrapper had fallen to the carpet. She often seemed to forget to take her pill and kept a supply of condoms in the drawer on her side, but they hadn't done it for a fortnight, or three weeks. It hadn't seemed important at the time. He hadn't seen Matthew again, but the woman had been Gaby and they'd met at least once a month for the past five years. He reckoned he could run rings round her, if he had to.

'Don't think to play fast and loose with me, Mr Exton, or you'll find I have a short temper and am not pleasant when crossed.'

He threw in a couple of ties because that was Timofey Simonov's image of an Englishman. Who terrorised him most? Gaby, or the people up the hill when there had been deep fog and no back-up? He zipped the case and heard the drill whine. Hard bastards: they'd have used the drill, might have enjoyed it.

He'd done the fire. In most houses the woman did it, but Malachy Riordan had made the fire for his mother, and when he'd married Bridie he had continued to lay and light it. The house then would be quiet around him, and he'd listen as the boy, Oisin, struggled for breath. He was relied upon. Brennie Murphy, Bridie's uncle, talked of strategies but had no idea how a mercury tilt switch should be handled and didn't understand the way a bullet travelled across four hundred metres of open moorland and how the wind affected its trajectory. He would think and plan. He would try to imagine where the surveillance would be, where there was weakness, and how to use what he had.

The fire burned well and the peat smelt sickly sweet and raw.

There were two boys, Kevin and Pearse, aged twenty and eighteen. Kevin's father had been a volunteer in the eighties, had done time, then gone to England and was last heard of on building sites in Glasgow. He sent no money to his family. Pearse had a child's face and a child's body, and seemed so anxious to demonstrate commitment. There were others who lived in Coalisland, and in the villages north of Castlecaulfield, and men in Stewartstown and Cookstown, but the pressure on the Organisation was fierce. Most men that he could call out spent half of every day looking over their shoulders for police tails. He liked the boys, accepted their youth and inexperience. There was a pipe bomb in the barn, a target and an opportunity. Could he give it to them? Could they do it if he wasn't there? There was an opportunity to hit the O'Kane house on the Pomeroy road on Wednesday, because it was the mother's birthday and her Catholic policeman son, Eamonn, would be down from Belfast. His car could be hit. Were Kevin and Pearse capable? Should the opportunity be let go?

She brought him tea. He smelt cooking. He heard her go up the stairs to wake and dress the boy. Oisin would never be a fighter, as his father was, as his grandfather had been. Oisin would not match him at that age. Neither were those boys equal to how he had been. Was either Kevin or Pearse able enough? They were the future, not the old bastards who stayed in the bar, talking of great days – and had capitulated.

He would not be there. He would be on foreign territory with people he didn't know. The knot was back in his shoulders. He stood, stretched, and went to fetch more peat blocks. The dogs greeted him.

Sebastian said, in Danny Curnow's ear, 'He's the most capable they have in East Tyrone and Mid-Ulster. Each of the active areas requires a strong leadership personality. That matters more than the ideology. When the full weight of the Provisionals had mobilised in their day they had an internal structure of discipline, which was rarely challenged.'

He allowed the man to talk. Patronising, but well meant.

'What counts now is charisma. I'm told he has it. Of course, we've contacts among men who killed and bombed before the ceasefire, and who've taken another path. Now we throw money at them to keep them on it, but they all speak well of him. There are men in the former Special Branch who knew and respected him before his twenty-first birthday.'

He wasn't a big man, but he had the strong shoulders Danny would have expected of a young man growing up on a farm; his mother had been widowed when he was a child so he'd have heaved bales, sacks, buckets and jerry cans. Mousy hair, inclining to fair, a tanned face.

'I've studied him, he's in my sector, but I've never been in a position to linger on him. I've seen camera work, from the last gear we put in – that tree-trunk in the hedge by the lane gate. It ran for three days and we saw him a couple of times. The last day there was a view of him striding towards it with a chain-saw – God knows how he knew. He cut down the tree at the ground. You were at Gough so you'll remember the wall round it. He parked on the pavement, close to the security cameras, near the gatehouse sentry bunker, and lobbed the camera over the wall, as if he was giving it back to us. We had that on camera too. Some in the county detest the agreement and the way the old IRA has gone into government, but they say they're not ready to resume armed struggle. He's trying to locate those in the community who don't buy into that. He has to find the ones who'll put life and liberty on the line. Nobody wants to come out of the shadows and hook up with a loser, but if there are new rifles, armour-piercing stuff, explosives and detonators, the recruits will show. Just so you understand where we are, Danny, it's not like the old days here. I can't sign up a hairy-arsed lunatic, with a big mouth, and put a rifle in his hand. We'd be charged with conspiracy to murder. It just doesn't happen . . . We have five hundred people from Five living here and we're on the back foot. We regard him as a prime enemy.'

The dogs would have worshipped him, were close at his heel and came to his knee if he flicked a finger. He gazed around him. Danny understood. It was the man's home, as the house in Caen was his. He wouldn't have travelled. He had read the file on the flight between Northolt and Aldergrove and there was no mention of trips abroad. It was clear to Danny why the man must go to Prague: they'd put an RPG launcher in his hand – capable of destroying an armoured police vehicle – a sniper rifle, a box of military detonators, with Semtex or American equivalents, and he would test-fire and test-explode, then give the gear a clean bill of health. He sensed the unease in the walk to the open gate where the farm track met the lane.

'The first file reference to him has him aged nearly four. He kicked a detective on the kneecap and fractured it. They'd come to take his father. The detective had to take three months' sick leave – that's why it's entered. About a year later they came again for his father and he threw a plate at a woman officer, breaking her glasses and splitting her forehead. That's in the file too. It's said he was traumatised by the death of his father – I don't wish to pry, Mr Curnow, but I assume you played a part in that. Teachers suggested he needed counselling because he was so introverted. Everything changed when he was thirteen. A man was bludgeoned to death a couple of miles from here, and local word was that he'd informed on the mission Padraig Riordan had gone out on. The file's interesting here. There's a big red star at the side of that entry and someone has written 'Is that really so – dear oh dear?' and initialled it MB. Anyway, the boy changed. Fair at school but a potential star in Gaelic football, and school staff were saying he'd turned a corner. Too much to hope for.'

The child came out. Danny saw the love. The boy jumped awkwardly but the man caught him easily and swung him high. A little shriek of excitement reached Danny. Those years before it had been hatred. He reflected: most intelligence people were never privy to anything personal in the targets' lives. They saw them, fleetingly, in balaclavas and combats, with an AK assault job, or brought from a prison wagon to a courthouse, heads ducked, or in a car park when information came one way and banknotes went the other. Or they saw them dead in a ditch with their shoes off, burns on their skin, and a plastic bag bulging over their heads with bone and brain. Few saw them as Danny did now, and that was what he had run away from.

'That part of the mountain never bought into the peace. Another man articulated what they felt: "Did we have all those men killed and all those men locked away in the gaols, their youth lost, so that a few could parade in government and boast that they'd achieved power sharing?" Malachy Riordan had come under the influence of an activist, Brendan Murphy, a sort of surrogate father. He packed in the sport. He became a part-time haulage contractor, mostly trans-border smuggling, and a part-time guerrilla fighter. Forgive me, Danny, but I don't make the judgements that require me to call them terrorists because we'll likely end up negotiating with them one day, as we did fifteen years ago with the Provos. It's as if this lot believe they alone carry the sacred flame, nationalism, and the former crowd are turncoats and traitors. He's blown up a courthouse, he's knocked the back off a local-government office, he's wounded a detective with a Dragunov. We've been waiting for a mistake, but it hasn't come yet. He's good at what he does, and behind him is Bridie, his wife.'

The father put his son down, held his hand, then let go.

Sebastian murmured, 'Apologies for not bringing a flask . . . Maybe going off the mountain, off Altmore, is his mistake, being somewhere his reputation hasn't reached, among people he won't easily impress.'

Had he been preparing to address a seminar of recruits that afternoon, Matthew Bentinick might have observed that 'The controller should always be aware that personalities, characters, individuals, never heard of before in relation to the mission, will spring to prominence. The presence in the scenario of some will be mildly welcome and others will be intrusive and a damn nuisance, may even put the show in jeopardy. Be aware. You may consider your planning has been faultless and dedicated, but things happen, events that cannot be foreseen. People will aid, obstruct and surprise. Ignore their interventions and you will fail.' He did not, however, do recruits' seminars, was sparing with advice to anyone, and among the remotest men in the building. He believed that 'Strangers will always slip into the spotlight, usually as a damn nuisance.'

No knock. She came in and kicked the door shut with her heel. 'Is the big picture in focus?'

'I think so.'

'Who has it?'

'I do and you – the whole picture. Vagabond has most of it. The young woman will have the small-screen picture, which is adequate for her. The boss on the top floor, not a lot. He can't worry about what he doesn't know.'

'There'll be a local boy.'

'Comes with a good pedigree. He'll know it all. You were right. Vagabond came without a bleat.'

'I usually am.'

And she was gone. His eyes beaded on the file.

His employer, Timofey Simonov, was up the hill behind the villa walking the dogs. He thought Simonov, who had been a captain, with little prospect of promotion – and was now a multi-millionaire – cared more for his dogs than for him. The former brigadier, who had seemed to be fast-tracked towards full general, was now a manservant ranked below the Weimaraners. He couldn't kick them because they would betray him. He ran a vacuum cleaner over the rugs in the first-floor salon. It was a fine morning.

Why the sour mood?

He had sat in the church through the concert. At the end, Simonov had networked with others prominent in the town's Russian community and from the embassy: the brigadier was not an equal and had been sent to the car to wait. He could remember hearing of the collapse of the regime and the dismissal of scores of intelligence-gathering officers, and realising that a world had ended. He had knelt in his office on his Afghan prayer mat and wept. It was of the finest workmanship, from the bazaar in Herat, prize booty from his service there. He had sobbed: he was no different from a conscript kid in a forward fire position with the savages closing in. He had survived that war and had gone as a star to Milovice, senior on the Central Command staff, but had been a casualty of the peace. He had felt hands on him and heard a soothing voice. His head had been against a uniformed chest, that of the junior captain, Timofey Simonov. He'd nowhere else to turn. Now he could have left him, had the resources, but the villa in Karlovy Vary was his true home. His wife lived in an apartment close to the embassy in Prague and they had two children at the school there, but his home was with his employer.

He not only kept the house clean, waited in the car, as a chauffeur should, and dried the dogs when they came in from running among the beeches on the hill: he had responsibility for day-to-day matters affecting Timofey Simonov, such as deciding when the Englishman would be permitted to visit them, when the 'cargo' might be examined and where . . . Also, other matters: in Yekaterinburg, a man had risen too fast and had forgotten to pay respect. Within the next hour he would be taken off the street, or his car rammed, or his apartment entered. A garage waited, with a cut-down oil drum, and dry cement, water, a chair and some rope. The brigadier had learned the ways of the gangs when they feuded. And, because of the arrangements he had made, a marksman – a Bosnian Serb – would that morning be taking delivery of a Rangemaster calibre .338 rifle with a killing range, in the hands of an expert, of up to 1500 metres. It had been tested in some fly-blown sheikhdom or emirate in the Gulf, and had disappeared. Then, from a land of corruption and camel shit, it had become available and had been taken into the United Kingdom. That morning, it would be in the marksman's hands. The brigadier had made the arrangements and found the man who would fire the shot. The captain had negotiated the contract by *siloviki* figures in Moscow: a former official in the tax office now had the life expectancy of a tethered goat in a tiger reserve.

The brigadier, Nikolai Denisov, could moan in his head about his life as a virtual servant. It was a reversal of roles on an epic scale. In public, his fall from high rank was not mentioned: he existed with it. That day he wore a floral apron. But he would organise killings and would kill himself to protect the man who fed him.

He saw nothing that interested him. He was thirty-four, had a middle-ranking job and earned a middle-scale salary in public service. The life of Karol Pilar ticked over.

He heard nothing that enlivened him. That morning the sun shone. He was already tired. Before dawn, his alarm had gone off in the studio apartment where he lived, courtesy of an uncle. It had been converted from the roof space of the once grand house in the middle-class Prague suburb of Vinohrady, said to have been designed in the style of Paris. He had dragged on the first fag of the day as he looked out of the window and saw the statue of Svatopluk Čech, a writer, who had died at least a hundred years ago. He had been on the road before half past six.

The files put in front of him on the first floor of the principal police station in Karlovy Vary, on Krymska, had told him nothing. Karol Pilar was probably of average ability, was certainly of average height and average build. He stood out among his many colleagues for his commitment to his work. He was a dedicated detective, who took obfuscation and obstruction with dogged calm. He was not a uniformed policeman who battered down doors and carried a high-grade machine pistol. A detective, plain clothes, he struggled to make an impression on the organised-crime desk from an office in the centre of the capital. His speciality involved the gangs originating in Russia: they would likely still have connections to the Solntsevo people in Moscow and the Tambovskaya group from St Petersburg, but there were also links to government and to personalities with influence in the Kremlin, close to the seats of power. His department, UOOZ, mostly hunted down small-time criminals involved in drugs, prostitution, stolen cards and the trafficking of children from the east towards Germany. Occasionally it looked for Mafia leaders who had taken residence in his country – and there lay the difficulties. He had seen the files, spoken to local officers and learned nothing that justified his early start and the drive from Prague. He was walking up the hill on Jiriho, and round the next bend he would see Timofey Simonov's home. He could devote one week in four to matters affecting the Russian community that had bought up the best properties in Karlovy Vary, and one day each month to maintaining a view on the affairs of the former GRU officer. There were difficulties. The town was said to be a fiefdom of Russian Mafia money, and Russian control of the country's economy grew each day. Russian piped gas provided three-quarters of the energy needed to keep people from freezing in winter, at a carefully negotiated price. Russian bids were about to succeed for the construction of nuclear reactors worth twenty billion euros. The force of Russian espionage agents based at the embassy wasn't there for cocktail-circuit gossip but to influence government policy and for a back-door access to the secrets of NATO and the European Union. That business was far above the level of Karol Pilar and his pay grade. Somewhere at that level Timofey Simonov lived quietly, apparently without criminal contacts, but he was worth one day each month of the young detective's time. The chance of a major investigation, which might ruffle far-away feathers and cause inconvenience, was remote.

The sun was warm on his face. The street was clean, swept of fallen leaves. There was no litter on the pavement. The villas on either side of the road were Russian owned or rented: a month's rent might add up to Karol Pilar's annual salary. They had bought judges, local officials, politicians, even senior policemen. To them the town was a 'safe-house'.

When he came to Karlovy Vary, he walked up that hill for a simple reason: the file reported Timofey Simonov as a former captain in Military Intelligence, with a small pension, yet he lived in a house that would have been priced at four or five million euros by any of the town estate agents negotiating with Russians. Where had the money come from? Organised crime – arms sales in Africa, drugs sales in Russia, sex sales in the old Europe of the West, and the sale of services to the regime currently holding power in Moscow. A considerable target.

But a target that was presently 'untouchable'. There was a little garden opposite. Later he would shop in the souvenir stores for Jana, his girlfriend – something pretty but cheap – and he would talk to the people he paid for information. There was one in the telephone exchange, another in the town's main hospital, and a Customs man at the airport. He sat in the garden. Most of the colleagues of his own age, who had inklings of ambition, had resigned and either gone abroad to work in security or had joined private consultancies. He had stayed on, plodded forward. There was a new memorial in the garden, dedicated to Anna Politkovskaya, journalist and human-rights activist – she had been assassinated eight years ago. With her investigative writing, she had been a thorn in the arse of those inside the Kremlin. A grim irony had sited her memorial in this Russian enclave. He saw the man.

Almost prematurely aged, but only fifty-four, a survivor of hard times and now basking in the success that had brought him millions, he would have accounts, Karol Pilar assumed, in Dubai, Gibraltar, St Kitts and Nevis, those atoll islands in the Pacific, Cyprus and probably in the City of London. The phone rang in his pocket. He lit a cigarette. 'Untouchable', protected by a 'roof'. The detective could dream – the ram, the door swinging open, the charge of masked men, dawn coming up, flashes from press cameras, and the man being brought out in handcuffs. To dream was free. He answered his phone. He was told by his line manager where he should be, when, and his duties. He no longer argued. He had talked the last summer with a British officer, a contact that was made to seem by chance, had spoken of his special interests and must have made a fair impression. What was it about? He was told. He ground out the cigarette close to the monument for the murdered woman. He let the man pass him – the dogs lunged at him – and Timofey Simonov crossed the road, went into his garden and climbed the steps to the door. It was opened. A 'servant' stood with the towels to clean the dogs. He had been a brigadier. The door closed.

To Karol Pilar, it was humiliating that there were 'untouchables' in his country, who strolled beyond his reach.

She flew from Belfast to Stockholm. A second passport, not in Frankie McKinney's name, and a change of appearance for the CCTV would take her out of Sweden to Berlin, then a connecting lift to Prague.

She had dressed as if she were going for an interview at an investment bank or a firm of international lawyers. She would have seemed – as those who had tasked her had demanded – to be one of the scores of young women with professional jobs who flocked in and out of Europe's airports. Her makeup was subdued and her jewellery discreet: they had said she would be seen but should not be noticed. She felt consuming pride that she had been chosen for the mission, and would work alongside one of the Organisation's principal fighters.

Malachy kept his hands clasped behind his back. It was because of the graves that he continued to fight. He would never give up on the struggle. There were graves in the Six Counties for volunteers of the Provisional wing of the IRA, the Real IRA, the Continuity IRA, the Ulster Defence Association, the Ulster Volunteer Force, the Ulster Defence Regiment, the Royal Ulster Constabulary, the Royal Irish Rangers and the Police Service of Northern Ireland. There were the graves of those killed by 'mistake' and more graves for those who had strayed into crossfire. They were spread across the length and breadth of Northern Ireland. Nothing was forgotten or forgiven. The dead kept alive the conflict.

His grandfather's grave was further down the hill in a churchyard nearer to the Townlands and Dungannon. He stood in front of the plot where his father, Padraig, lay. He was often there and was well known to the workers at the church and the Parochial House. A grave-digger had discarded his pickaxe and leaned on the handle of a shovel. He smoked quietly and wouldn't disturb him. Another man had stopped spraying the gravel with weed-killer. Both men would have thought that soon the mourners would come along the path from the church to put him down beside his father. The lettering was in gold on the black marble headstone: *Padraig Riordan 2nd Batt East Tyrone Brigade Irish Republican Army Killed on Active Service 28 April 1989 Aged 36.* The marble was expensive, quarried in South Africa, China or India and imported by a stone mason in Armagh City. He had heard the gravedigger tell a man, who had been planning for the future, 'Order the best, spare no expense, because you're not around to pick up the bill.' Also on the stone was *Mary, Queen of the Gael, Pray for Him.* He would not have considered the call for people to 'move on' with their lives.

It seemed that every village, every parish, owned its own grave. It was not possible for any man of honour to step back from the graves, he thought. Many had. They had been in the hedgerows with the rifles and at the end of the command wires but now they sat in lonely bars and lived off handouts, benefits and pensions. Many times each week he drove his lorry through the village of Cappagh where the biggest monument stood, with words engraved on the ebony marble from Patrick Pearse, executed by the Crown ninety-eight years before: *This is the Death I should have asked for if God had given me the choice of Deaths, to die a Soldier for Ireland and Freedom*. He had not been there, but had been told of a plaque in St Anne's, Church of Ireland, in the centre of Dungannon, for soldiers of the part-time Ulster Defence Regiment, shot dead or bombed by Malachy's people: *They died before their day but as soldiers and for their country*. One day, perhaps, he might go and read it.

He could remember being in bed and his father bending to kiss his forehead, then turning out the bedside light. The big roughened hand had rested a moment on his shoulder and he had heard footsteps on the stairs, then low voices, the kitchen door opening and shutting . . . and he could remember the priest coming with the dawn. Anything other than what he did would have been 'sell-out', the worst betrayal.

His cheeks were dry. He walked past the gravedigger, who straightened and stood almost to attention, and went to his car.

They couldn't move. Danny Curnow felt irritation well in him. The dawn had come and the day had moved on. She was a powerful woman.

He was trapped, and there was nothing that he or Sebastian could do about it. They were in the hedge, squashed together. The target, Malachy Riordan, had kissed her, then heaved the kid under his arm, and they'd all laughed. Time to move, but she had blocked them. She had gone through the house, then appeared at the back door, stepped into her boots and picked up a bucket, then a sack. First she'd fed her fowls, then moved up the lower field. The cattle had stampeded towards her as she'd shaken the cake sack. She had the dogs with her.

They quartered the field, followed scents – foxes or rabbits, perhaps a hare, and there would have been badgers. Danny Curnow had no more to stay for: he had seen his target, locked onto the body language and thought he had learned more than pretty much any file could tell him. He had squirrelled away the relevant points and—

'Excuse me.'

'What?'

'You were here? Right where we are now, in this hole, the night the father was killed?'

'And if I was?' The cold was in his bones, made worse by tiredness and hunger. He hadn't slept or eaten.

'It's intelligence work, FRU work, and there was an ambush waiting for the father?'

'Try a back number of the *Tyrone Courier*.'

The woman, Riordan's wife, was some hundred yards from them and what wind there was blew up her skirt and punched at the sack. Most important, it was behind her so the dogs were not alerted. They would be if Danny and the young man rose from the hedgerow and headed off.

'Did the father and the others who were killed have a chance to surrender?'

'There was a war.'

'So they were fair game?'

'It was what we did, the way we fought.'

'Worthy of pride?'

He flared. 'Hindsight's great, but not if you didn't experience it. It's how we were and it's what we did. A tout fingered them and I ran the tout. Did he get much? No. Lucky if I paid him a hundred quid a month.'

'Your agent was . . . ?'

'You've read the file.' The woman shook the last of the cake from the sack and moved confidently among the beasts. Some nuzzled her but most searched for the last crumbs of food beside their hoofs. She was a good-looking woman – Danny would have called her handsome. Padraig Riordan's widow had been attractive. He had not seen her that morning, when the priest had come up the lane and broken the news to her, but knew her from previous surveillance. He thought that both women would have strength and dignity. They would not cave, would likely take a sack of cake, go up the field with the dogs and weep there – but not where they could be seen. She moved sideways. He wondered if she considered whether danger – beyond its usual scope – was closer because her husband was about to travel. The young man had spoken of the risk of a *mistake*. It would be difficult if she kept on wandering about, came to their hide and the dogs found them. She lingered, but her back stayed towards them and the dogs hadn't caught their scent.

'Your agent was X-ray 47, Damian. He had learning difficulties but could manage simple carpentry. He had a small funeral but the day was noticeable for the address of the father, who took it from another priest's remarks at a Belfast informer's service. He spoke of "secret agents of the state with a veneer of respectability on their dark deeds that disguises the work of corruption. They work secretly, unseen, making little victims whom they can manipulate". It was pointed out to me when I took over the Riordan file. Today we don't send informers to unpleasant deaths.'

'And you're not winning.'

'Five years later the family blamed a different agent – a bakery driver, Aidan.'

'Another was better protected, more useful.'

'You would have swung out of bed in the morning, had a mug of tea and gone to Operations for the day's schedule. As I see it, you'd have been flicking the pieces round the board, deciding which one stood and which was sacrificed, pawns slotted, knights and bishops preserved.'

If she found them, how would she react? Would she go for their eyes? No chance. She'd look down at them with contempt and say nothing.

'The more valuable the asset, the better he was looked after.'

'One man would be denounced so that another stayed in place.'

'Obvious.'

'The piece that fell over on the board – you knew what would happen to him.'

'It was a war, and we were winning. I did what I was asked to do.'

'The teenage boy killed the wrong man.'

'An unpleasant man had his career cut short. Used to shift stuff with the loaves. He was trusted, and we dropped a couple of hints, in a roundabout way, so that suspicion fell on him. It's good when they feel threatened and betrayed – it makes them panic.'

Abruptly, she went briskly down the hill. They were strong women on the mountain. They didn't whine and were loyal to their men.

'Totally forbidden now. For that I'd be before a court.'

'We were winning, and you aren't.'

'A last question.'

'Shoot.'

'Your call-sign was Vagabond.'

'A long time ago.'

She was past the barns and smoke veered from the chimney. The dogs tracked her. The young man had started to gather together the kit and Danny passed the binoculars back to him. They were later than he'd expected, but had not yet missed the flight.

'I was with some old Branch men, chewing over the Riordan family. Did the work, went to a bar. They spoke of a call-sign, Vagabond, and a guy who was a bit of a legend, a handler who ran agents.'

'You shouldn't gossip, Sebastian, not in taxis, on the phone, in clubs and bars, at football matches, at home with friends, anywhere. "Whatever you say – say nothing." The Provos made posters with that printed on them.'

'The Branch boys said of you, "He was the best because he was the coldest, not a degree of warmth in his veins. The best because he'd no sense of mercy. A man wants to come out, but can't. A man wants to back away, but the hooks are in him. A little man's death may protect a bigger asset – so it's time to book the hearse, the priest and the grave-digger. The best because he'd no feeling." I think we can move.'

* * *

If Matthew Bentinick had been preparing a lecture for young officers on launching a mission, he might have said, 'Those working under you do not need chapter and verse on aims and end games. What they need to know is what is expected of them in a field, however narrow. That way they are less likely to be confused with ethics – always a substantial enemy.' But he did not lecture young officers.

The tourists would have arrived at Dunkirk. They would have been sobered over an early lunch in the bistro on Place Jean Bart. Stories of the town and the significance of the battle fought there, seventy-four years and a few months before, would have been etched in their minds. They'd be driven from the bistro up a narrow street named after a resistance fighter, Louis Herbeaux, who had been executed by firing squad in 1943: some of the men on the minibus would have wondered in silence how they might have been, or their fathers, if an army of occupation had moved into their town. The evacuation of Dunkirk, in the last days of May and the first days of June, had been controlled from a nineteenth-century fortress by a quayside, now a museum. They'd have been there in dull light and could hardly have failed to imagine the terror and confusion of the last stage of the retreat. A film played, black-and-white images, with a soundtrack at full volume relaying the scream of the diving Stuka bombers. They would see the rifles and machine-guns that old relatives might have handled in a desperate defence of the harbour, the dunes and the beaches. Within an hour of entering the museum, a few might have shivered. They would have felt better, already, to walk alongside the men who had suffered in that place, and a guide might have spoken of the nation's debt.

Dusty had come by taxi. A cloud had gathered over him – like that moment of warning before disaster struck, when tyres lost their grip on black ice and roadside trees loomed in the windscreen.

He had gone, long past midnight, to Reception at the Ibis. A sleepy porter had passed him the envelope. He had travelled 380 kilometres from Caen to Dunkirk and escaped with a fare of four hundred euros, but the driver had been Algerian and he had done a good deal. He had found the keys to the minibus with the thousand-euro float left for him. He hadn't slept.

It was 1998, the night the FRU team at Gough heard that a bakery delivery driver had been beaten to death. The driver was Aidan. Quite useful to the armed struggle. There had been another man who, it was felt, was facing growing suspicion, and was valuable to the FRU.

A discussion had been held. They might have been strangers, talking about putting down an old dog. Something had to be done. A way was found to pass the necessary information. The people on the mountain would be devastated that a trusted individual had betrayed a martyr of the status of Padraig Riordan and three others. A 'useful' man would be removed. Mistrust and suspicion would thrive.

The reports coming in to FRU said that Aidan, the bakery and weapons-delivery driver, had died slowly under a rain of blows from a lump hammer. He had not confessed, as demanded of him, between the frenzied attacks. He couldn't confess because he knew nothing. It was said that half the mountain, an exaggeration but with some truth, had heard his screams.

That evening, Dusty Miller had gone to Desperate's room and found him on the bed, silent and bowed, the bag packed at his feet. He had left an hour later. The shouts of Captain Bentinick would have been loud in his ears but went unanswered. He'd had moments to decide his future. Dusty had gone into his own room, stuffed what he owned into a rucksack, then hitched it as he'd run to the gate, Bentinick yelling at him, 'Good man, just bring him back. We all feel the weight of it sometimes. Get him out and drink a bar dry, then bring him back.'

He'd caught him at the bus station on the far side of the Mall. They'd gone to Belfast docks and sailed with the night ferry to Heysham. He had never heard Matthew Bentinick's voice again until that late afternoon. Now he sat in the minibus and waited for them to move on towards the sands above the Dunkirk beaches. He thought it cruel that his man had been recalled. And that it might break him.

* * *

'I just want you to know that you shouldn't worry about us. We'll tidy up after you. However much shit you leave scattered around, we'll clean it away. Have a good trip, Danny – or Vagabond – and we'll be there to pick up the pieces.' The sarcasm was rampant.

Danny Curnow went up the aircraft's steps.

5

He muttered something that was half of an apology. He was told it was nothing to worry about.

The pilot seemed exhausted and Danny Curnow felt the same, but he'd slept from the time the aircraft had left the runway and it was only the jolt of a good landing that had woken him. They had taxied and he'd blinked, and he'd seen the carpet under his feet, then retraced the drying mud on his way to the cabin door. He apologised again for the mess.

'No worries, sir. I take people to some funny old corners for the Service, but I'm not at the sharp end. Look after yourself, sir.'

There was a brief handshake. It was unlikely they'd meet again, but he appreciated what had been said.

A car took him on. He had documentation ready but no one seemed to want to see it.

They came in on a big dual carriageway. He recognised nothing. He had not been in London since he'd moved to France. Dusty Miller and he had spent a year in digs outside Salisbury and there'd been some awful work for an agency that specialised in surveillance operatives: marriage break-ups, industrial espionage . . . Then he and Dusty had taken a ferry from Portsmouth to Caen.

He had no feeling now of coming home, or any sense of being alongside the people he served again. When his life might have been on the line – or Dusty's, or those of any of the team working from the Portakabins at Gough, or those of the men he had squeezed dry and slipped money to – he'd never reckoned it was done in their name: they drove and walked around the car at traffic lights – none knew of him or had cause to thank him. He would have found it hard to justify what he had done, but it had seemed right then. It was his burden.

He had been a West Country small-town boy, and London didn't appeal to him.

Tavistock was an old community, laden with history, on the south side of the moor. His father was a coach driver, his mother a school-dinners lady and he had gone to the local school. There was a big private place on the way towards Mary Tavy and Peter Tavy but his school had no contact with it. He had hated the kids who went there, spoke differently and thronged the town on a Saturday afternoon. He had hated pretty much everything. Until he had met Barnaby. A recluse living in a foul-smelling bungalow, Barnaby had been a corporal in 40 Commando. When Danny had first met him, the ex-marine was half starved, as was his dog. He'd come across the place wandering on a lane above the railway that had been closed eleven years before. Danny didn't speak to strangers, but he was entranced by the old warrior. Barnaby had sprained an ankle: he took money from a biscuit tin under a bed and gave it to Danny, who had gone to a shop and brought back food for Barnaby and the dog. He had handed over the receipt and every penny of the change. He grew – almost – to love the man. He had listened in awe, spellbound, to the wry stories of going ashore at Suez, patrolling Cypriot streets and fire spats in the Steamer Point crescent of Aden. No teacher had ever roused such interest in him. He had listened and stayed at school. He had won a cross-country cup, to general astonishment, but had walked the course and learned where to skive off into woods and where to rejoin the route.

Barnaby had said he should not be a 'bayonet-pusher', that he was too intelligent for it. He had taken exams and done well, then joined an infantry regiment but with his future mapped out. He had gone to see Barnaby in his uniform, with a shine on his boots, and the old guy had wet eyes. That had been the last time he had seen him.

In the regiment he had applied and been accepted for a sniper course, which signalled him as a man without sentiment, and had done a tour of four months in a sangar on the roof of Flax Street Mill, looking down into Ardoyne. He had never had occasion to fire and kill. A switch to Intelligence Corps, at an officer's recommendation, then into FRU. He had gone to work for Matthew Bentinick.

They were in heavy traffic and inched their way south towards the river.

He had been back to Tavistock once since he'd joined up. The only time he had left Ireland to go on leave from the Province was after a call from a funeral director. There had been a sealed envelope on the ledge above the fireplace, along with the final demands. He hadn't gone to see his parents but had been at the crematorium, with a representative of the Royal Marines Association and an ethnic Afro-Caribbean social worker. He had owed Barnaby so much. That was where he was rooted.

They came past Parliament.

He didn't know the issues that troubled Britain. In Caen, Danny Curnow never tuned a radio to the BBC and did not buy British newspapers. If they were left in the minibus by clients he treated them as rubbish. Now he saw the Rodin statue, the burghers whose lives had been saved by an English queen in 1347. They had offered themselves to the English forces so that their town, Calais, might escape the sack and pillage. He had learned French history. They came to Horseferry Road. He expected to be dropped at the front entrance but they pulled up and the driver leaned back to open the rear door. 'This is where I was told to drop you off.'

He saw, in a side-street at the back of the building, two armed police patrolling with machine-guns and kit sagging on their belts. He saw the park, the tall, leaf-heavy trees, and a side door to the building. The driver pointed to the café further along the street. He climbed out and heaved his rucksack after him.

He went inside, sat down, asked for a glass of water and waited to be granted an audience.

Time wouldn't wait for him, and Brennie Murphy hadn't helped. He felt pressure building on his shoulders, weighing him down.

Brennie Murphy had hugged him, wished him well. The car door had slammed and Brennie had driven it out of the field gate and up the hill. Should the kids be allowed to lay it? Malachy Riordan was uncertain, and Brennie Murphy had only shrugged.

It was called EFP. It had been a long time coming to Ireland. An Explosive Force Projectile was standard for Hezbollah in south Lebanon as a defence against Israeli armour; it had been big in Iraq when the Iranians had flooded the country with them, driving the Yanks and the Brits off the roads; it had been refined for Afghanistan. At school in Dungannon, he had not got far with physics, engineering and chemistry, but he had made two – used precious resources in putting them together – and had test-fired them on the crest of the mountain by Shane Bearnagh's Seat, where the wind was hard and diffused the sound of the blasts. Each had been aimed at a sheet of metal, a yard square, a quarter of an inch thick, and five yards away. Each time it was punctured. It had come in a pack from a man in the south – Brennie had known of him. There had been enough PE4 explosive in each of the rinsed-out baked-beans tins to bring down an airliner.

The first time he had followed the handwritten instruction on a sheet of paper. The second time, after he had burned the paper, he did it from memory. The device was in a shoebox. When fired, it would penetrate with ease a car or Land Rover reinforced with plates against conventional bullets, kill the driver and passenger. It was new, the best. It was right for use against Eamonn O'Kane, policeman, visiting his mother. But the boys who would fire it were raw and untried. Brennie said that the explosive was 'sensitive', to be handled with care – which meant it was fuckin' dangerous. He had been sweating when he'd put the thing together for the test by Shane Bearnagh's Seat.

He went to see them.

Pearse was grinding out his fag and Kevin was smoking. They were in trees and a beat-up car was off the road. He came, parked and walked towards them. Kevin threw down his cigarette, let it smoulder. Malachy's phone, of course, was off.

He told Pearse to pick up his cigarette end, Kevin the same.

Their faces fell. They would have understood the simple mistake they had made – they had been told often enough about DNA, how places where they met could be bugged and . . . They were in awe of him. In their eyes he had star quality and they were gutted when they realised he had caught them out in something so small. He pointed to the car. Kevin nodded and made a sweeping gesture. Malachy had to trust that it was clean of bugs and of an audio system.

Could they do it? They talked together. They could. Didn't he trust them?

What to believe? He saw the defiance in their eyes. They were three years out of school and unemployed. Both – he recognised it – lived for the Organisation and for the chance to be volunteers under his control. He knew their wider families, and Bridie would have known their mothers well.

He needed to be gone, but the opportunity to take down a policeman was huge. The effect on morale on the mountain would be massive, but he didn't know if the boys were capable of it. Time was short.

'And I'm not here myself, I'm away. Do it for me, and make it count.'

Two young faces stared back at him. To doubt them was to insult them. He left them and drove away. In his mind he saw his father's grave, the bold lettering in gold. When he left the mountain to go on 'active service,' he would go through the villages to the west where the big memorials were for the martyrs. He went to put together a bag at home, then hold her, kiss her and leave her. He'd blow another kiss, and see, perhaps, a moment of shy affection from her.

She was in Berlin, at Tegel, and took a taxi the few kilometres into the city, to the Charlottenburg district. She was no longer Frankie McKinney, and that passport was lodged in the lining of the wheelie-case. The bank was on Kaiserdamm, where it merged with Bismarckstrasse. She went in confidently. She wore a headscarf, tinted clear glasses and a lightweight raincoat that had been tightly folded in her bag. On presentation of the second passport she was permitted to transfer the monies, now almost half a million euro, to a bank in Prague. Her confidence came from the trust invested in her.

Her life had veered onto a different track three years ago, towards the end of her second term at Queen's University.

She had gone with the Enniskillen girls to a party up by Finaghy, close to the motorway, near also to Andersonstown. She had never been to the sprawled estate in West Belfast because a girl from the Malone road, though sharing Andersonstown's faith, had no reason to be there. Looking back, she had been targeted and identified, it would have been known she was a Catholic, with Protestant friends – but they'd gone. She'd been left behind. Drink had flowed, the music had pounded and the air was heavy with smoke. She had felt a rare excitement, sucking in the music and the mood. A woman had been close to her elbow. 'You said your name was Frankie? Well, Frankie, what have you ever done in your life?' Nothing. 'Enjoy the emptiness, do you, Frankie, of doing nothing?' There might have been a thrust in her chin or a flash of her eyes. Others watched as she answered. The music dinned in her head, smoke was in her nose and the place had taken on a heady wildness. The woman, the interrogator, looked hard into her eyes, challenging, then half turned and beckoned a man, older than her. The woman murmured that he'd done time in the Maze as an eighteen-year-old – 'Which was doing *something*, not nothing.' She'd spoken to him, then disappeared.

He was a full inch shorter than Frankie and wore just a T-shirt, jeans and open sandals. She saw on his bare right forearm a tattoo of a pistol. Frankie was against a wall and he said in her ear – and she bent to hear him better, 'How would you describe your life, Miss Frances?'

'It's Frankie. My life, if you must know, is fucking boring.' She had had two boyfriends in her fifteen weeks at the university: a boy who was in the hockey second team, who thought she should stand on a touchline and watch him; another who was second-year English and wanted to be an actor. A bit of sex, not much . . .

They'd gone upstairs. He'd said on the landing, 'Could you handle something, Miss Frances, that's not fucking boring?'

She hadn't needed to reply. There was a couple in a room and he told them to go. They grabbed their clothing and bolted. He'd closed the door and undressed her. She'd thought it was adult sex – amazing and sweaty, quite unlike the actor and the hockey boy. She reckoned she grew up. There was no curtain and a streetlight shone across the bed. They dressed. He had a biro wedged in his wallet, and asked her to write on his palm her mobile number. They'd gone down the stairs and into the music. All eyes were on him and her, and he manoeuvred a way through the crowd. They went together out into the night. He smacked her buttock roughly and half smiled, then went right towards Andersonstown. She turned left towards Finaghy and a bus for the Malone road.

She had never seen him again in the flesh. A month later she had been called and contact with Maude established – a good name: Maude Gonne McBride had been the wife of a patriot executed by the Crown, firing squad, in 1916 after the Rising. She had seen his picture, though, on television: the police called his arrest 'significant'. He was Tomas Doherty, held on remand at Maghaberry. He'd chosen her and she had passed the initial tests. She had no regrets.

She told the clerk at the Dresdner Bank, showing him her passport, her account number, and gave him the details of the bank in Prague to which the monies should be transferred. She spoke briskly, as if the movement of funds on that scale was not unusual.

Then Frankie took another taxi, back to Tegel, and checked in on the Prague flight under a different name.

It would be good to see the man when he came: they would be partners. He would need her for the negotiations.

The restaurant served only Russian food: the waiters were immigrants. He had enjoyed his morning walk and now Timofey Simonov was with those who thought they were his friends.

A table had been booked at the back of the restaurant. Across the room, plate-glass picture windows gave a view onto the street, the river esplanade and the tall spa villas from the end of the nineteenth century and churches, the whole topped with the trees changing colour and clear blue skies. He had ordered *golubtsi* to start: cabbage stuffed with millet. He would follow with *kurniki*: chicken pie with rice, hard-boiled egg and mushrooms. He would drink mineral water bottled in the north Caucasus, and would talk in Russian. The conversation would be about grandchildren, though he did not have any, the price of property, political developments at home and the influence of the *siloviki*. He would neither contribute nor share opinions. He would laugh when others laughed. He told them about his dogs and when they had last put up a deer in the woods behind his home. He was different from all of the four men around the table.

He couldn't see the window: his back was to the door. The other four had jockeyed for positions where they could observe who entered the restaurant. He thought that, still, they kept to the habits of the Motherland. One had successfully founded a bank in Cypriot Limassol; one had sold a Siberian oil well to the state – the money transfer had been honoured; the third had been a KGB officer of the old regime and now did cyber work from abroad for the SVR, his former employer's successor. The last had owned a group in St Petersburg. It had been taken over, he had been rewarded and had escaped with his life. All four wished to face the door. Each had two bodyguards, one on the street, the other at a nearby table. They would be armed: arrangements made with officials in the town for the issue of legal permits. He had left the brigadier behind. There were firearms in a floor safe in the basement office at the villa, and ammunition, but they were seldom taken out. He did not regard his life, security or freedom to be threatened.

They knew little of him. They knew something of his wealth but not its extent.

They would have realised he had a solid 'roof' in place, but did not know whether it came from government, intelligence or organised crime. They might have wondered if their conversation bored him because there were moments when he seemed distant from them.

He had a keen imagination and good insight.

He saw the lock-up garage near the Iset river. A young man, no more than a youth, sat on a hard chair, his arms tied behind his back. He was stripped to the waist and his body showed the tattoos that came from gaol: he would have been under the needle to demonstrate his importance as a criminal, a badge of honour. His shoes were off, his socks beside them, and his jeans had been cut with a knife at the knees. It had drawn blood there. His struggles were lessening, and he made shrill grunting noises through the tightly tied gag. His feet were in an oil drum of which half of the sides had been taken off, leaving a ragged edge. A man now emptied a sack of cement into the drum, covering his legs. A second man filled a bucket with water from a tap against the garage's back wall. He would tip it onto the cement. They would not need to stir it into the cement as the leg movements would thicken it. The young man was asked no questions. He could not save his life though confession. His death was assured, authorised by the former intelligence officer, now eating chicken pie, whom he had crossed without knowing it.

Timofey Simonov drank only water. He could count the years since he had last been rendered incapable of coherent thought by alcohol. He had been with Ralph Exton – a true friend. Another thought. It was less clear in his mind because he didn't know London.

He had seen a passport photograph of the Serbian but – of course – had not met him. A slim man, tall, with a crop of close-cut greying hair, a master of his trade, which did not come cheaply. An arrangement had been agreed. From the embassy there had been an envoy, a meeting, a budget, and what intelligence had been gathered was handed to him. There was neither a paper nor an electronic trail connecting the diplomats to him. He thought the marksman would now be driving an airport car far out from the British capital. There were supposed to be wildernesses in Wales and the remote moors in the extreme west. The rifle would be in the hatchback, stored in a case with polystyrene shapes to hold it secure on the journey. He thought the Serb might fire four shots to satisfy himself of the calibration of the telescopic sight. His own share, after payment to the marksman and the purchase of the weapon, was a hundred thousand American dollars – and he would also win gratitude.

He sipped his imported water. When Ralph Exton came, he might drink alcohol. The deal was ridiculous, as the brigadier had said, and he had accepted it only because Ralph Exton was a true friend.

The engine seemed to be misfiring, and was spewing dark fumes. Ralph Exton intended to drive to Heathrow. The size of the last taxi bill, coming home, had frightened him. Most of his accounts were overdrawn, most of his bills outstanding, and what was due to him from the Irish, when the deal went through, would be more than welcome. He needed a new car. Trouble was, what with the bills, he could have spent the Irish money three times over. The car sounded sick.

He drove away from home.

His wife, *extraordinary*, was out. She'd come back briefly, changed and gone again. They'd exchanged pleasantries: her appearance, the weather. Tomorrow, or the day after, was their wedding anniversary. He hadn't bought anything. Would she have something for him? Would her parents have remembered and put a card in the post? It was unlikely.

He might have let slip to some that he was a central part of the community from which the duchess came. He would not have said he knew her well, but had implied they were on nodding terms. It had helped with a deal for Bulgarian furniture that should have done better, except the shifty bastards had skimped on the glue, and the out-of-sight joints were the worst fitted he'd ever seen. There were people down on the Costa who put stuff his way and liked him.

He drove towards Reading. Ralph Exton thought he might phone home the next evening and hope to speak to her. He would wish her a happy anniversary, and hope she'd had a good day . . . It hurt. He pretended it didn't – put on a brave face.

There was a pub off to the left, fronting onto a village green and a duck pond. They'd had a meet there. Him, Gaby and Hugo. It had been important enough for them to hang on what he'd said. He passed it and saw that the car park was full. There were the golfers, the guys who'd sold their Ford dealership franchise, others who ran property portfolios, and they'd been nattering. In the corner, under some horse brasses, Ralph had told his handlers what was now asked of him. He was still in shock. He'd come off the first plane of the day from Málaga. The proposition had been put late the previous night. He'd spluttered, 'You are joking?' The three men had said, their voices covered by the *folklorique* musicians, 'Never been more serious, Ralph. Right thing for you, and you're a man who can deliver. Not something we'd joke about.' They didn't want Marlboro cartons by the crate. They were looking at assault rifles, grenade-launchers, big machine-guns, military explosive and detonators. It was all written out – atrocious handwriting. Trouble was, he hadn't said, it was beyond him. His reply: 'Might be able to do something. Might have a man who could fix that sort of business for me. Give me a moment.' He had gone outside, into the gardens, and rung the villa. He had talked to Timofey Simonov. *For you, friend, for you, Ralph.* Should have kept his mouth shut.

Could he pull out? He remembered asking it, his nerves frayed.

Hugo had said, 'Hardly the right time, Ralph.'

Gaby had said, 'We really value you, Ralph. You're special to us. What you do saves lives. Ralph, we're here to look after you. We take your safety very seriously.'

They'd treated his anxiety as if it were a joke, dismissed it. When would have been the right time to demand to quit? But he had no cards in his hand: they had the power to lock him up. Might as well have had a ball and chain attached to his ankle. Later the envelope had arrived with the postman: the photograph of his front gate and house. He'd told them, but they hadn't seemed to register it. Five had him, and the Irish had him. Timofey Simonov was his friend, and that was another matter. He reflected that it was a small miracle he didn't run into a lamppost. He was on a treadmill, it was speeding up, and he didn't know how to get off. *Ralph, we're here to look after you.* He had to believe her.

A young woman came in, caught his eye, then ordered at the counter. He had sat for more than twenty minutes, staring at his empty glass. Around him people were eating. Danny Curnow was tired and grubby. He thought he probably stank. Every other table was taken but at his there were two empty chairs. She had two cardboard beakers, paid, stared at him, decided the link was made and jerked her head for him to follow her out.

She went through the door, held it open with her hip. He sat in his chair and had his elbows on the table, with the empty glass. She made the contact again, but he stayed in his seat. Others were now looking at her, wondering how long she intended to hold the door open, letting in the draught. She was short with dark hair, jeans, a sweater and an anorak. Danny assumed she thought that a suitable uniform to demonstrate she was not an analyst at a desk, but actually at the business end. Bentinick had said only that Danny would work with her.

Annoyance in her face. She let the door swing back and walked over to him. He looked up at her. In Caen, at the house, it was almost impossible to anger Lisette or Christine. Neither had tantrums, and neither wanted authority.

'You're Danny?'

'Are you Miss Davies?'

She said, grudgingly, 'Can we go outside?'

He had had no allies at Gough. He could remain inside the family and still have no friendships. He had accepted Matthew Bentinick's leadership, and Dusty Miller as his sidekick. He stared back at her, then stood, hitched his rucksack over one shoulder and chicaned between the tables. She led. At the end of the street there was a park, prettily kept, with benches around an outer path and old gravestones. She sat and passed him a coffee. He could have said he didn't drink coffee, but saw no point. She had a north-east accent and told him the garden had been used by one of the acknowledged stellar personalities of the Service for meetings, that she'd smoke incessantly and curse but was gone now. There were two gardeners on the far side, clearing beds of summer flowers, raking and filling a barrow. One had a wan complexion and a limp.

She told him that she was Gabrielle, usually Gaby. She said she had been yesterday in the Province and that she handled an agent. She expanded on him, as if he was her property: cheerful, probably one of life's losers, a minor crook and a major dealer in anything that showed a profit percentage, light on his tax and VAT if he qualified, heavy in dealings with the new Irish. He had started with cigarettes coming in off trawlers to the south-west, a Kerry port, or containers into Cork harbour. He was trusted . . . trusted enough to be asked – as a dealer in about anything – if his contact book went as far as a weapon supplier's name.

He sat and listened, holding the beaker in both hands and gazing at the man with the limp, whose back was straight enough for him to be ex-army: another damaged and discarded guy who now gardened for a living. He listened. She had been there the day before, with a guy who was on a higher grade. The agent had gone forward in fog and had had fuck-all back-up. Her boss – 'wanker' – had given a demonstration of post-traumatic stress disorder, and was now on sick leave. She was to lead; they were going that evening. It would be an exodus. The Joe was flying out and would do the business with a Russian from far back in his life, the vendor. The purchaser was in County Tyrone.

Danny Curnow did not say where he had been, or why.

She would manage the operation from the ground, would have control. Danny – for reasons not explained to her – was going on a separate Prague flight with Matthew Bentinick. Did he go back with Bentinick? He saw no need to answer. She drained her coffee. He declined to pass judgement yet on whether she was good, bad or indifferent. There had been women in the Force Recce Unit, good and not pushy. Also – he had never met her, but stories were legion – there had been a Five girl who worked out of Belfast and ran a Joe called Mossie Nugent on the mountain. They'd taken down a big man, and he was in one of the graveyards. Mossie Nugent was in the same one but his plot was on the far side; the Nugent widow still lived there, shunned. He had not met the Five girl, but had been with Special Forces and they would have gone through fire for her. He had also heard that she was a shell of what she had been. That was what the Province and the job did to the handlers.

Had he any questions? None. Her coffee was finished, and she stood. 'Sorry and all that, but I can't bring you inside. Security protocol, you understand.'

'Of course.'

'I think Mr Bentinick will come and pick you up from here when he's ready to leave. Anything you'd like to say, Danny?'

They probably taught that approach – bank manager to a client – to the young people coming into the building. 'Only one thing.'

'Please, go ahead.'

'You seemed to imply I'd be behind you, that you'd lead.'

'I did, and I will. What's the one thing.'

'Miss Davies, if I'm behind you then the temptation to kick you hard in the butt and out of my way – no offence – might be irresistible.'

He assumed there would be a look that might have killed, but his back was to her. He went to the bin and dropped the coffee beaker into it. He thought of where he should have been, pictured it, and the safety of the place.

They always formed a little cluster close to the guide. Such a vast place, from the harbour jutting into the sea to their left and the expanse of the dunes to the right. In front of them was the beach, and the tide was out. The guide would try to convey the noise and crisis of those days when 400,000 British and French soldiers had been there without any vestige of cover. He would speak of the small mercy of low cloud cover on some of the ten days of the evacuation, a hindrance to the dive bombers. The tourists would look towards the sea and conjure images of burning or listing ships and of the lines of soldiers stretched towards and into the water. They might imagine how many had drowned when the tide had ebbed in. Always a guide mentioned how close Great

Britain and Northern Ireland had been to the catastrophe of defeat in total war, and how the King had led prayers for the nation. Big ships and little boats had come in, through the inferno, and had taken off around thirty-five thousand men each day for ten days. The tourists were always quietest when told of the sacrifice. Whole units had fought with their backs to the beach, had resisted the panzer forces and held a blood-soaked perimeter line. They had done it so that others might get home – might fight again. A third of the 350,000 were French, and they had sailed for the Kentish ports. They had gone back to France from Portsmouth, in time to re-enlist, then crumbled again and surrendered. Men had died to give them that chance. Little gasps came from the tourists when they heard that.

A young couple jogged near the water line and three men were in the low surf, riding two-wheeled carts drawn by frisky horses, and far out to sea, halfway to England, container ships and tankers edged north and south, to and from Rotterdam. So little to see and so much to imagine. The tourists would struggle to compose pictures for their little cameras that did justice to the events of the place. The chaos and suffering would have been so great.

Dusty watched them, and the guide's reedy voice was carried to him over the wind. He thought he might have lost a limb.

Bad to be without Danny Curnow and not to know where he was. Danny would have been at the edge of the group, not interrupting or interfering. A wise guide would catch his eye and Danny would inject a little dose of truth, perhaps about the French who had gone back, resisting the chance to stay in England. They had returned to their own military, then spent the rest of the war in prison camps or as forced labour in factories. Dusty listened to the guide and remembered the day when playing God had led to success, and others when it had left the handler scarred. He remembered what Desperate had done.

An active-service unit had planned to hit a bar in loyalist Bangor, where the Union Flags flew and the kerbstones were red, white and blue. The tout was on the team that was going to drive out from west Belfast, well armed. The bar would be full and they'd spray the bullets around. If they put a ring of steel and road blocks round the bar then it would be obvious to the ASU's people that there had been a leak – the tout would be fingered, break under torture and end up dead in a ditch. All the handler's time spent on him, and the money, would have gone to waste. Desperate had come up with a counter-plan, and Captain Bentinick had sanctioned it. They knew what car the active-service unit were using to come into Bangor, and the action would take place when it passed through Crawfordsburn. Time would be tight – a road accident. Two undercover police cars had a shunt outside the bar, glass in the road, wings and sides dented. The blue lights were there fast, sirens and an ambulance. The boys of the ASU, with the tout on the back seat, gripping his AK, came up the street, saw the lights, the chaos and the watching crowd. They did a three-point and got the hell out. The best result. A new lease on life for the tout, and God wasn't bothered.

Dusty saw the tourists start to meander up the beach. A few took a last photograph, and all were subdued.

'It's intolerable. He's rude, boorish, and probably a dinosaur.'

'An interesting evaluation, Gaby.'

'It's a delicate mission, high stakes to play for.'

'Quite.'

He let her speak. An infuriating tactic Matthew Bentinick employed was to continue to work at his screen, seeming to listen but apparently paying little attention to what he was told. The outsider was left to stand. Perhaps she was amused that an old hand would play games of precedence. It was a dreary room, but Gaby Davies, from a north-east city where money was tight and interior décor minimal, was no expert in wallpaper designs and lampshades. She wondered why any vestige of humanity in the man was so artfully hidden: no family photographs, no pot plant on the windowsill, no painting of a rural scene. His jacket hung from a hook behind the door, with his raincoat and a trilby; his waistcoat was unbuttoned and his tie loosened. There was a floor safe and two padlocked shoulder-high filing cabinets. The leave chart was stuck to the wall: the last time she had been in the room she had checked her name and seen the dates entered for a break she planned in northern Spain at the end of October; and his column was bare for the year. His wife must have been a saint, or detached, and she'd never heard of children. It was the indifference he showed, and the failure to respond to her accusation of rudeness – *then the temptation to kick you hard in the butt and out of my way – no offence – might be irresistible* – that riled her most. A direct threat of physical violence. She pushed on.

'I'm suggesting, Matthew, that the cowboy world of Northern Ireland twenty years ago has had its day. He doesn't seem to understand that I will give the instructions and—'

'If you have ten minutes to spare, Gaby, before getting your bits and pieces together and hitting the road for the airport, why don't you go into Archive? I'll send authorisation ahead of you. The file you'll want is called VAGABOND. Some definitions of the word – disreputable, worthless, a rogue and a knave or having an uncertain or irregular course of direction. Call in before you go. Thank you, Gaby.'

He was typing.

She thought fleetingly of the woman who was married to him, lived in a suburban street and was surrounded by neighbours who thought of her as 'martyred', eking out a life in a loveless marriage. Poor woman.

She went out and closed the door after her. From what she had heard, only Jocelyn down the corridor could work alongside him. Hadn't much time, but could slot ten minutes. She took a lift down.

Jocelyn had sidled in. She could talk, listen or prompt.

Bentinick said, 'I have to have him there because the agent is the key. But who would trust an agent? Not me. An agent is a liar. He must lead us forward, but he'll want marshalling – he needs a collar round his throat and a restraining leash. Vagabond will hold the leash and keep it tight. He'll attempt deceit because of his terror of the Siberian rock and the east Tyrone hard place.'

'That's why I said you had to have the best.'

The place had the atmosphere of church. She was in Archive in the basement. The days of the card-index system were dead and there were two central piers. On either side there were cubicles and two women to open and close specific files. No voice was raised there, and the only sounds were the clicking of keyboards and the whine from the air-conditioners. The building worked on 'need to know' and Archive protected that agenda. She flitted over screen pages and glimpsed photographs. Other men's features were distorted, but Curnow's face was clear. He had barely changed in twenty years – even the haircut was the same. The eyes still lacked warmth.

A brusque middle-aged woman had opened the file, offering no small-talk, but Gaby had tried: 'You had the authorisation from Mr Bentinick?'

'Yes, which is why I'm opening it.'

'I work with him.'

'I gathered.'

'Have you known him long?'

'Probably from his first week with us. There you are. VAGABOND.'

'Is there family?'

'I'm sure Mr Bentinick tells colleagues what he wants them to know about his family. At your grade you can't download or print this file.'

She saw what had been written about Danny Curnow of the Force Reconnaissance Unit: the call-sign he'd used and the day-to-day name, 'Desperate', the man who had looked after his back, had been driver and protection; there were referrals to the testimonials of ranking army officers and a commendation from Special Branch, which was usually blood drawn from granite. There were the code titles given to agents – she scrolled past them and was able to read how long they had been on the payroll. A red cross against a name indicated 'deceased'. The final agent had been listed as dead on a date in late 1994.

Danny Curnow's face was not that of a thug. Gaby Davies had spent time, on attachment, with the international police in Bosnia and had searched for the last war criminals against whom secret warrants had been issued. There had been Serbs, Croats, Muslim Bosnians, and some among them had the faces of beasts skilled in brutality. Danny Curnow's was not a brute's face but it was lifeless, as though part of its owner had died. She could have said, as the woman from Archive closed down the screen and shut away the file, that Curnow and Bentinick shared the same absence of animation.

'Does he know I'm in charge or not?'

She stood in the doorway. Bentinick sat. Their eyes did not meet.

'I'm sure, Gaby, it'll all shake down.'

'Archive says he ushered a whole host of men to premature graves. In case everyone's forgotten, it's our job to protect our sources. We're responsible for our agents.'

'Anything else to get off your chest, Gaby?'

'I may be out of order, Matthew, but it's worth saying. You've pulled an old army chum, who'll have prehistoric attitudes, back into service. To me, that's insulting.'

Now Bentinick looked up. His eyes ranged the room, then found hers. He said, 'You have a good relationship with your agent, Ralph Exton?'

'Yes, and you know it.'

'Co-operative, relaxed, friendly.'

'I think so.'

'And productive?'

'Very.'

He was playing with her. It shouldn't have happened in the modern, inclusive Service. His voice was softer: 'Sorry, Gaby, I didn't quite hear that.'

She took a step forward, then another. She saw, from the

corner of her eye, the pair of dirty trainers, mud still on them, remembered them from the gardens, and the muddy jeans. She had told Danny Curnow that an outsider couldn't be admitted to Thames House.

She raised her voice. 'I said "very". I have an excellent relationship and it's productive.'

'And the source of the weapons that Riordan will test-fire?'

'A Russian. You can read my reports.'

'Vague, Gaby. You have a name and precious little else. He has deflected you on the background to their dealings. He's not coming bearing gifts, is he?'

'He will.'

She thought she had sold herself short. Ralph Exton had sat upright and hadn't looked at her. He had watched Bentinick – the source of patronage. Quite crude, really. She had been elbowed aside. The truth: each time the source had been queried, Ralph Exton had eased the question into the long grass. The fact: she had the name and little else. She was Exton's friend.

He spoke with an edge: 'Third floor, west wing, room ninety-one is where you'll find the complaints desk and counselling for bruised-ego syndrome. You'll be alongside him, and you'll listen to what you're told and learn or, Gaby, you're out. Fancy being given the same treatment as the wretched Woolmer? Please yourself. Stop whining or step aside. I can guarantee you won't be missed.'

She was Exton's friend and had hoped, with time, to win him over. She knew too little about the Russian. There was a coffee machine in the corridor outside, and she had on 'sensible shoes'. She kicked the base of the machine. She had extracted too little from Ralph Exton. Now she was running late – and her foot hurt. She hobbled away.

He waved Danny Curnow out of his office and into the corridor. Once the door had been shut and he was alone, Matthew Bentinick picked up his phone and dialled. She answered. He said he would be away that night, and probably on Tuesday. He didn't like to be away, but the mission was important, and one day he might tell her about it. Curtly, he rang off. Better to be quick and strong.

There was a wholesale greengrocer, who also had a stall in one of Reading's old alleyways, with whom Ralph Exton had done a good deal a half-dozen years before, vegetables coming in from Turkey. The man had offered him the parking space in the wholesale section. Useful. He didn't often use it but it seemed a good idea today. Did he want coffee, tea, mango juice? He didn't. How was life? He was hanging on, he said, grinned, and was rewarded with a slap on the shoulder. How long would the car be there? A week, no more. If he wasn't back in a week to collect it, he'd be either in a Prague mortuary or in the intensive-care unit of some clinic with the team digging for fragments of .38 calibre bullets and probably on his way to the mortuary. He walked through the streets towards the stop where the airport coach would pull up. Who did he fear most? The Irish would blow him away. The Russian? Not much difference. There were few certainties in life, he thought, as he went down a high street emptied in the dregs of recession, but the woman – Gabrielle, Gaby, who dressed like a derelict, wanted to be liked and seemed, to Ralph, as lonely as sin – wasn't up there with them. Decent kid: he didn't have to fear her. Small mercy.

He wasn't going to war as most would know it: they were not in an armoured car. He sat alongside the driver of the Ford Mondeo and Bentinick spread himself out on the back seat with his evening paper. No crowd would be waiting, with growing apprehension, in an operations room for a patrol to come back from hostile territory, and there would be no parades through market towns where the regiment recruited handlers, precious few medals and no reunions. They didn't do reunions because few who had done the work wanted to stir up old memories and admit to the past. Handlers couldn't josh and brag about the Service years in a corner of a pub with other veterans or in a British Legion bar. Talk of running agents, and losing them, was off limits. Danny had no flak vest and no firearm, and the only man he would trust to keep him clear of ambush was – a glance at his watch – at the wheel of the minibus, leaving the dunes and the quiet. Others might have told Matthew Bentinick that they'd no interest in his proposition, but not Danny. It was clear in his mind: whatever the risks to his own hard-won mental stability, he would never have turned down a request – instruction – to return to the fold. He would have walked on hot coals to be there. The rush-hour traffic was building, and the light would soon fail. There was a rustle behind him. A newspaper was folded untidily, then dropped onto the seat.

'Desperate, are you all right?'

'Thank you for asking, Mr Bentinick. I'm fine.'

The hand rested on his shoulder and the fingers went for his muscles. 'Desperate, you know what I told the Boss? Oscar, you're deaf.'

The driver answered, 'See nothing, hear nothing and never knew anything, Mr Bentinick, same as always.'

'Desperate, I told the Boss we're going to nail that bastard to the floor. Nobody gets in the way of us doing that. We nail the bastard to the floor. Nothing less.'

'Yes, Mr Bentinick.' A tough war, and dirty, like the ones he'd fought before.

6

And Danny Curnow did not go to war in a troop carrier with an Apache flying top cover and squaddies all round him, the aircraft, which might have been targeted with a surface-to-air job, corkscrewing down to land. It was an Airbus that carried him and Matthew Bentinick into Václav Havel, the Prague airport. The flight was not quiet, as it would have been if squaddies were entering a combat zone. It was a war, and Danny had no doubt of that, but removed from a battlefield. There were two stag groups on board. The ones at the front of the cabin were from Swindon, in Wiltshire, and the ones at the back were from Kettering, in Northamptonshire. The team from the West Country were Liverpool fans and the one from the East Midlands supported Wigan Athletic. They all drank heavily, and the prospective grooms were already half cut. The flight attendants had given up on them, and a couple of the Swindon boys had thrown up in the aisle. Danny drank little. He had a small beer or two in the Dickens Bar on the rue Basse with a game of cards or a newspaper, and hadn't drunk when he was at Gough. He handled and manipulated agents, and felt no loyalty to those who betrayed their colleagues and took whatever money was on offer. There was no way that any of the guys with the stag groups would have noticed the middle-aged man in casual clothes and muddy trainers. They wouldn't have registered him. He turned men into puppets, and could sentence or reprieve them. He thought of where he should have been, and with whom.

There was weight on his shoulder and he could smell pipe tobacco. They were on descent. Ahead of and behind him, the cabin crew were attempting to take the names, addresses and seat numbers of those who had vomited. They were also swabbing, and some older passengers had started to complain. Matthew Bentinick slept, snoring. His head rested easily on Danny's collarbone. Danny wondered how often Matthew Bentinick slept without disturbance. He sensed exhaustion in the man – the burden of work perhaps. His belt wasn't fastened. Danny leaned across. With care, he lifted Bentinick's arm, no resistance, and found the end of the belt. He lowered the arm on to the belt, found the second length and fastened the lock. It gave him a degree of satisfaction that the man hadn't woken as the aircraft yawed on the final approach.

The stag groups yelled support for the pilot, for Liverpool Football Club and for Wigan Athletic. The wheels hit.

The head jerked up. He was awake. His fingers locked together and he flexed them so that they cracked. Danny wondered whether the burdens on the mind of Matthew Bentinick were as loaded as his own, or whether he was better able to bear them. The mood changed.

The smell from down the aisle was rank.

The agent would now be in the air, up from Heathrow. And he had not learned lessons because they had not been taught in the curriculum Gaby Davies had followed.

'Are you all right, Mr Bentinick?'

'Of course I am. Why should I not be?'

'You been here before?'

'Never. No call to. I'll say it once, not again.'

'Say what, Mr Bentinick?'

'Where I work, Danny, there is a fault line. Two organisations that spend most of their lives in combat mode. There are the "modernists" and there are the old fogeys. There are the calculatingly ambitious and they regard the other crowd as idle, conservative and unwilling to embrace new practices. I was shut in a toilet cubicle when I heard someone say, "The old fool! Do you think he was with Harry Hotspur at Shrewsbury in 1403, giving bad advice that cost Harry his head? Probably he was getting it wrong then as often as he gets it wrong now. No idea what the DG sees in him." As I did in Ireland, Danny, I do things my way, tried and tested. With me?'

Danny Curnow had the rucksack on his shoulder and nodded bleakly. He followed Bentinick, who led with the stride of a man who owned the place.

Bentinick's phone warbled. He eased away, stopping short of the passport desks, the phone to his ear. He listened. Danny Curnow was house-trained, gave him space.

He had said, 'Yes?' at the start of the call, then listened. He did not need to write down what he had been told but committed it to memory. At the end, he omitted to thank his caller. He switched off his phone.

He was close again to Curnow. 'Our boy from the mountain, Riordan, is on the move. That was his travel schedule. Won't be here before tomorrow evening. All slotting down well.'

A young man came forward. He had the high cheekbones of an ethnic Slav, and was wrapped against the cold in a heavy anorak and a tartan scarf. The face fitted the photograph, and the coat matched what he had been told. The accent was central European but he spoke fluent English. Bentinick had heard about him and asked for him – Karol Pilar. Danny gave only his first name. Pilar addressed Bentinick as 'sir'. The face seemed sour.

They went through the passport checks and Pilar flashed a card. His group was waved through. He seemed sullen, his eyes hangdog.

Bentinick challenged him: 'Was it inconvenient to meet us, Karol?'

'No.'

'You weren't at the end of a shift and having to stay late?'

'My grade don't work in shift patterns. Very few in the UOOZ do regular hours.'

'Did you know we specifically asked for you as our liaison?'

'Yes.'

'For your skills and knowledge.'

'My skills in dealing with Irish terrorism are limited. My knowledge of Irish affairs is zero. I'll do my best.'

And Matthew Bentinick understood. An approximation of a smile flickered across his lips. They were through the exit doors. What he liked about 'Desperate' was that he stayed back and did not intrude. He took Pilar's arm and, as they drifted towards but not inside a coffee outlet, he told him. A smile lightened the man's face. The sourness and sullenness slipped away. He had said what he needed to say. The Czech detective was in his early thirties, he estimated, poor as a church mouse, his career withering because he was not corrupt. He talked of targets, and won the man. They went out into the early-evening light.

It was a decent enough hotel, halfway along the north-east side of Wenceslas Square. The policeman said it had been used by the general leading the Soviet invasion in 1968 as his headquarters. There were no drunks reeling in the hall, but a coach full of South Koreans had beaten them to Reception. Danny did not intrude.

The Czech had Matthew Bentinick's attention. Danny knew from long ago that information would be shared when Bentinick decided it was needed. The tiredness was catching up with him. When he had his key, he left them in the lobby and took the lift to his room. He didn't know why the Red Army had invaded a fellow Warsaw Pact member country. He had been a kid at school when it had happened. He fell on to the bed. On both sides they asked when it was possible to turn a clock back and step away. The agent couldn't. Once an agent had taken their money he or she couldn't walk out on them. It was as difficult for the handler to take flight if – when – the guilt rose.

There were old truths from his military time: 'Better to be asked than not to be asked' and 'Better to be volunteered than to be ignored'. Danny Curnow was desperate to sleep, but not with the nightmares. He was far from home and the few for whom he cared – and knew where he should have been.

Dusty stood by the gate. The cemetery was on rue des Fumes, and they were late – the guide had let them take too many photographs on the beach, and then there had been roadworks outside the line of fast-food outlets, which had been closed at the end of the season. Dusty had done some smooth talking and slipped the curator a fifty-euro note: the gates would stay open for another fifteen minutes. It was a place Danny Curnow liked – he could find a little calm there, shed some of the burden. He found space among the headstones.

Most of the time the burden was crippling.

Dusty smoked a cigarette and the memories came to haunt him. Not that he had had direct responsibility: if he had, the burden would have felled him. A couple in the village of Ardboe, a Republican family, were seemingly uninvolved in politics. They lived quietly and the husband was in work. Then a traffic accident – he was drunk, in his van. He would lose his licence and his job at a time when jobs were precious. He was in a cell, weeping, when the door clattered open and a man was standing there, with short hair, jeans, trainers and an anorak; a holster was visible beneath the coat. It had been easy enough for Danny Curnow to pull that one off, and the man was almost blubbering his gratitude. He kept his job, wasn't charged, and a hundred pounds a month went into his pocket. In return he offered the back bedroom of his house to the Organisation.

The couple went to the coast for a weekend, leaving the house empty for a night. The FRU brought in the bugs people. They heard good stuff, week in, week out, but never acted on it. The couple were lovely. Dusty saw them at each meeting – always so polite. They didn't know it wouldn't last. There was to be a hit. A chief inspector of police would be going to a country church in Fermanagh for his great-nephew's christening. The service was cancelled. Not all the congregation had been warned – people were milling about in the rain by the gate into the churchyard, and the team was there, weapons on the floor, but had no target. Danny Curnow hadn't known that the detail for the hit was talked about only in the back bedroom. Another team arrived, security, and the couple sat on the sofa downstairs as the back bedroom was ripped apart.

A bar outside Ardboe put on country-and-western every Friday.

There was always a big crowd and the car park was full. Danny used to meet them there, while Dusty sat in the Gough car with an H&K across his knees, two magazines taped together in the *soixante-neuf* position. They'd stayed away that Friday, and the next, and every Friday.

It had been three days after the final 'no-show' that the couple turned up. He'd been shot first. She must have freed her hands – there was blood under her fingernails – and then she had been shot. The military and the police in Fermanagh had been told to look for a guy with tram-line scars down his face.

Danny had told Dusty that the couple had come up with little of any importance. It had been an aberration for the Organisation to brief so comprchensively for a hit inside a single room. A full 'relocation programme' couldn't be justified – 'Very pricey, Dusty,' he'd said. The chief inspector was unlikely ever to have known what his life had cost. Dusty didn't know how Danny Curnow bore the guilt, or Captain Bentinick.

The cemetery always shocked the tourists. They might have been to First World War burial grounds but they were now almost historic. This was tangible and most of the visitors would have known men who had fought in the conflict – fathers, uncles or grandfathers. The guide would fill in the core detail at the start: there were 4,500 graves with 'unknown warrior' carved on the headstones and 600 for named dead. The cemetery was beside a busy main road. Many of the graves were of pilots who had attempted to give air protection over the evacuation beaches, British, Polish, Australians, Canadians and New Zealanders. Some visitors might be in tears as they hurried in the failing light back to the minibus.

The flight was called. Malachy Riordan waited for the surge to build, then strode towards Departures. It had been a complicated journey to Dublin.

Brennie Murphy had moved him up the Pomeroy road. Bridie had met him in the car park of the town's Gaelic Athletic ground and had brought him his bag of basics. There had been a brief hug, and she had told him to watch himself. Another car, engine idling, had been waiting in the shadows of the pavilion and he'd been driven off on the next leg.

They had gone down the mountain, leaving behind the territory of the 'rapparee', whose fights with Crown forces were familiar to every child brought up on the hills dominating Dungannon. Malachy knew each stage of the man's persecution, rebellion and success. He knew, too, about his death and in which lough his body had been dumped.

A woman drove. She said nothing to him but had nodded when his belt was fastened and driven towards the fast roads running south, for Armagh City, the border, then on towards Monaghan in the Republic. At first he knew the roads well – and saw the lane to Mossie Nugent's home. They careered through old battle sites: a crossroads where his father had twice fought paratroops, a culvert near to a primary school where a bomb had tipped an armoured police car on its side, injuring two of its passengers seriously – his father had done that – and a whitewashed farm where his father had sat motionless in a ditch for thirty hours and shot dead the farmer's son who had gone to get pigs' fodder in Cookstown and was a corporal in the Ulster Defence part-timers. He could still see, smell, feel the touch of his father. He couldn't escape him, could only strive to match the expectation his father would have had for him.

Malachy had seen his father before the coffin had been closed. His mother had tugged him forward and he had seen the holes in the forehead, throat and upper chest. All his life, from the day of the funeral, he had yearned to hear his father's praise.

There were places where Malachy had killed, at a stone bridge over a wee stream, at the back of a transport depot, at the entrance to a neat housing estate on the Middletown road. And places where he had failed to kill but had wounded, where the weapon had malfunctioned, or the device had failed to detonate because the Semtex was old. Then, he had thought of his father's disappointment in his boy. His mother had been a handsome woman. She had owned land and a business but had never looked at another man. She had kept the spirit of her husband alive, and flowers beside his photograph. There could never be an escape for Malachy.

In Monaghan they had stopped at a service station. She'd motioned for him to stay in his seat and parked away from the pumps, then gone inside to the toilets. She hadn't offered the facility to him. He supposed he could tell her to stop in any farm gateway where there were no cameras, but he didn't. They went through Castleblaney and hit the motorway at Dundalk – where big men, in the old days, had plotted and where jealousies had ripped apart friendships. The woman had the look of a housewife. She could have walked past him in any town he knew, anywhere in Tyrone, Fermanagh or Armagh, and he wouldn't have reckoned her as committed to the struggle. She wore a wedding ring. He wondered if a husband was minding the kids, doing homework with them, making a meal for them, and wondering how late she would be.

She had stopped well short of the airport terminal, rummaged in the glove box and produced the passport, Irish, with his photograph in it. She showed him the name, which he repeated twice to himself, then a strip of paper on which was written an address in Drogheda, which they had bypassed a half-hour before. She took the paper back and screwed it up.

She reached across and opened his door. She didn't wish him luck. He took the bag off the back seat, climbed out and slammed the door.

Malachy knew nothing of the woman, had taken her on trust. He could not know whether she would go home to her husband and kids, whether she would be off to a meeting with her handler or whether she would do it on her mobile. The Organisation was rotten with them. That was why he had demanded that the trip to the Czech capital took place immediately so that others, presently outside the loop, wouldn't hear of it. That was also why he had allowed Kevin and Pearse, kids, to do the bomb on the policeman, Eamonn O'Kane. He could take precautions, as his father would have, but at the end there had to be trust. Who to trust?

He had gone into the bright lights of the terminal. His passport was glanced at and handed back. He was in the flow and walked towards the gate.

Pearse drove a short-handled spade into the grass, eased it forward and backwards, making a V six inches deep, then moved sideways, on his hands and knees, and repeated it. Kevin would drop the cable into the V, then close the indent with his hands and put the grass back. A slow job. They would not have dared to rush the work, risk failure and incur Malachy Riordan's wrath. It was dark and they were close enough to the house to hear, when the wind gusted, the television programme those inside were watching. A hoarse whisper from Kevin: it was the same hospital programme his ma would be in front of.

Pearse responded: 'Fuckin' crap. Who wants to watch hospital misery?'

The exchange marked their nerves. Neither of them had been given such responsibility before. The house was up a lane, a hundred yards from the minor road. The end of the cable would lie ten yards from the road where there was a thin hedge.

They had walked the last quarter-mile. An owl had hooted as they'd approached the lane, then floated away to hunt. They'd gone as still as statues when the man of the house, Eamonn O'Kane's dad, had put the dog out of the front door and had stood on the mat to smoke a cigarette. The dog hadn't gone far enough to pick up their scent.

It was good that Malachy had faith in them. They'd do it right and show that his faith was well placed. They would kill a policeman who would come back for a party to celebrate his parents' golden wedding anniversary. It was said that the policeman, O'Kane, was hard, a Catholic, a man who hated them. Neither Pearse nor Kevin had ever seen the body of a man killed by a bomb.

They would on the night after next. They were sure of it.

He could see her. She was at the front and Ralph Exton was at the back. It might have been the first time he had seen her out of her uniform of jeans, T-shirts and anoraks: she wore them year-round. He didn't know whether she was reading or asleep. Himself?

A few things in his life needed sorting out. The right time to order his affairs would be the day after he got back from Prague: mortgages, bank overdrafts, school fees, the dentist, and finding something that would give him a more regular income. The biggest issue he had to sort out involved the Irish, and linked to them was Gabrielle, eighteen rows in front. It might just mean a visit to an estate agent, who would laugh at the prospect of flogging a semi-detached house that was almost within the boundaries of the royal village.

Nearly there. He could see lights below. Last time he'd raised the possibility of quitting, Gabrielle had laughed. 'We decide when you walk out, Ralph. It's not your shout. We're taking good care of you, and national security needs you in place. This is not the time even to think about it. Put it out of your mind and let's go back to work.' A little tap on the hand had followed, implying that he was a reasonable man, receptive to clear logic, and they were friends.

What was there to look forward to? Not a lot.

Ralph Exton was the eternal optimist, the sort of man who'd bank on fixing cheap motor insurance, then writing the car off, faulty engine and all, on an icy road and getting a payout for a new one. Always an opportunity around a corner. The landing gear was coming down. His old friend Timofey Simonov, now a multi-millionaire.

They hit the ground. Who did he play for? Whose shirt did he wear? Timofey's, Gabrielle's, or that of the boot-faced bastard who'd have used the drill on him? He came off the plane. He could always seem relaxed, at ease, even when his knees were knocking. He thanked the girl at the door. Gabrielle was ahead of him. She hadn't turned and caught his eye.

It had been quiet on the flight – but it wasn't a no-frills airline: the boozers would have been scared off by the prices. He fished his passport out of his pocket and headed for the formalities. She was through.

It was about guns. Guns and death jogged alongside each other, and there'd be pictures on TV of coffins being carried and denunciations. He checked that his bag was on the correct shoulder and straightened his tie.

She recognised him. He wore the orange and green striped tie, the sort that rugby guys at Queen's might have worn on a half-formal night, and had a bag on his left shoulder – most men would have carried it on the right. She had been told he was a lynch-pin for the Organisation. He raised money through cigarettes and had a lengthy contacts list in Europe. He knew a man. He walked lightly, carelessly, as though nothing threatened him.

Frankie McKinney had been at the airport for an hour. She knew all of the menu tariffs at the fast-food places. She had felt, without reason, that she stood out. Her throat was dry. She had arrived as drunken British kids were arguing in the taxi queue, had had two coffees and had seen the cameras that covered the concourse. She had been told by Maude that she should watch carefully when he came through for tails on him. There were three possibilities, but Maude had dismissed them: he was a tout and worked for the intelligence service; he was honest in his dealings with them but had aroused suspicion and was therefore being watched; he was clean, had no tail and was to be trusted. Her hotel was out to the south of the city, massive and impersonal, and her room had a view of the bridges that spanned the Vltava river; the man from Tyrone, the fighter, had the room booked next to hers for the following night and onwards. She knew his name, Ralph Exton, and readied herself. He would stay in the centre, on Stepanska, but the Radisson was beyond her budget. They had told her how to greet him. She would come forward, holding a newspaper, and look past him. She would seem not to see him and they'd bump into each other. A good enough excuse for half a dozen words. She could see no tail.

Ralph Exton, to her, was insignificant. She knew about the weapons, and their importance, the difference they would make when imported. Recruiting would climb, and in the wake of it more money could be raised. With firepower the administration would rock, crumble. Maude had talked about it. A big breath. She made the calculation of where, at his pace and hers, they would collide. She began to walk, holding the newspaper loosely. He loomed towards her. She did not know what description he had been given: a black trouser suit, a Vuitton bag her parents had given her, a loosely tied silk scarf, grey, and her hair pulled back. It was the moment they'd meet and—

Ralph Exton sidestepped her. He did a little swerve and she'd gone past him. She stood alone while men and women, passengers and airport staff, went by and round her, and more flights were announced. She took another five steps. Shit. She turned. Frankie saw his back as he went out into the night. She glimpsed him take a taxi. Her phone – the one Maude had given her – rang. She snapped it open.

'Sorry and all that, just didn't think it was a good place. I'm a bit bushed. Tomorrow morning, yes?'

When he had been in the queue a taxi had accelerated past and he had seen Gabrielle's face in a window seat. He thought his loyalties were fractured, his allegiance uncertain. He had seen Frankie as soon as he had come into Arrivals. A great-looking kid, taut and upright, like a bloody lighthouse – a fair chance that the sharp-eyed Gabrielle would have spotted any contact. God, they were thin on the ground if they'd sent an apprentice in street craft. He owed her nothing, but had protected her. All about self-preservation, Ralph. The taxi brought him into a city clogged with evening traffic and they crossed the river north of Charles Bridge.

It was quiet at the hotel desk, soft music playing, and the rate he'd be charged was confirmed to him, which made him shudder.

He went to his floor. Ralph Exton, one-time entrepreneur and prodigious salesman of second-hand and dubious merchandise – furniture, fags, china ornaments, computers, vegetables, pirate DVDs, and top-label clothing that came from sweat shops on the slopes of Vesuvius – could enter a first in his CV. He had never before tried to broker a deal for machine-guns that fired 50-calibre rounds, Russian-built sniper rifles, warheads that could take out a vehicle with armour plating, modern military detonators, explosives and assault rifles. It was a new world.

What had he told them when they had threatened him with the drill and the burning cigarette? *I need the money*. He went past her door and heard the British TV news.

He came to his room. He wondered where his wife was, and with whom, and where his daughter was, then grimaced and flicked the key card in and out. This job would be a good earner, had to be. His bag landed on the bed, and he kicked the door shut. He dealt with people he regarded as exceptionally ruthless, who would do to him things that were best left without description. All of them were good for business and at the apex of danger.

Rosie Bentinick had made a shrine at the back of the first floor. It was where she came each evening. She walked into the room at the time when her daughter would have got in from school, a south-west London comprehensive, and later from the college where she had trained as a teacher, specialising in remedial.

The room was as it had been on the day that her daughter loaded the bulging canvas bag into the car and they had set off for the airport. The parents had seen their girl through the gates, and had watched as they had closed on her.

He'd gone to work the next morning as if nothing had changed.

She worked part-time for the British Legion in the heart of the town, a red-brick edifice that sprang to life each autumn with the approach of Remembrance Day. They paid a pittance. She had had time to climb the stairs, go into the back room and tidy it so that when their girl came back it would be exactly as she had left it – except that the bed was made, the washing basket cleared, the clothes ironed and put away, the picture frames dusted.

That first night, flowers had been put in their daughter's tooth mug from the bathroom, then changed at the end of the first week of her absence and every week, on Thursday, for the last seven years. The pain never lessened, not for Rosie or her husband.

There was a chair by the window and part of the seat was filled with teddy bears, but there was room enough for one of them to sit during the evening vigil. Then a candle was lit, summer or winter. The cat would likely be asleep on the bed and the dog, older and arthritic, would be across her feet or her husband's. Visiting was worse.

The only light would be the candle and it would play on a photograph on the dressing-table that showed the girl, blonde and happy, with the children around her.

Timofey Simonov lay in his bed and his mind wandered. He thought of the hood who would be in the darkness inside the lock-up garage. The cement from the bags would now have solidified around his legs and ankles. His toes would be numb and the weight of the cement would drag at his knee joints.

He thought of his father, a junior officer in the Interior Ministry force that had had responsibility for the security of the camps for convicts. His father went to work each morning in a threadbare uniform at the camp that was Perm 35, and his memories were of the stories his father told him.

The man in the garage who had shown disrespect would survive the night but not the following day. Timofey Simonov, who regarded himself as a successful businessman, had long been fascinated by the ways, habits and punishments of criminals.

His father could have moved on from Perm 35, gone back into the main ranks of the Interior Ministry force and sat at a more comfortable desk. He could have been away from the awful damp, perpetual cold and misery of winter, when light was barely visible above the trees around the camp, and the summers of heat, flies and mosquitoes. But his father would not move, and his mother had not demanded that he transfer or quit, and all the time that Perm 35, the logging camp, was open, he had stayed. His mother had been a bureaucrat in the administration of the camp's hospital. He remembered, from the stories told him, the obsession of his father.

The criminals would have understood why it was appropriate for a man to go into the river, feet in set cement, as a punishment for disrespect. They would have recognised the retribution of death by shooting, at long range by a marksman, against a man who had broken the rules of conduct. But he did not see himself as a criminal, merely as a businessman whose value was recognised in the corridors of power. The town of Karlovy Vary was the right place for a businessman to be, and he did not seek out the company of criminals.

He thought of his father's obsession: the security of the camp. The man had become deranged in the isolation of Perm 35, 1,600 kilometres to the east of the capital. He had feared a breakout and was unwilling to relinquish control. Timofey Simonov had watched his father's growing madness. His whole childhood had been spent in the garrison part of the camp with criminals, whose faces showed no hope, and horizons of endless forests. The breakout had not taken place at a camp where his father had served, but his father had been called there when reinforcements were required.

Timofey Simonov would have been angered had it been suggested to him that he, too, was a criminal.

The camp was at Kengir in Kazakhstan. It was in the spring of 1954 that a guard had killed a prisoner, whose friends had called it murder. An uprising had followed and unchecked anarchy. The guards were slaughtered or had fled. For forty days the prisoners had ruled their own ghetto camp, formed a provisional government, attempted to barter for freedom with the Interior Ministry force commander, who led the military surrounding the perimeter. It was suppressed. Intermittent negotiations were entered into and bought time for the transfer to the nearest railhead of tanks and artillery pieces. When they were in place, talks were suspended. The military had attacked the camp. His father said that only a few dozen of the convicts died as the camp was retaken: the convicts had claimed between five and seven hundred were put to death. Timofey Simonov liked the stories of the mutiny and its suppression. He was grateful to his father for telling them. The lesson he took from Kengir more than half a century later: the prisoners had not shown sufficient respect for the administration of their camp. That was intolerable – and the convicts, grudgingly, knew it. For lack of respect a sniper could shoot to kill, or feet could be put into an oil drum as cement hardened.

Timofey Simonov had great wealth. He owned a villa overlooking Karlovy Vary with fine views, and the road was the most sought after in the town of Russian *émigrés*. He had accounts in discreet banks scattered across the globe. He had the protection of a man who had once been a brigadier. Soon an old friend from the days when he'd struggled would be close to him. None of that lulled him to sleep. He lay in his bed, listening to distant traffic and the quiet of his home.

The key, his father said, to retaking the camp was recruiting informers. They had been among the convicts, but slipped out notes detailing the names of the leadership, where the weapons were and the weak points. Informers, traitors, were a danger to convicts, the state, and to any businessman who traded at the edge.

It would be a long night. Many were.

'It's a city of the dead. It has a history of brutal killing. Can I say that to a visitor?'

'Feel free.'

'Here, where we stand, by this plaque, twenty-seven revolutionary leaders were put to death, noblemen, four hundred years ago. Twenty-four died at the hand of the same executioner. Perhaps he was too tired to deal with the last three.'

'Tiring work, killing people,' Danny Curnow said softly.

The night was cold. It was past two, the stag parties were gone and the sightseers from across Europe had dispersed. The policeman stood close to him, then took his arm, and they moved across the wide space of the Old Town Square, stopping by a huge memorial, a man of God, in greening bronze. An hour and a half before, Danny had come down from his room, sleep having evaded him, and found Karol Pilar dozing on a sofa in the hotel lobby. Why was he there? 'It's my job to be here.' Wasn't there a girl, someone important, he should be with? 'She understands – I thought you or Mr Bentinick might need me. It is a privilege for me to work with you.' Danny had thought him sincere. They had gone out into the night and tramped the emptying streets, a chill wind gripping him. It had been his intention merely to go round the block, then head back to his room. He was shown the sights, had his own guide. When he was on the battlefield tours some of the guides held bright parasols aloft. The policeman stayed close to him. When a beggar had loomed from the shadows, Karol Pilar had pushed him aside.

'The statue is of Jan Hus. Two centuries before those nobles were slaughtered he was burned alive for spreading heresy. In this square more than fifty of his prime supporters were put to death.'

Danny Curnow imagined, where he stood, brave men dying, not giving those who killed them the satisfaction of showing fear.

They walked on. There was a wide old pedestrian bridge, the river flowing briskly through the arches below.

'Charles Bridge. A saint of the Czech people died here, John of Nepomuk, the Queen's confessor. In 1393 Wenceslas the Fourth had him thrown off the bridge and drowned because he would not tell the King what she had said to him in the confessional box. You good to walk further?'

'Fine.'

They looked up at the huge illuminated wall of the castle.

'It was the custom in Prague, six hundred years ago, for the mob to attack the seat of power. Officials of the Crown or tax gatherers were thrown from the upper windows – those windows. Come on.'

They retraced their way, then Karol Pilar took his arm and stopped him. The water flowing below the bridge was deep and should have contained secrets.

'The Nazis were fleeing. Their executioner brought the guillotine he had used to the banks of the river and had it thrown into the current. He hoped it would never be found. In two years that man, Alois Weiss, had beheaded by guillotine more than one thousand Czechs. It was retrieved. There were bloodstains on the wood frame and the blade. He died, an old man, in Germany.'

The traffic noise had faded. Rats scurried in the gutters, derelicts snored in doorways, and another day started. The street-sweepers were out and rubbish bins were emptied. The first lights lit office windows. They were under the prison walls.

'We had the tyranny of Fascism and replaced it with the barbarity of Communism. A woman opposed the Soviet regime and its Czech sycophants, Milada Horáková. It was announced she had been executed by hanging. In fact, she was strangled. Each time she was near to death they stopped and loosened the pressure. They took seventeen minutes to kill her. Should we go further?'

Sparse traffic was now on the roads and the first trams. Men and women were starting to spill from the metro entrances. They were back in the long square onto which Danny's hotel fronted. There was a statue, many times life-size, of a figure astride a horse, in armour. Karol Pilar said it was of Wenceslas I, then pointed down to what seemed to be a cross embedded in the cobbles. It was twisted and broken. The policeman's face was sober. 'Most people accept the hardship of a vile dictatorship, from the left or the right, but a very few do not. Jan Palach was studying history and economics. He protested against the Soviet occupation and the Czechs who collaborated. He poured petrol over himself, lit it and died days later in great pain.'

'Why are you showing me these places?'

'I can take you near to where I live. There is a street corner where a man was shot dead. His crime? He had the same car – same make and colour – as a man condemned by a rival gang. It was a mistake. The court case against the assassins failed. Why? You should understand that here, Mr Curnow, life is cheap, so people in my country are not careless about their survival. Be careful.'

He thought of the innocence of the young men – British, Canadian and American – who had been on the beaches along the coast of France from Dunkirk, their lack of cunning, and of the many who lay there. He thought of the pastures stretching up towards the forestry and summit of the mountain, the narrow lanes running down to the Dungannon road.

'Karol, in your family, were they victims or executioners?'

'My grandfather was at the Pankrác gaol and fortunate to escape the axe room. He died nine years ago, much loved by his family and respected in his community, but he was not a clever man. He had been careless.'

They had coffee in a Costa lounge. Around them young men and woman were readying themselves for the office. The sight-seeing expedition had not been tourism: every action, he always assumed, had purpose. It would have toughened him. The agent would be subject to his discipline or they might fail. It was not that Bentinick was short of men or women who could have done a decent job. Bentinick had been looking for a man of proven ruthlessness, which was what Danny had been and for which he had paid a high price. He went back to the hotel, and the policeman settled on a sofa.

7

'You know why we're here, Danny?'

'I expect you'll tell me, Mr Bentinick.'

'You're here, Danny, because I worry that your exile in France, among the dead and the battlefields, may have softened your resolve.'

'You're never found me wanting.'

'A different war here from those beaches, and no Geneva Convention on prisoners. It's merciless and for high stakes. "The end justifies the means." Our sort of language at Gough, Danny.'

They were on a wide street on a hill with busy traffic. They had crossed the road – Bentinick walked straight across, looking neither right nor left, ignoring horns – and stopped a few yards short of a church that was flush to the pavement. Baroque style, mid-eighteenth century, the stonework was clean: it was important. Karol Pilar was behind them, silent. Danny had lain on his bed for an hour until the phone had erupted beside his head. He'd had three minutes to get down to the lobby. The policeman must have borrowed a razor: he was clean-shaven but in the same shirt, alert, suffering no ill-effects from the night tour of the city.

'Here, Danny, and in another place, we find evidence of courage, treachery, collateral, and the ruthlessness required of agent handlers. We hit the old brick wall, the one that has to be passed through. Was it necessary?'

The stonework up from the pavement showed bullet marks. In relief there were man-sized sculptures of a paratrooper and a priest; between them names were embossed on a stone slab.

'A little group of men, Danny, saved a country. A German was in charge of Prague, Heydrich. He was reviled and feared. The plan was to subsume most of Czechoslovakia into the Reich. As an independent entity, with language and culture, it would have disappeared. The Czechs had a government in exile, in Buckinghamshire. Some of their men who had escaped to England were trained as assassins, then parachuted into Czech territory from an RAF flight, with firearms and explosives. Heydrich drove in an open-topped limousine, no security escort, from his commandeered residence to Prague Castle in late May sunshine. He was attacked, with grenades and pistols, wounded and died a week later. His killers fled, disappearing off the face of the earth. Reprisals followed, but that'll keep. That's collateral – the responsibility that handlers carry. The man hunt ended here. Seven of the parachutists were hiding in the church, given refuge by the priest.'

'What am I supposed to say?'

'Nothing, Danny. Just listen.'

He wondered if the Czech would interrupt, but he did not. They went past the monument, then ducked into a side entrance to a cellar area. The Czech flashed his card at the curator, who gave a shrug of resignation: they did not have to pay. The walls were lined with photographs and dummies in British-issue Second World War uniforms.

'An informer, Kurda, brought the German military here, several hundred of them. He gave information to the investigators, but his motive was to halt the savagery of the reprisals. He would have been what you'd have called, in your Vagabond days, a "walk in". He came off the street when the hunt had gone cold. Three died in the nave, and the remaining four took refuge in the crypt. Follow me, Danny. Informers – we can't do without them, but they're seldom admired.'

Danny Curnow followed Bentinick into the crypt. Against the walls there were bronze busts of the seven.

'The last four were where we stand now. The fire brigade was called in to flush them out – flooded the place. Grenades were thrown in. They tried to tunnel out to the sewers under the street, scratching with their hands. At the end, some took poison capsules and some had saved a last round for themselves. None was alive for torture and execution. They were trained in England, handled in England and controlled by men who knew that savage killings would follow. The chief man was Jan Kubis. His mission started at Leamington Spa and ended here. His handlers knew what would happen, which didn't deflect their determination.'

They went out. Back in warm sunshine, the traffic swept past them. A girl pushed a pram, and a couple held hands as they walked briskly towards the metro. Each had a laptop bag slung on a shoulder, and no one had time to glance at the church façade. Danny Curnow understood the place, and the men who had been in the crypt – but they had not been part of as great an army as had been on the beaches. Matthew Bentinick lit his pipe, struggling in the breeze. Danny had no wish to be gone, and he lingered.

Karol Pilar hovered and watched. He was a man without illusions.

His office was in the Criminal Police section on Bartolomejska; the southern side of that street was taken up by buildings occupied by detectives of different agencies. Many would slip out at lunchtime for a meal and a drink in the bar opposite. Karol never went before seven. Then he would leave his Russian unit desk, go to the Konvikt and drink a bottle of Pilsner Urquell, then head off into the evening to the mini-mart and buy something for supper. The Sherlock and the Al Capone bar were on the same street but he used the Konvikt, only occasionally. He had little option: he earned the equivalent of one thousand five hundred American dollars a month, and his expenses were hardly a bonus. Then, with a plastic bag in his car, which was an old but well-maintained Skoda, he would go back to the studio flat he shared with his girlfriend and they'd eat what he'd bought. She was studying accountancy at college and did bookkeeping at a café to help with her fees. He could have earned more.

He did not interrupt them. Mr Bentinick had won him over. Danny was cautious and serious, perhaps suffering still from a wound inflicted long ago. Where could they have coffee? He shrugged, pointed down the hill, away from the church and towards the river.

A detective who attached himself to the political élite or a member of the judiciary could make a good living. And openings gaped for those prepared to ally themselves with the city's gang leaders – Russian, Albanian, Georgian, Armenian, Azerbaijani, any of them. Those who worked on surveillance teams were also in demand. He was clean. Many in his office thought him unnecessarily squeamish. There was a saying, deep-rooted in the country's culture: 'If you don't steal, your family will stay poor.' He occupied a middle-ranking position with the Russian desk. It was about resources, or the lack of them. On occasion he could go to Karlovy Vary, less frequently to Mariánské Lázně – prettier, with the same sulphurous springs and classic villas – which was second favourite with the Russians, with their suitcases of money. He could talk there to local police and underpaid informants and did the same in the capital where big men lived close to the Russian embassy and schools on the north side of the river. His seniors had given him the job of escorting Mr Bentinick because it concerned an Irish matter and he spoke good English – and while he was investigating the Irish he would have no opportunity to meddle in satisfactory arrangements. He thought Mr Bentinick a clever man.

They reached a café. It was cool, bright and a wind was blowing off the Vltava, as usual, but Mr Bentinick had decided they'd sit outside. Pilar was given two hundred Czech *koruna* to buy coffee. At the church of St Cyril and St Methodius, Mr Bentinick had spoken of ruthlessness. Karol Pilar did not doubt that he possessed it.

They were on the road and far out of Nürnberg, running late on the schedule. The driver seemed reluctant to burn some rubber, even though they were on the E51, a dual carriageway. There had been fog at the airport and they had spent more than an hour in stacking circles. When they had come down, his knuckles were white from gripping the top of the seat in front.

Malachy Riordan had been met. The fog had made a close wall around the car park and terminal buildings.

They had crept away and at snail's pace. It was rare that Malachy Riordan was a passenger on a long-distance journey. He was in the front seat, belt on, and the car was an old Mercedes, with more than two hundred thousand kilometres on the clock. In the fog, great lorries with trailers had surged by – intimidating. He didn't know where he was, recognised none of the place names, knew nothing of the old German Democratic Republic. Eventually the fog lifted and they had got stuck in Dresden's rush-hour traffic.

The driver talked but Malachy Riordan didn't. He ached for silence.

He knew the driver's name: Sean. Knew his age: twenty-seven. His job: he worked as a barman in an Irish-themed pub in Nürnberg. His origins: the family was from the Ballymurphy part of west Belfast and his father was a walking no-hoper after interrogations in the old Castlereagh barracks: an uncle limped from a wound above the knee where he'd been shot by a paratrooper; his mother had a cousin who had not bought into the war of the volunteers, and the martyrs. Malachy could not comprehend why the driver thought he would be interested in all of that. He could, of course, tell him to shut his face, but then the man could have pulled over onto any hard shoulder opened the door on the passenger side and said, 'Well, fuck you, man. Find your own way.' He could have been dumped on a roadside not knowing where he was or how to move on. He sat and endured.

Malachy Riordan never asked a question about the job in the Irish bar or whether the man had a family in Nürnberg. He didn't have to: he was told. The man leaked information. He imagined how it would be when the driver was back on his own territory. It was a mark of how far the Organisation had declined. In the old days, before the betrayal and the sell-out of the so-called 'peace process', people had been going regularly to the States, and for negotiations with the regime in Libya for weapons shipments; a delegation had gone to Colombia to teach workshops in mortar building and wiring. It strained his faith, but he knew nothing else – there were few days when he didn't go to his father's grave, and few weeks when he didn't pause in front of the monuments in Cappagh or Galbally on the slopes of the mountain. He couldn't imagine his faith being broken.

If the faith went, he would have to face the black marble

headstone that bore his father's name and blurt that he had compromised. He would follow the bastards who had gone into politics or who supervised the crossing in front of a school. He had never crossed his father, had always done his best to please and had hoped for praise.

Bridie was a hard woman. Brennie Murphy said she had the strength of granite. She might spit in his face and walk out on him, with the boy. So he let the man talk as they went towards the rising sun.

He learned more about the bar, the beers that were drunk, the bands that came over from the west of Ireland, the English football that was shown on TV, and buttoned his lip. Finally the driver had run out of small-talk. He asked, 'I suppose a man like yourself – they didn't give me a name, only the type of coat you'd be wearing – is important. Does that mean you're a soldier? You're a fighter, aren't you?'

They were in the fast lane and he watched the German traffic going about its business.

The driver said, 'Don't mind me. I know when to keep my mouth shut. My family always told me it's the touts you have to watch for.'

Malachy put the man's drivel from his mind and thought of home – Bridie would have taken the boy to school. Then he thought of his army.

The boys lived close to each other, were almost inseparable. Neither had work and neither was studying. They hung about together and most days were in each other's kitchens. Every adult in the village knew why they didn't have jobs or go to the college on the far side of Dungannon. It would be Pearse's mother's kitchen, or Kevin's mother's, and the other kids of the two families were gone for employment, training or to school. The boys were set apart, neither criticised nor encouraged: the subject was off limits.

It was Kevin's mother's kitchen. Physically, the boys were different. Kevin had red-gold hair and was tall, with spindly limbs. His voice had a reedy twang. Pearse was shorter, heavier, and had a deeper voice. His hair was jet black, Celtic, and curly. Kevin was quiet, Pearse more outgoing and overtly confident. The last time they had been taken to Gough they had sat in separate interview rooms and a detective had said to Kevin, 'You're sharp enough to keep better company. You'll bring ruin on yourself if you run with the shites and failures we see you with.' In another interview room, a woman detective had said to Pearse, 'Do you not realise that the time for killing and maiming people has gone and that you should be thinking of your future? It could be better than staring at a closed cell door, because that's what it'll be if you stay with Riordan and Murphy.' The last time they'd come out almost cocky, and had taken the bus back home to the mountain. In their different ways they had felt a new confidence.

That morning it had ebbed.

The kettle whistled. Kevin's mother was at work, cleaning the community hall, and the smaller kids had gone to school. The radio played the local station. There had been stone throwing and bottling in east Belfast, a boy had been shot in the kneecaps in Brandywell, Derry, and a 'viable device' had been found under a pile of rubbish at a tax office in Antrim. Normally they would josh and mess and be their age, but both were subdued.

It was the day when, alone, they would take their own length of piping, and the linked wiring for the detonation to the cabling hidden under the hedge, then wait for the car to come – Eamonn O'Kane's – and blow him away. They drank coffee, ate biscuits, and watched the hands of the clock on the wall crawl round.

It was as if there had been a death in the corridor.

Early in the morning, there should have been a strip of light under his door, with the indistinct glow from the ceiling distorted in a frosted-glass panel beside it. Jocelyn went by: no light, no voice speaking into a phone, no rattle of the keyboard, no hacking cough. She wore lightweight flat shoes and shuffled towards her own door. From anywhere along the corridor, she, and any other occupant, would have identified the metal tips clattering at the toes and heels of his brogues. The absence left an emptiness.

There were men and women on that corridor, senior management, who went to conferences and seminars, travelled internally or abroad, and left their rooms locked and darkened. They weren't missed. His window looked out onto the river. The glass was reinforced and supposedly shatterproof against a car bomb in the street. It was not supposed to be opened, but Jocelyn had heard reports of someone hanging out of a fourth-floor window, pipe smoke obscuring his face. She hated him to be away, was almost desolate in his absence.

She fancied she knew more about him than anyone else who worked there. When she was in that office she took no liberties. She would not slouch in a chair. She would not gossip or expect him to. Neither would she share what she knew of him. Jocelyn understood. She had been told once, and once was enough. It was a damp morning in central London and she had her raincoat draped over her shoulders. She made no concession to fashion and had never considered that dress might make her marginally more attractive to him. Both would have seemed, to strangers, emotionless, but they were bound by a fierce, unswerving pursuit of end-games.

If there had been a strip of light under it, or a whiff of pipe tobacco, she would have knocked courteously, would have been called inside and they'd have talked. They did so four times a day, at least.

She went past. It would be a big one. A high-value target was on offer, the most important in two or three years. She walked down the stairs, unwilling to wait for the lift, then through the lobby and past a desk where her card was read by the machine. A barrier opened, and she was out of the side door into the street. She could smell fresh coffee and bacon grilling from the café.

She didn't stop. The wind blew the sides of her coat hard against her. She cut through side-streets and headed towards Petty France, where buildings had privileged views over the parks and were close to the seats of power. She went through an unmarked doorway. A screen was consulted, her identification checked and a card issued. She went up two flights.

A young, smartly dressed lawyer was waiting for her. She shook his hand and was led towards a far room. The window that would have looked down into a central well was masked and the blind drawn. She had been told that this man, barely out of university, was a prime expert for the Ministry of Justice in areas affecting warrants, sealed or open, powers of arrest, the courts in which a case might be tried, and matters affecting international borders. He made coffee and offered biscuits. They settled. She assimilated advice, guidance, as Matthew Bentinick would have expected of her.

They finished.

He said, 'I was once taught, Jocelyn, the legal creed. "Be he ever so mighty, no man is above the law." Any observation you'd care to make?'

She said, 'We're not offenders. In the old days, we used "little people" for the nasty bits and let them run far enough to be out of sight. Then we couldn't account for what they'd done. But that, of course, was the old days.'

He'd sat in his room. She hadn't come or called: the mountain and Mahomet. He had gazed out of his window at the street opposite, a few chimneys and some satellite dishes. Nothing there to excite Ralph Exton.

His breakfast had been brought up on a tray – coffee, juice and a croissant. At home he was usually up early. When he was downstairs and dressed, Fliss and Toria still in bed, he had his desk in the dining room to himself and could shuffle the brown envelopes, make the decisions on which bills to pay and which to slip to the bottom of the heap. He could also consider new deals. Furniture always paid well, and he'd heard that there were good lines in clay garden pots from Vietnam – it was simple enough to run off the FairTrade stickers the garden centres liked. That was the trouble with Ralph Exton's life: money. When he was away the brown envelopes couldn't follow him. Maybe Fliss and Toria weren't at home. Maybe Toria was with a friend, and maybe Fliss had an early appointment in the chair, before the nurse arrived. Some men would not have accepted his wife's behaviour – they might have gone at her with an axe. There were men who stabbed or strangled their wives, then hanged themselves in the nearest woodland. That did not appeal, and the dentist was welcome to her. What did appeal to him was the next *big* deal, something that eclipsed the arrangements he had with the Irish for the cigarettes and was way bigger than the weapons he was brokering for them. It was elusive.

He could harbour an idea, then see it retreat into the mist when he dissected it. In the meantime there was business to sort out with Miss Gabrielle, and something rather firmer in the way of remuneration. He reckoned, with her in Prague and away from Thames House, he stood a better chance. It was the moment when they needed him. The mountain had not come to him, although he thought she liked him. He needed a pay-day.

He had a sheet of hotel paper, from beside the phone, and had made some calculations on it with the hotel's pencil. In his home bathroom there was a glass jar from a jumble sale, filled with hotel soaps, shampoos and shower gel. He was a serial pilferer and would slip the pencil into a pocket, then the replacement that the maid would leave.

He would be Mahomet. He left his room. The corridor was quiet as he padded its length. At her door he stood for a few seconds, listened, and heard the TV playing an English-language channel. He took a breath and knocked. 'Who is it?'

He looked up and down the corridor. 'Ralph.'

'Hold on a moment.'

He had his back to the door and kept a watch on the corridor, with the lift entrance at the far end to his right. It opened behind him.

'Yes?'

The lift came to that floor. Two girls walked out. They were Vietnamese – or Chinese, Japanese, Korean or . . . He turned. Gabrielle stood just back from the door. She was dripping. A towel was wrapped round her and her calves glistened. She seemed small, and the skin on her arms was white, as if it was never exposed to the weather. She stood there, legs a little apart, and stared up at him.

'Well?'

'Sorry, I'll come back.'

'Don't be ridiculous. Come in and make some coffee – milk and no sugar for me.'

He thought, couldn't be sure, that the towel had slipped an inch. She went back to the bathroom. There was a kettle, a bowl of coffee sachets, teabags and little milk pots. He boiled the water and poured. He heard her in the bathroom, clattering, then the whine of an electric toothbrush.

'Ralph?'

'What?'

'There's a pile of my clothes on the chair by the window – I put them out for today. Could you bring them here?'

He did so. Her hand came out and she took them from him.

'I was about to call you.'

The kettle had boiled and he made the coffee. There was no book beside the bed and the sheets were barely disturbed. He reckoned she had slept well. Why should she not? She would have thought she had control of him. He poured. She hummed to herself in the bathroom.

'What couldn't wait for me to contact you, Ralph?'

'I need to talk to you.'

'What about?'

She was in the door of the bathroom. Her jeans were on, fastened at the waist but not zipped, and her bra. She was towelling her hair.

He said it quickly: 'My future. I don't have a budget from you. We have an arrangement, week to week, day to day, and—'

'I can't offer you a wage, Ralph.'

'I need something better in place.'

'Are the Irish not paying up front?'

'My future is when I come out. Where's the exit?'

She pushed him down onto the bed, then brought over their coffee. She sat beside him.

'We'll look after you, Ralph. It's about trust, and you have good reason to trust us. You're really important. All the people in our building who need to know about you are rooting for you. All of them. We really admire what you're doing.'

A sweet voice, the burr of her accent, and nowhere near to an answer. His phone rang. She eased back, stood up and carried her cup to the window. He answered it. 'Hello . . . Yes, that's me . . . Yes, I have it. I'll be there.'

In his mind he saw the young woman he had walked past at the airport, a fleeting memory. He hung up. 'Gaby, we never seem to consider it appropriate to discuss my future.'

'That's for London, not here. How often do I have to tell you, Ralph, that we're all committed to you.' She put on her T-shirt. 'You worry too much, and there's no need for it. You meet her and come back to me. Your future? Well, that depends how all this shakes down.'

'Of course.'

She was alone and lonely. Frankie McKinney hadn't anticipated that. She was dressed and ready but had nowhere to go for two more hours. She felt like a wallflower at a dance for teenagers in a community centre. He'd sounded distant. There had been no enthusiasm in his voice but she lacked the street-level tradecraft to know whether it was basic procedure or meant crisis. It would be good in the evening when the Big Man came. She lay on her bed. She had an idea of how he would be: inspirational. When they went to the place where there would be test-firings, she would ask if she could go first, charge the adrenalin, see the flash as the cartridge case was ejected. Or better: shoot the launcher. Then she would meet the Russians who were far beyond her understanding. Two hours to kill.

On the hill among the beech trees, Timofey Simonov was content. His dogs had picked up the scent of deer and were quartering as the autumn leaves fell around them.

He had an agenda of sorts to go with his walk, matters he should consider. The *future*: the call from his friend, the meeting that would be arranged for the next evening, the journey for collection, then the test-firings and Milovice, the camp that had been his home. It would be good to be with his friend because he had no others.

He loved the dogs, but nothing else. The *present*: he could take satisfaction, as he walked on the dried leaves, that the hood in Yekaterinburg had spent the night strapped into the chair, his feet tight in the concrete. About now he would be moved. His disposal would take place in daylight, seen by many. Because it would be witnessed, other young men with ambition would step back from interference in the existing order, and the booths from which narcotics were sold would not be trashed. He did not think that the sniper would shoot that day in the London suburb because his computer had told him the weather was bad in that area. If it rained the man would not step outside, would not offer a target. An invitation had come that morning by email. His company was requested at a dinner on Saturday at the Grand Hotel Pupp: the charitable cause was repairs to the roof of the main Russian Orthodox church. He might go or he might send the brigadier with a cheque. The present was calm.

The *past*: that was where he spent many of his waking hours. He was with his father and mother at Perm 35. His childhood, with so little company of his own age, had shaped him. When the leaves or needles fell in the forests surrounding the barbed-wire fences, winter was approaching, the season most feared when snow settled on the fences and gates, and the watch towers where the guards shivered. The life expectancy of young men existing in the tundra communities was as little as thirty-five, and when they died many of them had already suffered a crude castration from drinking home-brewed alcohol in the depths of winter, then needing to piss, going outside and exposing their genitals to the ravages of frostbite. Amputation was required. His home was in the heart of a gulag for criminals, for those designated insane, and for men convicted under Article 70, which took in the failed escapers from the Union and the dissidents. Sometimes, not often, a dignitary would come from Moscow – a thousand miles away and a four-hour drive from the airport. At this time of year the first snow would have fallen and the chill was gathering strength; half-frozen men would have splashed paint on everything static in the camp. He had been educated among the younger prisoners.

For three years, Timofey's best friend had been Mikhail, who wanted to be a musician and had mauve-dyed hair. They had studied mathematics. Others had learned chemistry and engineering. More of the criminals had worked at his parents' home, cleaning, washing, cooking. They tended the small garden in summer and were trusted prisoners. Some had talked to him, out of his father's and mother's hearing, of the criminal underworld, and others had told stories of *samizdat*, hidden printing presses and smuggled manuscripts. He had grown up without loyalty, either to the state or to his family, with the lesson dinned into him that the greatest crime was to be caught. His response had been to join Military Intelligence; its motto 'Greatness of Motherland in your glorious deeds'. He had turned his back on the wire, the convicts and his parents, and had ridden in a bus down the one-way road to Perm and the outside world. He often brooded on the past when he was walking his dogs.

Sunlight dappled the leaves. He had made a near-perfect life for himself.

Tension crackled. Its source, Danny understood, was Matthew Bentinick. They sat at an outside table, and the pipe was lit.

It had not mattered to Danny, inside the sealed compound at Gough, that matters were kept from him. Some saw it as an insult to their integrity – as if trust was withheld. It was obvious to him that confidentiality existed between Bentinick and the Czech policeman. In the unit there had been demarcation lines between teams. The names of agents were not shared, and biographies were not gossiped over in the bar: the talk spread only when a man was found in a ditch and a country lane was sealed.

Bentinick's coffee was cold, and the biscuit in the saucer uneaten. He stared out at the fast traffic on the riverside road, the bridges and the castle on the hill. There was no small-talk, but there never had been with him. Danny had drunk his coffee. The Czech had bought mineral water and was sipping it.

Bentinick's face was screwed up and the lines at his mouth were deep, as were those on his forehead. He didn't blink. A hand came up and the thin white fingers drove through his hair. All those years before, in the operations room and in the building that doubled as canteen and bar, in good times and bad, Danny had not seen stress build in the man who had commanded him – and still did. Standards were adhered to – had been then, were now: the shirt was clean, the chin close shaven, the tie centrally knotted and the shoes polished. Emotion, not hidden this time, gripped the man. The quiet between them was broken.

The cold coffee was drained, the mark of a man to whom waste was abhorrent. Danny could not guess at the demons – he had had his own, had struggled in confronting them.

The lines on the face cleared, as if Bentinick had wiped them away. He said, bright, brusque, 'Karol, time for you to do back-up. Get behind Miss Gabrielle. We'll be fine. But my friend is short of some history and maybe needs another cup of coffee. Thank you, Karol.'

The Czech stood, bobbed his head and was gone. Danny Curnow recognised qualities that he had once had, which the policeman had shown: there for a moment, on the pavement and his back to them, then gone. Seen but not noticed, merging and lost. It was a skill few possessed. Danny appreciated the art-form, respected the man, and had no idea why they had spent most of the night tramping pavements in the cold and visiting sites of barbarism. He wondered why they had skipped the Church of St Cyril and St Methodius, and whether Matthew Bentinick had manipulated it.

He had much to learn. He bought more coffee. The pipe smoke billowed.

Dusty parked the bus. He'd rung Caen before they'd left and spoken to Lisette, said that he would be back on Saturday, in the early evening, but still didn't know when Danny might appear. Dusty worried for him. There would have been an accumulation of guilt, well hidden at the start but later rearing. He could remember each of the losses, and Danny had seemed not to care. Life had gone on in Gough, in their inner compound. Joseph, from Armagh City, needing to better himself, had been a big one. The idiot had wanted to be a businessman and required capital to buy a shop window. Maybe the limit of his ambition had been to join the Chamber of Commerce, if they'd admitted Taigs. He'd wanted to be an estate agent. Few Catholics in Armagh City could buy and sell, but they could rent. He'd been set up in business. Nice enough guy, pretty wife and three wee kids he adored. He liked, he'd told Danny, to get up in the morning when half the street was still in bed, put on a laundered shirt, knot his tie, and go to open the agency door. Property was always brilliant. He had empty houses that the active-service units could use for briefings and as hideaways. A familiar story, a well-travelled road. Nothing too serious, but lives would have been saved and killing weapons put under surveillance. He was a cheerful man and wore his worries, apparently, easily. Used to bring the kids to meetings: the handlers and back-up people started to take sweets for them. Great kids. But he was a useless businessman and the FRU had to decide whether it was worth pumping in more cash. There'd have been a meeting about it and a balance sheet would have been on the table. *Income*: the intelligence they gained from him. *Outgoings*: what he cost. He would be cut adrift. The decision was taken and Danny Curnow had not objected.

What would happen to him? Well, the agency would close, leaving a trail of debts, and he'd have to start again. There was a scheduled meeting that evening, in the back of a pub off the road between Aughnacloy and Ballygawley. The team had stocked up with sweets for the kids, and Danny would have been the bad-news messenger – but the tout hadn't showed. He didn't show for a week. When he did, he was in a ditch, no shoes or socks, trussed like a Christmas bird, his teeth out, body covered with bruises. His life had been ended by a single shot, .38 calibre. As Captain Bentinick had remarked, 'I think we'll find he just had bad luck.'

Too right. Volunteers had used a house. They'd had a coffee grinder that reduced fertiliser nitrates, for explosives, from granules to powder. It had blown a fuse and burned out the wall plug. One had been a fairly competent electrician. He had unscrewed the plug and found the hidden microphone. Bad luck. The kids had been at the funeral, close to their mother; not many others had turned out. The local TV always featured touts' funerals. That night everyone in the ops room had watched the news. Captain Bentinick and Vagabond had put on a class act of stiff upper lip, pretending to be unmoved. Three great wee kids.

Dusty waited for the tour party.

Too many men had been on the beach at Dunkirk and were now in the cemeteries. The guides liked the cattle byre at Wormout. It was Danny Curnow's place. He'd have been off to the side, listening carefully but not intervening. A simple story, and the guides would get it right because of the ample documentation. The group would have been cheerful, with initial alliances forming, when the coach left Dunkirk. Then they'd be hit. They'd be gathered together in a close group, then told that sixty British soldiers, overwhelmed on the perimeter line defending the beach evacuation, had been taken into the square, lined up, had faced a machine-gun on a tripod and been mown down. It would get worse and nerves were shredded. The fighting was brutal: a British officer threatened other officers with death – he'd shoot them – if they broke. He was as good as his word. The order on that sector was 'Tell your men, with their backs to the wall, that the division stands firm.' The integrity of the beaches and dunes was maintained long enough for the evacuation to take place. They would take a country road out of Wormout for a mile, then a turning to the left up a lane, and go on foot along a track to a place named La Plaine au Bois and a hut – in good repair because, as a monument, it needed to survive. The hut was open at one end but had no windows. It was fifteen feet square.

Around a hundred men, mostly from the Warwickshire Regiment, had been herded in there by their captors: their resistance had become hopeless through exhaustion and lack of medical treatment for the wounded. Also, they had run out of ammunition. They were shot, five at a time, then grenades were thrown at them. A private, Bert Evans, only nineteen, survived and lay for a few minutes hidden by bodies. He and a captain, Lynn-Allen, crawled out and tried to get to the cover of trees down a hedgerow. They were spotted and fired on. The officer died

– but, extraordinarily, Evans lived. He was found by French farmers and taken to a civilian hospital, then to a POW camp.

The troops who carried out the killings were from the Liebstandarte SS, and their commanding officer was Captain Wilhelm Mohnke. It wasn't until 1945 that Private Evans was able to tell the story of the butchery, after his release from the camp. At the end of the fighting Mohnke was a general, and spent ten years as a prisoner in the Soviet Union, then came back to Hamburg. He was never prosecuted: a wall of silence in the SS unit protected him. He lived for sixty-one years after those men had died in the little hut.

Everyone would be quiet, shocked, upset. It would seem impossible for an act of such barbarity to have taken place in a scene so tranquil. They would go back to the minibus, numbed. It was a good place, on a Tuesday morning, for Danny Curnow.

He walked. It was a wide street, the best sort. She was a hundred yards behind him on the far pavement. It was the sort of street that Gaby Davies's instructors used for recruit training. She did not have to be close to her agent but could observe him. Years ago, at Essex, she had been a historian, with an American bias, but at school she had loved modern European history. She was following Ralph Exton on his way to his meeting with the girl. She had the little compact camera in her bag and a fag in her fingers. There had been a teacher at school who had done the Second World War with them – she remembered a Churchill quote: *Now this is not the end. It is not even the beginning of the end. But, it is, perhaps, the end of the beginning*. Appropriate. Her agent was walking across the city to rendezvous with the opposition's paymaster and bag-carrier. The building blocks were in position, and in two or three days, it would climax. She allowed a little excitement to well. For Christ's sake, why did they do it, if not for the buzz? What were they there for, on the floors of Thames House? Not Crown and country, or Keeping Our Streets Safe. It was about the raw pleasure of seeing a mission move on from the *end of the beginning*.

He walked briskly, with a good stride.

He showed no nerves, looked around him only when crossing a

road. She hadn't said she would tail him and he might or might not have assumed she would. She thought he had been through fire. There had been a trace of a quaver in his voice when he'd relayed the story of the drill but he'd stayed calm and she thought him almost a hero. His fingers had been shaking when they'd pushed the book of photos, the rogues' gallery, at him, but there had been no histrionics when he had picked out Malachy Riordan, then Brennie Murphy: 'A bad bastard, that one.' She thought she managed him well.

The sunlight was on him.

His wife was a total cow. He deserved better. There was a big hotel ahead. His daughter was another cow. Gaby Davies reckoned Ralph Exton deserved not grief but a medal.

She should have known more about the Russian end but he'd done well for them and was worth the investment. Was she being followed? Did they do counter-surveillance? Riordan wouldn't hit town until the evening, but did they have other people? She'd done all the checks – doorways, shops, bus and tram timetables near the Pankrác prison – and would have sworn that neither she nor the agent was being watched.

It would be a feather in her cap when she went back to Thames House and the mission was put to bed.

Matthew Bentinick stood up, put a tip on the table and covered it with a saucer against the wind. He walked to the kerb. 'Come on.'

Danny followed him.

He waved down a taxi. Danny watched. The driver was given a destination and his face warmed. Then Bentinick asked how to get there by metro and bus. The driver gave a clipped answer and sped away.

'Before you ask, it's to complete your education, more history. Have we time to go by bus and train? Today, yes. Not tomorrow.'

Bentinick led.

8

'This is it.'

'The French have one of their own, Mr Bentinick, another village that was destroyed. Is it going to be important?'

'If not, I wouldn't have brought you here, Danny.'

The sunshine warmed them. The light fell on a sloping green expanse broken by a few trees, some ornamental shrubs and distant statues. High above, a buzzard wheeled and called. There were small groups of tourists, mourners or the curious. A few held guidebooks and most had cameras. The grass was mown as it would have been on the fairway of any above-average golf course. Danny Curnow knew of similar places close to his home in Caen. Other than the buzzard's call, the only sounds were from Vaclav Havel airport, the thrust of engines as aircraft powered up. Behind them were a café, a museum and the toilets. They stood on the grass, and Danny understood that Matthew Bentinick would not be hurried. It was where a troubled man might come, sit on the grass or on a bench, be with ghosts and find calm. There was a man-made lake to the right that would have been a reservoir for the village, which had been gone for seventy-two years. There would have been carp in it for Christmas dinners. Danny had known army people who couldn't see a stretch of water around any of the Irish towns where they worked without imagining what bait would best attract a leviathan. He had never fished. A river ran through Tavistock, had torrents and dark pools – it was said there were salmon in it. Here, a pretty lake, with swans and ducks, was flanked with reeds. An overflow stream cut across the grass at the lowest point. It would have divided the centre of the village. He tried to imagine how life would have been there on 27 May

1942 when the attack had been made on Heydrich. A traditional village in good agricultural country, transport would have been by cart and bicycle. The focus of local life would have been the church, with the school close behind; the community would have consisted of labourers, small farmers and one principal family.

There were places in France that were no different. They straggled along the north coast and had been the location of extreme gallantry and barbarity. He had chosen to live among those sites, and the people who wanted to share the history. The fumes from Bentinick's pipe wafted to him.

In front of him, down the slope and up the far bank, some of the visitors had brought small children. Two little girls wore floral dresses and their hair in ponytails. Danny wondered if they had a blood link to Lidice, or whether they were just filling an hour before resuming a journey to the airport.

'How was it?'

'On which day?'

'How was it, Mr Bentinick, on the day the sky fell on them?'

He took his time, seeming to savour the moment. His fingers were on the pipe, where the stem joined the bowl. Danny thought that everything Bentinick did was a choreographed performance. A foot was raised, a leg bent, the pipe was rapped against the heel of the shoe, ash spilling from it. The fingers worked in a tobacco pouch, then pressed the threads into the bowl. A match was lit and smoke was carried away on the wind.

'Am I boring you, Danny?'

'No.'

'The church was dedicated to St Martin, founded in 1352. The shell survived from the Middle Ages. There was a village hall and a mayor. The main farmer was called Horak. His family owned land, large buildings and a house. The priest would have wielded the greatest influence on that community, Father Josef Stemberka. Lidice was home to five hundred villagers. For many hours after the event they would not have known of the grenade thrown at Heydrich's car, perhaps not until the end of the day when people came home from the fields, or collected the children from the school, and the radio might have been switched on. Why should they have feared for their lives? They had cause, but it was tenuous.'

'Go on.'

'A farmer's son had fled years earlier to England. He enlisted in the RAF. It was known he flew with the enemy, and payback time had arrived. They had not, at that time, found the men hiding in Prague. The village was surrounded by troops and sealed off. They took a list of the inhabitants from the mayor's house. That night the men were separated from the women and children and taken to the church of St Martin. They would sleep there. Come on, Danny. She can do without us at the moment. We'll be in place when we need to be.'

They went down the hill towards the Horak farm, and the statue of grieving innocents, and to where the foundations of the church were.

He was behind the young woman. To Karol Pilar, her tradecraft was poor.

If she had been on any squad of detectives he had been training to the standards required for the surveillance of organised-crime gangs, he would have failed her. She was insufficiently aware of what was behind and around her, concentrating merely on staying in touch with her target. He would have sent her back to her unit. He smiled as he remembered the cake his wife had made that day for her mother's birthday.

The four police officers – a sergeant and three constables – had been briefed by their lieutenant on what was expected of them. They had been into the canteen for sausage, bread and cheese, and had drunk some bitter coffee. That southern corner of Poland was dank and wet but the radio said the sun was shining below Jelenia Gora and across the frontier. It was September when autumn rushed in so they were well wrapped up because they would be out of their heated cars. Wrocław was their base, and their barracks was in Podwale, on a fine, tree-lined avenue, but the fresh wind was stripping off the leaves. They took two cars and drove out of the yard into traffic. When they reached the main road they would set up the block. They had drawn weapons from the armoury: it was usual in such circumstances, and with the intelligence provided from Warsaw, to have handguns, light automatic machine pistols, CS gas and a 'stinger' of chain and spikes to be thrown across the road if a vehicle attempted to break through the checks. They would put on the bulletproof vests, now standard issue for such work, when they reached the designated point. They were experienced men, all with long years in the police, and possessed the wry gallows humour typical of their profession. Some days were interesting and others were dull. Some stood out and others were instantly forgettable. None had any idea how that afternoon would shape. They smoked, and in each car there was grumbling about the failure of government to raise the rates for overtime pay. Then more important matters rose to the surface: the coming weekend's home game against Lublin, and whether Śląsk Wrocław, going well at the start of the season in the Ekstraklasa, their top-ranked league, would win or drop points; there was doubt about the fitness of the principal striker. They took the road from the city towards Jelenia Gora, and were aware that they were part of a major operation in which ultimate control rested with the national police headquarters. Each man trusted his colleagues, and would depend on them if the business became difficult.

Ralph Exton gazed around him and saw her. *What's a pretty girl like you doing . . . ?*

It wasn't unusual for him to spend time checking faces and locations, the clothes he'd been told they'd wear, the paper they'd be carrying. A terraced garden separated the hotel and its forecourt from a suburban road

Is that the best you can do?

It was good to watch and bad to hurry. She was in profile to him, strong features and naturally gold hair. She sat upright and didn't look behind her. The clothes were good. He remembered that in Armagh, city and countryside, the women had looked worn-down and their clothes had been cheap. A stereotypical memory, but it was there. She wore the black business suit he had been told to look out for, a white blouse and a small green scarf knotted at her throat. No other decoration. Where she sat she would have had a good view down the slope to the curve of the river and upstream towards the castle. She smoked. The cigarette betrayed her nerves: as he'd noted at the airport, she took little snatches at it and blew the smoke straight out of her mouth.

Small mercies – as he'd noted at the airport, she was easy on the eye and wasn't one of the thugs who enjoyed switching on power drills.

They'd not told him her name. He went down the steps and through the upper part of the garden.

She dragged on the cigarette again, stubbed it out on the side of the bench, then flicked it, accurately, towards a rubbish bin. It had been laid down that they would meet at the airport, but if not the airport, then mid-afternoon, the following day, in the garden.

Ralph Exton's loyalties were governed by the need to keep lit fags off his skin, a drill bit out of his knees and eyes, and avoid being adjacent to a cell door swinging shut. The majority of his loyalty was to himself. He came behind her.

'Morning. Nice place. I'm Ralph. Good view.'

She spun round. 'Where were you?'

He had his hand out. 'I wasn't given a name.'

'Frankie. Where were you?'

He said that at the airport concourse she'd stood out and he hadn't been happy with the place. 'Can't be too careful.' A little shrug.

She stood up, came to the side of the bench and took his hand. Hers was hard, cold and bony. There were thicker shrubs up a little path and a hut where the gardeners would have kept tools. Out of sight. She stopped and faced him. Her face was no longer pretty but lined and hard. There was a snap in her voice. He was to hold out his arms.

Ralph Exton did so.

She frisked him. Armpits, waist and belt area, inside the trouser leg, down to his ankles. Then she unbuttoned his shirt. Fingers against his skin. He asked her if she was forgetting the belt but she didn't reply. She stepped back, brushed her hands, and left him to do up his shirt.

'Now you,' he said.

'What do you mean?'

'Your turn – Frankie.'

A blush, almost crimson. Her arms went out. He took his time and did it just as Miss Gabrielle would have done it. Nothing left to chance, each orifice checked. He felt her wince.

'You finished?'

He stepped back. 'Yes. Can never be too careful, as we agreed. Five makes very sensitive kit these days, so I'm told. I imagine it's your first time on the road.'

'What's that mean?'

'If you'd been around longer you'd know what I've done for your people and the risks I've taken.'

'I was told precious little about you.'

He said, 'And when the big man comes in tonight, will you strip him down to his boxers? You can never be too careful.'

He laughed quietly. She did not respond. He thought her humourless. Hugo Woolmer had once said, 'The women are the worst, Ralph, because they have no fun in them. Just deadly serious. The Bundesgrenzschutz, in their manual, suggest it's always best to slot the women first. Usually have big doses of ideology.' She was quiet and the hardness had gone. Ralph read people well. She was *first time*, prey to nerves – but fetchingly good-looking and the touch search had been a bonus. They went to have coffee.

They sat in a café, a far corner. She spoke of the big man who was coming to the city that evening. He went over with her what had been on the list of items they'd purchase, and the cost. She talked him through the detail of the bank arrangements. Together, they bickered over when payment should be made, the timing of a credit transfer: she tried to fight her corner – cash after the test firings – and he shrugged. The impression he gave was that she could take the responsibility for screwing the deal if she wished to. He thought her clever, probably a graduate, and on the team because they were short of quality. She'd have been what Miss Gabrielle would call a 'clean skin'. He doubted he would get another chance to run his fingers over her and satisfy himself that she wasn't wearing a wire. She was distant when they parted. He wondered what had triggered her enlistment. She talked with reverence of the big man who was coming in that evening.

Ralph had said, straight face, 'A useful man to have around the house, handy with a drill.'

He told her it was a fine city and she might get in some sight-seeing, or do a guided tour. He said, too, that he'd be making final arrangements the next evening, would meet the supplier. He asked her if she would be queuing up for a turn at the test-firing, the rocket-propelled grenade launcher, the machine-gun, or the rifle with the big telescope screwed to the top of the barrel, but added it would be painful if her shoulder was bruised by their recoil. He said how the next contact would be made. He called the tunes, not her. His schedules . . . Maybe she knew already that he had no respect for her.

What should she do, hours to kill until the next stage?

Ralph Exton said airily, 'As I suggested, see the sights, take in a concert, tramp round a gallery or entertain the big man when he turns up.'

He left the table and walked out into the warm afternoon air.

Miss Gabrielle was sitting on a concrete wall, reading a woman's magazine. Not much in the fashion pages had rubbed off on her. Unlike Frankie, she was a mess. She'd looked better with only the towel round her. Shit, he felt old. The stress was catching up with him.

How much should he tell his handler? That was the big problem. How much should he keep from her, and at what cost? How much should she know about Timofey Simonov, his old pal and mucker?

What the hell had they been up to? She had no idea. They had met at the bench, then gone walkabout into the bushes. When they'd reappeared he'd been grinning and her face was red. Then they'd gone into a coffee shop, and everything had returned to normal.

The girl had followed Exton out. Gaby Davies had no trace on her: no photograph and no file copy. She wasn't confident. A fine chain hung round her throat, with a tiny crucifix: visible now, hidden before. She'd taken a loop from the chain into her mouth, as if it was something to hold on to because the going had been rough. A new kid on the block. As Gaby had been. The only kid from her school ever to win a place at a half-decent university, the only young woman with a provincial accent to leap the hurdles at Thames House. She'd climbed over Hugo Woolmer and gone up another rung . . . But there were confusions.

Danny Curnow was one, and the boss, Matthew Bentinick, was another. She didn't know where they were in the city or what they were doing.

They weren't team players, and had been dismissive of what she had achieved over the last five years in milking information from Ralph Exton, and building a relationship she reckoned to be rock steady and profitable. Bentinick should have been put out to grass years ago. Danny Curnow should never have been brought back and put on the payroll. She felt alone. She knew that Exton had seen her. A tiny flutter of an eyebrow, recognition. They'd meet that evening: she'd have more than a bloody towel on her back, and they might get a chuckle out of her "showing out".

He was gone.

She watched the girl, who seemed lost in thought and insecure.

Bentinick was a bigger confusion than Danny Curnow, a cold little man, harbouring attitudes from the Dark Ages. A miserable, desiccated creature. Had he ever been seen to laugh? Not that she'd heard. How would Bentinick be in his suburban street? How would a wife put up with him? How would anyone touch any sensitivity in him?

The girl left the café and Gaby tracked her. It was hard to understand why the two men had ditched her and disappeared. She didn't know what they were doing, or why.

* * *

Danny Curnow, walking slowly, learned of the destruction of Lidice.

After a night locked in the church, the men had been taken to the garden at the Horak farm. The executions started. At first five at a time, then ten were called forward to face the firing squads. Apparently all had refused to be blindfolded, facing the rifle barrels and the men behind them. Those killed at Lidice numbered 173. Another nineteen died at the firing range in Prague. The priest was among the last.

Bentinick said, 'There were men in London who decided to launch the attack, called for volunteers, trained them and parachuted them in. They knew that reprisals would follow. They bore the burden of it. A different scale and a different time, but I took the weight of it and so did you. Different scale, same story. We did the God bit because someone had to.'

The children were taken to a concentration camp at Chełmno where most were gassed: seventeen lived and seventy-one died. The village buildings – homes, church, hall, farms – were destroyed by explosives, the ruins burned with motor fuel.

'The attack on Heydrich brought respect to the people. They would have talked about the 'greatest good for the greatest number'. That was what you and I did, Danny. You did it well so I called you back.'

They were at a group statue. It stunned Danny Curnow in its complexity. Life-sized children with universal expressions of numbed resignation, dignified, and showing no fear. He thought it the most moving memorial he had ever seen. It was humbling. He no longer heard the buzzard's cry, or the song of any other bird.

'The women went to Ravensbrück, north of Berlin, as forced labour. Most survived but twenty-one died there. The village is merely a memory. Could you have taken responsibility for training the paratroopers, equipping and despatching them? Could you have persuaded yourself that a bigger picture needed to be painted? . . . Shall we have some coffee?'

The sun was bright on his face, the grass was a brilliant green and the falling leaves were golden. He felt no warmth and the beauty was lost on him. 'Why did you bring me?'

'Time to kill, Danny, don't you know? Time to lose.'

As Dusty Miller had seen it, if Desperate had hit him back, one of them would have ended up in A&E, then been on the way to an intensive-care unit, or worse. It was after they had lost Gerry Prentiss, taxi driver, in Coalisland. He did nights mainly, and his cards were all round the bars in the town where the Provos and their supporters drank. They needed cabs to get them, pissed, home. FRU needed to know who they travelled with, gave lifts to, and where they were dropped off. Low-level stuff. A passenger had been arrested, a coup, then passed on to the crime suite for interrogation and charging, a triumph. A big fish was caught in a small net. The big fish was a marksman and spent most of his nights in Monaghan town across the border. He'd been talking in the bar with an asset, an agent who also led an active-service unit. They were not idiots: those who had known where the marksman would sleep were the taxi driver and the ASU leader. The ASU leader was handled by Vagabond call-sign: he belonged to Desperate and Dusty. The taxi driver had lived with his mother, who was crippled with arthritis and housebound. She was isolated but for her son. The fifty pounds a week he brought home from his handler, Vivian, paid for some of the minimal comforts the woman enjoyed. He'd been found that morning. The usual scene: no shoes or socks, money stuffed into his mouth, a hole in the back of his head, burns and bruises. No argument: an ASU leader would always carry the day, not a taxi driver of occasional use.

Captain Bentinick wasn't in evidence – might have been at Brigade. Support gathered around Vivian and plied him with drinks. Late that evening, Desperate and Dusty had come back from a meeting and were ending a shift. Alcohol and anguish were the ingredients in the cocktail.

A volley slurred at Desperate. He thought himself the big man. The big man did not have to worry about regulations and small print, rode roughshod over them. The big fucking man who always had an excuse for letting a Joe go to the wall – actually, to the mortuary. The big fucking man who didn't give a toss about the consequences of choosing who lived and who went to the knacker. An old woman, disabled, helpless, had no son to care for her, and it was not as though the taxi driver had volunteered for the fifty pounds a week. It was a well-worn trick: the police would pull over a delivery driver, an ambulance driver, a taxi driver and he'd breathe into the kit. They'd shake their heads, look concerned and cart him down to the station. There'd be an FRU man – or girl – there, so kind-hearted, only wanting to help, dishing out sympathy and tearing up the 'evidence' on the machine's printout, then seeing him back into his vehicle with a deal done. The taxi driver might have been over the limit and might not, but had been recruited. So had an estate agent, with three kids and—

Maybe Desperate's silence in the face of the taunts and gibes, the insults, had boosted Vivian's righteous anger.

Dusty had been a pace behind him. Desperate had stood his ground but his hands were behind his back and he'd looked straight into Vivian's eyes. Dusty knew the mask of indifference was a sham. Vivian, a fellow sergeant, had thrown a punch.

Desperate had ridden it, but the fourth or fifth had caught him in the face and split his lip. If Desperate had hit him back, they would have half killed each other. The hands had stayed clasped behind the back.

The captain had come into the mess. He'd have heard about a 'nutting' in a lane and would have expected it because the deal on priorities had been effected in his office.

Captain Bentinick had said, voice never rising, 'Probably enough, lads. If your jobs were easy I'd not be looking for special men. I could pick any riff-raff bayonet-pusher out of an infantry crowd. It's not easy, and I admire and respect you. Don't carry it through to the morning.'

It was never mentioned again and the lip had healed, but not the wound to Desperate's soul. Dusty had been witness to the damage done, which had built on what had gone before. The sea crashed on the shingle and the surf surged. It was where Desperate would have been at this time, on this day, of the week.

The beach, Plage de Puys, was to the north of the harbour and town of Dieppe. The bus would drop the visitors on a concrete esplanade beside a considerably ugly restaurant, closed because the season was over. A slipway for small open fishing boats and pleasure craft divided the wide expanse of loose shingle. That was where the tourists gathered and their guide addressed them. The village was situated along a winding road that dropped down fast towards the sea, and the valley walls were littered with weekend cottages for an affluent élite. Either side of the beach there were sheer cliffs, white and similar to those of the Kentish coast. Many of the householders had adapted defensive gun emplacements of reinforced concrete into patios or sheds: too well built to be dismantled. The guide would deal with the facts.

Six hundred troops of the Royal Regiment of Canada had come ashore. When the evacuation was ordered, the raid an abject failure, only 240 had made it back to the ships waiting for them; the rest had been killed, wounded or captured. The defenders seemed to have known what was coming and when. The tide had been low when the fifty tanks accompanying the ground force had waddled ashore but on wet sand they'd had almost no traction. Those who reached the shingle found it scattered under the tracks and marooned then, stationary and helpless. The guide would say that the sole value of the Dieppe raid was that the planners for the great invasion two years later had been shown the dangers of a contested landing from the sea. No laughter among the visitors, no jokes. A sad, grey place.

Many heads were shaken in respect of the tragedy.

Mountain troops, scrambling up ropes to reach the batteries, had made heroic efforts to silence the guns on the clifftops but they had lost their explosives in the ascent.

The driver would usually stand to the side here and not contribute unless invited to by the guide. His eyes were often on the pebbles and he always looked for those that were bright red under the retreating surf. A good one would go into his pocket: all men who'd worn a waist holster had kept smooth pebbles in the pocket of the jacket that hid the holster.

It was a dour little place that lowered the spirits. Everyone was glad to leave it.

The man who drove Malachy Riordan was silent. A message had been passed to him that conversation was unwelcome.

Malachy had no experience of a mission of this sort. He did not know the full range of intelligence gathering that would have been at the beck and call of his enemies. He understood what they could do on the mountain, and on the roads and lanes from Dungannon to Cookstown, Magherafelt and across to Omagh, and Brennie Murphy had taught him the procedures for meetings. Many times he had stood in the middle of wet, wind-lashed fields with others' ears pressed to his lips. At times, indoors, he had written everything in a notebook then pushed it towards the other men, seen their replies, then thrown the notebook into the fire. He practised best procedure with phones, and sent messages written with a fine nib on cigarette paper. What they could achieve at airports, how much they could get from overhead cameras in a concourse, was beyond his knowledge. Had it been necessary to fly to Nürnberg, not Prague, then to have made the long diversion through Germany and into Poland when a direct road linked the German city to the Czech capital?

His legs were cramped, his knees constricted, his joints locked. His stomach growled. His view was of drab countryside and a high mountain range on a far-away horizon.

His concentration had been dulled by a radio station playing country-and-western. Sentimental shit – as was the stuff put out by most of the groups in the back bars of the drinking places tourists might come to in the countryside of Tyrone, Fermanagh and Armagh. The quiet ate into him. He couldn't offer to drive but the other man's weariness showed. It had been worse during the night because of the fog and the headlights of the lorries coming at them.

He saw a church and, in a reflex action, crossed his chest, then a roadhouse and a mini-market, a *pension*, a sodden garden centre, and bare fields from which the harvest had been taken. A pair of distant deer was grazing on the leftover grain. Then, at a clump of trees, the road seemed to veer right.

A police car, and a queue of vehicles – lorries, saloons, vans.

They were past the police car and an officer stood beside it, big in a vest with a machine-gun slung at his neck, and his hands on its body. Malachy thought it one of the many variations on the Heckler & Koch. He could have recited rates of fire if it were on automatic or on single aimed shots. They slowed. His driver chewed gum. Malachy felt sweat on his neck and his gut tightened. The driver had the heater on and wore no pullover or jacket. His jeans were held up with a narrow belt of imitation leather; he did not wear a firearm. They crawled. Half of the road was blocked with a police vehicle parked at an angle. A uniformed officer was checking the papers of some drivers and waving others through; commercial vehicles were not stopped. An easy pattern to recognise. Saloon cars were inspected. One had its boot open. Another officer stood back and covered his colleague. Further ahead, a hundred metres beyond the block, another officer was on guard, his weapon ready in his hands. There were ditches at either side of the road, and, anyway, there had been heavy rain on the fields. His breathing was faster. The driver looked at him, curious, then shrugged. In low gear, they edged forward.

Malachy Riordan had often wondered how it would be.

Not at home, not when the dawn knock came – always civil then. Polite to Bridie, careful with his boy and correct with himself. He didn't think the men from the crime squad, who came to the farmhouse and took him away every few months for interrogation, would have said they *hated* him. The uniforms, yes. The men at checkpoints who would never achieve promotion, who'd have reckoned he looked at them as a hangman would – they would have *loathed* him. Three cars in front, one lorry, then the block. He wondered how it would be if they took him out and tried to put the cuffs on him. Would he struggle or try to break and run, chancing their aim? How would it be in the cells of a Polish police station, with the Five people coming to see him and laughing in his face? A boy from Dundalk had been taken down in Lithuania and was looking at cell walls now. He'd rot. Malachy would be no martyr, as his father had been – as the men named on the monument at Cappagh had been. He'd be forgotten and rotting. His breath came faster, and his legs felt leaden. If he ran they would shoot him. The turn of the lorry now, waved on through. The car ahead was driven by a woman and Malachy Riordan could see her blonde hair. She was waved on. The police officer gestured for them to stop. Malachy saw that the finger of the one who was covering the colleague was against the trigger guard. An impassive face. Bored? Perhaps. He wouldn't be bored if Malachy flung the door open and started to leg it. A ditch, and water in it from the rain. And a field with no cover.

Who would have touted on him? So few had known the timetable of the journey.

'The car – is it clean?'

'What you mean?'

'Is there a shooter in the glove?'

He was reaching forward, hand wavering.

His hand was knocked aside. 'Course there fucking isn't – what's your problem?'

He saw the gun, the magazine slotted into it, the finger on the trigger guard. Sweat ran. His father would have had a weapon in his hand, and his grandfather. No one in his family had gone quietly, like a bullock at the abattoir on Crew Road in Dungannon. The window was down and the driver was offering his ID, his licence and was asking a question. The glance at the paperwork was momentary, and the bulk of the man filled the window. An answer, short, a wave for them to go forward. The window went up.

The car pulled away.

Past the last police officer, he saw the stinger on the grass between the ditch and the road. Up through the gears, and an open road ahead. The driver turned, grinning. 'Fuck me, you were scared.'

He sat silent.

'I thought you were a big man, a fighter. Fucking scared.' He laughed.

He couldn't hit him – he wanted to, but he couldn't. They were accelerating. The driver might have realised he had stepped over a line. Silence fell again. Malachy Riordan was, already, beyond the reach of what and who he knew.

The boys came down the hill, were off the high ground. The device was inside the curve of a spare tyre, which was in the boot of the small car. They had driven up to the Riordan farm, had gone to the barn where the tyre and the device were, and had loaded it. They had come out and it would have seemed to anyone – police, military, Five – that they were there to collect an old tyre. The child had been at a window, staring out at them: a lifeless little bastard. Warnings rang in their ears.

They drove down a lane. The rain was heavier. The water flowed in rivers down the tarmac, and was funnelled into two courses because the centre of the lane had gone to grass.

Because of the rain and the low cloud, which was already heavy over Shane Bearnagh's Seat behind them, dusk had settled. A fox crossed in front of them and the lights caught the colour of its coat. It seemed not to care about the intrusion they made on its territory. There was a lone bungalow off to the right, with peat smoke billowing from a chimney: the home of a man who had done eight years in the cage but now supported the Shinners. He took the Sinn Féin money for driving hospital visits, and he had done time on an active-service unit with Malachy's father. They barely saw the fox and neither commented on the home to the right. Their eyes were on the road.

They were looking for holes.

In a lane such as this, remote and barely used, there was little call for council work teams to fill ruptures in the surface. They had deepened after last winter's snowfall, and repairs had not been made in the spring or the summer. When there was rain the holes filled with water. Pearse drove and Kevin scanned the surface for him. It was not possible that either could judge the depth of a filled hole. They had been told that the chemical in the detonators was dangerous, unstable, and should be handled with extreme care. Kevin had said that it was what they used to propel the airbags in cars. Big deal. Who needed to know? What they did need to know was that a slide at any speed into a pothole was more than sufficient to explode the device. It was being ferried down the hill towards the home of Eamonn O'Kane, policeman, and was intended to take his life.

In each boy there was a rise in tension. They talked little, but the headlights glimmered in the water ahead and they searched for the small lagoons. The can that was loaded with the explosive charge, the copper disc and the detonator rested on an old cushion and was wrapped in towels. They went at barely fifteen miles per hour and searched with increasing anxiety for the gleam of water covering a hole. Nothing to say. The firing of the main charge was well in excess of what was required to demolish their car, and probably enough to spread their body parts up the hedges on either side.

Before the silence had enveloped them, Pearse had told Kevin the story of a girl, Doloures, whom they had been to school with and whose father drove a post-office van. Doloures had told Pearse about a disco at the community centre by the church in Donaghmore. Would he come with her? The date was given. It was a Friday evening: they worked with Brennie Murphy on a Friday evening. They did tactics and history, and the legends of the Organisation and the ideology stuff. She'd said Friday. He'd said he couldn't make it. They needed to do tactics because in the field they might come face to face with the C4 Special Operations Branch, who had firepower and special-forces training. Pearse wouldn't learn how to fight at a Friday-night disco. Maybe she had been set up to invite him, perhaps by a teacher or the priest – because she might test his faith. He'd repeated that he couldn't make it. She'd said, as if she knew, 'Get a life, why don't you? Because you're with the old guy, Murphy. Because you hang around the Riordan man. It's over, what they do – or didn't anyone tell you?' She was a great-looking girl, and he thought she'd have gone the whole way. He'd told Kevin and his friend had punched his arm. They were solid, joined at the hip.

They went down the hill, further but slower. The dusk closed around them, but there were lights ahead, to the left. Kevin reached across in the dark to put his hand over Pearse's. The target area was in front, and the track that led to the home of the policeman's parents.

'We got there.'

'We fuckin' did – and no holes. I was near shitting myself.'

A florist came with two bouquets, ordered from them by phone for delivery before a party started.

The caterer's vans arrived with tables, chairs and food. A Transit followed them and a pair of lads unloaded the speakers for the DJ session. An electrician was trailing cables through the cherry trees beside the driveway from which the celebratory lights would hang. A boy from an adjacent farm had brought some long stretches of canvas – they had once covered a silage pit – to spread in the field as a foundation for an overspill car park.

A neighbour, as he had promised because he was a worrier, had circled the property in the last hour of daylight. He had served in the Ulster Defence Regiment twenty-two years before and reckoned he knew a security risk when he saw one. He had done the perimeter of their land and pronounced it clean. He hadn't seen the trace of a buried cable, or the innards of a maroon flare, or a black mass secreted in a hedge, or two young men lying on their stomachs in a copse. They had a good view of the road approaching the track and had been told what make of car to look for.

The sun was dipping. The birds had gone and shadows were flung wide on the grass. In the distance Danny Curnow could see the bright colours of a wreath. Bentinick had said that a German politician had been there the week before and laid it. A small group remained beside the children's artwork.

Abruptly Bentinick slapped Danny's shoulder. 'It's you because you're an agent handler. They're liars, deceivers. They have no creed but "self". At the crisis stage, this will depend on you holding the agent in place, a bloody rod up his spine. Not in our time, Desperate, but the name of the game now is *evidence*. Photographs that prove association, complicity, then conviction in a court of law. The route to that process is through the agent. The going will get hard, dirty, and dangerous. Are you up for it?'

'Yes.'

'Whatever it throws at you?'

'Yes.' It didn't matter to him whether he believed the effort worthwhile and the risk justified. He was pleased to be asked. 'And, Mr Bentinick?'

'Yes.'

'What I did, used to do, I'm not apologising for it.'

'Why would you? For bringing you in, Danny, I'm out on a limb.'

Danny Curnow smiled ruefully. 'You always were, Mr Bentinick, when the target seemed worthwhile.'

Many walking alongside the river that divided Yekaterinburg, fourth biggest city in Russia, administrative centre of the Sverdlovsk *oblast*, would have seen it.

There were policemen nearby and families with small children who threw bread to the ducks. Some posed loved ones against the the rails where boys put padlocks, then threw away the keys as an expression of eternal devotion, and there were shoppers.

A van pulled up in the centre of a new bridge. A policeman could have waved it on because stopping the flow of traffic was illegal, but his back was to it. Another officer saw two men get out and go to the back but did not reach for his personal radio or make any attempt to contact his headquarters. A man, bound and gagged but not blindfolded, near naked but for his underpants, was dragged out. He was heavy and difficult to manoeuvre because of the concrete that encased his legs below the knees. He was heaved up. For a moment he seemed suspended, feet over the rail, backside on it. Then he toppled. There was a splash, and he was gone. The river in the centre was deep and the current strong. Those who had seen it would have disbelieved what they *thought* they had seen.

It would be reported and talked about. A young man had climbed too fast and given offence. That would be remembered.

The head came round the door of Jocelyn's office. 'Heard from our man?'

'Hello, George – only at sparrow fart this morning. Right now he'll be out on his rounds.'

The eyes sparkled and the mouth had a trace of mischief. Few in the building – no one else of Jocelyn's rank – knew the director general by name. She could have analysed the long-standing friendship between him and the withdrawn, distant Matthew Bentinick. To George, Bentinick was 'our man'. She knew that George came by often and would hear in her room, if the door was open, the light tap at Bentinick's window. The men were opposites but respected each other. She fancied that the director general envied the loose reins on Bentinick's activities, and sanctioned them. She'd heard others on the corridor and on different floors refer to the closeness of the relationship as 'inappropriate'. Now he came in and eased the door shut.

She grimaced. 'I can only offer you water.'

He shook his head. 'You understand the motivation?'

'Once we had names in the frame, places and dates, the focus was sharp.'

'As expected. It won't be about some personal vengeance – legitimate targets and legitimate motives.'

'A good target, George, and worth the effort.'

'He said something to me about nailing the miscreant to the floorboards. Big nails.'

'He won't do it, of course. Flies out of there tomorrow and it'll come to climax a couple of days later – unless we hit a head wind.'

'The man he took . . . ?'

The mischief had left the mouth and the light the eyes. Jocelyn found it hard to imagine her director general with a killer streak.

'Matthew knows what to do with him. He's taken him out for the day. They're doing the rounds of age-old atrocities. I think Matthew was concerned that in the years since he went adrift then—'

She was interrupted, quietly but firmly: 'What's his name?'

'We called him Vagabond.'

'I remember.' Fingers together, joints flexed. 'Matthew spoke well of him.'

'He was damaged by the old work – enough were, but he was the best. And Matthew needed the best this time.'

'He's got a nice girl out there, promising, but probably squeamish with a thumbscrew. Matthew said her Joe was stringing her along, but Vagabond wouldn't allow it.'

'Vagabond's being toughened up today before things start tomorrow and catch fire. Matthew's confident he'll do the business.'

'Thank you, Jocelyn. Always good to be in the picture.'

'Any time, George.'

The door closed, and she again opened her screen.

They waited at the bus stop across the road from the entrance.

Nothing much had changed. He was even wearing the same shirt and socks as he had at Gough – and registering the same sensations. He recognised them.

It was always slow at the start. They used to say, 'Prior Planning and Preparation Prevent Piss Poor Performance.' The seven Ps were part of the creed. In place in good time. A look at the ground and a tweak to the motivation. He didn't complain. The pace would quicken. It always started slow and the trick was to squash down impatience. When the climax came it would be at the pace of a scudding storm. It always was. He thought he was ready.

They were two of a kind, who did not do small-talk, not even about the weather. They stood, at first in silence, neither looking at his watch to see if the bus would be along soon or was running late. Bentinick's pipe smoke smelt good. Bentinick would never have fiddled his expenses, but that might be where honesty ended. As minutes went by, they began to talk. Suggestions and refinements, how it might happen at the end, if the cards stacked well. A query from Danny, and a nod from Bentinick. Much was uncertain, but a plan had been hatched before the bus came.

9

It had been Matthew Bentinick's idea.

They had gone past the cobbled space with the sculpture of the half-buried cross. Karol Pilar, who had shown it to Danny, had not remarked on it this time. Danny had followed Bentinick up the steps, into the muscum, a relic of empire and grandeur, for a concert.

He seldom listened to music on the radio and never at the house in Caen, though it would be switched on in the kitchen. He had the car radio tuned to pick up traffic warnings when he was alone. He could not have said what music he liked and disliked. Bentinick had the tickets and the programme.

The seats were in the front row. There was a pianist; a solo violin – the star; two more violins, a viola and a cello. Danny knew the names of the instruments because Bentinick told him. The programme said they would hear works by Bach, Vivaldi, Mozart, Bizet and Brahms; the concert would last sixty-five minutes, about Danny's tolerance limit.

The double bleep for Bentinick's phone sounded twice.

Savage glances were ignored. The artists never spoke. Not that he'd have understood them if they had.

Bentinick said, 'Music is good for the soul. It reduces stress.'

He listened.

Bentinick said. 'You'll enjoy it when we get to the Bach. It's the Gavotte BVW 1068, an old favourite of mine. Weren't you accused at Gough of dancing on graves, Desperate? What about doing a gavotte on a grave, putting some welly into it?'

He thought Bentinick was moulding him, as he would a piece of wet clay. There were the leaders and there were the followers;

the roles seldom crossed. They had once, and he doubted the 'dance' insult was yet forgotten, ever would be.

'He's good on the violin. For God's sake, Danny, you're supposed to be enjoying yourself – and we go to the countryside tomorrow.'

His buttocks ached and his stomach was cramping. He sat and suffered.

'You know how it'll be – one moment quiet, tranquil, and the next all hell breaks loose. When it happens, Danny, I don't want you mucking about in your head – *What do I do now?* Go for the jugular. Get him down and disabled and have your boot across his throat. I told my lord and master we'd nail him to the floor, but that's afterwards. Lovely, isn't it? Restful.'

He had led once – when it mattered. Him in the front and Dusty Miller behind. They had gone out of Gough and up the road to Belfast. They had quit and he had led. He'd heard Bentinick's voice, only time it was ever raised, bellowing into the night for him to come back. Bentinick would have gone inside and told the boys in the bar, and Julie who did the paperwork, that Desperate would be back soon enough. Certainly by the time the bar closed. As Danny Curnow imagined it, the steward would have been kept in the Portakabin half the night. Two empty beds at dawn, and an agent rendezvous that would not be met that day by the man's handler. Desperate had led.

'Nearly there, Danny. We might get a bite to eat after this. You'll be all right tomorrow when the pace speeds up. My favourite, Danny, is next. It's from Vivaldi's Four Seasons, written in 1723. We're getting Concerto Number Two in G Minor, Opus Eight. It's *Allegro non molto* and you'll enjoy it. Remember what I said. Your boot on the jugular, and later I'll do the nailing to the floor.'

A woman clucked angrily behind Bentinick. A man leaned forward and rapped Bentinick's shoulder. Both were ignored.

'About taking responsibility, don't expect to be universally thanked. Many said that the Czech officer in exile who set up the killing of Heydrich had the blood of thousands on his hands – those killed in reprisals. But you never looked for thanks, Desperate, did you?'

He knew that, two or three months later, Dusty had called the steward who ran the bar. The man was a better filing system and intelligence collator than Julia who looked after the card indexes. The steward had told Dusty that the life had gone out of Gough, and the success had stalled. They'd lost people who mattered, and Captain Bentinick was moving on because his FRU command was a 'busted flush'.

The musicians completed their programme and were applauded. Men and women scowled at Bentinick, and were rewarded with his smile. Danny understood the purpose of the day's exercise: he had been withdrawn from normality and put on a pedestal next to the one Bentinick occupied so that he could look down on them and feel nothing. Danny Curnow had no father, brother, best friend, or lover, and knew he would follow this man into Hell. Bentinick said he was hungry, and smiled congratulations to the artists.

'That's what I want to know.'

'Is "please" not in your vocabulary?'

'I use it where appropriate.'

'And I'm not appropriate?'

Gaby Davies had not been invited to eat. Matthew Bentinick had a bowl of goulash in front of him and a plate beside it with bread and dumplings. He was drinking a glass of a local wine. Her anger was directed at the 'blow-in', Danny Curnow, who had once been Vagabond. He spoke evenly, which inflamed her fury.

'I don't say "please" when you should be making up for failure.'

'What failure?'

He shrugged, seemed to tell her it was obvious. Her room and Ralph Exton's were in a hotel on Stepanska. Cosy: handler and agent on the same corridor. She had no ally. The Czech policeman was by the door, nursing a Coke out of earshot. Matthew Bentinick wasn't standing in her corner either. The food in front of Danny Curnow remained untouched.

Her failure irked: she had been unable to answer the questions put to her.

How much contact did Ralph Exton have with Timofey Simonov? When would they meet? Where? What weapons were required? How many would be test-fired by Malachy Riordan? Would a full exchange take place? When had the relationship started? What drove it? She had no answers.

She said, to Bentinick, 'Do I have to repeat what I said? I'm coaxing. It's a friendship, goes back for ever. All I know is that the Russian was on the floor and our Joe gave him a first step up – it happened before the cigarettes, and before the Irish showed up. They go back. I'm getting to it, but it's slow. Of course he's reluctant and – believe it or not – he's actually quite an honourable man. He wants a pay-day, his marriage is in bits. The truth's hit him – where he is and why. He has some integrity, which sits well with his considerable courage. I'll get everything we need and . . .' She tailed off.

Danny Curnow was rapping a spoon on the table – the drumbeat of a *tricoteuse* waiting for the head-lopping to begin.

Matthew Bentinick wiped his mouth with a paper napkin. 'Very good – the goulash,' he said. 'Thank you, Gaby. Eloquent and put with compassion, except that we are not Work and Pensions. So, would you, *please*, go to work and unlock him. Soon.'

It was dark and raining and they wore cheap clothing – military camouflage but not of good quality. They had gone together round the edge of the field and had taken the bomb to the wire's terminal point.

They were soaked, their hair slicked down on their foreheads. They had no firearm between them. They had done some practice up beyond Shane Bearnagh's Seat where the ground overlooked the western part of the county and Omagh town. They might have fired two dozen rounds between them, at twenty-five yards' range. Most shots had missed the cardboard target Brennie Murphy had brought for them. They were not yet trusted with weapons. Might get to use rifles when Malachy Riordan came back and the new supplies reached the mountain. Unarmed, Kevin watched, and Pearse made the connection.

Cold wet fingers.

It looked like nothing that could hurt. Just a can, with bubble-wrap round it. The end shone, where the copper piece was, and there was a light by the outer gatepost, good enough to alert the guests that they'd reached the turning to the track and the home of the O'Kane family. Pearse took his time. Twice, Kevin hissed at him that he should get on with it, but the joining of the wires – twisting them together and keeping them dry with the black plastic sack – was difficult. He couldn't use a torch, and there was only the light from across the track and the cattle grid. More vans came, the caterers again, the headlights raking through the hedge.

It was done.

They went back on their stomachs across the grass and the mud, where the cattle had gathered for cake, to the cover of the trees. They had the wires there, and the battery that would power the signal. It was about doing the terminals, groping under the plastic sheet that covered the battery, and to each of the wires was attached a Sellotaped strip of cardboard, for positive and negative. Pearse didn't know much about electricity, and neither did Kevin. They knew little of the ideology of the movement, the history of the struggle or the politics of past and present. Both knew about excitement, and the pleasure of having been chosen. When they had done the terminals and the wire ends, it would fire.

The word was, as Brennie Murphy told it, that Eamonn O'Kane would use his wife's car, the VW Golf, light green, and they had its number scribbled on paper. They'd have two opportunities to identify it – did it matter that the policeman's wife would be in the vehicle? Should it? And what if another car was alongside it, arriving at the same moment? Tough. They could identify the car, at a hundred yards, when it slowed to hit the cattle grid and was in the cone of light from beside the gate. There would also be an earlier opportunity: down the lane, near to the trees where they sheltered, was the home of Mrs Halloran, widow, and her daughter; they kept a light on in the porch that fell on the lane. It would warn them, give them time to be ready.

The darkness cloaked them, rain pattered on them and their

fingers were chilled. They heard music from the house, and waited for the guests to begin arriving.

They were trusted. It was their chance to prove the trust had been well placed.

It was war. They were soldiers. The biggest comfort to the two boys was that Malachy Riordan had trusted them. Others might not have. Others, with Malachy called away, would have cancelled the hit. But Malachy had placed in them his trust, and they carried its weight.

He was at a corner of the night operations room, shielded by screens. His computer screen glowed. The evening shift were across the work area, their voices hushed. In his ear the voice grated and was distant. Sebastian, bright young figure in the Five firmament of Belfast, listened to what he was told. He had never seen the source, knew him only by the code given him, *Antelope3B8*. The calls came regularly, and the cash went to a Gibraltar-based account. He was told what he needed to know, queried it for confirmation, was given it again with emphasis and the connection was cut. He remembered when he had been on the mountain slope beyond the Dungannon to Pomeroy road, and the man he had lain with in the shallow scrape under the ditch. He had chided a man who had played God.

He went to the machine for coffee. Then, back at his desk, he made a second call and received the curt answer to his question, the same as he had been told an hour before. In an hour's time, if he called again, it would be repeated. It was going to be a long night.

Frankie took care. She knew how she wanted to look. He came with a reputation. The contact, Maude, knew of him, and spoke highly of him.

She did not think she would have been chosen unless she fitted the role offered. It was not for Frankie McKinney – in her room on the eleventh floor of the conference hotel in the south of the city, the castle walls floodlit on the far side of the river – to consider the cause, its origins, aims and end-games. The ideology of the struggle took second place to the excitement. There was nothing better than the exhilaration of having the AK at her shoulder – to hell with the bruising – and feeling the recoil, or the chill in her stomach on going through Passport control with forged paperwork, smiling at the official, ignorant, behind his desk and being passed through. And there had been pleasure in the upstairs room at a house, with a party below, when she'd given herself to a man now in Maghaberry gaol. She might get to fire the grenade launcher if Malachy Riordan agreed.

She wore good jeans and a white blouse. She had put up her hair, exposing her neck, and had tiny studs in her ears. She thought her look casual, relaxed, in control.

She shivered. Where would they be, the girls with whom she shared the house in the road opposite the university? In a bar with other students, or at home, talking about their courses? Her parents' home was up the Malone road, and where would they be? It was Tuesday night: maybe they were at a bridge evening, or her father was at a charity committee, her mother at a Pilates class.

She waited for him, and was proud to have been chosen.

It was Pearse who saw the VW Golf go along the lane in front of Mrs Halloran's bungalow. He had good eyesight and caught enough of the registration to match it with what he had been given. He gasped, and tapped the shoulder beside him. Best friends since each could remember, dependent on each other, they were bonded. It would be the first time for both of them. He had been thinking, lying in the dark with the rain on his back, staring beyond the wall of darkness into the light in front of the bungalow, watching the cars passing – plenty of them now, all turning into the O'Kane home – of Doloures and her invitation, whether he could ask Brennie Murphy if it was possible to miss a Friday night.

'It's him. It's the policeman.'

'You sure?' Kevin hissed.

'Course I'm sure. I saw the number – most of it – colour, make. It's him.'

The headlights tracked up the lane. Pearse thought it one of the last cars to reach the party. The driveway was full and cars spilt into the field that stretched towards the small copse.

'You ready?'

'Yes.'

No moon, only low cloud and rain, but a dull light reached them from the front of the house and the lamps strung from trees growing at the hedge that flanked the field. It was enough for Pearse to detect the copper at the end of the plastic-coated cable, divided wires, positive and negative. The battery was mostly covered from the wet by the supermarket bag, except for the terminals.

'You know which?'

'Course I fuckin' do.'

An idiot question: the wires had a tag each, one of red paper and one of blue, and the battery top had the same colours stuck to it beside the terminals.

'You going to be good?'

'If you stop the fuckin' talk, I will.'

The two wires were, perhaps, an inch from the terminals. Kevin's hands shook and the wires wavered. Pearse had his head up, then straightened his body. He was kneeling. The car had slowed and would be at the gate to the track, where the light was, within four, five seconds.

Pearse counted it down.

They were there because of Malachy Riordan's trust in them. It was a disgrace that a family from the mountain had a son, a Catholic, who had joined the enemy, was a policeman. He deserved no mercy, nor his wife. He had seen the pattern: each car came to the gate slowly, braked, then went at snail speed over the rattling cattle grid.

The headlights were on the gate, the bars of the grid, the post, and swept through the hedge where it was thinning. He saw the policeman's head. A tight haircut, what policemen had, and a flash of blonde from the seat beyond him.

'Do it.'

'Now?'

'Kevin, fuckin' do it!'

The wires snaked close to the terminals. Blue had contact, then red and—

Pearse cringed. He screwed his eyes shut.

He heard silence. Then the noise of the cattle grid's bars. The VW Golf powered up the track to the house.

Pearse looked at the bag and the battery. The copper was against the terminals and the colour codes were right. 'What happened?'

'How'd I know?'

'What didn't happen?'

'It was him, him and his wife.'

'It was Eamonn O'Kane.'

They saw the brake lights come on at the top of the track where a place must have been kept by the guy who supervised the parking. Pearse saw the shadow of the policeman's back and his wife was on his arm. They went in through the door and music spilt out. The door closed.

'What'll we do, Pearse?'

'Wait till he comes back and try again.'

The driver brought Malachy Riordan into the outskirts of Prague. Not a word had passed between them since the roadblock near Wrocław, but often enough, in the daylight and in the evening when oncoming headlights had swept over them, Malachy had seen the curl of the driver's lip, the sneer.

They'd stopped at a fuel station. The driver had pointed to the sign at the side of the building. Malachy had needed a toilet but wouldn't have asked to stop. Once, inside the outer limits of Prague, the driver had pulled over, dug into a map, then pushed on. They went through a tunnel in heavy traffic. He was depending on people he didn't know who he hadn't chosen. They drove onto a modern bridge.

The driver broke the quiet. 'The roadblock? Thought you were going to wet your trousers. Wanting to know whether there was a shooter in the glove. You know what it was about?'

Malachy didn't answer.

'Want me to tell you? They've had bank robberies in Gdańsk and Szczecin – that's up on the Baltic – and they're looking for two Albanian boys. They think they're going south. That's what the roadblock was for.'

They went over the bridge, which spanned a wide river, bigger than any he'd seen. He was a man of stature and importance at home, but here he was a stranger.

A Tuesday night: if Matthew Bentinick had not hunted him down, Danny would have been in a corner of the small bar at a decent hotel in the old port town of Honfleur. He'd have had a Coke or a coffee in front of him. The clients on the trip would have been around him and he'd have completed his stalk of Hanne: some days he successfully erased her name from his mind, other days he failed to. He would already have followed her from the gallery where her work was exhibited. He would have trailed her with the expertise he had learnt on the pavements of Irish country towns, merging with the shadows if she'd paused at a dress-shop window. Much of what he did on Sunday evenings and Tuesday nights shamed him. She never looked behind her. It was to him a mark of confidence in her new life – one without him. The clients, if Danny Curnow was lucky, would keep away from him. He could have found another town further up or down the coast, turning his back on the gallery and the pavements leading to the alleyway where the small terraced home stood. He could have avoided the chance to see the girl . . .

He was in the lobby. Matthew Bentinick had gone to bed, and the young Czech had left to walk Gaby Davies to the hotel where she and the asset were staying. Her job, for what was left of the evening, was to rip detail from him. Later, Karol Pilar would be back and would stay until the small hours. They might again go out for a walk together.

It was agony for Danny to think of the French town, the tang of the sea, the tinkling of halyards against the yachts' masts and the girl. He had not known how to compromise.

* * *

In Honfleur, the clients always began the bonding process. Little groups would form in a couple of restaurants, wine would be ordered, and there was a determination to put aside catastrophe. On the Tuesday evening, they would agree that the worst was over. There was an expectation that things could only get better. They'd swap edited life stories: health, grandchildren and other holidays. As the evening wore on and tongues loosened, they'd discuss the guide. Respect for the historian, with reservations about his communication skills – and the driver.

'He's an oddball.'

'Lives somewhere over here.'

'Knows his stuff backwards. We're just here for a flavour of it, but he seems to live it.'

'There's a past, has to be. A past he's locked into. Poor beggar. The past doesn't allow escape.'

They'd be friends by the end. Most would swap addresses and they'd have the guides' email links. They'd know nothing of the driver, Danny Curnow, and would go to bed remembering it was an early start in the morning.

'I'm Dusty. I doubt you've heard of me.'

She stood in her doorway and the light from inside was thrown into his face. The geraniums in the windowbox were an exquisite scarlet. 'I haven't.'

'I know you, though. You're Hanne. I know you through your pictures. I'm a friend – we go back a long way – of Danny Curnow. I know your pictures because where we live he has the room next to mine and it's full of your work.'

Dusty thought her a lovely woman. They had told him at the gallery where she lived so he'd had his meal, seen the clients back to the hotel, then gone to the house. She had a robe wrapped around her.

She allowed herself to smile and shrug. 'They tell me each time he is in, and what he has bought. It is supposed to be secret. He chooses well and badly.'

'They're on the walls of his room.'

'He would not give up on something. I don't know what is "something". I took second place to it.'

'It's what he did before, and me.'

'Dusty, why did you come?'

'Miss, not sure it's any of my business, but it was about a chance of breaking free.'

'I am not a therapist for the complaint of whatever it was that he did before. I was in second, maybe in third or fourth place to it. I am sorry, Dusty.'

'He comes here every week.'

'He watches me and follows me. I am not supposed to know.' She chuckled, rich and soft. 'He is behind me. I can set my watch. On a Sunday and on a Tuesday. One day, I tell myself, I will stop and I will turn round and I will walk back. You want to know what I would do, Dusty, when I came close to him?'

'What would you do, miss?'

'I might kiss him, and I might take him by the hand, and I might lead him here, and I might cook for him, as I used to, and I might pour wine for him, and I might . . .'

'Yes, miss.'

'And I might again be second.'

'Where is home, miss?'

She tilted her head to look towards the clouds and the gaps where small stars were. 'There are islands and there are fish, eagles, whales and snowstorms. In the winter it is dark all night and all day. It is very far away.'

'One day, miss, will you ever stop and turn?'

She didn't answer but he saw the pain in her eyes and how it creased her mouth.

'He was called back, miss. A man came for him. He was taken again to do what he did in the past. He was good at it, and it half beat the life out of him. It's why you didn't see him tonight.'

'I wondered if he was bored with the game.'

'He's been taken again to do what he used to do. It damn near broke him. Not your problem, miss, and maybe I shouldn't have bothered you.'

'We were good together at the start – and I could believe I had softened him, until we came to the line. The red line, not to be crossed, of commitment. Thank you, Dusty.'

She stepped back into the room behind the door. He thanked her for her time and spun on his heel. He didn't want to linger and see the tears. As he walked away he heard the door close behind him. He wondered where the islands were. His own life was uncomplicated and comfortable, his relationship with Christine warm and happy. He thought the man he loved was tortured. He supposed that so many were who had been in that place and done things there . . .

'I'm hungry,' Kevin said.

'My ma does great cocoa,' Pearse said.

'And mine makes a great pie.'

'The best pie.'

They had to talk nonsense because it kept some of the cold out. A wind rustled the leaves above them and the rain was heavy. Kevin kept in his mind the face of Malachy Riordan. Without Malachy in his life he would have been an ordinary shite, nothing special. Since he was a kid he had craved to be noted and chosen, able to walk taller than others – except Pearse . . .

The door opened across the field, over the hedge and past the parked cars. They were pissed, the men, warm and smart, the women. He saw Eamonn O'Kane, couldn't miss him because he did a job with an umbrella and sheltered the women as they scurried to the cars. There was music, louder, from inside, and shrieks of laughter. He wondered why so many had come to celebrate with the mother and father of a policeman – and all of them Catholics. The cars made a queue down the track from the garden and the noise of the cattle-grid bars was constant. The stream went down the lane and through the light from Mrs Halloran's bungalow.

Now the parents hugged their son and kissed his wife. They stayed in the porch and a dog yapped at their heels. The son and his wife ran to their car.

The track was clear.

'You ready?'

'Course.'

'You want me to . . . ?'

'No.'

His fingers – numb with cold – were on the wires, held poised by the terminals. Pearse would do the watching for him. Pearse told him when the car started, when it moved and when it was close to the grid. He heard the rattle of the bars and used his will to hold the wires steady. He had them beside the terminals.

'Go for it.'

He made the contact. He could imagine the pulse that flashed from the battery and down the cable, under the ground, then up to the surface in the hedge and into the maroon that was the charge to fire the detonator. His head tilted up. He saw the VW Golf caught in the gate light. It paused, rolled a few feet and then it was gone. He barely saw it go through the light from the Halloran house.

Kevin could have cried. Pearse swore. The door of the house had closed.

Kevin said they'd have to get it. Pearse said that Malachy Riordan would likely half kill them if they left it to rot in the field. And Kevin said they had to get it because his prints would be over it – he couldn't have worn gloves because his fingers were bolloxed with cold. And Pearse said, with defiance, that it wasn't their fault, they'd done what they'd been told to. Kevin said that the man might come down his drive, under his umbrella, to run the dog before shutting up the house. Pearse said they'd wait before they went to get it. Kevin said that he had pictured the flash exploding out of the hedge, the car swivelling round it, the fireball taking hold. He'd seen it too many times. Pearse said Malachy Riordan would kill them if they left evidence in the hedge. Their voices were choked, as if tears weren't far away.

The quiet fell on them, but for the rain and the wind, and they waited.

The car pulled in. The driver leaned across Malachy Riordan and opened the door. Nothing was said.

He could have spoken out: 'When my business is done I'll come looking for you. I'll find you and fuckin' break you.'

The driver could have replied: 'Don't come looking for me because there might be a roadblock, with cops, and you'd shit yourself.'

No thanks and no good wishes. He took his bag, straightened up and kicked the door shut with his heel. By the time he was on the paving, he heard the car accelerating away.

The hotel building was monstrous. A wall of glass towered ahead of him. He saw clusters of men and women at tables. He thought he saw her. The glass made the image indistinct and there was a swell of smart women and men in suits, who swirled about the foyer and in front of thc wide reception desk. She stood and glanced at her wrist, checked the time and gazed out. She seemed nervous, ill at ease. He hated the place. So many tables and so many people. He couldn't read what was safe and what stank of risk. Throughout the last stage of the journey he had turned in his mind the dangers of where he was. He couldn't judge the men and women here. She fitted what he had been told. He reached into his inner pocket and took out his wallet. The photograph was where any man kept his sweetheart's picture. There was no doubt that it was her.

He went forward a few paces and a porter came towards him, a decent-looking kid in a flunkey's uniform. He asked for a sheet of paper and a pencil. The porter found them for him. He wrote on the paper, and folded it. He took a ten-euro note from the wallet, gave it and the sheet of paper to the porter, then pointed out the woman with the golden hair. He was thanked. Had the porter a street map? No problem. He was given the map, large scale, city centre, and told where they were. He asked a last question; the boy giggled and pointed at the map. He was gone. He didn't look back at the girl, but was satisfied to see the porter go through the big doors with the note in his hand. It was a precaution, and his freedom depended on suspicion. He stepped out into the darkness, heading for the city's heart.

* * *

'You have to tell me. This is fast becoming ridiculous, Ralph.'

'I can't tell you what I don't know.'

'When you meet, what weapons will be test-fired?'

'It's not decided yet.'

They were in her bedroom. He had been in bed when she'd phoned him. With a rasp in her voice, she'd told him to dress, then come down the corridor. She had laid on coffee. He had dressed, as instructed, and she had tried, at first, to sugar it. She had been pleasant and – she reckoned – businesslike.

Her reward was vagueness.

'You're telling me you don't know when you'll meet your contact – it's Simonov? You don't know?'

'Not really.'

'You've been here a night and a full day and you don't know? The girl's in place. We reckon Riordan should have hit the city by now. You're the middle man, the facilitator, but you don't know when there'll be a meeting? Level with me, Ralph.'

'I haven't been told and that's the truth.'

He wore his helpless look, usually a winner. She was close to believing him. 'What about the location?'

'Not yet.'

He wasn't meeting her eyes. He had given her chapter and verse on the Irish girl and had had the wit to gossip with her: she was Queen's, a graduate, lived at the bottom of the Malone road. They had shown each other their passports. Gaby would be able to furnish Thames House with enough details by midnight for the computers to spit out her identity, the accounts where the cash was held and the bank address. All good, except the core of what she needed. She remembered the face of the man with Matthew Bentinick. She had thought it unforgiving, merciless. Ralph Exton was hers and had been since she'd trailed to that provincial police station and lugged Bentinick's file bag into the interview room.

'I'm trying to help, Ralph. I've played fair with you over the years. Everything I've done for you has been based on honesty. It's no time for you to play fast and loose with me.'

'Would I do that, Gaby?'

'This Simonov, it's the old thing, "the devil in the detail": where's the detail? When do you meet, where do you meet, what do you fire? I can move on – where is he coming from in your life, how are you hooked to him and—'

'I've always given you everything I've known, Gaby, kept nothing back. The weapons may not turn up. What if they don't? Riordan a killer. What'll he do to me? That drill was right in my face. I don't know how much more I can take. Don't you believe me? After all I've done . . . I'm a little cog in the wheel, and I get frightened.' His head was in his hands.

She was out of her chair. God's truth, what was he? An asset or a colleague? Her hand was on his shoulder. 'We'll do all we can, Ralph. Your security is hugely important to us, a main priority. Anyway, the detail. We'll try again in the morning.'

She helped him up and took him to the door. His head was still down and he was breathing fast. She took him along the corridor and he gave her his key-card. She let him in and helped him on to the bed. She closed the door quietly after her.

Not bad. He rubbed his arm over his face. Not bad at all. He had both of them, a level of fear and a level of allegiance. Attached to each was the name of Timofey Simonov, his friend.

He heard, below and at the back of the house, the door, then the dogs stampeding up the stairs. It was the brigadier's task to take them out late at night, sometimes into the woods at the back of the property and sometimes on the pavements. If they went into the little park opposite, dedicated to the memory of Anna Politkovskaya – troublemaker – who had been assassinated in Moscow, and if the dogs crapped on the grass he would leave it. The Weimaraners appeared, and the brigadier came a few minutes after them with a tray of hot milk and biscuits.

Timofey said he had spoken to his friend. The brigadier would collect him from Prague, bring him to Karlovy Vary for the night and take him back on Thursday morning. He had told his friend that they would meet in the new forest that had grown over the old base, Milovice, on the following evening, Friday. They would do business where he had been a junior officer, and the brigadier had been in a position of authority. He made the pilgrimage regularly, and it was a good place to be. Few, he believed, knew the routes to the hangars as well as he did. Some were frightened of it. To Timofey Simonov it was as familiar as an old home, which it had been.

Happy days, after a fashion. As a member of GRU staff, Timofey had lived on the base in a dormitory for essential staff. The generals who conducted exercises from the underground command bunker had known his name and loved to banter with a bright, committed young man, for whom no job was too great, no shift too long. Exemplary work always left his desk for theirs. And around him there had been the entrenched power of the Union of Soviet Socialist Republics. Great days bordering on magical. The long lines of tanks heading towards the live firing ranges, the power and thunder of their engines, the belch of diesel smoke . . . The deafening noise when the fighter bombers came onto the runways, raced for speed, then lifted off. He was Military Intelligence so he was privileged to stand with the senior officers on a viewing platform and watch the tanks manoeuvring. He could go to the control tower when the aircraft were scrambled in a mock emergency. In the command bunker, at the great table where the maps were spread and the counters moved to designate red and blue forces, his opinion was sought: 'What is their speed of reaction, Timofey?'; 'If they push into Poland, having breached the German lines, is that a feint or the main thrust?'; 'Their armoured crews, Timofey, how much battle preparation have they had?'; 'I leave on the train for Moscow the day after tomorrow, Timofey, and would like to have with me a crate of good champagne, if possible.' He had known all of the answers – could quote statistics and intelligence debriefs with brevity and clarity, and could produce champagne, perfume or silk, whatever. He had loved Milovice. It was not mentioned there that his father was a gulag security officer, that his mother treated criminals for typhoid, TB and knife wounds in a gulag hospital. Everybody who had any degree of influence or importance knew him on the base, as he walked, jogged or drove around it in his assigned open-top jeep. He had thought himself a part of the great power that was Milovice.

It had first shocked but now disgusted him that in all of the many visits he had made to the old base he had never met another Russian. Why not? There were no monuments either, or veterans' reunions. Timofey went there and took the brigadier with him.

He drank his milk. Tomorrow evening he would be with his friend, and they would laugh till they cried. It was always good to be with a friend. He had reason to be grateful to Ralph Exton.

That night, in the room that had become a shrine, Rosie Bentinick had lit the candle. It had been a long, busy day. The cat slept on the bed and the dog's head lay across her ankles. She spoke aloud, telling the stories she thought would be of interest, as the cat purred and the dog snored. It was hardest for Rosie when she looked at the pillows on the bed: empty. She couldn't escape the photograph on the dressing-table: the excitement of the children and the contentment of her daughter. It was a painful ritual and it would be her husband's turn tomorrow. They couldn't move on. The day after tomorrow, Thursday, they would visit, she and her husband. They always did on that evening, never missed.

A tale was told. A summer evening recalled . . . Karol Pilar had walked at the speed of the target. He had been led away from the main streets, the lights of the bars and fast-food places, and was among old buildings and narrow lanes. They were dark. Several times, without lighting he had lost sight of his target – the man's shoes must have been rubber-soled because they were silent on the paving.

No warning – pain creased his shoulder and back. The blow, from a lead-tipped cosh or wooden truncheon, had come down with full force on the bone between his neck and his shoulder socket. He swayed, lost balance and wheezed out a small cry. The second strike was to the other side of his neck. He went down and the kicking started. One had builders' boots, steel-toe-capped, another had conventional lace-ups and a third wore light leather shoes – they might have been snakeskin or crocodile. The blows caught his stomach, testicles, kidneys and the base of the spine. His face was not touched. Nothing was said.

Nothing was taken from him except his police pistol, the CZ 75, locally manufactured with a good reputation. One said, 'Enough.' They walked away.

No one came near him. A man approached with a torch, identified his shape, then crossed to the far side of the street. He lay there and the pain soaked through him, then the disgrace that he had been so vulnerable. He recognised that he had been warned. One word only had been spoken: Russian language, European dialect.

It might have been an hour later that he started to move. He crawled, a great effort, and found the pistol in the gutter. He used his phone to call his girlfriend. She came for him in her small car. Its lights found him because he had talked her there on the phone. Her shock: had he called an ambulance? He didn't want one. Where were the police? He hadn't called them.

How had a target, moving late at night between cafés and bars, spreading word of deals done and arrangements pending, known that a single officer was on his tail? He hadn't shown out – he was certain of it. Who in his office, in his unit, had taken money in an envelope? A target could be untouchable. Which senior officer nurtured hopes of a villa in the countryside, with forests, quality fishing and early retirement because a meagre police pension had been augmented?

She took him home and helped him up the stairs. Then she phoned in to the detective unit on Bartolomejska. He had influenza, a nasty strain. He'd had to leave work early the previous evening and apologised for not completing his shift. The influenza had taken a week to clear.

He told the story quietly.

'And you went back to work?'

'Yes, Danny. No mark of what they had done showed on me. It was assumed I had learned a lesson, would know my place.'

'What did you learn?'

'I learned that the day would come when I would fuck them and the codes we were taught at the academy would go out of a high window.'

'How long ago?'

'Twenty months. It was never mentioned in the office – as if nothing had happened. I was not transferred. I did my job, and was sidelined whenever they could assign me elsewhere. Now, it's liaison on an Irish matter. That's good. What harm can I do on an Irish matter?'

'It's filthy work, Karol.'

'I think so – and for me it is necessary.'

They were on the third or fourth circuit of Wenceslas Square. They walked at a measured pace, the rain stayed off, and the only eavesdroppers were the homeless people in doorways. The clubs and restaurants were shuttered.

Danny said, 'It's what we're asked to do that people don't want to know. We're outside any world that has rules and conventions. The people on the streets, who pay us through their taxes, are happy to know that an element of criminality has been nicked. They're unhappy to know what had to be done to achieve it. We don't expect thanks, and if we get hurt we shouldn't expect sympathy. We're out of sight. Good to work with you, Karol.'

'I want to destroy them.'

'Stick around.'

'You want a drink now?'

'I want to get to my bed. They'll be hurt, and one day you might learn why. Go back to your girlfriend.'

They hugged, maybe too tightly. Karol Pilar gasped, but said nothing about old wounds and pain. Danny Curnow watched him walk away till he was past the museum. He expected no thanks and no sympathy.

10

He thought it as pretty a town as he had ever seen. The spook was from the embassy and had driven Danny Curnow and Matthew Bentinick across country along winding roads flanked by fast streams and steep-sided valleys where the trees had turned gold. After a dawn start, they'd made good time in the Freelander. What did he want, Bentinick had been asked. A rough reply had made the spook chuckle: Bentinick wanted only to see the man. They were there by eight, parked the vehicle and walked.

They had gone to an apartment block where the spook had rung a bell and spoken quietly to the grille. Bentinick had lit his pipe and Danny had gazed around at the fine buildings of the spa against the autumn colours. It looked to him like Paradise. The door opened, an elderly woman passed out through the gap with a straining dog on a tight lead. The spook took the dog, a spaniel, and the woman closed the door behind her. The spook said that her father had been at Aylesbury, in Buckinghamshire, with the Czech government in exile during the Second World War and that the dog was useful. It was not trained but it led them at speed.

They went past clinics and the spa buildings, saw magnificent old homes and streets from the days of Austro-Hungary. The flowers were in bloom, the river ran clean and the dog led them. Danny approved. The best surveillance people always said a dog was a jewel. He saw the Russian names on the shops, restaurants, mini-marts, and the logos on delivery and builders' vans. The gold of the orb on a church roof glowed in the first low sunlight. The spook talked to Bentinick – Danny caught snatches. They spoke of 'endemic corruption', 'fear of the Russian bear and its corrosive influence', the 'energies, expectations, of young people', the 'hold of organised crime', and '. . . no cull happened for the old counter-intelligence men of the Cold War. They're still around, fêted by the Russians . . .' He heard what was said, had no interest in it. They went up a road and to their right were huge villas, splendid in their preservation. There was a small park, and they sat on a bench.

Bentinick's pipe was lit. The sun rose steadily and the shadows shortened. Opposite, there was a detached villa, and a quality Mercedes was parked in front of the steps up to the door. The spook and Bentinick faced it, and Danny was left side on. The spook would have been mid-thirties – moderate height, moderate build, moderate brown hair – and was dressed in jeans, a battered waxed coat and a sweater with loose threads. Bentinick, true to form, was suited, with a waistcoat and his watch chain across it.

The spook said conversationally, 'The Ivans think we're yesterday's stuff. That's what I find here. We don't matter and therefore can be ignored. They don't change, which sort of goes back to Joe Stalin and the Vatican – how many tanks does the Pope have? They have people based on the top floor of a block over there, behind the St Mary Magdalene church, and keep a weather eye on the millionaires and billionaires who favour the town. To the Ivans we're ready for the scrap heap. I don't think the Chinese – they're here – even know we're still on the planet. The Americans are down by the river. I'm sometimes taken for a coffee, but nothing's shared. It's a bit lonely, really, to be a Brit here. Trouble is that it's a melting pot of views and intelligence gathering. It's a place where you can, just about, see the changing status of people – whether they're officials from Moscow or the hoods, the parasites of the *siloviki*, but I only get down once a week. What are we hoping for the end result – not just the sighting to-day?'

Smoke billowed from Bentinick's pipe. He said, assured, 'To demonstrate we're capable of administering a sharp kick to the shin, where it hurts.'

'You can achieve that?' Doubt, but respect.

'I like to think we are still able to direct a steel toecap in the right direction. Cause a bit of grief.'

'They'd be powerfully angry. There was a charity bash the other night for the nobs of the Russian community. The ambassador had an arm round him. He has status . . . And where does the Irish angle come in?'

Bentinick gave a light laugh, then stiffened: the dog was alert. Danny saw the door open across the road. The spook had pulled his scarf high over his face, natural in the chill. A man came down the steps, two dogs with him, and walked past the Mercedes towards the pavement.

Bentinick mouthed: 'There's no traffic. Let the dog go.'

The spaniel, a roan, was across the road and sprinted. Bentinick called it – didn't stand a chance. The spaniel charged at the other dogs, then danced round them on the pavement. They joined in and their leads were round the man's legs.

'He's Timofey Simonov, there so his shin's measured,' Bentinick pushed himself up.

Another man was behind Simonov.

The spook murmured, 'That's a former brigadier of GRU, Nikolai Denisov, his chauffeur, butler and bodyguard, with a legally held firearm, I fancy he's carrying it now. He was once considered a formidable opponent but, as they say, nothing is for ever. He's a sort of trained chimpanzee now.'

Danny watched. Bentinick was across the street, scrabbling for the loose lead, spinning it out, close to a high-value target. Nothing more natural than a bumbling Englishman, incapable even of catching his dog. It lay down, seemed to know the part it was playing. Danny heard Bentinick ask the ages of the dogs that licked at the spaniel and pranced round it. He heard him praise their fine coats and excellent condition. Danny didn't need to be closer. He could see the man, each wart and blemish on his face, his build and the slouch of his shoulders. Then not overstaying his minimal welcome, Bentinick had the lead and had pulled the spaniel to heel, made an apology and was back across the road, the spook tailing him but inside of the target's eyeline. Danny

Curnow understood that a sighting far outweighed the value of photographs.

Bentinick and the spook returned, neither glancing back at the two men going up the hill with the dogs, then turning into a side alley and disappearing.

They reached Danny. Bentinick asked, 'What do you think?'

'Insignificant. Ordinary enough.'

'They don't get to live in a home like that on charity handouts. Don't undersell.'

And that was it. Back to the car park. He locked the memory of the two men's faces into his mind. They were often like that, insignificant and ordinary, and he had seen enough of them in his time, enemies and assets. Bent in the back and with a pale, pinched face, no indication of the brains required to put together a personal portfolio that might hit a half-billion American dollars. It had begun, in Danny Curnow's mind, to take shape, and he understood the role, valued, that Malachy Riordan had been awarded. The spaniel was dropped off, then the spook drove away fast. He had a plane to catch.

Malachy Riordan woke up. It was extraordinary that he had slept. He stretched and yawned, then felt the ache in his stomach.

After he'd been dropped, he had used the map to cross the city. He had been through smart and cheap residential areas, then the business quarter and the tourist sector, where the big squares were and the monuments. He had gone on past the railway station, quiet and shut down, then the darkened bus terminus. He had paused every two or three hundred yards to check the map, and if he had gone wrong he had doubled back. The porter had giggled when he had asked for the red-light district where the girls could be found. He passed girls on the streets, and their pimps. He hadn't been with another woman since he'd married Bridie – these girls frightened him and he pretended not to hear them as they called to him. There was a cross on the map for the street the porter had suggested. He had reached Prokopovo Square, and had seen the turning. He could have chosen six or seven hotels or guesthouses. He could not have said why he had chosen this one. He had beaten on the door, fist clenched, until a guy had opened it, half dressed, foul-tempered. How many nights? He had paid for four, with an additional fifty euros, and had not been asked for identification. He had climbed three flights, stripped and slipped into the bed, between sheets that lacked crispness. It was where he wanted to be.

His mind had churned: the journey and the future. He had tossed and turned: the driver and his contempt, the girl in the hotel lobby, her flustered anxiety as she waited. A couple had begun above him. When they had finished, another pair started across the corridor and the woman squealed.

There was a cubicle with a toilet and a shower that he needed to contort himself to get into. The water dribbled. He had only gone to sleep when exhaustion had cleared the worries from his mind. He could not be followed and found here.

When he was dressed, Malachy Riordan went down the stairs, with his bag, leaving nothing personal behind. There was a breakfast room. A couple were bickering in German. He went to the desk. His story was that his mobile's battery was flat. He asked to borrow a phone. A drawer was opened that held a dozen, or more, and the man gestured for him to take his pick.

He rang the girl. He had the map in front of him and told her where to be and at what time. She might have wanted a conversation, but he rang off.

He handed over another note, was rewarded with a smile, and pocketed the mobile.

He went out into bright sunlight. Later he would find a bar with satellite TV and learn of the death of a policeman. The warmth felt good on his skin.

A core had stayed on, three cars.

They moved late.

Pearse's idea was that they could get it done in darkness by touch.

A wet grey morning had replaced a wet black night.

Twice they had been about to leave the trees to crawl across the field and down the last part of the hedge to the gate where the device was laid. Each time, the door had opened, people had come out and there had been shouting and laughter. Kevin said that it was because they'd been at the whiskey. The three had gone, no more cars. But the O'Kanes didn't sleep in. He was outside early with the dog and his first fag, and she brought black bags out of the back door to stack them around the wheelie-bin. There was a mist over the grass.

Pearse had said that the caterers would be back early to clear up and shift the stuff they'd left overnight, and Kevin couldn't deny it. Then Kevin had said they might leave the thing in the hedge till that evening and come back for it at next dusk, but Pearse had disagreed: they'd get the thing now.

They began the crawl across the field, both already sodden. Pearse knew it was no different for Kevin, that they shared the hunger and thirst, the weakness and exhaustion.

Then, Christ, they had some luck and perhaps they were owed it.

There must have been places on the lane where anyone looking from a car window would have seen the two of them, in the crap camouflage tunics, crawling through the cow muck and thistles. But no one did. More luck: no one came out of the O'Kane house – if they had stood on the raised step by the door and gazed towards the big lough, they would have seen the kids.

They went fast on their knees and elbows. Pearse led, and Kevin was breathing like an old pig. Was Kevin all right? He mumbled that he was.

They made the hedge, leaving a trail of bent grass. He would have liked to take out the cable, maybe a full hundred metres of it. A sprig of the hedge caught his cheek and ripped it. He wiped it with his hand and saw blood on his fingers. He had forgotten to do the proper clear-up search of where they had been in the trees. They might have left a sweet paper or a bus ticket. For that, he reckoned, Malachy Riordan could have trashed his balls. Through the hedge he could see the gatepost, and the light now was strong enough for the lamp on it to have been switched off. More worry: their car was parked where it could be seen from the road. It was a good enough place when it was dark, but not in daylight. They needed to get the job done fast and be gone.

They'd half buried it and couldn't find it. He felt a pinch and turned.

'What you doing?' Kevin hissed.

'Looking for the fuckin' thing, what else?'

'Can't you see it?'

'If I could, I'd have it, you eejit, wouldn't I?'

He found the can. He had his hand on it. He groped for the end where they had connected, last evening, the cable to the maroon charge that activated the detonator. He found the contact point and eased the can back. He reached for the connection and remembered that it had taken effort to slot it. Again he felt the pinch.

'For fuck's sake, Kevin, what you think—'

He twisted round. Kevin didn't speak but held up the cable close to where it had been cut. Cut. Not ripped apart by a fox or gnawed through by rats, but cut, left with clean, not frayed edges. Kevin gaped at him. Pearse understood that they had been touted: the weapon had never been live so no plug of molten copper would have hit the car driven by the policeman or his wife. The urine ran hot over his thighs and he was shaking. His hands were stiff, the fingers unresponsive. He felt the scream well in his throat. He dropped the can. He snatched at it, missed and—

He would not have heard the crows rise and scream. Neither would Kevin. They would not have seen the smoke that hazed over them.

'It wasn't very good.'

She had come to his door. He was mostly dressed, using an electric shaver and sitting by the window.

Ralph Exton mimicked her: 'What "wasn't very good"?'

Gaby paced, her hands fidgeting. He saw how stressed she was and that she could barely control her temper. He knew how to play it.

'Don't mess me about, Ralph. I'm not in the mood.'

'Serious stuff.'

Fight back, deflect and provoke. He knew the big card he would play. Trouble was, she was a lovely kid. He fancied her and it might have been mutual. He reckoned it was time to hit hard.

'I want answers, sensible ones. Has it crossed your mind that I'm trying to protect you as well as myself?'

'I tell you as much as I know.'

'Ralph, are you being honest with me? Because if you're not, I've got a big problem.'

'Can I tell you something?'

She softened. 'Shoot.'

He thought Gaby Davies had a lovely throat, but he went for it. She was, he reckoned, the least of his problems. So reasonable and calm.

'You weren't there. Where were you? With that snivelling creature you brought to Ireland? You weren't there when they switched the fucking drill on. You know what happens to bodily functions if the sphincter muscle goes slack? There was a drill in front of my face. Where were you? Did you have a "big problem"? Not as big as mine was.'

'I'm right with you.'

'Yes.'

She'd backed off. He'd thought she would. A nice girl, but no match for a decent shite like Ralph Exton. Nothing decent about Timofey Simonov, whose reach probably spanned continents.

He put on his saddened look, as if she had hurt him with her disbelief. She touched his arm. He let himself slump, a man reeling under the strain.

Gaby said, 'We're on the same side.'

'Yes.'

On his screen, in his study on the first floor, with his dogs beside him, Timofey Simonov could check again the house to the south-west of London. Not that the image was recent – in fact, the satellite camera had recorded the picture on a clear winter's day when the trees had lost their foliage. But he could see the house and the gardens at the front, rear and side, and could make out the raised ground further to the west, where, he assumed, the marksman awaited an opportunity.

It was raining. On his screen, there were lawns around the house, and paths and places where a man might sit – as Timofey did in high summer – but not in the rain. He cursed. He had taken money, given assurances, but the contract had not been fulfilled – and it was raining.

Timofey Simonov's marksman waited. He was now on his third day in the country. He had found a good place with a clear view of the back lawn and the patio. There had been days in the snipers' nests overlooking Sarajevo when the autumn mist had settled in the valley below and he had struggled to find a target. Some days he had fired at anyone who moved, not calculating whether or not a target had military significance or was a grandmother struggling with a plastic bag of wood and any food she had found.

He was close to a path used by dog-walkers, cyclists and schoolkids. He was well concealed, away from the path, and protected in the cavern left by the roots of a fallen tree, but too many people were too close – and his hire car had been parked for too long in the same place. It was unsatisfactory. But he held his position, was obliged to.

There were puddles on the patio, alive with ripples. The man would not come out in the driving rain. The marksman needed to do well. He was in a competitive market. The trade, whether it involved a sniper, a bomb-laying under a car, a knifing or a close-quarters pistol shooting, was saturated. Too many kids coming from his own Serbo-Croat background and from Montenegro, Bosnia, Albania and Moldova for too little work. And the way to further work was not to complain that a job couldn't be done, when money had been paid up front, because it was raining. He stayed in place, waited and watched. Sometimes dogs came close but the wet must have deadened his smell. He was not aware of any crime his target had committed. The men and women on the streets of Sarajevo – with rifles or shopping bags – had been guilty of nothing that he knew of.

The rain fell and the target did not come. He had been recommended and failure would bring recrimination – or a knife or a bullet. It was that sort of trade.

'We'll go – come on. I'm ready. Hurry yourself.'

The dogs would now be shut in the annexe off the kitchen and the inner doors fastened. A woman would come in later to let them into the yard, but would not compromise the security of the interior. He was paranoid about security, acknowledged the weakness in himself and occasionally laughed at his obsession: it was, their mayor said, the safest town in all Europe. Few thieves would have had the boldness, or stupidity, to rob the rich and infamous of Karlovy Vary. He stood by the passenger door of the Mercedes and shouted back at the front door. 'I want to go now.'

The brigadier – a jack of all trades who knew where the skeletons lay – emerged, locked the door and came down the steps. Timofey slipped into his seat.

The man ran the last strides to the car. Did Nikolai Denisov, brigadier of GRU, *enjoy* his position as servant to Timofey Simonov, captain of GRU, or did he simmer with resentment? It hardly mattered. The engine started and the car pulled out of the driveway. He felt good to be working again. There had been times, this year and last, when he had worked too little and been bored. He refused to accept the advance of age. Small matters stimulated him. The brigadier had advised against the action he was taking with his friend. He had ignored him. He had ignored most of the cautionary advice offered by his former senior officer.

They came out of Karlovy Vary. Their destination was a town to the south-west, Český Krumlov, but they went north towards the German frontier, a basic precaution. He settled into his seat. He could never fault the brigadier's driving. It would be a round trip, but worthwhile. He was comfortable. Timofey had ignored the brigadier's advice from the day their relationship had changed when the man had been on his knees, clinging to the trousers of his junior officer. The photocopied letter advising him that his post at GRU had been suspended lay on the floor.

There had been pandemonium in the camp. Extra trains were added to the daily one back to the USSR. Efforts were made to strip the base of everything that was of value. The cranes and haulage lorries that shifted broken tanks were used to drag down the streetlights so they could be sent home, items of value, with weapons, technology, computers and paper files of a base that had had power across the continent. Not everything, though, went onto the inventories of the transport officers.

He had taken advantage of an opportunity when the morale of others had collapsed. Conscripts were his labour force; the brigadier was his bookkeeper.

The first wealth came from what had gone under the wire. The perimeter fence was endless, running through woods and along roads. There were places beside the air strips where Czechs could come in their Skodas, Ladas, Wartburgs and Trabants. He sold cans of fuel at half of what a local garage asked. He had tankers backed up to the fence and the containers were pushed underneath. The cash, in dollars, went through the wire's mesh.

The petrol trade was the best, but there had been more. The heavy transport lorries were waiting for the long journey east, in convoy. Some, while they waited, had been diverted. Office furniture went under the larger holes in the fence, with computers and sophisticated optics from the infantry's stores. There was food too. Wonderful times. He would go every week to the new French-owned bank that had opened in Prague and deposit the contents of a big black plastic sack in a numbered account. At the counter, he found a temporary girlfriend: she received petrol for her extended family; he had time in the big bed at her parents' home in the Florenc quarter.

In the last few days, before looters swarmed over the base, what was left went out through the main gate. He had said to the brigadier, 'You are mine. You do what I tell you to do. You give me absolute loyalty and I'll look after you and your family.' The man had wept on his shoulder in gratitude.

They had gone back to Mother Russia, where they had heard of men of his rank and the brigadier's who were digging potatoes, driving taxis and guarding the new regime of gangsters. Would it last? They didn't know, couldn't judge, and had spent too freely. His memories were of the excitement and flush of success. He loathed the British, with one exception, and would take his hatred to the grave. He had loved the camp that had housed Central Command at Milovice.

They went into Germany, then swung south.

At the airport there was a display of the edgy formality Matthew Bentinick offered. He stepped out of the Freelander, opened the boot and took out the bag. He shook hands with the spook, his gratitude crisply expressed, and for Danny Curwen there was a slap on the arm. Danny thought it unchanged from Gough, a quarter of a century before, when he and Dusty had been about to drive out on a difficult, perhaps dangerous, mission. No theatre, no schmaltz, only the briskness. He'd swung away from them, heading towards the terminal. The slap had been hard enough to sting his arm and might have been, Danny felt, the sole indication of the reliance placed on him. Near to the doors, Bentinick paused but did not turn to wave. Instead, he rooted in his pocket and Danny saw him retrieve the pipe, fill and light it. The smoke wafted behind Bentinick. It was no more than a dozen steps to the doors, where he rapped the pipe on his heel, shook the debris into a bin and was gone.

The spook drove Danny away. Without Bentinick, there was a loosening. The spook's name was Morrison. Danny gave his. Something about the weather, then the economy – dire. Something about the countryside, the local wildlife, then a few words about the Freelander's engine, and the spook's last holiday, white-water rafting with his wife and kids in the Samava National Park. The spook talked and Danny learnt a fair amount about him, but gave only his name. The Green Slimes and FRU, agent handling, the beaches and graves were off limits. Only Bentinick had that detail and could have called him back.

The spook had been in Prague for two years, had been with Six for fourteen. And Curnow? Old caution kicked in. He didn't trust strangers, whatever their credentials. The weather, the economy, wildlife and engine were acceptable. He'd done 'a bit of this and a bit of that', was a vagabond – rootless, shifting, restless – and the spook had realised it was all he'd get. They came into central Prague. Where could he be dropped?

Pretty much anywhere. The wheel swung, the vehicle stopped. They were beside a pavement. Danny opened the door, then gave his hand to the spook.

He was questioned: 'You said you were a vagabond and I'm wondering what sort of life that goes with. Comfortable or tough? Right for a bit of this and a bit of that?'

Danny said, 'It's what suits me. I liked the dog – clever. Thanks for the ride.'

'Danny, we have a good little station here, quiet, calm and respected. Try not to embarrass us. Promise?'

Danny was on the pavement, tourists flowing around him and the Freelander was lost in traffic. He hoped the spook wasn't easily embarrassed, but he hadn't promised.

She took the call. He was in Departures.

She ate a mid-morning biscuit. Was he OK? He was fine. Her screen twitched. Jocelyn hit a key, wrenched the mouse and read. She told him the legal advice just submitted by that pretty young man.

'The eagles say it can be done. Do I ramp it up?'

He told her to build the case, then what time his flight would land. She said she'd fix the car.

He didn't comment. They were in her hotel.

Gaby Davies said, 'You have to understand that he's fragile right now. I'm treating him, Danny, with extreme care. What I fear most is that he'll just cave in. I've kept, in my mind, a ledger of what we've had from him – the names of those involved in the cigarette importation to Ireland at the Costa end, most of the names of those who do the smuggling routes, and the people who raise the cash for payments. Add to that the name of the individual who propositioned him concerning the firearms purchase and who made the arrangements for the meeting with Malachy Riordan, a committed terrorist and killer, and Brendan Murphy. Murphy is what I'd describe as a godfather. He calls shots, plans strategies, identifies targets. Also, we now have the identification of a 'clean skin', this girl, Frankie, and more of that'll drop into place. The ledger is very much loaded on the positive side. It's pretty good. The idea may not sit easily with you but I admire his courage in going through with this business and agreeing to come here – and I believe in Ralph's honesty. If he tells me, to my face, that he has no answer to a question I put to him, I believe him. I've worked with him for five years – I was there from the start. You've known him, what? four days? He's a major and quite critical CHIS to us – a Covert Human Intelligence Source – and I have bragging rights to him that I won't willingly surrender. I'm telling you to back off, leave Ralph and his dealer contact to me. Understood?'

He neither commented nor said where he had been, who he had seen and why a spaniel had been borrowed and taken for a walk. He thought she was hurt that Matthew Bentinick had not sought her out to wish her well before flying back. She'd have despised Danny Curnow, freelancer, 'increment' and vagabond.

'Sorry, I didn't hear you. Is that understood?'

He shrugged, rolled an eye. Understood? Yes. Shrugged again. Headed for the main door. She'd learn, and it would be a hard lesson.

Dusty said, 'I'll send him back.'

'I can't be in second place.'

'I'll do what I can – if he survives where he is now.'

'I'll be first equal, but not second. I'll tell you a story, Dusty. I once asked him who he was. He answered that he was Vagabond. Was that an army rank? No. It was a man who was rootless. "A man without commitment?" I asked. He said it meant he looked only at the target of the day, whatever was in front of him for those twenty-four hours. I asked if that was good for a soldier. He supposed it was. Is there a future for me with a vagabond? A good man, but damaged? A caring man? I have no one else. An honest man? I would like to believe but . . .'

'If he's worth having after he's finished what he's doing, I'll send him to you.'

She turned her back on Dusty. He'd found her along the coast to the west of Honfleur, in the dunes towards Deauville, overlooking the nature reserve and the seals.

'It's been grand to meet you, miss. The least I can do for him is send him back.'

She had a lightweight collapsible chair and an easel, and was working in watercolour. He thought that day's picture was hideous. He wouldn't have given it house room. On his own wall in the house in Caen, there was only a big photograph, framed, of all the guys at Gough – except one – he had served with. Captain Bentinick was in the centre, sombre, but all the others looked like a winning Cup Final team, and Julia was there, at the side. Only one had skipped the picture. And he had a calendar that each month showed a different view of the town. Nothing else. Desperate's room was covered with her pictures. Dusty could have loved Hanne from those islands, and thought it would be the best reward in his life if he could bring his friend back to her. He reached the bus.

They applauded, even the historian. What did they know? They were off route, along the coast, no explanation. They had turned up at a car park, empty but for one 2CV that was decorated in narrow blue and white stripes and was mainly red. He'd assumed they were the colours of the Norwegian flag. The applause rang down the aisle of the minibus as he started the engine again.

A voice called, 'Well worth the diversion, Dusty. Why didn't you introduce us all?'

He said, through the microphone, as he reversed, 'I was speaking to her on behalf of a friend.'

Another voice, 'Greater love hath no man than this: that he chats up a pretty girl for his mate.'

They headed for the next site, which Danny Curnow always appreciated.

A guide would have a rapt audience.

They were on a high plain and the sea was barely visible over the tops of the trees. When they left the bus they would have seen huge, half-buried, fractured concrete constructions, great tortoise backs protruding: the casements for the 155mm guns that covered the beaches and could have thrown monstrously heavy shells onto the landing craft on that June morning in 1944. Close to the concrete shapes was a single C47 aircraft. The British paratroops were dropped from them – the military version of the civilian Dakota. The airborne soldiers had been briefed that the prospect of the invasion coming that morning was in jeopardy if the guns were not silenced. The German defenders numbered 160, behind coiled barbed wire and minefields, or were deep in their bunkers with twenty machine-gun emplacements.

The drop was chaotic. Most of the British came down miles from the location. Eventually Lieutenant Colonel Terence Ottway led a charge of 150 men. The wire should have been flattened by RAF bombers but their ordnance had missed the target. The attackers, in the chaos of the jump, had lost their mine detectors and the white tape that could mark the engineers' cleared paths. So, they made the corridors by hand and touch. The battle was won before the beaches were assaulted, at a fearful cost: of the German defenders, only five survived. Of the British attackers, sixty-five died, and seventy were wounded. Fifteen were unhurt when the last shot was fired. Brigadier James Hill, 3rd Para Brigade CO, had warned, as they loaded into the aircraft at Brize Norton, 'Gentlemen, do not be daunted if chaos reigns. It undoubtedly will.'

And the guide would tell the visitors what Gordon Newton, a private soldier in 9th Para, said afterwards: 'I was not afraid. My only worry was that I might look stupid, shouting out or freezing. That would have been worse than being killed. I didn't want to let myself down and my family. Nor my regiment, nor my battalion. I wanted to do my job properly.' Respect would have been total. The old men and women who made up the small tour party would marvel at what the paratroops did, and the odds against them, on that morning. The guide usually quoted a remark Colonel Ottway had made: 'We were given a job and got on with it.'

One response, 'So different from any war of today.'

It did not come particularly fast to the Five people in their inner fortress at Palace Barracks. A duty man took the report first and forwarded it to the boss on the shift. Then it went to those who needed to know. Sebastian was coming back from the coffee machine and had a cellophane-wrapped sandwich. He would soon be finishing his duty.

The boss was older school, had been regular army in the Province before taking redundancy, ditching his uniform to join the Service. He was unreconstructed and had ignored the new disciplines. He called, across the open-plan office, to Sebastian: 'Hey, Seb, an explosion in their bloody heartland. Likely to be two of them. What we called, in my Fusilier days, an own goal. With me?'

He winced at the crudity, wondered if the barbarians were now at the gate and whether, in the Service, a new medieval or even Dark Age beckoned. He reached his screen. Information, sparse, flickered on it.

The previous day, a command cable had been located and neutralised. Antelope3B8 had come through with a categorical assurance that a device could not be fired. That morning, from the barracks in Dungannon, a search party had been prepared with enough personnel to secure a perimeter, dogs for tracking and the services of Felix – the bomb disposal man who needed a stack of lives – to dismantle the damn thing. A bit bloody late. A householder living adjacent to the explosion scene reported two cadavers. It was the hope of the generation of officers to which Sebastian belonged that a police operation, allied with class intelligence and forensics, would lead to 'the dissidents' being locked up and the movement withering. Deaths in the field fuelled them. They traded in martyrs.

He remembered the man in the ditch who had possessed that awful certainty of purpose.

The female voice was clear, not raised, through the partition wall. 'Usually it's the women who come, wives or mothers. It's the same in so many areas. The women go to the doctor about their men. But if the women come, and keep regular appointments, there's a chance the men will follow.'

Two elderly women sat in the waiting room and couldn't help hearing what was said. They knew each other by sight, were from the same community, but hadn't spoken or exchanged a glance for close to twenty-five years. Sickness had brought them to the waiting room together for the first time. They had been there for fifteen minutes, had been told that their appointments were further delayed because the director was briefing a journalist from the *International Herald Tribune*. It was hoped they would not be inconvenienced.

'You have to understand the scale of the Troubles. Quite apart from the thousands of dead, another fifty thousand suffered injuries. Everyone knew somebody who was killed or maimed. A time bomb is ticking – that's what post-traumatic stress disorder is. We're supposed to have had ten years of peace but the numbers coming through our doors continue to increase. For so many, the idea of putting it behind them is not a credible option. A dream but seldom fulfilled.'

It was off a side-street. A stranger would have struggled to find it – the sign advertising its work was small and insignificant. Those who counselled there didn't seek attention. One was the widow of Mossie Nugent; the other was the widow of Jon Jo Donnelly.

'The mainland and the rest of the world have forgotten Northern Ireland. Never cared about us that much and got bored with our problems. The window of compassion for outsiders is long closed. The damage is widespread. Those who brought violence to our streets didn't consider the aftermath. The equivalent of a dump of toxic waste. So many victims.'

Mossie Nugent's name was reviled. He had taken the money,

had given the information that enabled the troops to wait in ambush and shoot dead Jon Jo Donnelly. Ten or fifteen had been at Nugent's burial, and up to a thousand had escorted Donnelly to his grave. The widows faced each other. One kneaded a handkerchief and the other fidgeted with a magazine.

'It takes great courage to come in here and sit down with us, either one to one or in a group. Very few are from the ranks of what they like to call the armed struggle, the "perpetrators". So many of the gunmen and their families won't accept that they're victims of PTS. If they admitted it, they'd also have to accept that their efforts and sacrifices were for nothing. It's a huge step for them to come through our door.'

Both women were hurt. Both went, most days, to their husband's grave. Both had seen the body with the marks of the shots, the broken skull and the burns. Their eyes met.

'The traumas are desperate. A six-year-old child clings to his father's hand as gunmen break into the house. Then they shoot the man. The child is still holding his father's hand. That was thirty years ago. The child is now an adult and can't work. He's in bits and has no life.'

An acknowledgement. An understanding that neither had worn well. An acceptance that the wives of the martyr and of the traitor had suffered.

'There are the relatives of so many who were murdered. It's hard for them to understand how a stranger could feel such hatred for their husband or brother or father, quite a different reaction from a road accident or death from disease. We avoid, like the plague, issuing pills. We have chance-to-chat groups, and we go on country walks together . . . So many have no relationships, no jobs, are in isolation, can't even fill in a simple form.'

The wife of Jon Jo Donnelly, killed by the army, said that an English girl had targeted her man. The wife of Mossie Nugent, who had been tortured before he had made a confession of guilt to the security people of the Organisation, said that the same girl had gone after her husband, compromised and deluded him.

'Draw your own conclusions. Don't quote me. It was for

nothing, and some want to return to it. Incomprehensible. Did you hear the news this morning? Anyway, I hope that was of help.'

Attracta Donnelly said that her boy, now in his middle thirties, was broken and she missed her husband as if he had gone yesterday. The pain was 'as bad today as the day he was killed'.

Siobhan Nugent said that the damage had been done by the English woman, the recruiter who had handled her husband and forced money on him. 'The English girl killed my husband and yours. God burn them, the handlers.'

The journalist was American by his dress: he wore a bow-tie, with polka-dots, a heavy grey herringbone jacket and strong shoes. A big shoulder bag was slung at his hip. He thanked the counsellor for her time, and seemed not to notice the two women who sat on the hard chairs in the waiting area. He might have thought them irrelevant to the story he would write about the time-bomb. The counsellor carried out a tray of dirty cups and uneaten biscuits.

Jon Jo's widow said, 'The informers – touts – destroyed the boys. They made the killings happen. And how do the handlers live with it on their consciences?'

Mossie's widow said, 'They put claws into a man, never let go of him, exploit and manipulate. No one ever called by after his death. Pick a man up and drop him as if he's nothing – except that he's dropped into his grave. I might see you.'

The counsellor, a neat, busy woman, came back and gestured for Attracta Donnelly to follow her. Attracta stood, allowed a thin smile, and might have surprised herself. Jon Jo's widow said, 'I could call by.'

He'd done a turn of the square and was back at the top by the King's statue, near to the place where the boy had burned himself to death. Few knew him. Not Lisette and Christine at the house in Caen, not Hanne in her studio.

It might have been that Matthew Bentinick did not, quite, know Danny Curnow. It was possible that Dusty Miller did. He went past the shops that sold visitors' tat, the coffee places, a bookshop, and turned back into the street where the hotel was. His own was behind him, on the far side of the square. He reflected that Dusty Miller, alone, might have read him well enough to know whether anger was genuine or an assumed tool. Dusty Miller would have been behind him, with the H&K across his chest, a live one in the breach, when Danny had broken all of the rules laid down in the Green Book or the Red Book – whatever colour the book was that day – and punched Aaron Hegarty. Hegarty, unemployed and unemployable, was on the bread-and-water rations of a hundred pounds in used notes each month. He did a bit of message-carrying, was useful for noting car registrations, who came to which house on the estate on the north side of Armagh and up beyond the Gaelic ground – and Hegarty's conceit had gone too high. A problem with all of them: they thought they were invaluable. He had wanted a hundred a week, had stood defiant and been whacked. Hegarty had thought Danny's anger real enough and had believed he might face 'nutting'. He had crumpled.

Dusty had told Danny Curnow afterwards that it had been a good act – or had it been an act? The result: Aaron Hegarty had feared his handler more than he had feared the Organisation he betrayed, and his money had stayed at a hundred a month. It had gone into the account for a further eleven months, but had been cut the week of his funeral. A month later the widow had received a letter from a bank in the north of England, telling her that they'd been notified of her husband's passing, that there was an account with £2,500 in it and she was listed as a beneficiary. What had she done? She had cleaned out the account and sent the money to the Shinners' office in Cookstown. When Danny Curnow had hit her husband, the anger had seemed authentic.

It had been about fear, not about friendship. He took a lift and aimed to prove it.

11

He knocked on the door. There was a pause. Then he heard shuffling inside and the door opened. Danny Curnow faced the agent.

'I'm Danny.'

'Are you.'

'I run the show.'

'Do you.'

'She answers to me.'

'Does she.'

He went in, used an elbow to push the door shut. An untidy room, bed not made, a dirty shirt and discarded socks on the floor. An ordinary looking man. Danny Curnow knew about the meeting on the hill above Dungannon, by Shane Bearnagh's Seat. Ordinary enough, but with guts.

'I've a problem.'

'Have you.'

'And you're going to solve it, Ralph.'

'Am I.'

Danny felt as though he carried the plague. If he 'touched' Ralph Exton he would pass on the virus. He had touched men, and a woman, and they now lay in graves. Not in the ornate plots reserved for the paramilitaries, the black marble with the inscriptions in gold leaf. The ones allocated to them were unlikely to have a backdrop of a scenic lough or a mountainside, more likely had a view of the graveyard's compost heap. He had walked away into the night. One more pace forward, now, across a worn hotel carpet, and he would 'touch' Exton. He had run from it, had cleansed himself. For nothing. He had returned.

'You will. Yes.'

There had been the cringing ones, who had needed to get down on their knees and snivel about the loneliness, the risks; there were those who did it like a business transaction, expected to pocket or bank the funds, give the report and fade into the night. Last, there were the cocky little beggars, who were doing 'Vagabond' a favour. They reckoned to walk tall, grin and be what Dusty called 'piss-takers'. Ralph Exton was in the category of . . . He had slipped into the old routines effortlessly.

Danny Curnow slapped him – he did it with a smile: a sharp slap across the cheek and chin, hard enough to make his palm tingle and redden the skin. The man rocked. Surprise flared on his face. Some thought the system depended on their contribution, that they deserved red-carpet treatment, that they were continually owed compliments. In the case of Ralph Exton, that was likely to be true. Danny saw the shock spread.

He slapped him again. It was about authority. Danny would have said, in the old-speak of a former life, that it was necessary to create authority. The man was not a friend. He was not grateful to Exton. The man's heroics and the odds stacked against him were unimportant. The agent was the key. He sought to dominate.

A third slap. He had brought the plague with him. Why had he come back and why had he neutralised all the years of convalescing from the pain? He was a lemming, speeding towards the cliff edge. He re-created the hotel room from memories of the Portakabin at Gough, the dark car parks behind pubs and woodland walks where no tourists came. They had all cowered when he struck them. He had done it with his fists and his tongue and he reckoned he could make an agent pliable again. He was unsure, at that moment, whether Exton needed a fourth slap, a kick or a punch – and he didn't have Dusty Miller behind him with an H&K hung across his chest and a Glock at his waist.

'If you think you can play games with us, you are so, so, mistaken.'

The curtains were back. Sunlight spilled into the room.

'Fucking us about, chummy, holding back on your Russian friend, that's just not acceptable.'

Ralph Exton's head was in front of the light. He had missed the trick of reading the face.

'Good on the Irish end and crap on the—'

It hadn't happened before. Not just a couple of flailed blows but the anger of a street-fighter's attack.

The weight of Ralph Exton hit Danny Curnow. The sun had been in his face and he hadn't seen the response welling. A man possessed. He went down.

What would Dusty have done? Dusty would have powered forward, the shoulder stock of the H&K raised. He would have brought it down – required force – on the back of Ralph Exton's head. He would have flattened him. Then he would have levered Danny up, with that world-weary look on his face: 'What would you do without me to pick up the pieces, Desperate?' Dusty wasn't there.

The fingers were rearing towards his eyes. The weight was on him. Surprise first, then control, last the response. Unequal. He had the fingers out of his face, and the weight off him. He pitched Ralph Exton, the star agent, used to coddling, onto his stomach. Danny had a knee in the small of the agent's back, and he had the fingers and one arm against his knee, twisted round. He turned the fingers some more, and the cry was of agony.

Submission.

'You listening to me?'

'Yes.'

'You frightened of them?' Danny asked it lightly: as if real and total fear was everyday stuff.

'Do you know anything?'

'Telling you what I know.'

He kept the pain constant. Felt no pride in it.

Danny told it like he thought it was. 'I reckon it's about loyalties. You don't have any to me. Why would you? A nice life, pulling in the cigarette money, but the idyll ends when you get called into a police station. You're trapped, coerced, compromised. You work for the Irish and they're heavy with threat and could put a drill bit through your kneecap. You have your friend and you can see that the mistake you made was in involving him. Would he get angry if crossed? A mobster. A broker in arms deals. How angry? Who can inflict the pain? Who has the longest arm? I can, Ralph, and I have.'

He twisted the fingers. The unarmed-combat people had taught it. They were weathered old birds: tracksuit bottoms, white vests, stubble on their chins, hair cropped tight. They smelt of cigarettes, and knew about pain, the creation of fear. The trend, as he had seen on the local TV talk shows in Bagram interrogation centre outside Kabul and at Guantánamo, was to say that pain did not produce reliable results. Hurting people let them cough up any shit to halt the pain. They'd say *anything*. Not the way Danny Curnow knew it. Alongside the unarmed-combat instructors, there had been the guys who did the heavy interrogations at Castlereagh and Gough. Water, sleep deprivation or punches to the stomach where the soft flesh doesn't bruise. They'd talked. Not too much weight given to human rights or any Amnesty report. Good stuff spilled out. It was all about fear. His mouth was close to the agent's ear. He whispered, 'I am certainty. My arm is long and the pain I can inflict is guaranteed. No escape from it. You hear me?' The barest movement – enough to bring on the agony. 'Glad of that. The arrangements?' He loosed the hold. The agent gasped. Then Danny heard the hissed schedule for Ralph Exton's movements, when the pick-up would be and where he would be taken. Pretty much what he needed. He thought he could justify what he had done. Into the ear, 'I'll tell you what I'm not. I am not your good friend.'

He let it sink in.

'I am your last, best – and only – hope. Last hope, best hope, only hope.'

The door closed. Ralph lay on the floor.

He did not know where Gaby was. He thought he deserved a bit of her but was too drained to crawl to the bedside table where the telephone was. He had attempted to juggle loyalties and failed.

It was early afternoon. He rolled onto his back and tried to flex his hand, then massaged it until the feeling returned.

He believed. The long arm existed for the Irish on the mountain and for his friend, whose driver was due that evening. He did not doubt that the man who had inflicted pure pain on him had a long arm. The words sang in his ears: *last hope, best hope, only hope*. He crossed the floor, pushed himself up, took the phone. God, he needed comfort. Where to find it? He dialled for an outside line, fed in the international code and the digits.

She didn't answer. Neither did his daughter. A man answered. He recognised the voice.

'Hello . . . Yes? Hello.'

His own voice was stifled.

He heard, 'Don't know who it is.'

He imagined his wife reaching across the bed. An arm would have stroked a path across the dentist's chest – a bare arm – and the fingers would have cancelled the call. The whine rang in his ear. Where else to look? Only one place.

He vomited. Danny Curnow hadn't trusted himself to get from Exton's hotel on Stepanska to his own. He wouldn't have made it that far, then up the stairs, along a corridor and into his room.

Sick as a dog, a parrot or a squaddie first night on leave.

He heaved. By keeping his head low he minimised the mess. But the squaddie, the parrot or the dog did not throw up because of acute shame. He did.

He flushed it three times to leave it acceptable. He swilled out his mouth, but couldn't touch the shame.

He came out of the hotel door onto the street and hardly saw where he was going. He would have cannoned into her if she hadn't pulled aside.

'Where are you going? Where have you been?'

He looked into the face of Gaby Davies. A good-looking kid. Didn't wear any rings. He walked past her. Just at that moment he had no wish to mouth excuses, shed half-truths and fight his corner. His back was to her.

She called after him, 'What the hell have you done?'

He hurried, and the bile was climbing again in his throat. The shame outweighed the pride that he had extracted more of the necessary information, going hard, than she had by going soft. He texted Matthew Bentinick. The shame was for his self-inflicted wound. Of course it was dirty – whoever said it wouldn't be?

The priest watched from the lane, forbidden to enter the field. The two bodies were covered with tarpaulins. Alongside him, also waiting to be called forward, was the team from the undertaker in Dungannon. They had the body-bags and the metal boxes that would be used to remove the corpses. The priest had protested to the senior uniformed officer at the long delay during which the bodies were left in the field, but he was stonewalled. He was told that there were procedures to be followed and he must be patient. The rain was heavy and the cloud base low. It was unlikely to clear. The priest would have seen that a fingertip search had been made up the line of the hedge, that a tracker dog – an attractive black cocker spaniel – had gone back and forth across the field, and that a number of the search team were in the trees some hundred yards from the tarpaulins. The priest would have seen the parents of Eamonn O'Kane stand by their front door, sheltered from the elements by a golf umbrella: he had not received an invitation to the celebration of the previous evening but knew of it, knew many who had been there, knew their son and of his work. It was likely that when the bodies were dignified with names he would know those who had died in the pursuit of the armed struggle. He never used the word 'murder': it was inappropriate, and unwelcome to many of his parishioners. He could hear the cold remarks made by the police officers, Protestants, of course.

What he did not know was that the search teams had carefully retrieved two parts of the command cable, either side of the snip that had saved the life of Eamonn O'Kane. There were bomb-disposal troops on the scene, matter-of-fact and casual in their work, and they had filled small plastic sachets with metal scraps. He was familiar with the prosecution of the war. He had worked as a junior on the mountain, had transferred to west Belfast, then spent four years at a college in Rome for the Irish, on via dei Santi

Quattro. Afterwards he had returned to the mountain and had thought himself blessed. But a thread had continued. Men killed, men died. The aims had not altered. What had changed was that expertise had lessened. He knew well enough what would happen higher up the slopes of the mountain in the villages that had small estates of pinched family homes. For two wives or mothers this would be a time of growing anxiety, of spreading anguish.

He had heard the explosion. His knee had been painful so he had been up in the early morning, searching for a paracetamol, and he had heard it, faint, distant, had known the sound. In two homes there would be undisturbed beds. Two wives or mothers would be waiting. He did not know how much longer he would be kept behind the cordon. He could not tell the families on the mountain that it was for nothing: it was not his remit to lecture them. He also knew, from his experience, that when the priest was called out and ministering was needed, the work of an informer was close behind, like a hideous shadow. Here, as before, he sensed that evil in the dank air, and the presence of those who had fashioned it.

It was a hard landing. The aircraft shuddered on the second impact but Matthew Bentinick seemed immune to the white-knuckle mood around him. Others grasped armrests and the sides of the seats in front. Arms folded, eyes almost closed, he rode the bounce, flotsam on a wave. Then folded his newspaper and slipped it into the rack in front. He satisfied himself that his tie knot was straight, that his handkerchief was displayed the correct amount in his breast pocket and that his waistcoat was buttoned. He patted his hair to flatten strays. He did not join the scramble to be off the aircraft. He unbuckled his seatbelt when the cabin was nearly empty, retrieved his bag from the hatch above him, thanked the stewards and set off along the corridors.

He cleared the formalities. He switched on his phone. Oscar, from the driver's pool, was meeting him. They were away quickly. He read the text from Vagabond.

An afterthought from Oscar – were they heading for Thames

House? No, they were going home. Oscar often took Matthew Bentinick back to the suburbs late at night, knew the way, the street and the house. Sometimes Bentinick talked to him and sometimes he didn't. Not that day. He would go to the Five building early the next morning, Thursday, but would have to be away again in the early afternoon. Then . . . Well, by the weekend a small part of it would be over, God willing.

Selfish? Some might have thought so. He called Jocelyn, said where he was, what he was doing, and relayed the text message. Then he called Rosie and told his wife when he'd be home.

He sat back in his seat, closed his eyes and reflected that it had been a good decision to leave Vagabond to see the matter through. He had always placed his trust in the man, had cursed and loved him, had worked him to the bone and was responsible for him . . . The car had an uncongested road and made good speed. It was difficult, coming home.

Jocelyn beavered at the growing file. In the building, and inside the loop, only the director general had oversight of her work. In normal investigations there would have been a line manager, a head of section and an assistant director. They were bypassed. Jocelyn, now nearly forty-four, could have been described as 'plain': not ugly, not unattractive, but plain. In her fiefdom, she passed the hours of the day, and often of half the night, alone. Few of the men with similar rooms in the corridor, or in the open-plan area to the left on that floor, came to chat with her in the hope of future favours. She wore flat shoes, a shapeless long skirt that hid most of her shins, and a large sweater, likely to have come from a charity shop. She had no lover. Any affection she was able to give went to the cat that lived a mostly lonely life in her flat, with a litter tray, ample food and a radio station for company.

The file grew. She knew the story and there were times when she had wept, with her cat for company, at the thought of it. Few who knew her in Thames House would have thought her capable of tears, probably regarded her as 'a tough old bat'. She hadn't expected Matthew Bentinick back in his office that afternoon, and sensed that the pace of matters was brisk, that a conclusion beckoned.

'Because I need to.'

'Might be a good enough reason.'

'Because I want to,' he said.

'Might not argue with that.'

She pushed him away from her. Gaby Davies had been sitting in her room. The bed was made, the bathroom cleaned and the carpet hoovered. The biscuits and coffee sachets had been replaced. An antiseptic space. He wasn't much taller than her but was thicker in the stomach, and he hadn't shaved properly. She left Ralph Exton, went to the door and took the Do Not Disturb sign off the handle. She opened the door, hooked it on, then closed the door.

He'd come to her room and made the first move. He had stood in front of her and stretched out his arms. She'd allowed them to loop round her back. She could then have eased herself away gently so that his feelings were not bruised, and could have turned her face so that his kiss missed her lips and landed on her cheek or near her ear. She hadn't.

He'd said, *Because I need to*, and she couldn't have disputed that. Normally, with her Joe, she found irreverence, a cocky cheek, and a refusal to confront calamity. She had not gainsaid him because there was weariness in his face and pain in his eyes. Sorry for him? Almost. And she might have been sorry for herself. Gaby knew about Fliss Exton and a dentist. She reckoned his home was lonely, dark and cold. She knew about a house in Pimlico that was stuffed with women from the Service – high-fliers and back-sliders cheek by jowl. Some brought their guys back on Saturday nights and others brought girlfriends. Both would appear at the bathroom door, and for what seemed a bloody eternity no one had shared her bed.

He broke away, winked, then crouched by her minibar and took out the two little bottles of fizzy stuff. The two corks were allowed to cannon into the ceiling, leaving dents. He slipped a paper napkin over his arm, playing the waiter, and passed her a bottle. She swigged, and a wave of shyness swept over her.

'Any other service, ma'am, I can perform for you? Don't hesitate to ask. I'd be honoured to fulfil it.'

Her arms were round his neck. She seemed to hear the sound of that drill. Her life had started to lose purpose . . . And no one would know. They kissed. She'd have thought that with intimacy Ralph Exton might be a meld of clumsiness and shyness: instead she sensed awe and disbelief that she had chosen him. Her grip tightened. Too bloody right she had chosen him.

His lips broke from hers. 'You up for this, Gaby?'

'Just let's get on with it.'

'Have you got . . . ?' Which meant he hadn't.

'I have – always the optimist.'

She pulled away, went to the bathroom and rooted in her sponge bag. Among the junk she found the packets that had come, ages before, from the toilets at the Jugged Hare. She'd been there with a Six man. He'd seemed worth the effort but had gone home to his fiancée. Win some, lose some. She took out two and went back.

He tried to undress her and she tried to get the clothes off him. More important, Gaby Davies, top-level graduate entry and supposed star in the making, was breaking a rule that was considered sacrosanct, inviolable. The girls around her in the open-plan bit would have said, 'Christ, Gabs, what got into you? How could you be so bloody daft?' The men in her section, or down the corridor from the door to the coffee machine, would have said, 'Big mistake, Gaby. Didn't you think first?' Clothes came off, littering the floor, and his face – when it was not buried in her slight cleavage – showed wonderment. On any floor of Thames House, at any level of the Service, they would have gathered in a unanimous howl of disapproval. They were on the bed. She broke one open, put it on him and was underneath.

If it were known that she had seduced a Joe, a compromised source, recruited instead of going to gaol for aiding and abetting the fundraising of a terrorist conspiracy, she would have gone out of the building like a dead rat from an upper window. Sympathy?

Forget it. Understanding? No chance. She would be the source of mockery and sniggering for a generation.

First time wasn't special. Second time was. Gaby thought she had brought the spark back to his eyes, the diamond brightness.

She was across him. 'You all right?'

'Never better.'

'It was good?'

'You know it was.'

She did. It was unprofessional, awful in the scale of misdemeanours. The lectures at the training sessions had been about compromise. Women such as herself, targeted by the old East German secret police, the modern Russians or Chinese, would find that good-looking men picked them up at a bus stop or in a supermarket, would bed them, then ask for files. Could it happen? She was in his arms, and his breathing calmed. Gaby Davies could not have said which of them had needed it most. She slipped off the bed. He wasn't much to shout about, but he was what she had. She didn't know what consequences would follow.

She picked up the one on thc floor and he gave her the other. She went into the bathroom. 'I don't think we yell about that from the rooftops, Ralph.'

He called after her, 'I have to ask you, Gaby. After this, do I come into the warm? Do you all look after me? Is it a good deal?'

The toilet flushed. 'Not really the time, Ralph. But we always look after people.'

'I get bloody frightened.'

'You're doing so well. You're brilliant. Like I said, we look after people.'

She came back from the bathroom and scooped up her clothes, then his. She chucked Ralph's at him and he wriggled upright on the bed.

'And the deal? Gone to ground. New life and funding for it?'

'We pay what's appropriate. We always do.'

Why now? Hell of a moment. Bizarre to pick it. There had been, a half-minute before, a wonderful calm on his face. A mood had been fractured. She crouched over him and kissed his mouth. 'We look after those who help us. They're not disposable. We have a duty of care and take it seriously. What's the rest of your day?'

He took the clothes off the crumpled coverlet and began to dress. 'Not too sure,' he said. 'Sit by the phone and wait for the call.'

He left her. She didn't know what to say to herself. She could feel the weight of him. Her chin jutted – a moment of defiance – and she saw her face in the mirror. She finished her bottle, then the dregs of his, and tossed them into the bin. She wondered where a degree of love ended and a basketload of idiocy began. Time could not be rolled back.

It was a pleasant enough avenue. A bin lorry, coming towards them, blocked most of it. Matthew Bentinick had Oscar drop him outside 151 and he'd walk to 77, his home.

The houses were a mixture of three-bedroom, semi-detached, and four-bedroom, minimally detached. All had garages. Trees grew on the grass verge at either side between the pavement and the road. In the spring they were a joy of cherry blossom, but as autumn came they had the tiredness of the season, and the leaves were scattering. There were small front gardens, all tended because it was that sort of community. The houses had brick façades on the ground floor, then pebbledash for upstairs. At the back, out of sight of the pavement, the rear gardens were around 120 feet long. Rosie Bentinick had chosen it when he had come back from Ireland and left the army. Both had swallowed hard and begrudged the cost of property fifteen years ago, but it had seemed a sensible house in a sensible street and right for a teenage daughter.

He knew all the other residents by sight, name and work. Matthew Bentinick was the only one in the avenue who wore a three-piece suit, winter and summer, and carried a furled black umbrella. No neighbour knew anything about him, and Rosie could steer away conversation when he was mentioned. There was the wife of an advertising man, bringing a child home from school, and he nodded to her politely.

It was raining but not hard enough for him to put up the umbrella. His home was where the burden was.

And his home was where he had an appearance of normality, might have seemed just another Whitehall Warrior, eccentric and outdated, doing something in Environment or Pensions or the Treasury. He could reflect, on the avenue, that those men and women who lived, worked, existed in the shadows were likely to be as conventional as the society they served. But their lives were of critical importance in keeping bombs from the streets and handguns from the front doors of the prominent. They were not thugs who inhabited the netherworld, were not the shaven heads that populated Millwall's football ground, the Den. Good men and women did the work and were crippled by it. Not many cared. Not many were able to care because they were not privy to the work done in the darkness at a price. It incubated stress. It gnawed at their hearts and could destroy them, as it had his Vagabond.

He was at his door. He opened it. She would have heard the key turn. 'Hello, Rosie. Had a good day? Flight was on time.'

He could be torn apart, as so many were, but would refuse to show it. He faced the stairs. How had his trip gone? She wouldn't expect a vestige of detail. Up the stairs lay the purpose of his life and Rosie's.

'It went well. I think we're on the road to where we want to be.'

The journey had been through German territory, then into Austria at the control point on the Passau to Linz road, and from Linz north and a return to Czech territory at Stiegersdorf. On long journeys, Timofey Simonov always sat in the back seat. He let Denisov drive and be alone in the front. So, using Route 157, they had reached Český Krumlov. It had been a simple procedure. No Czech police surveillance team could cross, if no prior arrangement existed, onto German territory. No German police tail cars could follow a vehicle into Austria, unless clearance had been given. No Austrian police units could travel over the border and into the Czech Republic without consultation and the bureaucratic niceties. Caution flowed in the bloodstream of both men, ever-present: they had no reason to believe they were tailed at that time but caution was a necessary part of their mutual makeup.

It was almost all they shared. The car park they used at their destination was wide and long, designed to cope with the massive influx of visitors who came daily to the heritage site in the tourist season, which was over.

Denisov had parked the Mercedes at an extremity where the weeds grew. They had waited and the van had arrived.

It was driven by a man Timofey knew from long ago, a trader. The back had been opened, and Timofey – as his importance decreed – was given a helping hand by the driver, from Azerbaijan and of total integrity in such matters, and Denisov. It had been a formality, but a part of the choreographed game. Weapons were always inspected prior to purchase. Not that Timofey Simonov or Nikolai Denisov, presently engaged in cash-laundering, the protection of a narcotics market, state-sponsored assassination and whatever made good money, understood the workings of battlefield firearms. But they had to show due diligence. One AK47 rifle seemed to Timofey pretty much the same as the next. One RPG-7 launcher was similar to another, but he couldn't understand how the big machine-gun – the DShKM 12.7mm – would be used in that theatre. The Dragunov SVD 7.62mm sniper weapon seemed lightweight, decent and in fair condition – the protective oiled paper was still tight on it. The ammunition had not rusted. There were two boxes and he could barely move either of them. Squashed into each was a reported twenty-five kilos of military explosive, with a recent date stamp. The Azerbaijani talked him through each collection: two hundred grenades, RG-42 and high explosive, also of the 4.82mm mortar tubes and ten rounds for each, and the maximum listed range was three kilometres. The Azerbaijani lived in the neighbouring state of Slovakia, and had dealt first with Timofey some fifteen years before when surplus stock had clogged a satiated market. They trusted each other. Hands were shaken, a deal was concluded. Timofey had crawled out of the back of the van and a delivery schedule was agreed. The van had driven away.

They had gone for lunch.

Guides said it was the most attractive small town in the Czech

Republic. He liked it. The childhood of Timofey Simonov, in quarters that were little more than log cabins, with smoking wood stoves and misted windows in winter, the mosquito swarms in summer, and the buildings on the far side of the wire that had lasted far beyond the intention of their designers, had learned no perspective of history. He had not known in his youth about fine buildings designed by architects of quality, or about the rugged castles placed on clifftops above winding rivers. Now he could have bought a good part of the town, paid for it and not noticed it. He preferred to visit.

Nothing about Timofey Simonov was ostentatious. He was at the old inn on the square and it was warm enough to take an outside table.

There was a pretence that the one-time brigadier bought the one-time captain's lunch. The cash would come from Denisov's wallet, with a tip that was acceptable yet not flamboyant, but it was drawn from a bank in Karlovy Vary that dealt with accounts held in the name of Timofey Simonov. It was a ritual, and when the meal was finished he would thank the older man, dead pan, for his hospitality.

He had a glass of wine, and his 'host' had sparkling water. Timofey had asked, 'You still oppose it?'

'I see no need for it.'

They had eaten pork and now cheese. 'You remember how I was treated by the British officers? Like I was shit – like we were all shit.'

'I remember. I remember also that it is not wise to shit in your own yard. Or to tease authorities whom we expect to leave us alone.'

Coffee would be brought, and the view for Timofey was of the castle high above: formidable. He was comfortable, close to home, and he felt the power in his body. 'It's for a friend.'

'At home, it isn't advisable to mix friendship with risk – ever.'

'He was a friend when we needed a friend.' The waiter refreshed the cheese platter. He added, 'I think it's still raining in England.'

* * *

The afternoon wore on. Water dripped on the marksman's clothing and the dip where the tree's roots had been was filled with stagnant water that did not drain. The lights were on in the house. No one, he was sure, would come out in that rain at dusk for a walk or a smoke or to gaze at the skies. He cursed. He folded the weapon, bagged it and crawled up the last part of the slope. He paused by the path, looked around and saw no walkers, no kids, no dogs. The rain pattered on him. He walked back to the car. He had survived the siege of Sarajevo but this place unnerved him. He would sleep in his car, had nowhere else. If he failed, he would not work again. He would be back in the morning, and would hope that the weather had changed.

They walked to the car, his brigadier following him. He walked first and his protection was close behind, wearing a shoulder holster with a Makarov PM, semi-automatic.

At the collapse of the regime, the man had been a psychological wreck. They had gone back together to Moscow. He had thought niches would open. The brigadier had a wife to support and small children – she was fat with thick ankles, but he was devoted to her. Initially good times had been within reach – but they had been too long in Milovice, too many months away from the power struggles. They were too distanced from the new wave of gangsters and the money men who profited from the state-utility rip-offs, and they did not comprehend the extreme violence required to rule a sector. The new cars were sold off at knock-down rates. The twin apartments in a smart suburb, the Frunzenskaya quarter close to the Gorky Park, were given up. The money had gone. Doors were slammed in his face and the brigadier's. It had been Timofey Simonov's idea that they should decamp to Amsterdam. The wife and children were left behind, crammed into her parents' three-room apartment. They took a bus to Amsterdam and were beaten up because it seemed they were trying to muscle in on the cannabis trade. They were beaten again for looking at tarts by a pimp impatient with gawkers. They spent two nights on the streets and took a good kicking from a pair of police. The last coins in his pocket:

enough for one beer to share. Then it would be in God's hands as to what they did in the morning.

The arrival of the Englishman, confident and warm. Maybe the little man had done a good deal. He offered them a drink each.

They spoke a little English because they were GRU-trained and had taken language classes. What did the benefactor do? 'A bit of this and a bit of that,' with a smile and a shrug. 'Sometimes not too much of this and not enough of that, but right now it's good.'

More drinks.

Timofey Simonov had recognised something in the man. No posture, no play-act, no lies. He had whispered to Denisov, 'He's honest, I guarantee.' Another drink was ordered. They explained their circumstances. They had no bed that night. They had no clean clothing and hadn't found a tap where they could wash their underwear, socks and shirts.

'What might you be able to do?'

The told him about backing fuel tankers up to the base perimeter fence, the queue of Czechs with plastic containers, and the office furniture. He had said, 'We can trade, but we need a start. We don't know how to begin.'

After the man had produced a wad of notes from his hip pocket and paid the bill for the drinks, he had bought sandwiches and pies from a stand. They had wolfed them and got into his hire car. It had been swerving across the road but the chance of not meeting an oncoming police vehicle had seemed minimal. They were drunk and had had to stop twice beside a dual carriageway to pee. The arrival at the airfield. An introduction. They were brought to a little work ghetto of Russians. Nods and understanding when they had given their ranks in the GRU. An opportunity.

First thing, that night, they had showered, and every stitch of clothing they had possessed had gone into a washing-machine.

All because of Ralph Exton. The start of a new life. Timofey Simonov was not one to forget. They reached the car. He would see Ralph Exton that night, his truest friend. He would hug him, his truest and best friend, who seemed to have fallen on hard times, needed help and was trying to push through a pitiful deal. It was for his friend.

Ralph Exton felt good. He'd had a romp with a woman and thought he'd said the right things. His back ached but he felt fine. He posed the question in his mind, repeated it, tried to get the right tone – desperate or casual, matter-of-fact or at crisis point. He didn't know how Timofey Simonov would react to it: theirs was an old relationship based on a helping hand of long ago, and times had changed. One thing was appropriate for a business deal, another for a favour.

He could dream. That, at least, was free.

He had an understanding with Gabrielle Davies that he required 'space'. She shouldn't have them trailing round after him. Different from when he had been on the mountain and the fog had closed in: there had been no close-quarters back-up. He didn't think she would put a tail on him.

Ralph Exton went out of his hotel. A coffee in the Costa on Wenceslas Square. Across to the big basement bookshop opposite and a browse before he left from the back exit. A walk past the building that was now the Ministry of Trade and Industry, but bore a plaque that denounced it as the former home of the Gestapo in the city. He passed a money-exchange booth, a Toni & Guy hairdressing salon and a Vodaphone outlet. There was a little park nearer to the railway station, with indestructible bunkers among the lawns and bushes. He sat there and waited.

He had lied. Her question: what would he do for the rest of the day? His response: *Not too sure. Sit by the phone and wait for the call.* He would be picked up from where he sat. A small victory because the outline of his itinerary was with the man. Only an outline. He owed them nothing because she had opened her legs. He owed himself survival. Endlessly, he repeated the question in his mind. He was satisfied, and thought his precautions satisfactory.

Unprofessional.

Had Karol Pilar assessed his target's performance it would have failed. He watched the man on the bench – he had taken a paperback book from a pocket and was reading.

His target's efforts to observe possible foot or vehicle surveillance had been poor. Pilar was thirty metres away, sitting on a graffiti-daubed wall. A hand rested on his shoulder. Karol Pilar did not take his eyes off his target. A set of car keys landed in his jacket pocket. 'Where is it?' he asked, in English.

'Just in the slip road. Right behind you.'

'He has a book and has checked his watch twice.'

'He's slippery as an eel. The girl bought the line he peddled – that he doesn't know about his pick-up. He told me he was getting a ride down but not from where or when, which says he lies. You alright?'

'Of course. Be in the car.'

The hand slid off his shoulder. He knew him as Vagabond and thought him hard. He didn't know if his 'soul' had left him. His girlfriend, Jana, said the soul was important, that she couldn't live with a man and love him if he had lost it. It was almost impossible to do his job and cling to it. That weekend they would go to her mother, with the cake she was making. Then he would, however briefly, have broken free. The cake was a symbol: he was not totally owned by the job but thought that Danny Curnow was.

He watched. The afternoon faded and the crowds thickened as they surged towards the railway station. He thought he was risking much. If the mission, as described to him by Mr Bentinick, ended as planned, then the anger he would have aroused in the offices of Bartolomejska and in the Convikt, the Capone and the Sherlock would be hard to deflect. A man came close and stood near to the target, who got to his feet.

Malachy Riordan gazed down at him. Frankie was behind him, and he'd made that little gesture with his fingers that told her to stay back.

He was used to it. Men cringed when he spoke to them, if they knew him. They would avoid his eye and look to the side. At the bungalow on the mountain the gaze had been steady. The drill had moaned in his ear and the man had held his nerve. He had seemed to have the balls, guts, 'face' that Brennie Murphy responded to. And Malachy? He had thought Ralph Exton a chancer. But the man had shown no fear. Himself? He was unsettled.

Malachy had the girl with him. A smart tart. Near to Shanmaghry, to the east, was the Dungannon to Pomeroy road, which crossed the Gortavoy Bridge, an old stone one. Under the bridge there was a clear river pool, where kids had caught trout. He would have liked to take the smart tart, in her city clothes and makeup, to the water there and have her scrub her face. His Bridie didn't use makeup. The smart tart wore scent and gazed too often into his face. He trusted neither of them and needed both. He had no faith in the girl, or in the man who had insinuated himself into the Organisation and carried the commendation of men and women senior to himself . . . But they needed the weapons. Without them they were dead and lost. A big man in intelligence in London had made a public speech, and it was reported on the television because he had listed the priorities for protecting Britain: cyberattack at the top, and Al Qaeda in some shite desert next, then home-bred jihadists, animal-rights people – and finally the armed struggle in Ireland. To be so dismissed had fuelled his anger. Without increased firepower, nothing would change.

She looked at him too often.

He didn't know the Malone road and had never been inside the campus of Queen's University. There were girls in Coalisland, Cookstown and Dungannon, from the housing estates, who hung round the boys who might get invited in as volunteers: some could be used for 'dicking'. Some might get pregnant and fetch a weapon in a pram under a swaddled baby. The girl seemed to think herself his equal. She would do the logistics of the journey and leave the weapons checks to him. He'd scrub her face and get the paint off it.

Him on the bench . . . Something about him he couldn't pin down. There was always a bullock in a field that couldn't easily be put in the wagon for the trip to the abattoir. Something in the eyes of the beast would tell him which it was, but only when the wagon was backed up to the farm gate and it was late for its slot.

He was told what would happen. The girl had come closer to him, as if she were a part of him.

Danny Curnow sat in the car's passenger seat. On the windscreen he could see a slip of official paper that the Czech had said would see off any traffic police complaining about illegitimate parking.

It was Wednesday evening and he was at the heart of middle Europe, with a decent view of the man and the girl. An age had passed since Monday morning, just hours before, when he had lain in that scrape and watched the man with his family. Now he read him: ill-at-ease without the certainties of home.

Dusty was by the bus. It seemed half a lifetime ago that he had driven to the parking area above the dunes and found her. He might have spoken out of turn, or not. Gloom trapped him, and he remembered the woman who had walked into the barracks at Keady, near the border, asked to see an intelligence officer and given her name. Desperate and his boy, Dusty, had scrambled to get down there and weave the web round her. Lovely woman, great-looking and with a sense of humour. Why her man had cheated on her was beyond them. ' "Hell hath no fury," ' Mr Bentinick had said.
They were at Pegasus Bridge.

The bridge was grey-painted, small and insignificant, yet each of the visitors, on every tour that stopped at Pegasus, knew of its significance in the battle for the beaches. The guide helped as best he could, but most of the men and women wanted to walk beside the river, in the shadow of the bridge, and imagine how it would have been when the gliders navigated their free-fall to the landing sites. They had come through horrendous bursting flak barrages, and stories are told of airborne officers cocking their revolvers, standing behind the pilots and demanding that they go through the spraying shrapnel and on to the targets. Some of the gliders, ugly beasts, were so expertly put down that

British soldiers were on the ground and sprinting across the bridge before the defences had been alerted.

The clients also loved to hear of Piper Millen leading Lord Lovat to the bridge, with commandos who had come ashore that dawn and legged it through farmland to relieve the paratroops. Lord Lovat had apologised for arriving a few minutes late. Within a hundred yards of the end of the bridge they would see a tank, German gun emplacements and a small field where two gliders had landed. Awful casualties in 6th Airborne: four thousand men killed, wounded and missing. The gliders were sixty-five feet long and eighty-five feet from wing tip to wing tip; many of the boys squashed into them would not have been out of their teens. The visitors would have seen one across the road and marvelled . . . Then they would have gone to the Pegasus café, drunk coffee and bought cheap souvenirs or postcards.

The girl was gone, as was Malachy Riordan, whose father Danny Curnow had killed. The darkness had thickened. The road beyond the park was filled with crawling traffic. It was a background that reeked of ordinariness.

Twice policemen had come and smacked a closed fist on the window. He had pointed to the authorisation and had been left alone. He had never believed any informant he had run. He had acted on what he was told. Sometimes lives had been saved; at other times they had been lost. But he never believed what they said to him. He could barely see the Czech detective, but sometimes a cigarette was lit and the man on the bench was a faint outline. When it happened, it would be fast – always was.

12

He peered into a dappled sea of lights for one slowing with a winking indicator. The traffic was solid. Danny Curnow could no longer see the Czech, and it might have been twenty minutes since a cigarette had been lit. His view of the target was vague.

There should have been four or five men and women on the ground, and two cars, engines ticking over. It was cheap-skate – usually was where he had worked. It was why, he assumed, he had been called back, an *increment*, outside the areas where health and safety and obligations of due care, all the modern shit, ruled. Dusty had a 'Make Do and Mend' mug in the kitchen at Caen, and had bought a mug for Danny that showed a ration book. He never used it.

He sat in the car and his hand hovered close to the key in the ignition. He could only peer in the direction of the target – Ralph Exton, liar, twister, temporarily useful. He was in darkness.

A basic law of handling agents: they lied to friends, families, colleagues in war – and to their handlers. Anything the agent said should be tested for provenance. But laws were backed by resources and provenance cost money.

The last years in Ireland, with FRU's budget shrinking, had been Make Do and Mend times – as they were now.

A car indicated. He saw the Mercedes. He had seen one in Karlovy Vary. He cursed: he hadn't memorised the number-plate, but it was written on the pad now inside his anorak. If he fumbled for it he would lose sight. He should have had the number in his head or on the dash. The vehicle slowed and crossed a lane, a volley of horns protesting. The target, visible now, stepped forward, almost jaunty. Ralph Exton was on the kerb and the car was closing on him.

The bloody engine coughed, failed to fire. Danny tried again, heard it catch. Old skills, if not practised, died. Dusty would have had it quiet and ready. He left to Danny the glamour work with the agent. Fumes spewed back. The Czech came towards him, fast, and twice peered back over his shoulder. He flung the driver's door open and gestured to Danny to get out. Danny saw the interior light illuminated the seats of the Mercedes as Ralph Exton dropped into the passenger seat. He had a fast sighting of the man at the wheel – a brigadier, who was now a manservant and carried a legal firearm. The man had pepperpot hair, cut short and thick. The traffic was blocked.

Danny Curnow was pushing himself up but his shoulder was grabbed. He was hauled out and stumbled. His hand caught the bonnet and then he was round the front of the vehicle, tugging the passenger door, the car already moving. He was half in, half out, his left foot trailing.

'Get out.'

'I'm coming.'

'You're not needed.' From Karol Pilar.

'I'm coming.' Danny Curnow's old stubbornness.

'You have no authorisation.'

They were into the traffic. Danny sat straight-backed in his seat and looked for the tail of the Mercedes.

'Why did you come?'

'Because I need to see for myself. Then I can be confident.'

'You don't trust me?'

'I trust you, but I trust myself more. I can't see it.'

'I have them. I don't share well, Danny.'

'It's a habit of the trade.'

'What did you do, back where you came from?'

'Walked into people's lives, fucked them, squeezed them for what was needed, walked out on them – never a backward glance. A few lives saved, a few lost. I think I can see the car.'

Gaby Davies would look after the Irish. He had his own job to fulfil. It was about the priorities laid down by Matthew Bentinick. He had his cigarettes out and put two between his lips, lit them and passed one to the Czech. The pace quickened, the road opened and the lights towards a bridge favoured them. Now the Mercedes was wedged behind a long-distance bus and could not avail itself of its engine power. They dragged on their cigarettes and smoke billowed around them. He did not expect to be thanked for riding shotgun – and unarmed – on Bentinick's business.

It was that time in the evening. If both were at home, one would always, without comment, leave what they were doing and go upstairs. If it was Rosie, she would put down the paper with the crossword or close her laptop. If it was Matthew he would put away the file he'd been reading, or pour himself a meagre malt, then slowly climb the stairs. As he was at home it was his turn. His suit jacket was on a hanger in the wardrobe but he had kept on his waistcoat and tie. When he reached the landing, he paused – always did.

It hurt as much as it had on the first day – weeks, months, years ago. The pain was constant.

So few knew – Rosie's sister did. Matthew Bentinick had no relations he was close to, but at work he had shared the matter of his daughter, what had been done to her, with George and Jocelyn, who was a confidante and a friend. Both had shoulders on which he could lean. The matter was not discussed between himself and Rosie. They felt it would hurt even more if they continued to go over it.

He hesitated at the door, then took the handle. The sign was still there, purloined from a hotel in the Lake District where they had stayed in the spring two months before she had gone away: *The Room Is Ready for Tidying*. A joke. Their daughter had never left her bedroom trashed, with unwashed clothes and an unmade bed. He opened the door, went inside and closed it behind him. The room was a raw wound.

He sat down in the chair where he had read aloud – back from the Province on leave – Beatrix Potter, *Winnie the Pooh*, even bloody *Ivanhoe*. An only child and . . . Hockey stick still there, the one for lacrosse and the school-team photographs on the wall. It had broken the bank to keep her there. He scratched in his pocket for his lighter, lit the candle and saw the picture of her with the children. The tears streamed down his face but he wouldn't allow them to choke his voice. He never had and hoped he never would.

'Hello, my love, not a bad day. I'm just back from Prague. You'd have liked it – a modern city in old clothing, crawling with young people drinking themselves to death and smoking for an early grave. But my pipe caused interest. Grand buildings and lovely churches. Unlike Warsaw and Budapest, Prague wasn't fought through. It survived the war intact. Nice place, and I'd like to think that, one day, we might get there, all of us. Anyway, Mary, you don't want to listen to my ramblings. Best you get some sleep. By the by, I think my visit to Prague will kick up some interesting developments but we'll have to hang on for another couple of days to find out how interesting. Sleep well, Mary . . .'

He let the candle burn. There was a big rucksack in the corner behind the sports kit. He'd carried it downstairs for her when she'd gone and had carried it back upstairs when she'd returned. He never tried to staunch the tears, just let them flow.

In a couple of days, if it went well, he'd tell her about it.

A light knock, and George's head was round the door. 'Hope I'm not disturbing.'

Jocelyn thought him economical with the truth. Other than to see her, there was no earthly reason that the director general should be at her door. 'Always a pleasure.'

'Possible to ask? When?'

'Seems to be twenty-four hours away, or forty-eight. Won't be longer than that.'

'And you're confident, you and Matthew?'

She faced him and a smile lit her face. 'As confident as we can be, George. It could go well, but then again . . .'

No one else could speak to him so boldly.

He said, 'I feel I'm at the helm, and a storm's in the rigging, but I'm betting that by hook or by crook we'll make harbour.'

Did she laugh with or at him? 'Of course, but it won't be

Windermere on a Sunday afternoon when the gale's blowing. I think it's falling into place, but not without risk.'

'Matthew's put a good man in place.'

'He may need to be better than good. Thank you, George.'

It was always the way when control slipped further from the centre: predictions meant less, and luck was valued more.

The ride in the Mercedes was smooth and comfortable. Neither man spoke before they were out of the city. There were lorries ahead and few opportunities to overtake.

Ralph Exton had known the brigadier since the man was in the gutter – had seen him at the bottom of the heap.

'What is it? Fifteen years since we met up? How is Timofey keeping? Well, I hope.'

'When he is sensible, he is well.'

'He's always sensible, isn't he?'

The former brigadier spoke so softly that Ralph Exton had to strain to hear him. The heater was on and its warmth lulled him.

'He is sensible when he listens to me – not always sensible when he does not.'

'Sorry, that sounds outside my area. I asked if he was well.'

'In good health when sensible. Sickening when he is a fool.'

'So, right now, he's well or ill?'

'I think he is not well.'

'And the cause? A virus? A diet problem?'

'You are the problem, Mr Exton. You give him sickness. It is because of you that he is neither well nor sensible.'

'Meaning what?'

'He should not have business with you. He should have ignored your request for help. A silly little deal for which he gets *nothing*. For Timofey Simonov to trade weapons with you in a quantity that a leader or an organised-crime group would consider irrelevant is not sensible. I told him to dismiss the idea. My advice was ignored. He does business with men we think we trust, but cannot be certain, here in his own quarter, and compromises himself. You are here and should not be. You are not worth the possibility of danger.'

'Eloquently put.'

'May I tell you some things, Mr Exton?'

'It's your car and I'm captive. Feel free.'

'Do you know of the city of Yekaterinburg, the gate to Siberia?'

'If you say so.'

'Listen very carefully, Mr Exton, and do not interrupt me.'

'I'm all ears.'

'A young man in Yekaterinburg did a deal to buy a considerable quantity of heroin resin, brought from Afghanistan via Dushanbe. He borrowed heavily to make the payment and must trade quickly so that the debt is met. To sell more quickly he believes it necessary to remove competitors in the city and the kiosks they use. The owner of the kiosks, though, is a man of substance and he has old arrangements in place in the city, and the arrangements are with people of influence. The young man sits in a chair through Monday night of this week and into Tuesday morning. His feet are in wet concrete, which by the morning has hardened. Yesterday he is taken, with the concrete that weights him, to a bridge over the Iset river. Many people are within sight of the vehicle that brings him to the middle of the bridge. He is taken to the rail, lifted over and dropped. He did not treat the man who had the kiosks with sufficient respect, and now the fish eat him, but not his toes.'

He was driving at the same speed and his voice had not risen, but there was a light laugh at the end of the story.

'May I continue? Respect is always important. Respect should never be withheld. A man is given a contract by a *siloviki* group. He works in a finance division of a central ministry and wishes to denounce malpractice in Moscow. He does not make the accusation in the capital where prosecutors can examine the claims, but goes abroad and will be well rewarded by banks who allege they were defrauded. To go outside the state's frontiers was an act of treason and the reward – usually – for treachery is apparent. At this moment a sniper watches that man and awaits an opportunity. Where he is, the traitor, it rains and he does not go to the garden. It will not rain for ever. The man believes he has found a place of safety, is confident of it, and so, when the rain stops, he will go out into a pretty garden for a cigarette and will be shot by a sniper. He did not give respect. And the individual who makes the arrangements for this to happen, and is discreet, is well rewarded.'

The lorries in front of them had turned off. The road was open, empty.

'The Albanians are serious people. I hear their new punishment for any occasion when sufficient respect is not shown them involves the stripping of a man, then the use of a mastic sealant and the gun that squirts it. The nozzle of the gun is put into all of the orifices, big and small. Water goes after the sealant and it will expand. The process is irreversible. I hear the Albanians say that the pain is terrible and death is slow. I would find such people if respect had not been shown.'

'Would you now?'

'If, Mr Exton, through your Irish dealings, you have brought a form of bacteria to Mr Simonov, I will be angry. You understand levels of anger? Acutely angry. That level of anger equals concrete on the feet, a sniper who demonstrates the length of the arm, or the swelling effect of a builder's sealant. That is easy to understand, Mr Exton?'

He did not back off. 'For a chauffeur, you talk too much, Mr Denisov. Why should your boss demean himself by dealing with these Irish people for minimal sums? Because I asked him to. Good enough. I'm his friend and I earned that friendship when you and he were on your arses. You were pitiful. I helped, and I'm his friend. Cut the crap, because you're yesterday.'

Nothing more to be said.

Sometimes there was a vehicle behind and sometimes there was only darkness. It was because of Gabrielle that he'd summoned the aggression to hack back at Denisov. He thought of her and a smile wreathed his face.

It was poor procedure. She boiled with resentment at what was handed down to her. On the surface, Gaby Davies was another young woman – indeterminate age, nationality, profession – who loitered on a street. She wasn't a whore because she glared at the men who slowed their cars on passing her and the others who hovered near her. It was more as if she was waiting for a date who had been delayed in traffic or at work – or stood her up.

She should not have been there alone. There was no central control to move players on a board and shift new faces onto her pavement. Bentinick had flown out. Danny Curnow had disappeared, taking the Czech liaison man with him. She had eyeball on the pair.

They were in a café. He didn't know her and she had little understanding of him. That much was obvious to Gaby when she came past the window and stole a glance at them. They had a table in a corner and the girl had cleared her plate, meat and chips. He had eaten sparingly. She had ordered a glass of wine, while he had water. She followed with fruit and cheese, and he had only coffee. Easy enough to see that Malachy Riordan and Frankie McKinney shared nothing.

They were the prime priority of the mission. She was alone. It made no sense to her. The chill settled on the evening. The girl talked. Malachy Riordan said barely a word.

'Go on! So what's it like?'

Frankie thought he possessed none of the stereotypical qualities she would have looked for and had known. He did not display the brutal certainty of the man she had met at the party, been recruited by, and who was now in a Maghaberry cell. He had dynamism, but there was no sign of that in this man. He was top dog. She had been told that but couldn't see it.

'I mean, you're close up, you're not a wee kid. You've done it so many times – what's going on in your head?'

He seemed to bite his lower lip.

'When the recoil comes through your wrists and into your shoulder, or you're watching at a distance and see the explosives blow, is it fantastic?'

He seemed to writhe. She had not met anyone like him, not from the country. Her parents had no friends in the villages and small towns. They knew people in Dublin, across the border and the south, and they lived in Belfast's good-quality inner suburbs. She didn't know Dungannon, had been to Armagh only once to visit, with a school party, St Patrick's Cathedral. No reason to go near Coalisland, Cookstown or Carrickmore. She sensed his strength – his muscles seemed to ripple – and his complexion was weathered.

'You have a hit. How do you celebrate?'

After a pause, he said, 'You go home. You get in the shower. The wife has an oil drum out the back and she's lit a fire in it. You wear overalls, and they go in the drum. When you're out the shower, and the clothes are well gone, she'll make some tea. You don't talk to her about it. Maybe the kid needs lifting back from school or taking to a friend. It's what happens.'

Incredible. A guy blown away, and it was about the wife going out the back to light a fire in an oil drum, then the school run.

'Hasn't the adrenalin kicked in, like speed?'

'We don't do drugs. We put dealers out of the community – we might shoot them in the knees first.' Then a smile, wafer thin. 'We sometimes take a cut from the dealers and they pay for protection from us.'

She leaned forward, elbows on the table. 'When you hit, do you hate them?'

'It's not personal. You think about the way out. That's what matters to us.'

Not winning a battle, then. Not watching the TV that night and seeing the panic spread. There might as well have been a debt-collection guy in Short Strand or up the Newtonards road repossessing the TV. 'Nothing personal.' And ripping off the dealers because that was as good a source of cash as any. She knew that: some of her funds in the bank would have been from coke, cannabis and amphetamines, but most was from cigarettes. She saw the strength of the hands, which fiddled with the spoon in the saucer.

She gazed into the man's eyes. 'Do you think you'll grow old, Malachy?'

'My dad didn't, nor his. I hope to.'

'But you'll not give up, like others did – like most of them did?'

'You get the bill.'

She wondered how it would be for a man or a woman who did not grow old. Was there 'good' and 'bad' death? She had her purse out and went to the counter. She didn't know where he was staying in the city – she hadn't been trusted with a hotel's address. She paid. He waited for her at the door. She wondered then if it had been a daft thing she'd asked him, whether she herself would grow old – and how, for her, it would end. 'Good' or 'bad', quick or slow, heroic or humiliating.

The cold hit her. Out on the pavement, he looked around him. There was a woman up the street saying gazing into a hardware shop's window. It wasn't lit, and who needed the price of a hammer at that time in the evening? Otherwise the street was deserted. He said where he would meet her in the morning, and was gone. A few steps then shadows closed on him. He was beyond her experience.

Long after the light had gone, the priest was allowed into the field.

He would have liked to bitch at the senior officer, but they had brought him beakers of hot tea and meat sandwiches, and he had been told it was about the 'contamination of a crime scene'. The undertaker had waited as long as himself, and they had offered him cigarettes. He had postponed a meeting with a couple from west of the mountain planning marriage – they'd be lucky to fit it in before the birth. He usually went to choir practice, but had made an excuse.

The grass was sodden. A policeman held a wide umbrella to shelter him. It was going to be a poor autumn for the farmers: the arable ground was drenched, the grazing fields would be scarred if the cattle were left out any longer, and the sheep would have foot rot . . . He walked and a torch guided him. A generator chugged and the area beside the hedge, protected by makeshift tenting, was brilliantly illuminated. Men and women stood around, uniformed and in the kit for harsh weather. He sensed that few were of his faith and would harbour no great sense of tragedy – more likely 'best place for the murderous little bastards'. At the site he was greeted with formal politeness and apologies that he had been kept waiting all day in the lane. He saw stern faces, the weapons held ready as if they thought themselves quagmired in hostile territory. Had the 'peace process' built bridges? He saw few signs of it.

A flap was opened for him.

The army had been and gone. The forensics team had left. He was last on a list of priority visitors, and the undertakers would be hard on his heels. The hedge had been damaged and the earth, where the explosion had taken off the top soil. Their heads were not covered. Neither face was marked but the expression on each showed the last moment of panic and terror. The eyes were huge and the mouths gaped. There was ripped clothing, scorched, and the holes in the bodies were deep and deadly. He saw the face of Pearse, a fine boy at heart, almost angelic when in school uniform and at communion – not often there, but always a polite boy. The other was twisted in his fall to the earth and the priest could see only half of his features. That was enough. He would have expected it to be Kevin, a pleasant enough young man, an attractive personality, with a future if the clasp of the Organisation had not grappled him. He knew their mothers and their family histories. He had administered their first communions, and those of their siblings. He would bury the boys. At the foot of the mountain, far below Shane Bearnagh's Seat, was Castle Caulfield, a Protestant community. He had hardly ever been there, and long ago a bishop's efforts to get contact between Catholics and Protestants had foundered. It had a fine church, not that he had ever entered it. Charles Wolfe had been a curate there, ministering to the new Ascendancy that had squatted on Catholic lands, and had written a poem in 1816 on the death of Sir John Moore at the fortress of Corunna. It often ran in the priest's head at a time of death in violent conflict:

Slowly and sadly we laid him down,
From the field of his fame fresh and gory;
We carved not a line, and we raised not a stone,
But left him alone with his glory.

He enjoyed the words' bleakness and they were free of the false sentiment he lived with.

He gave the names to the policeman who had led him forward.

As he stepped out of the tent, the undertakers were waved forward with their bags. It was understood that he would go before the police to the necessary addresses. He had done it many times in the past, but not often now.

Which household to visit first? A dilemma. He might almost have sniffed the air.

Policemen and -women around him smoked fiercely, and the undertakers started their work. He heard the purr as the zips of the two bags were opened.

Had he sniffed the air, he might have smelt the stench of informers. The Irish curse of betrayal was always present. It would have turned the priest's stomach.

Dusty dropped them at the hotel. He would go now to the secure car park on the quai Vendeuvre to clean the interior of the minibus, hose the outside and empty the rubbish bags. And then? Desperate would have walked round the bassin Saint-Pierre, then cut up the venelle Maillard, by the plaque to the guillotined Charlotte Corday, to rue Basse and Le Dickens Bar to take a beer. He pushed through the door and regulars saw that their friend was not with him. Jaws seemed, momentarily, to slacken.

The hours he spent without Desperate were hard for Dusty. He felt his absence and feared for the future. Not a future that involved Hanne, despite his efforts at match-making. That night he would go into Desperate's room on the top floor with a duster and glass-cleaning spray to polish the pictures that crowded the walls. The fear was based on where Desperate was now, the handling of an agent and the price to be paid. The first beer didn't touch the sides so he had another.

The fear stayed with him.

A quartermaster had been married for eighteen years and his wife had borne him three kids, two girls and a boy. The wife and children lived in the family home, in Augher. The quartermaster was, to preserve his liberty, across the border in the Republic and had a bed-sit in Monaghan town. He controlled the weapons and explosives for the active-service units and was responsible for the hardware and the caches in which it was hidden. The quartermaster was lonely. There were plenty of women in Monaghan, other men's wives and girlfriends, plenty of temptation. The quartermaster had fallen for a pretty girl who didn't bother him with talk. His wife seldom came from Augher to Monaghan because she spent so much of her time caring for an aunt with chronic emphysema. The quartermaster visited his family occasionally, and was high on the list of wanted men.

All was well within the divided family until the aunt's brother had gone to Monaghan to buy a new lawnmower – cheaper in the Republic. He had seen the quartermaster in a bar with 'the painted floozy' and had watched them kiss. Outraged, he had followed them to a terraced house on St Macartan's.

An immediate response from the wife: she had driven to the barracks at Dungannon, had demanded to speak to an army intelligence officer and had recruited herself. A lovely lady, they all said. Demure, polite kids, an elephantine memory and a hatred of her husband. She knew so much.

Weapons were 'jarked', FRU-speak for disabled but left on site; others were fitted with homing beacons; cameras were laid in plastic logs on the approach to the caches.

She knew where her husband went, where the bunkers were that kept the kit dry.

Arrests were made in a dribble.

For Desperate and Dusty she was a prime and valued souree. A bank account was kept ticking over.

She wasn't satisfied. The money was good, the kids had better clothes, but she hadn't yet 'put my foot on the bastard's windpipe and stamped'.

Should the man be arrested and caged, or should he be left at liberty while his life was scrutinised? She could be a good laugh and, sometimes, a flirt. She was offered help to get to the mainland and take a new identity, but it would have meant leaving the sick aunt in Augher so it didn't happen. Dusty remembered the day she had given Desperate her answer, grimaced at him and driven off. Desperate had said, 'Too good to last. Never does. Always tears at the end.' And it had been.

He asked for a last beer.

The fear Dusty had for Desperate was genuine: he had been called back and the undertow of the past was too strong to withstand. The old wounds were there to be reopened.

A night off for the tourists, a chance for them to ease away from history and wander the sites of Caen. Tomorrow would be a big day, but that evening they could relax. On offer for those who wished to walk would be the school where Charlotte Corday, killer of the revolutionary Marat, was educated. The grave of Matilda, diminutive wife of England's William the Conqueror, could be visited at L'Abbaye aux Dames, in the church of St Gilles: she had been four feet two inches tall and had initially refused him – wouldn't marry a 'Bastard' – but he had dragged her out onto the street from her father's home and beaten her until she had accepted his proposal. They might also visit the flattened ruin of Le Vieux St Gilles, begun in the eighth century and a place of worship until the RAF had bombed Caen in 1944. They would have time to walk under the walls of the castle from which William had ruled Normandy. For those with a surfeit of culture there were restaurants close to the hotel, the Abracadabra, the Santa Lucia and the little Armenian place round the corner.

As they walked in the historic quarter they might find themselves on the rue Haute in front of a dark old stone building that was notable for exquisite carving of little flowers and sprigs of cherries. Had they seen it they would not have known about a room in the house where the walls were covered with pictures, that it was the refuge of a man troubled in his own way by war. Last, they might have seen their driver, thoughtful and subdued, walking home from Le Dickens Bar.

He checked his watch yet again. The house on the hill was ready for his guest.

Timofey Simonov understood the importance of friendship,

and the repayment of debt. It was part of the creed of the *zeks*, the criminals behind the fences. A stranger had helped him and gained little from his effort. From the airfield he had met Mr Vik, old air force, Russian, with an understanding of an entrepreneur's chances, blooming as the regime collapsed. Weapons were the new currency.

He'd have sluiced the toilets for work, and had the brigadier scrub them beside him. He had been brought inside an organisation. He had been trusted, the brigadier tucked away as baggage.

Weapons paid big-time, and old aircraft flew them where the rewards were richest. Never greedy, never critical. He was described as 'a man who delivers'. At first he was always a pace behind Mr Vik, carrying the briefcase. He was with the bodyguards who were old Spetznaz, with front-line experience of killing in Chechnya. Later, he was sent on his own trip, with the brigadier. A giant stride for him . . .

It was a new strip – he had seen it from behind the pilot's shoulder on the descent – narrow and red, with undulations. The aircraft was an Antonov and that it stayed in the air from Europe, via Damascus and Khartoum, was a miracle: engines had cut, then restarted, the pressurisation was sporadic, and the landing gear was a mystery beyond the understanding of the in-flight engineer. They had been round four times looking for the strip, then had seen it. They had brought in twenty-five tons. The brigadier had been behind him in a bucket seat, but had often gone to the latrine while they bumped in turbulence.

Without the help of Ralph Exton, he would not have been there.

As they careered along the strip, the brakes came on and the aircraft juddered, leaving a plume of red dust behind them. Before it was enveloped, he had seen the village and a crowd. There had been Africans in combat fatigues – he had thought of the NCOs who drilled conscripts at Milovice: they'd have had heart failure at the sight of men in military kit, assault rifles dangling towards the dirt, and the wide eyes of drug or booze abuse. There had been civilians too, men, women and children, who had stood back, huddled close, and didn't move. The pilot brought the aircraft to a halt, then made the sign of the cross over his once-white shirt. The engines were switched off.

The chief man appeared. No Mr Vik to greet him: that was left to young Timofey Simonov. He knew what to do: payment first, then the weapons. That was Mr Vik's rule. There was a pilot, an engineer, the brigadier and himself. They each had rifles and grenades, and there were twenty-five tons of hardware in the cargo area. The chief man had enough medal strips on his chest for a full general. He had a typed inventory. Timofey understood that if he gave credit, he would never fly again, would be out on his ear. The pilot kept the tail ramp raised. Timofey said what he wanted, had enough French for it. Payment first, then weapons. The men below him were festooned with grenades, some had belts of machine-gun rounds draped over shoulders, and there were loaded RPG launchers.

He was surprised that the Mercedes had not yet returned.

He had called down, demanding the payment. There were enough weapons around the Antonov to start a medium-sized war, and the plane could not lift off again if it were under fire. That was the moment when he proved himself. He stood at the open side hatch and demanded payment first. He could have been gunned down, could have had a swarm of men scrambling past him into the aircraft and stripping out the cargo. He had felt a strange sense of calm.

And it had happened. Another man had been called forward, an ethnic Indian, with an attaché case. It was passed up. He'd taken it, opened it, and looked into the cloth bag it contained, had seen the dull faces of the uncut, unpolished diamonds. He had smiled.

That moment had been decisive in his life, which from then on had led him to success.

There had been a semi-hidden safe deposit box under the pilot's seat. The cloth bag went into it. He had returned the case, and the pilot had again crossed himself. The hatch at the tail was lowered. A crocodile of men formed, not the ones in uniform but men from the village. The soldiers were in the cargo area, shifting the crates, but the village people had carried them. Ammunition was moved, with mortar bombs, grenades, light machine-guns and heavier versions. Timofey Simonov had little knowledge of which side in a civil war the sale would support, which faction would gain immediate advantage. He took satisfaction from the small dull stones stowed under the pilot's seat. They would end up in the diamond quarter of Amsterdam, en route to rich women's throats and fingers. A girl watched him.

He heard the car and the dogs stirred.

He remembered two people from far back in his life. There had been a poet at Perm 35, there for political crimes, who would stand at the fence and recite his work to the tundra – and there was the girl at the side of the dirt strip. Timofey saw her, he thought afterwards, only because he had the elevation of being at the forward hatch. She had been standing behind the local civilians and did not come forward to help with unloading the aircraft. When he saw her, she was alone. She wore flip-flops, and her shins and knees were reddened but not burned. She had on khaki drill shorts and a blouse with long sleeves in a quiet check. Fair hair protruded from under a woven sun hat, with dark glasses perched on top. Behind her there was a building of mud and wood and over the door a dual sign and two arrows: 'Clinic' and 'School', in French. He saw her very clearly: north European, twenty-two or -three, no rings on her fingers, no pendant round her neck, no earrings. He had not forgotten her expression. He assumed her to be an aid worker who had came to change the world, live rough for a few months and claim it as a 'life-altering experience'.

When the weapons had been lifted out there would be two boxes of Johnnie Walker, a dozen litre bottles in each. The boys, when they had their new toys, fought better if fortified by the Red Label brand. Looking at her, he had thought this would not be a good place for her when the sun dipped. The booze would make them 'difficult'. Kids flocked around her, thin legs and protruding bellies. Usually children smiled and waved but not that day: they took their cue from her. The look on her face was of contempt. Her target? Himself.

The crates had gone from the strip and a group of soldiers was at one of the cardboard boxes, but the chief man belted them away with a rifle butt. Her stare never wavered, and the contempt remained.

The engines caught, the propellers turned, and the chief man at the side broke off the beating and clumsily saluted. How could that girl exist there? The propellers spun, the dust rose under them and they taxied. He didn't see her again. The pilot took off.

The dogs were barking and he heard the door close, then the call, 'And how's my old cocker?'

They hugged. He was held tightly to register long friendship. His coat had been taken, the warmth of the room played on his face, and he looked around at fine furniture and fine art – because the blighter had done well. A useful man to call a 'friend'. They broke apart. 'It's wonderful to see you, Timofey.'

'You are, Ralph, so welcome to my home. A good journey?'

'Yes, with excellent conversation.' He assumed the brigadier was hovering, waiting for instructions, but might already have been gestured away.

'And all is well in your home?'

'Home never changes, Timofey.'

He was led towards an inlaid mahogany table, with bottles, glasses and an ice bucket.

'Not champagne, as I remember, Ralph.'

'No champagne until a deal is signed, sealed and delivered. For now, a gin and tonic – fifty-fifty, plenty of tonic. Just my little joke, Timofey. It would go down a treat.'

A good measure of gin, and it would be only for him because Russians did not drink gin. A refresher of whisky for his host.

A wide smile. 'So, Ralph, how is your "royal" village?'

'Never better.'

'You see her often, your neighbour who is the future tsarina?'

'I see the duchess often enough.'

'As I remember you telling me.'

They egged each other on.

'What is the price, Ralph, of "royal bullshit" this summer?'

'Interesting that you should ask, Timofey. I can do you a nice load of it, royal to the core and straight out the back end of the palace horses.'

They toasted each other. Then, as if a courtesy had been forgotten, they shook hands. Funny – the room was overheated and already Ralph Exton was sweating, but his friend's hand was cold. A calculation: Timofey Simonov had no warmth left in him, all squeezed out.

'You look well, Ralph.'

'Thank you. So do you.'

A pause. Silence between them. The room was quiet enough for him to hear a trapped fly. He thought of a man sitting in hardening cement, and another man waiting for the rain to stop so that he could walk into the middle of a garden, and of yet another man going into a DIY store and asking for a mastic sealant gun.

'Why did you come to me, friend, to ask my help?'

He lied: 'Just thought, Timofey, it was a nice little deal, something that might be fun for both of us.'

He had to look straight into the eyes when he lied and not flinch – the brigadier was by the door. Ralph was good at looking into the eyes of any man he lied to. And the business of 'escape', would keep until later when the serious drinking was over. He was waved to a seat.

They were at the back of the house on a bank beyond the track where they had sufficient height to see over the wooden fencing into the yard area, then down to the kitchen and the dining area. Karol Pilar's camera had a high-enough quality lens – better than FRU had been issued with at Gough two decades earlier – with a high-definition capability. The view was of Timofey Simonov at the side of the table and the back of Ralph Exton's head. Matthew Bentinick's instruction had been that evidence should be gathered. They had to get an image of Exton, full face or profile, and Timofey Simonov with him. That was a basic requirement, proof of conspiracy: the more important objective, not this time but soon, would be the personalities and the weapons, same camera frame. This was the start, and would whet jurors' and jurists' interest. They waited, shivering, and couldn't smoke. They had pictures of Simonov in profile and the back of Exton's scalp, but nothing that would be admissible in court.

'Does it matter?'

'I'm told it does,' Danny whispered back.

The dogs didn't bark.

The brigadier served dinner to his employer and his employer's friend.

They growled, but almost in silence.

Would he be wanted again? He would not. They had fruit and cheese on a sideboard, brandy and port. He ducked his head in respect to Timofey Simonov and ignored Ralph Exton, then took the plates and dishes on a trolley to the service lift outside the dining area, closing the door behind him.

The dogs padded downstairs, to the kitchen door. He let them through, and they scurried to the outside door. He crossed the utility area. They were fine dogs – some European police forces used them for their intelligence and their noses. It would not have been a fox that had disturbed them: the hackles were raised at the base of their necks – they would have yelped in excitement for a fox. He could barely hear the growl, but the curled lips and bared teeth showed him the dogs' suspicion.

He went to the cupboard on the landing, near to the front door, where he stowed his pistol – he had put it back when he had returned from Prague. He had driven many kilometres that day. The long journey, with the detour across two borders, to Český Krumlov, and the return to Karlovy Vary, then to Prague and back. His eyes ached. Tiredness caught him – as did his loathing of the man who claimed his employer's friendship – and the dogs warned him.

He shut the dogs into the kitchen, went out through the front door and down the steps. The pistol was in the pocket of his windcheater, and a power torch was in his hand – it was long enough to double as a club. He went up the street, then disappeared into the darkness of the alleyway, which led to a footpath behind the house. He moved warily, with care.

He was back and the Czech was forward. It had never had been Danny Curnow's way to allow another man to be on the ground, alone, doing work in his name. He was exhausted but he was there and would stay. Danny was among trees high on the bank and the path was below them. Karol Pilar had the camera. They needed a single image: two recognisable faces in the same frame. There would be a moment when the Russian and the agent stood up. Then the shutter would clatter and they could get the hell out.

It was cold and there was an owl about. Karol Pilar had a frog in his throat, the dreaded tickle of close surveillance. Little suppressed coughs.

Wood, a dry twig, snapped.

For half of his adult life, Danny had been away from surveillance and being alerted by snapped twigs. He was very still. There was no moon, and the lights from the house and those at either side did not reach beyond the fences. The path and the bank were dark. He strained to hear and see. He thought he knew where Karol Pilar was and the camera would be up to his face, lens focused, ready for the moment: two faces, same frame.

A softer, less intelligible sound.

Old habits and skills slipped back. The softer sound would be the pushing aside of a crisp leaf. He remembered the cat that had spent time with the old marine: the man and the boy used to watch it hunt in the undergrowth, once the bungalow's garden, moving with such stealth and weighing each move of a paw, understanding the significance of the noise made when a leaf moved or a twig cracked. Danny knew when a stranger came forward – unlikely in innocence – and probably brought danger. Karol Pilar's attempt to smother his cough was a thunderclap in comparison with the stick and the leaf.

His eyes had found the light's level and had made the compensation equations. It was a shadow, almost black on black. It had the frog in the throat to guide it. He could identify an object in a hand, and a shiny surface. He reckoned he heard the click of the camera. The shape passed in front of him and moved steadily towards the cough. Danny didn't know when to break cover. It was hard to steady his breathing, and he had no weapon. He heard a sharp oath, nothing he understood – and chaos broke.

A shout – it might have been Russian, not Czech – and surprise was lost. Two men grappled, black movement against black background. He could barely see. Danny launched himself. The mind worked well. It was the moment when an operation subsided into failure or came through. Failure was unthinkable – always had been. He went forward towards the squirming mass ahead of him. The torch came on – it threw light but had been dropped. The target between the two men, visible at the rim of the light pool, was the pistol. Danny reached them. Decision time. Which of them to belt when he intervened? The pistol was held high, the barrel pointing up, towards the slope of the woods. One man tried to drag his arm down so that the weapon was levelled while the other sought to keep the thing high. He realised Karol Pilar was the smaller and hit the higher shoulder with a chopping blow. The sort of blow the instructors taught, and that recruits reckoned was a waste of energy. He used the heel of his hand and heard the yelp. The fingers must have opened and the pistol fell. It hit the ground and bounced once, then rested in the torch's beam. Danny lashed at it, caught it on his toecap and it spun away.

Combat of a sort.

The torch showed a face he recognised. He kicked hard, punched, used his fingers and nails and, once, his teeth. Nothing more came back.

All done so quietly. No flashlights from the houses, no shouts, no dogs set free.

It was finished. The fight had gone out of him.

Danny eased himself up. The torchbeam showed a bloodied face. Karol Pilar knelt over the victim, stripped off a wristwatch and went through pockets until he found a wallet. He snapped it open, peeled out banknotes, and threw it down. He stayed on his hands and knees – his victim's eyes were tight shut – to pick up minute fragments of glass.

They ran as if for their lives. They left the torch behind, the pistol and the man who moaned and was long past an age for street scraps. They were gasping when they reached the car. The camera's lens was broken and the back screen was fractured. The light came on in the car. They were wrecked: faces bloodied, hands scraped, clothes torn.

'Are you happy?'

'I am if you have the picture, Karol.'

They heard nothing, saw nothing and knew nothing. Timofey Simonov kept the brandy coming, and Ralph Exton kept the level in his glass sliding down.

Voices slurred. Old anecdotes renewed: the story of the arrival at the airfield at Ostend was told twice, but the right moment to ask about slipping away and a changed identity was elusive. The night settled on them. The schedule was decided.

Ralph was content to slip into the booze haze and thought himself safe from the handlers who persecuted him. In the morning he would raise the matter of how to disappear.

Interesting, but half a dozen times, Timofey Simonov had left the table to gaze at the screen of a laptop. It was not locked onto the indices of the Far East markets, or the closing prices in New York, but to the meteorological assessments of the coming day's weather conditions to the south-west of London. They showed a likely break in persistent rain, but not till the afternoon, and the forecast was the same each time he checked it. Interesting. He would have liked to trust Gaby Davies, but did not.

They drank, and for both it was a way to forget. The house was quiet.

In the car, Danny Curnow thought the Czech had been hurt worse than himself but Pilar drove.

The road was dark, empty.

There had been two pauses on the way to where the car was

parked. The first was at a rubbish bin beside a pizza place. From a glimpse, Danny thought that the Rolex watch was worth three or four thousand sterling, far out of the price range of almost all of the tourists who came to the battlefields. It went into the bin and Pilar thrust his hand in after it and disturbed the contents so that it was not on the top. The second stop was at the big church facing onto the river and a charity box for the starving of East Africa. Close to four hundred euros went through the slot, all that had been taken from the wallet. Danny could have clapped. Good thinking to 'steal' a watch and empty a wallet because that was what a mugger did. It was not the behaviour of a trapped intelligence-gathering team.

They were well out of the town when they reached a fuel station. Pilar went first, a lightweight scarf covering most of his face. He didn't use the pumps or go into the shop but used the toilets. When he came back his face was wet from washing. They were beyond the range of the cameras for long enough to allow Danny to follow him. He cleaned the dirt and blood off his face. It would be a long day when morning came. A hard day.

He could be thankful. There was a damaged camera on the floor between his feet, but most of the detritus was in his pocket. It would never take another picture. No problem. Mission successfully carried out: there was – he had been assured of it – a good image on the memory tab. They passed the sign for Lidice. He remembered the children fashioned in bronze, the open spaces where a village had been. It had been about taking responsibility, living with it, and about ensuring that an enemy could never feel safe – wherever they hid.

The lights of the airport were ahead. He would be a changed man before he was there and knew it. He couldn't flee from it. He no longer felt either clever and competent or in control. He was on the treadmill, as he had been before. It spun under his feet and he was running so that he didn't fall. The pace was increasing, and wouldn't slow until the end.

13

'You had a fight with a door?' she asked, and rolled her eyes.

He didn't answer her.

Gaby Davies amplified it: 'Did it have big fists and hob-nailed boots? Did it win?'

They had met outside her hotel, walked fast towards the south of the city and tracked along the river. She had come out onto the pavement a minute before the rendezvous time and he had been there. He would be, she reckoned, the sort of man who was never late, had never missed a train or an appointment.

She had said, 'You're a sight. What happened?'

He had said, 'Something to do with a door.'

For a while, as they trekked, she'd left it. The wounds were clean and the cuts were already knitting but the abrasions were ugly and the bruises were colouring. His lips were puffed out of shape, and he'd looked at her through slit eyes because the lids were swollen and the bags under them grotesque. They'd crossed Resslova Street, and she'd pointed down it, indicating a tall church spire. She'd said, 'I haven't been there, but it's significant in Prague history. It's St Cyril and St Methodius. There was a shoot-out in the crypt, and some partisans were killed. It was after the assassination of a Nazi administrator and . . .' He had shown no interest and she hadn't bothered to go on with the story. Extraordinary, because she'd read the guidebook and wished she had time to go there, feel the place and sense the event. The hotel was huge, modern, glass and steel, without the heritage of the church behind them. She rated him a philistine, shorn of sensitivity.

She quit irony, did flippant. 'Will you tell me why you and the door were fighting?'

'No.'

'Make a habit of it?'

He glanced at her. The file in the archive said he had run agents but that was a long time ago. Life had moved on. Perhaps he'd gone out for a few drinks in the old town, been jumped and mugged. Not something to boast about. So bloody patronising, and he'd been beaten up. She wondered if he'd lost his wallet. Street-thieving in central London – Romanians, Bulgarians and Albanians, the favourite villains – was a constant moan in the office, the hassle of sorting out the damage. Police she knew in the capital told her that only idiots fought to protect their property. It was best to let the scumbags have it. He wouldn't have. It would impinge on his pride to cave. He'd been done over on a street in the Stare Mesto and his pride was injured. It was almost worth a giggle.

'I don't make a habit of fighting doors.'

'Glad to hear it.'

They were close to the hotel when he slowed, then veered off to the left and the wide car park. He said, 'Just a little query. Did you see our Joe this morning?'

'Exton? No.'

'Sleeping in, was he?'

'I checked his room, but didn't get an answer.'

'Last night, how was he? Standing up well?'

A gulp. Perhaps her irritation showed. 'I didn't see him last night. I did the Irish. Didn't you know? Followed her back. Saw her inside, then went to my room. Yes, I tried him – I opened his door and the bed hadn't been slept in. He wasn't there.'

'Wasn't there last night or this morning?'

Reluctant. 'Something like that.'

'Well, well . . .'

She saw the girl, Frankie.

'I'd have thought, you having a good relationship with your Joe, that he wouldn't go to the toilet without your say-so. Anyway, we'll close that down.'

They were at the edge of the car park and could see the route to the hotel's revolving doors. He didn't rate her; she didn't like him. Frankie had been in the black trouser suit she'd worn before and a neutral blouse. Her hair had been pinned up at the back of her head. She was new to it all, Gaby thought, naïve and stood out. She didn't take precautions.

She didn't need to say it, but did – as if it were important to prove her tradecraft. 'Standing out, obvious. My mum and dad used to take me and my brother to the Northumbrian coast, and on the Farne Islands there's a lighthouse, the Longstone. She was about as obvious as that is when it's flashing.'

'Do you reckon she's crap?' He had spoken quietly, as if her opinion was important.

'Absolutely.'

'You don't think it's intended?'

She was rocked. She felt as she had on the first day of the surveillance course when she'd spotted none of the people tracking her. She had almost failed.

She murmured, didn't know if he heard, didn't care, 'Fuck you.'

He thought it a test of wills. In Danny Curnow's mind there was a similarity between the places he knew best: there had been that trial of morale on the beach at Dunkirk, on the shingle slopes of Dieppe and on the wide sands in front of Hermanville-sur-Mer. He could have backed away or accepted the challenge. It was, of sorts, a game. At best, the reward for showing out would be the failure of the mission. At worst, if his efforts were inadequate and the tail was seen, lives would be cut short. The location for the game was the garden around the church at Vyšehrad and inside the fortress walls. He had not chosen the ground: Malachy Riordan had.

They made a good-looking couple. They seemed to chat and joke together. He led through a narrow entrance under a low arch and the defensive walls were high on either side. Gaby Davies followed him. He wasn't proud of the way he had treated her but had thought it necessary. If they showed out, everything that had been done was of no value. Why was he doing it?

He could have seen Malachy Riordan approach the hotel, swing away to the right, head along a residential street above the river and follow the signs to the castle. He could then have backed off. Dusty would have understood, Matthew Bentinick too. It was about superiority, claiming the bragging rights. He was doing it for himself.

A challenge issued and accepted.

There was a café to the right. Malachy Riordan took a seat and the girl, Frankie, went to a hatch and ordered coffee. He led Gaby Davies into the souvenir shop on the opposite side of the cobbles where she bought the necessary guidebook. He stuck himself at the postcard carousel, where he could see them. He and Gaby lingered, were fussy about which map they needed. When he saw, across the road into the gardens, that they had finished their coffee, he told Gaby to pay quickly. Then they went down towards a small church that was only a circular tower – she told him it was St Martin's Rotunda, a millennium old. Malachy and Frankie passed them – so close that he could see the stress lines at the girl's mouth. Had she joined up for this? Had she anticipated what participation in guerrilla warfare was about? Did she know what a prison cell looked like, how the food tasted? Had she imagined what it was like to be shot, wounded, down in the gutter with the blood seeping? He doubted it. They went on.

He told Gaby that they would leapfrog, and keep eyeball. Danny Curnow could not have backed off.

Bloody men, and their ego. To Gaby Davies there was a world of madness around her. She read it.

Malachy Riordan would walk with Frankie McKinney through the gardens of Vyšehrad and would use all the skills he possessed in anti-surveillance tactics, as practised and perfected by the experience of forty years' sporadic conflict on Altmore mountain. He'd look to see whether Ralph Exton had brought baggage with him and whether Frankie McKinney had a tail. She and Curnow did not have to be there – the madness merged to insanity. He had no reason to prove his skill other than feeding arrogance.

Or something else.

Fear?

Interesting. She was beside him. She had the guidebook. She had to talk for the sake of authenticity. 'It's about a woman who married down. She was Princess Libuše and this was her dad's castle site, more than a thousand years ago. He was Vratislav the Second. She insisted on marrying a peasant, Přěmsyl – might have been a ploughman. Their dynasty founded Prague. Fascinating. You riveted? Of course you are. Anyway, the main defences were put up in the late seventeenth century. Did you ever get married, Curnow? Don't answer. I didn't either. Do I have to keep going? Over there, that's the church of Sts Peter and Paul. Across the square – show some bloody interest – the statues are of Libuše and Přěmsyl. How are we doing?'

They were bronzes, more than life-size. He wore a close-fitting helmet, had a shield on his arm and held her close. Gaby could turn with her map, orient herself, and was well placed to see the two targets going towards the church.

'There's a cemetery for national heroes. Want me to book you in?'

He didn't rise, seemed calm enough, and other visitors drifted by them. A couple of kids had a football. She sensed a trap was baited but didn't know where or when. She could imagine how it would be if the teeth snapped shut on her ankle. She would go back to Thames House on a crutch, take a lift up and go past Jocelyn's cubicle. She'd see the expressionless face, feel the condemnation, and make her way to Bentinick's lair for the dressing-down. Unthinkable. How had it happened? The instructor who had done the early courses with her intake had told a story of a Soviet trade attaché who had been regarded as a top-priority surveillance subject and was supposedly in blissful ignorance of the fifteen men and women from A Branch who traipsed after him, buses, trains, taxis and on foot. There might have been micro-dots at dead letterboxes or brush contacts. Even had a big chief out of the office doing it. An edict: no showing out. It had ended in red-faced embarrassment one sunny spring afternoon by the Serpentine. The Soviet had turned, without warning, had walked briskly back. He had gone up to the 'big chief', identity a matter of national-security secrecy, and had told him that the techniques and procedures of his people were exceptionally poor, that the Syrians, even the Egyptians, would make a better fist of it. He had handed over his card and offered to arrange for surveillance training courses, then buggered off. She thought Curnow needed the adrenalin surge pound, that the game mattered more than the result.

The targets were sitting on a bench, facing a low privet hedge. Beyond it the fortifications cascaded down to the river. There were no seats, with a line of sight to them, where she and Curnow could park. He kept her on the move and they drifted towards the church. She did her map routine again, the excuse to turn through the full circle. The bench was empty. She had no eyeball.

'Bugger. I don't have them.'

'What can you see?'

'Nothing.'

'You look hard?'

'Of course – what for, Malachy?'

They were away from the bench and the views up-river, where rowers and scullers did their time trials, and down-river, towards the castle and Charles Bridge. They had tracked along a line of trimmed conifers that gave them cover and had gone into the cemetery. There was a covered walk on two sides of it. Heavy shadow there, and he kept back from the light. Near to them there was an exit towards the main body of the church.

'In London, from what I hear, it would be anything. Old and young, black women as likely as men in suits. Here, it would be the Czech police. They'd be given descriptions of us. There would be, perhaps, a Five man with them, but it would be done by Czechs, and it would be men.'

He had her hold up the mirror from her makeup pouch at an angle that suited him. He could see across to the cemetery's entrance. It was crowded with headstones, mostly marble. Angels pranced above the dead, and fresh-cut flowers brightened some plots.

'Are we clean?'

'I think so.'

She thought he said it grudgingly. 'Can we go?'

'Soon.'

'When is "soon"?'

'When I say it is.'

'Can I tell you—'

'Tell me what?'

'Are you always nervous – frightened? You're screwed up. How would I know? It's an infection and you've given it to me. That's how.'

She didn't know by how far, if at all, she had overstepped the mark. She felt for the muscles at the back of his neck and let her fingers work on them. The boy at Queen's, the one who had done sport, had calmed when she'd done that.

'Those who aren't nervous, or "frightened", which is what I call "aware", you want to know where to find them? They're in the graveyard, like the stiffs here, except they went too young. You know what else? Most of their names are forgotten, except by their mothers.'

She kept going at the knots in his shoulder muscles, but failed to untangle them. She thought he lived with death. She didn't know if she could. This was different from anything before: it was real, not a training run.

It was a slight. Kevin's mother had heard that the priest had been to the other house first, then come to hers. She had no husband with her – he was away in the south, avoiding the police, the courts and, perhaps, her. She and the other children had been in the house, dead of night, when the priest had come. A cold fish. No warmth to him.

She had taken the children to school. Where else? She had work to busy herself. Straight after she was back from the school gate the police were parking outside her home. Weasel words about 'tragedy' and more about 'There, ma'am, is an object lesson in what happens when wee kids are led astray', and talk from a sergeant – with a sneer at his mouth – about what should not happen at a funeral. The sergeant had told her that the police would not tolerate shots being fired over a coffin, and advised against any 'paramilitary trappings'. What in Heaven's name did he mean? A bigger sneer: there should be no black gloves on the coffin and no beret. 'If you don't want trouble, ma'am, it would be best to steer away from anything other than an ordinary decent funeral.' Talk, then, about when the body might be released. The undertakers would call by. She had not cried in the night but had lain in her bed, without her husband's warmth. She had fussed at the children over their breakfast, but had told them. They had been white with shock when she had nudged them into the car and driven to the school. No one spoke to her, all the mothers frightened and holding back. At home, she had seen his boots at the back door, his coat on the hook, the school photo on the dresser, the plate in the sink that she had not yet washed and had found flowers at the gate. Then she had cried, and no one had been there to hold her. She had closed the door after her, not bothered to lock it.

She would not have claimed to know Pearse's mother. Kevin was her eldest. Pearse was the woman's youngest. The rain had eased.

They approached each other on a collision course. Kevin's mother had wanted to be flushed with aggression when she met the other woman. Might have been a mirror of herself she looked at. Hair tangled, eyes swollen and red. Both walked in the middle of a road that was not wide enough to have a line at its centre. There was a tractor behind Pearse's mother and a delivery van behind herself. Neither mother made way. They met and held each other. The anger shrivelled and fell away.

'I would have said, and argued it to my grave, that it was the fault of your Pearse for leading him.'

'I came to yell at you that if your Kevin hadn't led him they would both be lolling in their beds.'

'At the O'Kane house, and he's no bigot.'

'A good Catholic man and his wife. Their boy did no harm to us.'

'Who led your Pearse and my Kevin? Who filled their heads with the rubbish?'

'Malachy Riordan led them, and Brennie Murphy stuffed their heads with the rubbish.'

'Brennie Murphy is a joke, full of the shit of the past and all talk.'

'Malachy Riordan would have turned their idiot heads.'

'They're dead, and what for? Why?'

'Because Malachy Riordan sent them.'

The delivery driver in his van hooted at them. The farmer in the tractor cab revved.

'They were just wee boys and knew nothing.'

'It wouldn't have happened in the old days when they used men – fine men – not kids.'

'Why were my Pearse and your Kevin taken?'

'For nothing.'

The anger was purged, and the two women stepped aside. The delivery van sped past and towards the Pomeroy road. The tractor went by slowly, as if the driver was mindful of the mud on his tyres and took care not to spray them.

His tongue? Better he had bitten it out.

Yes, I think I know a man, can fix it, who'll sell you gear. Better he'd never said it. He sat at the table in the back room of the villa in Karlovy Vary. The sun slanted in through the window and the warmth came over the hill, the woodlands, a back path and across the yard. Ralph Exton always agreed to a deal that would guarantee him a profit, and frequently opened his mouth when no profit margin was in sight. He won some and lost some, and right now in his life he was losing plenty. He might have to sell the semi-detached in the 'royal' village and the bullshitting would be over. He couldn't have said what he was doing in Karlovy Vary. He was hung-over.

The brigadier cleared the plates and had battle scars. He had taken a pounding. Ralph felt no sympathy, but sensed Timofey Simonov's irritation with his man's appearance. A mugging, apparently, an assailant prowling at the back of the property. A thief who had stolen a watch and a wallet – dumped but cleaned out of cash. Not police or detectives doing surveillance, but an opportunist thief. Timofey claimed that no criminals dared set foot in Karlovy Vary, and was confused.

They had discussed the detail, himself and Timofey, and had a time, a general location for the test-firing and the start of the transfer process. He'd thought he'd asked the question casually enough but he had been ignored.

The plates had gone, and within half an hour he would leave and be shipped back to Prague. He made the pitch again. 'I was wondering, Timofey . . .'

'What, Ralph?'

'I was wondering if you could advise me.'

'If within my power.' Wary. Not the warmth Ralph had shown those many years before in the Amsterdam bar.

He blurted, 'Timofey, how do I disappear, out of sight – go under the radar?'

The man sniggered. 'You want to leave the royal village and your meetings with the duchess? With your wife and daughter? Go where you have no contacts? How then do you trade, if you know nothing, nobody? Ridiculous, Ralph.'

'I thought you could help me.' He was deflated. He couldn't say he needed to get away from the Irish, that he was an agent of the security service and needed to escape their clutches. He needed also to be beyond the retribution reach of the plump, unsightly Russian – he didn't want mastic sealant up his rectum, his feet swilling in wet concrete, or a sniper stalking his garden.

'Just that sometimes events seem a bit overwhelming.'

'You talk nonsense, Ralph, and that is not you. I advise. You buy a dog. You have a dog. You cannot fuck the dog but you can talk to it. It will not complain to you or criticise you and will not contradict.'

'Thank you.'

Timofey stood. It was as if his attention span for his guest was exhausted and he wished to walk his dogs. Ralph bored him now. The deal rested on a sneer offered by a British officer at a Berlin seminar a long time before, and Ralph had heard it, chapter and verse, three times the night before. He was no nearer an exit strategy. He had dexterity, was fast on his feet. Think again, dear boy. The brigadier was called.

Ralph was hugged, and left. He thought the claws held him, and that the road to freedom was harder to spot.

Suspicion cut into him. Malachy caught hold of her. She was beside him but he tugged her in front of him, held her hard and high. He saw the shock spread across her face, inches from his. He turned with the finesse of a clumsy kid at a school dance. Her knees banged into his.

His mouth over hers, he tasted toothpaste. He kissed her.

If Bridie had seen him, or known of it, she might have battered him with a pan or walked out on him. It was an age since he'd held her like he held the girl, a stranger, and kissed her lips. She moved her body against his and he felt her weight against him. The warmth came through her clothing and she was tight to his chest and stomach . . . and down lower. She was like a bitch on heat, and had almost closed her eyes. When he had turned her the full half-circle he could see them.

Gardeners swept, pruned and raked, and mothers with children in buggies were nearby. A man walked with a tablet open in one hand, his mobile in the other, the two linked by cable. He saw an old man dressed like a tinker from home, German tourists with loud voices – four of them – and a couple: hardly remembered and barely recognisable. Nothing about them had stayed prominent but they had been there. He kissed the girl and she kissed him back. He eased her hair to the side and saw past her. They were arguing.

Malachy couldn't hear their voices.

He had seen them at the gate. Then, when he and Frankie had finished their coffee, they had been on the rampart walls of the fortress. He had gone with Frankie out of the cemetery, through the far exit from the old graves, and they had been twenty-five yards from him. He couldn't have said whether the argument was starting or prolonged. He saw them through the girl's hair, soft gold strands that fell through his fingers.

The woman prodded the man's chest with her finger, did a drumbeat on it. Made her point, emphasised it. The man pushed her away, open hand on her shoulder. She came back, closer, fury blazing in her eyes. He looked for the flash of a ring on the woman's finger. Nothing. The man broke away, turned his back and went towards the steps that led to the outer wall. Malachy thought he had seen enough. He kept the view of them through the hair that lay on his face and twisted in his fingers. The woman seemed to shake, as if tears were coming, and she went after the man, kicked at the back of his leg, missed and stumbled. He turned and held her. Event over.

Malachy pushed Frankie away from him and her eyes opened. He wiped his mouth on the back of his hand. He said, 'I reckon they're clean.'

'Who?'

She tried to take his hand but he put it behind his back. Then she must have read it in his face: indifference.

'They're clean.'

'What were we doing?'

Malachy put a hand on her shoulder and turned her forcibly. He told her that a couple, a man and a woman of uncertain age, had had sight of them round the Vyšehrad gardens.

He said, 'Thanks for that, making it all possible, you know.'

'Thanks for nothing. Please yourself. Any time.'

'Well, I had to, didn't I?'

Malachy didn't know if anything more should be said, except that there was time for a coffee before they went back into the city. He was satisfied, and had told her.

The fight was over. Danny Curnow had an arm protectively round her shoulders.

She grimaced. 'Was that all right for you?'

'You did well.'

'Are you good at rowing?'

'I try not to . . .' He looked to the left towards the steps up to the wall's parapet.

'Because there isn't anyone in your life to shout at?'

'None of your business.'

'No next-of-kin was listed in Archive.'

'I'm my own man. I don't like arguments.'

'You were pretty convincing.'

Danny Curnow softened, perhaps for the first time – maybe the last too. 'And you did well. We had the sort of argument others don't want to be part of. I'm talking to you so I'm turned enough to see them. We're off their eyeball. Don't think it gets easy. It never does.'

'As you know?'

'Yes.'

'If I could ask a question of Desperate or Vagabond or Danny, or whoever's shirt you're wearing today, did you prefer our performance or theirs?'

He said to her, 'If we'd shown out it would have been a death sentence for our Joe – and nasty stuff before.'

They walked towards the round tower of the church and the arch. He used Gaby to do their eyeball and he was talking with Karol Pilar. When he'd cut his mobile he repeated to her that she'd done well. He found it hard to give praise – it wasn't his style.

The death of the quartermaster's wife was a painful memory. It seemed to cut deeper than others. Dusty had parked the minibus and stayed with it. The tourists liked to feel it was secure, that they could leave their bags and coats without worrying. It was a sharp day and a wind came briskly up the Channel. The evening they'd heard that they'd lost the woman had been a defining one. Maybe, for Desperate, it had been a tipping paint. It was always down to politics when the world screwed up for them. The decision had been taken at Lisburn. It would have crossed a brigadier's desk, or a general's, and the secretary of state would have been leaning on him. A general would never tell a government minister to go fuck himself. They'd always had a laugh with the quartermaster's wife, and the guys had liked the pictures of the kids she'd brought with her. Her usefulness was shrinking, though – the locations of the caches were less relevant – but she'd be at the meetings, delve in her memory and come up with a new name each time.

The secretary of state had needed a coup with his counterparts in the South. It was a difficult time, strained relations, and the refrain was that the South did not do enough to seal the frontier and disrupt 'terrorist' operations; the response was that the intelligence rarely dictated where arms seizures could be made. A simple solution: photographs of the field in which a bunker was located, its interior and the weapons; aerial pictures and a map – 1:50,000 scale – with a cross. There would have been a meeting, and documentation passed from hand to hand.

Desperate had warned her, but she wouldn't leave. She had touched his hand and said, 'I'll sort any of the boys out, no worry. Nothing to it.' The internal-security unit would have gone purple at the knocking over of that cache, and that amount of gear, and would have worked hard to find the source of the leak. She'd known of it because the quartermaster had banjaxed his ankle, couldn't drive, and she'd taken him there a few months before the Monaghan exposure.

She'd been found in a ditch near Cullyhanna. The day before, her kids had been dropped off at the presbytery of a church. A lieutenant from the light infantry had come over to Gough and had photographs. She would have gone through many degrees of hell before the bullet in the head had ended it. The lieutenant's reason for driving that distance to Armagh City had been apparent from the pursed lips that barely held in the anger at an innocent's manipulation. He'd have been on a four-month *roulement* in the Province, had barely scratched the surface of the war and might not have understood that winning was seldom pretty. The biggest mouth in the FRU mess that night had been Harris Gates's, a sergeant, two years with them, who had gone berserk and called

Desperate a 'fucking murderer'. He had swung a punch before he was pulled back. A bitter moment, and Gates was gone by breakfast the next morning, never seen again. Not even Captain Bentinick had raked over it. The funeral had been on TV, and the kids had walked with an uncle. It was one of those days when the light went out and something of the unit's soul had gone walkabout.

Dusty watched them walking along the beach, where Desperate should have been.

The visitors, on a Thursday morning, are on Sword beach, always best when the wind whipped up, the waves' crests broke and the tide was not too far out. The guide has them captivated because this is what they came for. All of the bad talk about Dunkirk and Dieppe is behind them; Merville and Pegasus were comparative side-shows to the main event. They hang on the guide's words, and if he flounders the driver, not intrusive, could prompt as quietly as a stage manager in provincial repertory. The guide tells them about the moon's cycle, and its importance to the tide: not too high or they'd come in over the sunken obstructions and pitch down into the mines; not too low or the landing craft would drop the lads far out, with open sand, no cover, to traverse. The supreme commander, Eisenhower, had told the young meteorologist, 'On your decision, young man, rest hundreds of thousands of lives.' A tough individual, with the confidence of youth, stuck to his forecast. Eisenhower said to his commanders, 'Let's go.'

The armada, tossed by storms, met mid-Channel from a host of different ports in southern England, an extraordinary feat of navigation. From chaos came order as the host headed for Sword, Juno, Gold, Utah and Omaha. The first twenty-four hours would decide the battle. For months, German defences had been refined and strengthened under the direction of the formidable field marshal, Erwin Rommel. The Allies would land some 158,000 troops, and the defenders would reckon, for survival, to put them back into the sea.

The visitors are awestruck by the ordinariness of a beach where the season has ended.

The weather was too poor, low cloud, for the air force to provide ground-attack cover, and many staff officers feared a bloodbath and defeat. That it worked was a triumph of planning, heroism and – probably – a fair amount of luck. A must for any guide is the story of a piper. While he played 'Highland Laddie' and 'Road To The Isles', it was recorded that lapping waves raised the level of his kilt. The ladies always enjoyed that anecdote. They'd be running late for the other British and Canadian landing beaches and for the miracle of the Mulberry harbour or precast concrete blocks floated across and hooked together and the sole method of landing stores and vital fuel until a major port was captured. And triumphalism would have begun to rule, and only a few would stand on the soft sand and look for a perfectly smoothed pebble to take home, and think of the many who died – less than expected by doomsters – and many more who were mutilated and damaged and who fought for their lives; the men of both sides of the combat. The driver, usually there with the visitors on Thursday morning, would have spoken if asked to contribute.

It was bad practice, and had Jocelyn been a lesser personality on the fourth floor, she might have been reprimanded for putting that screen-saver image on her laptop.

It was there because, that day and that week, he was at the centre of policy and carried the weight of it on slight shoulders. She knew him as Vagabond. It was a top-shot picture, and she had expropriated it from the electronic memory of the ceiling camera at the side door of the building where he had been brought in. In her experience strangers always looked up as their ID was checked and they were waved through the barriers. His clothes were a mess, his face unshaven and his hair tousled. She had placed a rectangle over his eyes, blanking them out. She knew him, and Bentinick would have done, but his name was privy only to the director's immediate staff. She might, that evening, raise a glass and speak his name. If the matter was resolved it would be because of him, but if it failed, he would be blamed. She had no problems with the ethics of him being called back: she had few problems with the ethics of anything.

She had the laptop open in front of her, the screen tilted at an angle that prevented the man and woman opposite her from seeing it.

It had been a brisk, pleasant walk from Thames House along the river, past Rodin's *Burghers of Calais*, then the concrete teeth and black bollards that protected Parliament. She had gone up Whitehall and into the Treasury. They were waiting for her. In terms of deference it was a red-carpet greeting from Revenue & Customs. Strapped for resources, they could fund two teams only of investigators specialising in the international arms trade where British law was violated. They possessed a quality database and had access to each European capital lying to the west of the dismantled Iron Curtain. It was something of a crusade for them but their numbers were thin on the ground. Jocelyn was welcomed because she promised action and even a result.

She brought with her legal opinion and documentation, and sought reciprocity.

Her clothes were unironed and her legs bare but the Bravo team hung on her every word: both teams prayed for the chance to hit a high-value target.

That morning the weather cleared. There was no rain, but no sunshine either. There was not enough mist to interfere with the clarity of the telescopic sight or to prevent an inveterate smoker seeking freedom in the garden.

He had slept in the car, which had been parked in a field gateway away from house lights and any main traffic route. He stretched, grunted and coughed. He thought that, by the afternoon, he would be on a plane out of Heathrow airport, his fee assured. He was always, when he practised his trade, well clear of the scene by the time descriptions and media statements tripped from local police agencies.

He drove back to work. By that evening his employer would be satisfied.

Timofey had watched them go, then surfed the internet for news stories – dismal rainswept fields, a priest being interviewed, disturbed earth under a hedgerow – and walked his dogs. With them he had met two young women, often his companions among the trees on the steep slope above his house; they had talked about the weather and admired each other's animals. On his return home, he had checked the suit he would wear on Saturday evening for the charity gala at the Grand Pupp Hotel. He was not required to speak but he would contribute generously and his presence would be noted. The embassy people would have driven down from Prague. He had been very clear with the brigadier as to what was required from him, from them, at the bank at midday.

He sat down with some coffee. The dogs' coats had muddied the rug – he hadn't cleaned them as thoroughly as the brigadier would have done. Again, he checked the weather to the south-west of London, where the far edge of the city met the countryside. It would lift. The clouds would thin and the rain stop. He would hear that afternoon. He assumed that men from the embassy, on Saturday evening at the Grand Pupp, would sidle up to him and squeeze his hand, murmuring appreciation.

In Europe, the weather was an exact science and offered up few surprises. The nearest to a nightmare in his life had been a thunderstorm, with jagged lightning, torrential rain and turbulence that had seemed capable of ripping the wings off the Antonov.

Timofey's hands shook – they always did when he remembered it – and the coffee slopped onto his trousers, staining them. If he remembered that storm at night, in his bed, he could not sleep.

It had been the worst flight he had ever endured. The pilot might have been drunk or on an amphetamine high, but he had held his nerve and they had come through it. There had been worry about the cargo shifting: if twenty-five tonnes of weaponry had slid loose in the hold, they were doomed. He had been sick and rigid with fear when lightning had struck the fuselage. He had wept on his knees in the vomit because the bucket had tipped over but they had survived. They had come out of darkness into sunlight and the engineer had given Timofey a mop, cold water and a roll of kitchen paper to clear up his mess. It had been the second trip when he had been independent of Mr Vik, was his own man.

Now he dabbed at his trousers with a handkerchief, which spread the damp stain.

The pilot had made the landing. Timofey remembered the pitiable relief he had felt when the judder in the airframe told him they were down and alive.

So much was different from the previous month. There were no villagers. The unloading would be done by the uniformed rabble. 'Give them the spiel, Timofey,' the pilot had said, 'or we won't get out of here.'

No tail hatch would come down before the cloth bag and its lightweight contents were thrown up by the commander – probably a fucking field marshal by now: he'd been a full general the previous month – and checked. When Timofey was satisfied, the tail had grated down and the men had swarmed in to shift the crates. There had been maize fields, ripe for harvest, but the crop was flattened, and he saw shallow mounds the bright colour of the earth. The huts had no roofs because the thatch had been burned. The beams of the one concrete building were charred and skeletal, and round the windows there were the black marks of the fire. He saw the sign, scorched, that had indicated the school and the clinic. Bullet holes pocked the walls. He didn't see her.

There had been a clamour below the hatch close to the cabin. The pilot had said that the hold was empty. He'd thrown the switch: the tail had closed and the engines had engaged. Timofey had dropped the first box of Johnnie Walker down to the forest of reaching hands, then the second, and the engineer had swung the hatch shut. They'd turned, buried the bastards in a storm of dirt and gone. He hadn't seen her. Had never gone back there. It had been a smooth flight home.

Always remembered that day, the storm. And the girl who had not been there. It had been a good trip and had confirmed him as a favoured acolyte of Mr Vik.

* * *

The bank was off Wenceslas Square.

Danny Curnow made the contact with his mobile, and was told where to look.

He showed Gaby where the Czech was sitting, and saw her wince. She would have seen Karol Pilar's face. It might have been a mirror image of his own. They stood, uncertain, fifty or sixty yards short of the bank. She muttered that there seemed to be a disproportionate number of 'aggressive doors' in the city. He told her to shut up, and she chuckled.

She spotted them. They were on the far side of the street inside a dingy café. It was not the top end of the square, near the boutiques and restaurants, but there was a change bureau and a shop that sold fridge magnets. A tour party from Korea, Taiwan or Japan came by and the guide had an umbrella up as a beacon for them. Danny Curnow took Gaby's arm and eased her away, satisfied when he was beyond the line of vision they might have had from inside the café. He thought Pilar's face was more of a mess than his own. He wondered how bad it would have to have been for the Czech to pull out his firearm and shoot the guy. Catastrophe if he had. They were in sunlight, but he shivered.

She tugged at his sleeve. 'Why did you come back?'

'I do a job. I don't need a shrink.'

'Which might frighten you?'

He turned away from her. Anger rose in him – it was the tiredness and stress, the adrenalin of the fight. He couldn't see inside the café but had a good view of the door. He looked down the street, past the bank to the bench in the centre of the square. Pilar caught his glance. He flicked a hand, acknowledgement. Danny ducked his head. He liked the boy, valued the commitment he showed, and—

She tugged again at his sleeve. 'It's my business, why you came back. I want you to know, Danny, that I'll hold your hand if it gets tough. I'll see you through.'

'Don't talk shit.'

'Because it's pathetic.'

'I'm not listening.'

'It's pathetic, Danny, because it means you can't let go. You know those kids who go to university and leaving is the worst day of their lives? They hang around the lecture halls and the students' bars. They can't see that it's over. They've lost the team they were once a part of, and nothing can replace it. I imagine, you're lonely. I doubt you've got a woman. You should have, Danny. You should have left all this behind. You came too easily, and you were damaged before. God alone knows how you'll be when it's over and you're back to where you were. Maybe you thought us all incapable, and you were the only one who could do the business. In our place, Danny, every Friday night there are people who feed their ID into the security machine and it doesn't give it back. It destroys it so they can't come in on Monday morning. They're not a part of it any longer. Life goes on, like you never existed. The team sheet for next Saturday still goes up on the board for Accrington Stanley's first eleven. The X40 bus goes from Reading to Oxford and doesn't stop as a mark of respect to you. Nobody notices. Nobody needed you and you'll make no difference. Bentinick was a bastard for cold-calling you. It's a shame but you, Danny, are a victim.'

He spotted the Mercedes. It loitered in heavy traffic, but edged closer.

The couple came out of the café.

It was for the Czech to lead and he had a camera.

Danny Curnow shrugged, shook his shoulders, reckoned he'd ignore what she'd said. She slipped a hand into his arm, and they were another couple seemingly with time to kill in a tourist city, near to a bank, watching a Mercedes squeeze into a parking slot. He heard her laugh.

14

The laugh was brittle, humourless, and there was the scent of her growing superiority over him. Not much Danny Curnow could do to slap down Gaby Davies's new-found confidence.

He had good eyeball. The Irish walked briskly towards the bank. He saw the caution of the man and the thrust of the girl's stride: he looked around him and she did not. The brigadier was out of the car first. His face was marked, not as badly as Karol Pilar's or his own, and he hobbled as if his hips or groin were still painful. Danny thought that at the peak of his military career he would have been handsome, authoritative on a parade-ground. Now he was hunched and a scowl creased his features. Ralph Exton was behind him: uncertain, hesitant, hanging back. Danny understood his 'rather be somewhere else' look. He had seen it often. The agent is at a meeting of importance and the pressure builds on him to deliver. What had seemed an excellent idea a week or a month ago is now wrapped in hazard. Danny could not, then, get close to Ralph Exton and speak to him. He would do it with eye contact.

She laughed again. Danny and Gaby Davies were a hundred yards apart. For a moment his concentration broke and he cursed her softly. It was about the exercise of control – manipulation. For a moment, Exton had broken stride – had to. A snake of tourists followed the inevitable umbrella, perhaps listening to the history of Wenceslas, then three tall Africans with sports bags that bulged with handbags to sell on the street.

'A glance of death', was what Matthew Bentinick had called it. 'Necessary to have it, my boy, and necessary to use it. The chance to nail a man with a glance at a hundred metres as effectively as a sniper can,' he had said, while toying with a plastic beaker of coffee. 'Because it's about winning, and anything other than winning is unacceptable. He's more afraid of *you*, my boy, than any of the scumbags who float round him – he has to be, or you pack up and go home.' Vagabond had gone out into the soft rain of an early morning and had run to the car where Dusty had the heater on and the windows were well misted. Some men and a few women could deliver the 'glance of death'. Others failed, tried again and were ridiculed.

The Africans and the tourists did the work for him: Ralph Exton looked around to see if further ambushes would impede him and their eyes met.

Danny Curnow kept his head still, focused on his target. The only movement he made was to rock slightly on the balls of his feet. The target saw him, then moved on, checked further up the pavement for obstructions, and the eyes darted back. Danny held him. He had a useful prop: his face had the clear marks of the night's violence, which would further intimidate.

It ended. The brigadier had Ralph Exton's arm and pushed him forward. The girl came to intercept them – the man had seemed to shrink and his shoulders had convulsed. The moment was gone. The laughter beside him was stifled. She'd have seen her prize and her confidence would have ebbed. They went into the bank, after Malachy Riordan had paused in the doorway, spun on his heel, raked his eyes over the square.

She said, 'I see you shared the door. Generous. Don't I get in the loop?'

'When you deserve to – when your Joe doesn't walk out on you.'

She managed a smile, left him and walked to the bank.

Malachy Riordan hissed, 'That is serious money, but you're saying it's to be transferred beyond retrieving and we've seen nothing.'

The Russian, creepy bastard, his facial injuries playing havoc with his mood, said, shrilly, 'When it's transferred and cleared you'll see what is the merchandise.'

'Which might be shit.'

'You take that chance.'

'We pay and have no guarantee.'

'Wrong.'

Riordan was agitated, and the girl was confused because he had elbowed her aside.

Ralph Exton was cut off from the argument – it might have been almost funny, a Republican gunman and a former Soviet-era intelligence officer bickering inside a modern Prague bank about 'terms and conditions' for the purchase of lethal weapons and explosives, but it wasn't.

Riordan slapped a fist into a palm. 'You telling me that we pay when we've had no sight of what we're buying? Where's the guarantee?'

'He is. Him.' The brigadier jerked a thumb towards Ralph Exton. 'It's about trust.'

'I want to see what we're getting.'

Ralph Exton intervened: 'It's about trust, Malachy, and about me. You trust me and I trust the people with whom I've negotiated quantities and costs.'

'If I don't see, I don't buy.'

'If we all stay calm,' Ralph did a negotiator's smile, 'we can resolve—'

The Russian chipped at them, a chisel on stone: 'You think we care? You think this is business that matters to us? It is for sentiment. My employer's sentiment for *him*, for Mr Exton. No transfer of money and I go. Does it matter to me? It does not.'

Ralph saw Gaby Davies, scarf over her hair, big glasses masking her face, eyeing bank papers, and he had spotted the handler outside. His options were minimal. He stuck to the plan – he had no other. 'I believe, Malachy, that you have to concede on this point and trust them, or—'

'Where I come from, too many graves have been filled because of trust. I trust men and women I know.'

'I assume, Malachy, that you trust me, and I can only urge you, therefore, to trust the man I've introduced to you. Through my good offices you have available an excellent price per unit for materials you and your colleagues need.'

Ralph Exton had seen pictures of construction workers taking their lunch break on a spar while the Rockefeller Building grew in height in the years of the Great Depression. Eleven guys sitting on it with their sandwiches, no safety harnesses, the street 840 feet below. He felt now as if he was among them. His hands were shaking.

The brigadier said, 'No transfer and we quit. You accept or you do not. There is no trust. This is business. You will have no opportunity to deceive me. You transfer or I walk.'

And, for God's sake, it was a public place. People around them were drawing out money, sorting mortgage rates and paying utility bills. No one else was concerned with the purchase of assault rifles, machine-guns and bomb materials. He saw that the girl had gone white.

'Can we please show good sense and restraint, and—'

The Russian stared into Malachy Riordan's face. 'Do you want the deal or not?'

Ralph Exton wondered how long it had been since the Irishman had last ceded ground. Malachy Riordan said nothing but gave a nod. It signified the concession and— He saw Gaby Davies, still reading the bank's investment fliers. A man stood behind her.

It was as though a wheel had turned. The man behind Gaby Davies was outside the door but was peering in. He bore the marks of a street brawl on his face. Ralph Exton looked at the Russian and saw the same marks of violence round the eyes, mouth and across the cheeks.

Malachy Riordan saw them too. He was red with anger. 'What happened to you?' he spat, at the brigadier.

'I was attacked, a thief – I heard a prowler, I went to—'

'At your house? Not an agent? Not intelligence?'

'A thief. My wallet was stolen, then dumped with banknotes taken, my watch pulled off me.'

'Wait.'

He took Frankie's hand and pulled her towards the door. Her feet slid on the smooth surface. A man had blocked the bank's exit but was gone. Malachy's knee hit the girl who was reading brochures on investments. They went outside. Across the pavement, he tugged her close. 'What am I seeing?'

'I don't know.'

'There was a man outside with a bruised face.'

'If you say so. I didn't see—'

'Because you don't look. A man outside had fist-fight marks. So did the man in the gardens.'

'What are you saying?'

'That Russian is jumped. He fights. Who? A thief, certain of it. Wallet and a watch. Big deal. Two more now, same injuries. I'm not happy.'

'What do we do?'

'Maybe quit. I'm not happy. We can turn, walk and—'

'I'm not walking.'

'You have to walk if it's compromised. Don't you see?'

'I see you dithering. That's all.'

'I'm talking about turning my back on it because it stinks. When it's compromised, and you're lucky enough to see it, you walk away – or you go in the cage.'

'You walk. I won't.'

'You'll do as you're told.'

'Go back on your own, tell them you chickened out.'

A full-blown row in a street, men and women passing them. He caved.

She felt empowered. It was better than firing on the Sperrins, better than walking behind the guy, who was now in Maghaberry, through the press of the party, better than being told they had chosen her to travel. He seemed smaller, vulnerable. On the mountain, his territory, he would have backed his judgement and been justified, but he was not there. He had listened to her, was in her thrall. She led him back inside, took a pen from her bag and went with Exton and the Russian to the counter.

They made the transfer. He didn't speak, seemed numbed.

Gaby Davies brought with her the bank's investment brochures. She passed Karol Pilar, who looked through her, and went up the pavement to the corner, for Stepanska. Danny Curnow was beside a man who wore a sandwich board advertising an Irish bar. She joined him. He didn't ask her what she'd learned, which annoyed her.

'It's tomorrow night. The money's been paid. I'm not sure where it'll happen but I'll get that from Exton. Anyway, it's going ahead.'

Now Danny Curnow spoke: 'You have a photograph? Of course you do.'

'I got my phone out and asked them to pose. Don't be bloody stupid.'

He tapped her arm, pointed to where Karol Pilar stood, and the crowd of tourists that had gathered for a wide shot of the statue to Wenceslas. Pilar's camera was raised, and few would have noticed that its aim was away from the statue. They came out of the bank, the brigadier, then Malachy Riordan, Frankie McKinney and Ralph Exton.

'There's a difference between you and me,' she snapped. 'I have a future. You don't. My future is that I can walk away when I want to. I'm not a doormat for Matthew Bentinick—'

He left her, like a date gone wrong. Danny Curnow trailed Exton, while she moved closer to the Czech policeman and would follow the Irish pair. Each time she thought she'd done well, it seemed the success of the moment was illusory. There was something in Curnow to admire: he was dogged and harboured loyalties she barely understood.

Danny Curnow told him to keep walking. It was a long tramp. Sometimes Danny led Ralph Exton, and sometimes he was behind him, goading him on. Occasionally he was alongside. When Danny was at Exton's shoulder he made small-talk. It was a tactic to confuse the man, disorient him. It was where he himself had been taken in the night and he'd sufficient landmarks to guide him. They reached the gaol and the ring of walls, and across the road there were small businesses – a restaurant, a store selling industrial pipes and Erotic City. Opposite the gaol gates was the park, and he sat on a bench that faced the bronze bust of Milada Horáková. He told his man the story of the judge, her execution and how long it had taken to kill her. 'Don't get me wrong, Ralph. I'm not threatening you with strangulation, a guillotine or hanging. Nothing's likely to come your way beyond a hug from Miss Davies and the opportunity to float away. Good enough? Of course. So, what I'm waiting for – without any threats – are the when and where of the transaction. But I'm not Miss Davies and not easily deflected. I'm tired, Ralph, so I haven't much patience. Do I give a damn about your feelings and welfare? No. Some things annoy me quite considerably, Ralph, especially the ingratitude or arrogance that leads a paid informer to forget who puts money in his pocket. It annoyed me, Ralph, that you decided to slip off to your chums in Karlovy Vary and forgot to tell Miss Davies what you were doing. Let's put it another way. The Russians, your best friends, have a certain reach, quite long but not infinite. The gang from up that hill in County Tyrone have a distinctly shorter reach and you'd have to be excessively careless for them to locate you. Which leaves us, Ralph. We have big computers and limitless resources. We can find you any time and any place. You remember the old saying, 'You can run but you can't hide'? Joe Louis used it when he was going to fight Max Schmeling. It was also used in the Balkans when the war criminals seemed to be beyond the reach of the International Criminal Court. Do you know where they are now, the ones who melted into the Bosnian mists? They're in the penitentiary institution at Scheveningen in the Netherlands. That wouldn't happen to you, Ralph. You'd be at the mercy of a telephone call – Russia or Ireland, when an address would be given. Fuck about with me, Ralph, and we'd let you run for a while, but the tension and the fear of shadows would kill you. When you were on your knees, swearing suicide, we'd make the call. You haven't interrupted me, Ralph, with the answers to where and when.'

He smiled more broadly. Then he slapped – open fist across the cheek. No answer. He used the heel of the same hand across the bridge of the nose.

Ralph Exton gave him the answers. Danny Curnow used his handkerchief to wipe the man's eyes and the dribble from the side of his mouth. He saw the fear.

Danny Curnow had not hit an informer across the face in twenty-one years but he lived in the past and the old ways ruled. He told Ralph Exton that a number-eighteen tram, from outside the gaol gate, would drop him back in town, and was gone.

The end of an afternoon to kill, then an evening and a night. Frankie McKinney didn't rate Malachy Riordan as one for galleries or concerts. She could have done the castle with him, Charles Bridge, Stare Mesto, the Astronomical Clock and . . . He was staring into a shop window. She stopped ahead of him and saw the furrow deepen on his forehead. A man with shopping bags cannoned into her and hurried on without apology. Would he be more interested in the sites where freedom fighters had taken on the might of the Nazis? He was still at the window but she couldn't see what was bothering him.

Frankie edged back. The Mercedes had gone. The transaction was complete and the money electronically shifted. She had seen no tail. She remembered the knotted muscles in his shoulders, which she had attempted to relax in the cemetery earlier. She had not imagined that a man of his reputation would be so alone, so taut. She saw past his shoulder into the shop window. It sold television sets. They were in banks, showing the same picture. On a screen at the centre of the display, there was a crudely drawn map of Northern Ireland, with a star shape, red and orange, that represented an explosion. A village main street flickered on the screen, mourning flags hanging from upstairs windows. A microphone masked part of a priest's face. Then a rural view, with rain falling, drops on the camera's lens, and cattle grazing at the edge of a field, kept away from a hedge by an electric fence. There were tyre marks in the field beyond, a bungalow in the distance. A policeman, uniformed and bulky in a bulletproof vest, spoke into a microphone.

A pair of faces, young, one with pimples on his chin, the other a squint.

Malachy Riordan was rigid. The next map appeared. Baghdad was highlighted and the locations of five explosions. The film was of ambulances, devastation and blood.

A woman stood on the far side of Malachy, and Frankie realised she was studying the sets on display. He dwarfed her. Frankie went to her and asked what had happened – everyone spoke some English.

She was answered briefly: 'Another atrocity in Ireland. Two boys dead, their own bomb.'

Malachy Riordan had gone – he was shambling towards the lower end of Wenceslas Square. Frankie caught up with him. 'Did you know them?'

He walked on. His mouth moved, but no words came. They crossed a street. A policeman blasted his whistle at them and vehicles swerved, hooting. He saw nothing around him. She held his arm, almost running to keep up with him.

'Did you know them?'

He stopped in his tracks. He turned to her but said nothing. He had known Pearse and Kevin since they were kids at the village school, inseparable. They'd come up to the farm and messed in the barns while he was working, hanging on every syllable he uttered. He had known them long enough to put simple work their way: they had dicked for him in Dungannon, could kick a football or loiter with a bag of chips at a street corner and see the registration plate of a policeman leaving work. He had used them to go on their bicycles along lanes and check for him that cars were not parked in woods or gateways when he was going to drive that way with weapons in his car. He had sent them to Brennie Murphy and seen them blossom as they had learned more skills and tradecraft. They were the future. He had seen them, in his mind, with the RPG launchers on their shoulders or running along the hedgerows with the assault rifle. It was as if he had bred them. He had allowed them to take the device, lay and fire it. He would have rated them good or fine boys. He had laughed at how they had handled weapons with youngsters' awkwardness and then he had shown them how it should be done. He was their prime influence, had been in life and was in death. He said nothing.

She asked again, 'Did you know them?'

He'd known them well, and the priest who would have called to the field, then made the long journey to the front doors where the mothers would have known because beds had not been slept in. He knew the policeman who had been interviewed, had seen him on search operations and arrest sweeps, and in the corridors of the big barracks at Dungannon when he had been taken in. He knew the fields, and the farmer whose cattle had been grazing inside the fence. He knew the people who lived in the houses where the black flags flew. He knew too much. The boys would have been round after dark on the first night he was back, and they'd have gone together into the middle of a field. There, they would have crouched down and he'd have told them that rifles, machine-guns, launchers and explosives were coming. He squeezed his eyes shut, forced back the tears.

It was always informers. It was the curse of his people and their struggle that they bred informers. The graves in the villages were the evidence of it. Treachery. He scoured his mind for an answer. A bomb exploded when laid or when checked later. It did not carry the hallmark of a tout, but there would have been one. They spawned them. The bastards who took money were always there.

She held his arm tight, as if she was his friend.

Brennie Murphy was wary. There were two mothers he had no wish to see that morning. They were quiet funerals: these days, few would wish to involve themselves with masks and pistol shots over a pair of coffins. If the temperature of emotion was raised too high some awkward bastard would want answers. Who had sent out the boys? Who had known where they were and what they were doing?

He went in his car to the shop. He passed the flags, limp with rain, and in some windows there was the page from the Dungannon paper with the photographs of the boys. The first pictures issued had been from the police, custody pictures, not right for the day. These were from their last year at school.

There was always anger on the mountain when young volunteers died. The old who had guided them might be blamed. He needed to go to the shop because he had no cigarettes. He lived on his own. He had no friend to go for him while Malachy was away. Loneliness often gnawed at him. When it was too great he would drive away from the village to where no one knew him and he could drink. At the shop he parked, hurried from his car, shouldered past others and inserted himself at the counter. No one spoke to him. Sometimes the loneliness was almost unbearable.

The group of tourists he'd driven to Omaha from Gold, where the Mulberry harbour still lay as a ruin anchored in the sea, had gone forward to the German bunkers with their guide.

That afternoon the sun was shining. Dusty thought this part of the day, nudging towards early evening on the Thursday of the tour, was why Desperate had come across the Channel to this coast. This was where the fighting had been fiercest, the casualties heaviest, where the cemeteries were largest and the stakes greatest. Men had shut themselves away, so Dusty had heard and read, in abbeys and monasteries because the act of being there purged guilt: they dedicated themselves, as Dusty reckoned it, to cleansing their bodies and minds of any blame from association. It was all too heavy for him. He had done his job, jumped when told to, and passed no comment. Desperate was always quiet at Omaha, on the high ground above the wide beach – golden, flat, without a single rock that would have given cover. Dusty understood Desperate's torments. His loyalty was to Desperate alone, not to Queen and country, but to Desperate.

Dusty's war stories would have made choice telling. But there was no Crown and Anchor in Caen and no Royal British Legion. In any case they were censored and could not have been recounted with the Suez tales, or those from Bosnia, Basra or the Kosovo adventure. That he never told his share of anecdotes did not dull them in Dusty's memory. One of the worst seemed to warrant Omaha as a place for recall.

An uncle of Dermot Brady had died. An interfering old man,

and a nuisance on a grand scale, but the damage the uncle had inflicted had taken place after his funeral. In the will he'd left on his mantelpiece all his goods and chattels went to Dermot. A disaster at Gough: Dermot Brady was dependent on state handouts to keep himself, his wife and four kids alive. What Desperate gave him – twenty pounds a week – made the difference between a few pints on Friday and Saturday nights and no pints at all. Dermot Brady had been a taxi driver and had lost his licence. He had driven without it, was hauled in again and the magistrate threw the book at him. He'd go to gaol next time.

He was useful to the active-service units. There was to be a hit in Keady and the getaway car had to be fast to clear the roadblocks that went up immediately. He knew all the routes, was an expert in escape from hot pursuit, but the armed struggle hadn't the cash to see him right.

Desperate had met him outside the bar on a Saturday night, and offered him a lift home. It had pissed rain that night, and the first raft of notes had slid into Brady's hip pocket. He was useful, and most weeks he had something to give. They all knew him: the OC of Battalion, the OC of the company, the cell leaders, quartermasters and intelligence. His information was judiciously milked. All had gone well, until the uncle died and the will was read.

At the next meeting, Brady had played the big man with Desperate. He'd had enough, was packing it in. He'd finished looking death in the eye and hearing of touts 'getting nutted'. 'I've done my time and done it well. It's over.'

Desperate had responded. 'You've not done your time until I say you have.'

Brady had laughed and turned to walk away. Desperate had caught his shoulder, whacked him, then lectured him. Dermot Brady might as well go to the hardware store, buy himself a shovel, get down to the graveyard, dig himself a hole and lie in it. The PIRA would take it badly that their friend had screwed them over two years taking payment from the Crown. Desperate's conclusion was that Dermot Brady was as good as dead if he left the car park with no say-so from him. It seemed that Desperate had been persuasive, because the next five weeks' information came in and the profile of three active-service units was analysed. Desperate was reckoned to have done well.

It was a July evening and the meet was in a forest recreational car park, up behind Ballygawley and off the Omagh road. A breezy night, and there was a creak that Dusty had thought was a tree under strain. The shoes were level with their eyes. The body turned and the wind sang against the rope. His weight had almost broken the branch.

Desperate, in Dusty's opinion, was always quiet on Omaha. He needed the woman who painted on the Baie de Somme. It was a fine afternoon and the sunshine made it almost pleasant to be outside, even there.

The guide said they called it Bloody Omaha.

Forty-five thousand men went onto that beach, with an insupportable weight of problems: rough seas, the depth of the water when they were pushed out of the landing craft, too many tanks sinking immediately, the sea swamping the landing craft and men frantically baling with their GI-issue helmets, ineffective bombing of the strong points. Then there was a cliff to face, and half of the engineers, who were trained to scale those heights, were dead before they'd left the sand.

It was a cathartic moment for the tourists who stood high on the hill above the beach and watched sand yachts racing far below them. Around the group were the concrete strong-points and towards the horizon was the pure blue sea, the white crests of waves breaking at the shore. The guide would have quoted the words of Colonel George Taylor, of the Fighting 29th, when his men were pinned down at the cliff's base and the sector advance was stalled: 'Two kinds of men are going to stay on this beach, the dead and those about to die. Now, get off your butts.'

The group would have struggled to comprehend the scale of the casualties on the high ground and the beach. From V Corps at least three thousand men died, were wounded or posted as missing. An American lieutenant had yelled at his cowering men, 'Are we going to lie there and get killed or are we going to do something about it?' The guide said that 2,500 tons of supplies should have reached the beach in the first twenty-four hours, but only a hundred came ashore undamaged. The guide said, also, that it was a 'near miracle' that the landing succeeded on Omaha, and the final outcome depended on 'heroic courage'. Harry Parley, of the 116th Infantry Division, recalled afterwards, 'As our boat touched sand and the ramp went down, I became a visitor to hell.'

They group went back to the bus. They felt that being in this place, standing vigil, was recognition of the courage shown there. None wished to hurry away.

The afternoon promised and delivered sunshine. Drips from last night's rain pattered from the trees and bushes on the slope below the path that walkers used. When the drops fell on leaves from the previous autumn the sound was sharper than it was when they landed on the camouflage tunic and trousers into which small sprigs had been woven. The two sounds made a steady, remorseless drumbeat as the marksman waited. The rhythm might have dulled his sense of what was around and behind him, but his attention was locked on a gap between a beech and an ash: through the gap he had a clear view of the edge of the patio and the lawn with the gravel path across it. At the end of the path, there was a small can, which would be for cigarette ends. Voices, excited and young, came closer, but were on the path and he thought himself well enough hidden. There had been no dog owners and no rambling children in the vantage-points on the slope above the Jewish cemetery or the abandoned tower blocks or by the old Olympic bobsleigh course: Sarajevo was free of them . . . The man must come. He himself had smoked half a pack in the car during the night, and the rest while huddled on a bench, his ear phones playing music from home. He waited for the man and was certain that the addiction to nicotine would provide him with the chance. Then his money would have been earned and more work would follow.

There was a confusing noise behind and to the right. He stiffened, then slowly turned his head. His finger remained outside the trigger guard. He saw the dog and the ball. The dog edged warily towards him but had more interest in the ball than in him. He was about to look back at the garden and resume the watch through the lens when a child came. The marksman did not appreciate that the glass of the lens was uncovered or that his own eye shone in the light. The dog had the ball, then turned in response to its name. The dog and the child left.

His eye was back at the lens, the focus tight on the patio. The range was marginally less than two hundred metres. He expected to hit all targets even at 800 metres.

A woman had come out. She had smoked in the sunshine and a shoulder holster's straps had risen on her chest. Perhaps the man was trying to quit. He himself had failed eight times.

The man would come – the addiction would win – and he would be away.

The child was bright, the most intelligent in his class of six-year-olds. His mother and teachers often marvelled at the sharpness of his mind.

Neither a teacher nor his mother would doubt what the child said he had seen. Back from the path, the dog in the car, a call on a mobile: 'That's what he says he saw. If my son says it I believe him.'

It might not have been necessary to take such precautions, but Timofey Simonov met the man, a Moroccan known as 'Morocco', in a park by the river. In any other city he would have engaged in a business conversation at an outside location where bugs could not have been planted and where he was beyond the range of microphones and enhancing dishes.

That afternoon, as the sun lowered on the hill above his villa, he felt good, comfortable, confident. The message was through from his man that the transfer had been effected. They talked. More accurately, Morocco talked. Timofey listened. He rarely interrupted when he was given interesting information. He rarely took advice from the brigadier.

He was told, 'It would require financing. It's an opportunity for a person with prestige and cash to make an investment. They would remain in the background, then take a reward. It is what a Georgian group did in the South of France. In a year they did a thousand burglaries. They took iPads, tablets, laptops, good watches, anything electronic and small. The authorities in Cannes, Nice and Marseille did not recognise that an important organisation was behind the thefts. It was thought to be merely an increase in "minor offences". There was a warehouse where the goods were stored, then loaded discreetly into a container. It was taken east across the Mediterranean and unloaded at the port of Batumi on the Black Sea. The flea markets in Georgia were flooded, but the sale went well. The profit was in excess of a million euros. Serious money. I would like you to consider it. I would have thought that an initial investment of a hundred thousand euro would see the business launched and the return could be measured at three hundred to four hundred per cent. I believe also that the opportunity is particularly good at the moment because there are so many new models in the electronics field and demand outstrips supply. Also, the market could move from Georgia into Azerbaijan and possibly to Iran where the currency in exchange would be resin from poppies. The items' prices would undercut trade across the Gulf. The South of France would be good, but there would also be opportunities along the coasts of Italy and in the north.'

He was handed a slip of paper. A mobile number. He distorted it, entered it.

A pause and Morocco hesitated. He said, 'I would hope this investment will not seem too trivial to you.'

A smile of encouragement, and Timofey Simonov saw the ambitious entrepreneur on his way.

For a man such as himself there were seldom opportunities he considered too small to be worth his while. He could remember, far back, some of the imprisoned *zeks* of Perm 35 – they never had been too grand, his father had said, to turn aside business. And he had heard that the Italians from Naples, Palermo and Calabria did deals where the margin was small but would grow. The brigadier still had the mentality of a senior officer and would have said such an investment should be ignored. Timofey Simonov could value his assets and investments at a half-billion euros. Nikolai Denisov was able to keep his wife in Prague, pay her bills and the school fees, but was at the beck and the call of an employer. Timofey enjoyed small deals. Against advice, he had organised the sale of weapons – at a knock-down profit margin – via his friend. It would take him back to Milovice, where the ghosts were. It was a pilgrimage for him and he might fire one of the weapons when they were tested. He loved the darkness of Milovice, and its safety.

He walked home, another late-middle-aged Russian who took advantage of the conditions of Karlovy Vary. He did not want to be out on his own after darkness, even though the road to his home, Krale Jiriho, was well lit. Extraordinary that a thief had been prowling at the back with an accomplice.

He had a few animal carvings by African craftsmen, reminders of the gilt-encrusted days when he had flown into central Africa. They stood around the fireplace in the living room, in his bedroom on the windowsill and in his office. An elephant of dark hard wood and a gazelle were in the hallway. They recalled the days when money had come easily. His balances in unidentifiable accounts had swelled, and the élite of Moscow had sought him out. Good days, he had raked in his fortune. The agency dealing with properties had said this house was the best in the town on the market at that time. He had bought it. All because of his success in Africa, and the little cloth bags that were given in payment. And now thieves roamed at the back of his property. It was as if his security had been violated. It would be sad if he had to move on.

Matthew Bentinick drove and his wife had her hand tucked at his elbow. She was trying to reassure him. He appreciated that. Their destination was to the east of where they lived, tucked away in a rural suburb. It might once have been the residence of a captain of industry but was no longer the 'Grange' or the 'Manor'. The signboard at the gates read 'Clinic'. It was where the ambulance had brought her years ago. His wife's hand was on his arm because the wound was as painful that afternoon as it had been when they had travelled with her from Heathrow after the flight from central Africa. The driveway took them past a herbaceous border and a shrubbery. Matthew stared straight ahead, while his wife seemed to be studying the handkerchief crumpled in her spare hand. Their one child – now a grown woman of more than thirty – was only taken outside once a week because she seemed not to benefit from going more frequently. They had brought her here, had been with her in the closed ambulance, had come through the gates and seen her settled in the room where she now existed. A car provided by the Service had taken them home.

He parked. They walked across freshly raked gravel to the visitors' entrance. She did not hold his hand, not where they could be seen. Pain, for Matthew and Rosie Bentinick, was neither shared nor displayed. They came every Thursday. The staff did not encourage more than one visit each week, but the one they were allowed was sacred to them both. Three winters before, in the great freeze that had closed roads across the south-east, they had walked nine miles there, had seen their daughter and walked nine miles back to a home as empty as it had been on the first night they had left her there.

They were greeted at Reception and asked to wait. The staff on her wing would take a few minutes to make her presentable, as if she was a doll.

'You walked into a door.'

'That's what I said,' Karol Pilar answered.

'Not a Russian door?'

'A door in my apartment.'

'And there are no Irish doors in your apartment?'

'My apartment is in Vinohrady. The doors are home-produced, not from Russia or Ireland.'

He was disbelieved. His boss was left with the decision either to confront the lie or to let it go. A cigarette was lit, a voicemail was checked. His boss didn't like him. Karol Pilar was outside any circle in the detectives' building on Bartolomejska. He did not have mates in the building, or at the Sherlock, the Al Capone or the Konvikt. He was not marked down for promotion, but his work was sound.

'What do you want?'

'A back-up unit, guys from the URNA team.'

'Why?'

'Because I believe the Irish here are making a contact and may have the opportunity to test-fire weapons, probably tomorrow. I don't know the location or the supplier, so I want them on standby. Four would be sufficient.'

'And are you able to go forward discreetly on this matter with our British colleagues? Without surprises?'

'Yes. It's straightforward.'

'Watch out for doors.'

The phone was lifted and a terse instruction issued. The detail of armed men had been authorised. Pilar would do all he could for Bentinick. If it were fast and clean, discretion could be maintained and surprises kept to an acceptable level. He thanked his boss and backed out of the room.

They sat on a bench and the dusk closed around them.

Gaby Davies had guided him in, and Danny Curnow had homed in on her. 'I'll do the stag,' he said. He saw her surprise. Then she shrugged – as if it wasn't a big deal whether or not she resumed her watch on Ralph Exton.

'When'll I see you?' she asked.

He said later – he'd call her – and added something about the next day being fraught, and some rest would be good. Then his eyebrow had flickered. She left.

The targets were across the park, sitting on a bench, the towering TV mast in front of them. He had come through some pleasant squares, flanked by the grand houses of a century before. He doubted Malachy Riordan had noticed the gardens or the grandeur of the buildings: his head was down and his shoulders were bowed. She was an attractive girl – he reckoned she enjoyed the glamour and excitement of being integral to a conspiracy, that she was an innocent – her hand was back on his shoulders, working at the muscles. Maybe she should have stayed with her college books. Danny was learning to know her: he always grew familiar with targets he tailed.

He envied Riordan the fingers on the shoulders. The pictures were on his walls, and the hands that had held the brush and mixed the pigments could have been on his back if he had been prepared to commit. But it was as if the beaches ruled him, and the graveyards. He served the dead.

The light faded around him. The mothers with their prams had gone. Schoolkids came past, laden with bags, and the work force was on the way home, heaving shopping. The couple stayed in view.

The next day it would finish. Danny Curnow thought he knew how – hoped he did.

15

There had been a rain squall beyond the TV tower. It had melded with the last of the sun and had thrown a bright rainbow – Danny Curnow's pocket map told him it was in Stare Mesto and the Zizkov quarter. It would not be there for long because the wind was strengthening.

Frankie McKinney came back with a six-pack of cans and two hot dogs. While she had been gone, Malachy Riordan had not moved. Shoulders hunched, head bowed. Danny would barely have recognised him as the well-built figure at the farmhouse. He didn't need to see a man's face to recall him: his stature was enough. A can was opened.

The rainbow died. Danny saw rain advance and blanket the tower. It reached him just seconds after it had started to fall on them. They were eating, and Malachy used his hand to wipe his mouth, then swigged at the first can he had opened. Frankie sipped from hers. A woman jogged past him, trying to beat the worst of the rain home, and the wheels of a buggy threw up water that splashed Danny's legs. He had no need to sit in the open. Outside the small park there were the doorways of what had once been fine houses – he could have sheltered in one. From a bar behind him he'd have had a view of the backs of their heads. But it seemed right to share his vigil with them. He couldn't have said why.

She took the napkin from his hand as he wolfed down the last of the hot dog, stretched past him and dropped it into a bin. The first can went after it, and he opened another.

More men and women came by, umbrellas up.

Their heads and shoulders were closer. Twice he saw the girl wipe rainwater from Malachy Riordan's forehead with her hand. She threw the greater part of her own hot dog into the bin. Their shoulders touched. He thought he knew where Gaby Davies would be. He had given her full rein. He had a coat that kept off most of the rain from his shoulders and upper chest but hadn't unfastened the hood and had no cover for his legs. Malachy Riordan was on the third can.

He was a voyeur. Danny Curnow had acted that part often enough. He had watched people throughout the years he had spent in Ireland, and had been on courses to refine his skills. He had looked across parks and through windows and had seen men and women prepare themselves to kill and . . .

The woman who looked after the secretarial side of Bentinick's life at Gough had once been seen in a corner of the mess, nursing a coffee and reading from the poems of William Butler Yeats. She had been asked which one, and why. Something about an Irish airman with the Flying Corps in the First World War:

Those that I fight I do not hate,
Those that I guard I do not love . . .

The quotation had sobered the bar. Did they hate the Provisional wing of the Irish Republican Army, who bombed and shot their way deeper into a cul-de-sac? Did they love the Protestant civilians, with their bigotry, intolerance and stupidity? Little *hate* and little *love*. She had read on:

A lonely impulse of delight
Drove to this tumult in the skies . . .

Danny Curnow might not have been alone. 'The lonely impulse' had resonance. He remembered barely a word of any conversation from the Gough days, but the woman's voice, calm, quiet and respectful, had taken root with the words she'd recited. His was a 'lonely impulse'. He remembered how it had been in the gardens by the water at Honfleur, close to the lion statues and the small fountain, his stubborn refusal to abandon 'commitment', and her walking away. He remembered each Sunday evening when he drove through the harbour town to collect the battlefield visitors, and each Tuesday evening when he left them at their hotel to trail after her.

Frankie McKinney had her head close to Malachy Riordan's and there was more water for her to wipe from his forehead. Danny remembered the look of almost sad defiance as she had gazed into his face, grimaced and muttered something he hadn't quite heard. She might have wished him well. Then she had gone. Both, too obstinate to compromise. The rain slapped him. He was cold.

He watched them and thought of where he might have been. He knew the stories of men and women, once prominent, whose fortunes had corkscrewed: they had given up what they knew and had gone to act as witness to greater suffering. He knew where he should have been.

The German cemetery was always the second to be visited. First was the American cemetery. It was outside the village of Colleville and closer to Utah than to Omaha. There were two hundred casualties on the first day at Utah, but the mayhem, chaos and suffering at Omaha dwarfed that. The edge of Omaha could be seen from the cemetery grounds. There were always American civilians here. They moved stiffly, ravaged by obesity and arthritis, on sticks and frames, and would have come to see where their young men lay, nine thousand of them. The headstones were in geometrically precise lines, crosses and stars of David in Lasa marble from the South Tyrol, northern Italy. The quiet was infectious: the noise of the sea as it broke on the beaches was deadened by the bluffs of sand that the young soldiers died trying to scale. Many were from the talisman unit – the Big Red One, 1st Infantry Division – which held the motto No mission too difficult, No sacrifice too great. Duty First. *There were state-of-the-art museums and a magnitude of organised dignity. The visitors and the guide stepped warily here . . . and returned to the bus.*

It was a short ride only to the losers' resting-place. It was at La

Cambe, beside a fast road. There were twenty-six thousand graves and many were marked with the simple words Ein Deutsche Soldat. *The crosses marking the graves were different from those of the victors' dead. The guide did not point it out.*

The Germans lay beneath squat, stubby dark stones or under tablets of similar material. There were fine trees that threw shade and broke up the distances. The visitors by now would have been punch drunk with the statistics of the beaches and the strong points that the US Ranger units stormed high on the cliffs. They would have wanted to get away from the gloom of approaching evening and back into a new hotel in Caen. The guide said little but pointed out one grave. He was brief and tantalising about its significance. They were asked to remember the name Michael Wittman, an armoured ace from an SS panzer unit, buried here with the two soldiers who served with him in a Tiger Mark 6. The place had an air of dignity and despair. It lacked the nobility of the field in which the American bodies were interred, and the chance of seeing German families was remote. It was not on the tourist trail that Germans wished to follow.

The attendants wanted the gates closed, wanted to empty the parking area and close down the small building that passed for a museum. Back on the bus, the tourists were addressed by their guide. He congratulated them on their stamina and their attention during a long and upsetting day. They had earned a drink, perhaps two. There might have been a ripple of applause and the bus pulled out onto the main road. The gates closed and the darkness settled. The ghosts emerged, young men all of them, to light their cigarettes, talk about girls and beg paper for letters to distant mothers. Enmity died.

Dusty drove, as he always did, at a steady pace. He had never liked Thursday evening, but reckoned it the lifeblood of Desperate's week. He thought of him as a friend or elder brother – a troubled man, holding back the pain. Only Dusty, who had known him for ever and had walked behind him with the Heckler & Koch, loaded with a full magazine, thought of him as a rock, but now saw the granite cracked. He feared for his friend.

It had seemed natural for him to follow Desperate out of Gough

Barracks. He had not been asked to, but had never questioned his decision to go with him. The day before they had gone was sharp in his memory. He had walked into the outer office to hand in fuel receipts and the mileage list, and had heard voices through the chipboard door that led into Captain Bentinick's room.

A man had been left bare-arsed and it was inevitable what would happen.

Sorry, Desperate, but out of my remit and taken at a loftier level.

The man would be picked up within twenty-four hours, then be beyond reach. Their security had a line into him already. The man should have been shipped out.

I'm sure you know the factors that are weighed before there is an exfiltration, Desperate. It would have been nice to lift him clear but budgetary restraints forbade it.

Had the man been abandoned because there wasn't sufficient cash left in a relocation pot?

Let's not get emotional. Pockets aren't bottomless. We have to live within our means.

The man would end up with burns, bruises, and a piece of his skull blown out. Was there not a duty of care?

Never thought to hear you, Desperate, muttering that sort of mumbo-jumbo. You know what it costs: safe-house, armed protection, the new-identity stuff. Then they want their women shipped in – and later the women want to go back and do so. Then he does and he's nutted anyway. Hardly cost efficient. It's not considered worth the effort.

The man was liked. He was good company, and—

Hadn't expected you'd need to be told this, Desperate, but get a grip. Nothing is ever as bad as it seems. You're starting to feel sorry for yourself. You should take some leave and find a woman. Look, someone has to protect those wankers on the commuter trains and you're the best at it. Another day, another dollar. On your way, please, Desperate.

A bit late. They'd learn, through back-door channels, that the man was already in the hands of their security unit. Dusty had scarpered. He'd left his paperwork and was gone by the time Danny had come out. Dusty had only ever been into Bentinick's office to deliver a mug of tea because the girl was busy with a malfunctioning computer. There had been no family photograph on display, but rumour had it he'd been heard speaking to a daughter on the phone and had sounded almost human.

If Dusty Miller had been there when Matthew Bentinick had called him back he'd have fought it. But he hadn't. And already, before the call, his friend had been in a state of decay. It was sad to watch a good man weaken.

It was Gaby Davies's room. No trail of clothing across the floor, but two neat piles.

Bizarre. They had met in the corridor. Neither had picked up the phone and offered an invitation. She had come out, and so had Ralph. Both had closed their doors. He had brushed a hand across his hair, straightened his back and pulled in his belly. She had tugged at her blouse and done a wriggle with her hips. As if choreographed, they had moved forward and nearly bumped into each other. Her room was a couple of yards nearer.

The coverlet pulled back, sheets and a blanket rucked under them.

She had led, and both had understood where they were going. Neither held the initiative. So, an officer of the Security Service, with a future, was in the arms of a near-itinerant chancer. Ralph Exton had not crossed the Rubicon to be with her, and she had not seen him on the far side and waded out. It was as if they had held hands and stepped into the shallows together, had skidded and slid but held each other up. Well, something similar. They understood that time was with them, and a future might have beckoned.

He lay on his back, Gaby Davies half across him. Her head was on his shoulder and her fingernails worked in the hairs of his chest.

She said, 'I don't see it as two lonely people, needing to do this to feel better about themselves.'

'I see it as going forward.'

'Going where I want to be.'

'He said I could be found wherever I went.'

'What else?'

'They'd trace me. The *mafiya* would be told and the people off the mountain. He said I'd be looking over my shoulder day and night. He terrified me. Confession time, Gaby.'

'Tell me.'

A pause. 'I told you half of it, maybe a third. The Russian end – my friend Timofey, who's a devious and wicked little bastard – was where I filtered the truth.'

'I think I realised that.'

'It was threatened out of me. *He* did that.'

'I'd have had the same result. Slower but the same.'

'It makes me the great betrayer. A traitor to my friend, a traitor to the men with drills and burning cigarettes. Not to you, Gaby.'

She looked down into his face. Their eyes and mouths were close. His teeth were poor and hers imperfect. She would have bought insurance from him if he had cold-called at her door. If she had spun a hard-luck story about needing a taxi because her mum was at death's door, he'd have cleaned out his wallet for her. 'We'll find somewhere. A bottle of fizz every Friday night, and you'll put on a pretty frock, and I'll try to look my best. It'll be our place. Somewhere they don't reach.'

'We deserve each other.'

'Right word, "deserve". We'll be good for each other. They'll say in the corridor that I was a frigid bitch but developed an itch. God, the shock waves . . .'

'Can they reach us? I think he could, that he would fulfil a threat. He's hard.'

'Wrong, Ralph. Bad habit of mine. I call it like I see it. There was a woman at our place, Winnie somebody. She was involved in a big one and afterwards she bugged out. Up in the Hebrides, living at a backpackers' bunkhouse. She's surviving, and we can . . . You're wrong.'

'He's hard, as I said.'

'Wrong. We get taught profile recognition. He's lonely, nervous, twisted with emotion. I loathed him at the start and now I'm a sympathiser. He's a wall-builder. If anyone comes close to him, he's mixing mortar and slapping on the bricks. He's one of the men or women we have a use for but are kept outside the gates. They're increments, employed like street-sweepers. He's a creature of Matthew Bentinick and . . . What's the matter?'

His hands eased her sideways. 'Gaby, can we do it again?'

'No . . . I'm going back to the battlefield. Get some sleep – you won't tomorrow. It's always difficult when the betrayal gets called in.'

She kissed him and swung her legs off the bed. He wasn't much of a catch but he was what she had. Would anyone care? She went to her pile of clothes and started to dress. Probably not. Not even the agent handler if she delivered. Not even Matthew Bentinick.

The pattern was well established. There was a chair in the corridor for Matthew Bentinick. The door was left open and his shoes rested on the line where the carpets changed. Rosie was inside. Truth was, and he freely acknowledged it, he didn't have the strength to be inside the room for the weekly one-hour visit.

Nothing much changed. The days of head X-rays and magnetic resonance imaging scans were long past. Their daughter was in 'trauma'. In fair physical health but psychiatrically wrecked. She sat in an easy chair. She could swallow solids and drink. She could use a toilet with help. Most afternoons she was brought downstairs into a common recreational area. On dry summer days, once a week, she might be allowed to sit in the sunshine by a large lime tree under observation. But Mary Bentinick never spoke. Her mother and father had not heard her voice since they had met the air ambulance and hurried beside the gurney as she was wheeled through the airport passageways. She had the TV on: she did not watch it but stared at it. She seemed to recognise neither her parents nor members of the nursing staff. Matthew no longer bothered to quiz consultants. He had been told years before that his daughter had the acute symptoms of catatonic schizophrenia: *Catatonia is a state of neurogenic motor immobility and behavioural abnormality manifested by stupor*. That was enough. How long would it last? 'Sorry, Mr Bentinick, we have no idea.' The fee at the clinic was around a thousand a week and the insurers of the charity that had sent her to Africa paid a lump of it. The previous director general had done some creative accounting so the Security Service chipped in. A little more came from the Bentinick funds.

If she had spoken it would have been better. If they had been given an approximation of an end date it would have been easier. It was the blank stare that destroyed him. Much of the time he was there he focused on the carpet. Rosie had a cheerful voice and talked for both of them. She was describing now how well the tomatoes were doing in the greenhouse in spite of the aphids. Mary's condition did not change. When he imagined what had been done to her, the torture was almost beyond what he could bear. There could not be closure, but he hoped for redress. Maybe tomorrow evening.

'Of course, I wasn't actually there.'

'I think you've a good idea of events as they played out.'

'I suppose I have. It's like a nightmare, but not a dream. It happened.'

Jocelyn sat opposite him. He was the stereotype of an aid worker. She had travelled to his office that afternoon: too complicated to have him inside Thames House, and unsuitable for their business to be talked through in a public place. There was a small conference room at the back of the first floor of the building. She had a mug of coffee, and the charity's logo was flaking off – a child in its mother's arms against a backdrop of Africa. He had close-cut blond hair, sun-bleached, a wind-tanned face, and wore a safari shirt with frayed jeans. Her estimation: a grandparent's trust fund supported him. He seemed irritable, and she assumed that was because her questioning reminded him of where he'd been – useful, involved – and where he was now.

'She didn't make the radio link. She was supposed to do it whether she had malaria, was at death's door, in the middle of a clinic, taking classes or delivering babies. Two days without contact – we pressed the panic button. Mary Bentinick was important to us. She was conscientious, stubborn and played by the rules. She should have left, but had refused. The area director was scheduled to go up and drag her out by the hair if he had to. It was not something we'd have done lightly – two hundred klicks there and another two hundred back. We'd decided to bring her back after the first shipment had gone in. We left it too long. It happened, we think, a couple of days afterwards.'

Jocelyn took the note. The story was substantially the same as that told by the Revenue & Customs team, but the slant was different so it was useful.

'It isn't a pretty story.'

'I wasn't expecting it to be.'

'Her father's been told.'

'In the raw?'

He grimaced. 'With edits for sensitivity.'

'I'll take the unexpurgated version, thank you.'

'It was an Antonov plane and had been given an arrival time on an old strip – mineral explorers had built it. The Russians had a contract to provide the M23 people with more modern firepower, better weapons than the UN people down the road – where I was with the area director. The local commander was Brother Hastings – that was what he called himself – and he paid with illicitly mined rough diamonds. Twenty-five tons of hardware were ferried in. A Russian handled the transaction, a former intelligence officer named Simonov. There were people in the theatre who had big radios and could download stuff – spooks did it. Simonov brought the weapons in – threw in a crate or two of Scotch – and flew out. It was illegal. It violated a UN resolution and an embargo. There was a nun who nursed in the clinic and she's the main source. Don't ask for her email address. She kept a diary, wrote it down and fled. She was caught and butchered. The document was stuffed down her front – they weren't interested in removing clothing from above the waist so they didn't find it. Her body was located by troops of the UN force, Indonesians. They recovered the document. How are you doing?'

'Thank God my parents sent me to shorthand classes. I'm doing fine but I'll want a photocopy of the document she carried out.' Her coffee had cooled.

'The first night was tense. The M23 people were mostly blind drunk. Mary Bentinick stayed in the clinic and made it into something of a refuge. There were two nuns and a priest there, and patients who were recovering after minor surgery from the doctor's last visit. In the morning, apparently, they came looking for food and assumed the building was a good start point.'

She wrote.

'They took what food was there, went away for a couple of hours, then came back. Mary Bentinick could have done a runner, but she didn't. It's a familiar enough story for foreign aid workers in bad places at bad times. They're surrounded by the kids they've taught and nursed, and the friends they've made – they find it impossible just to leave them. So she didn't go. The priest was bayoneted, the nuns were raped. Any of the men who tried to stand in the militia's way were shot or clubbed. Then they got to her. What they did is in the document. I can't bring myself to spell it out.'

He lit a cigarette.

'In brief. She'd already have seen the brutality of the killings. At some stage she was clubbed across the skull or thrown down and hit her head on concrete. She was raped. It would have been a frenzy. Unprotected sexual penetration with more than a platoon of them. They were high on alcohol and higher on the power given them by the cargo brought by Timofey Simonov. I don't know whether she was HIV-infected – it'd be a miracle if she wasn't. There would have been a bit more of it the next day. The graves had been dug and the dead buried. The woman who had written up the document went that night, and other villagers left singly or in family groups. The militia still had the dregs of the whisky. Someone took her out but she was already wounded – had a bullet in the stomach. She was found by the Indonesians about five klicks up the road. She was sitting by a tree with her legs apart and her knees up, as if she were just waiting for the next in line and being ready meant it hurt less. The wounded man had bled to death. Do you want a full résumé on the UN mandate?'

'I think I know where you're going.'

'The Indonesians didn't think they had the firepower to win a decisive victory over the M23 people. They believed it would be inconclusive and they would take casualties. They never went as far as the air strip, but took her back with them, along with any survivors lucky enough to be close to the track. Those who were in the bush had to take their chance. You know the rest. Air-ambulance evacuation. I'm afraid I've lost touch with it. I do southern Sudan now. How is . . . ?'

'Not much changed. I'm grateful for your time.' Jocelyn gathered together her clutter, dumped her pad and pencil in her bag, and had her scarf out. She stood up.

He gazed at her. 'It was all because of those bloody weapons being sent in, some bastards making a fortune out of the trade. Are you actually going to do something about it?'

'Don't push me.'

'There've been enough weasel words over the years, promises of decisive intervention. The thugs of the bush and savannahs have never been better armed.'

'Watch this space.'

She headed for the door and the stairs.

It was not for an officer of her rank and standing at Thames House to discuss policy with a desk prisoner of an obscure underfunded charity. A young staffer in the analysis corner of the building had produced a paper three years earlier. It had dealt with internal threats to the UK's homeland. The staffer was of Pakistani origin, from the West Midlands, and reckoned a top-grade talent. Her paper had been widely circulated – the Islamist threat to British cities and lives, and to the communities of close allies in the country's inner cities, but was then franchised out to safe havens abroad. The safest of the havens had shifted from Afghanistan, Pakistan and Yemen to unpopulated wildernesses in Africa where well-armed war lords ruled. They held sway in Nigeria, Mali, Mauretania, the mountains of southern Algeria, Libya, Somalia and many other corners of destitution and Islamic fundamentalism. Their power was based on bullets and weapons. Their faith was fuelled by a perversion of Islam and the naked pursuit of power. The weapon in the hand was the strongest element of the equation. Crates of rifles and mortars loaded on pallets and airlifted into remote parts of an unpoliced and ungoverned continent would provide, ultimately, the threat in Britain's cities.

Each plane load tilted a balance; each illegal arms dealer was to be classified as an enemy. Her message was absorbed. The Americans – 'the Cousins' – had incarcerated Viktor Bout and had rejoiced at the success of an overseas operation that had netted the Merchant of Death, but Jocelyn and her colleagues worked quietly. She would never have considered hinting to the charity worker that the affairs of Timofey Simonov were on the point of possible closure. The problem was the lack of evidence to lay before a court. It was hard to find any – which meant that risks had to be run. She knew most of Vagabond's history and thought Bentinick had chosen well. It was not only about the assault on Mary Bentinick but concerned the threats posed to the United Kingdom and the need to expose an enemy. She took the bus back to the Thames-side building.

He prepared for his visit to Milovice, once the headquarters garrison camp of Central Command (Europe).

What had happened to Milovice was a disgrace. The brigadier was in the utility room ironing the grey shirt he would wear, and the tie that went with 'best uniform dress'. Timofey Simonov was at the smaller wardrobe of the dressing room that led off his bedroom. The larger one held the majority of his clothes. The other was for the two uniforms he possessed and the greatcoat of the Red Army, with headgear for summer, winter and a combat helmet.

Milovice was a disgrace that shamed the Czech people, who had shown no gratitude for their liberation from Fascism. Equally deserving of opprobrium was the Russian government, led by Gorbachev, Yeltsin and Putin. He would not wear the combat uniform with the camouflage pattern, but the one designed for an officer of his rank in the GRU. He fingered the material, pinched the tunic between thumb and forefinger.

The site of the camp had been allowed to sink into disrepair. It had become home to gypsies and squatters, then been abandoned. Trees grew where there had been tended grass, and undergrowth carpeted the areas between runways and hangars, control towers and bunkers.

Veterans' groups should have been there at weekends, with monuments to the different units of infantry, armour and air force that had been stationed there, and a museum to show the superb technology of the equipment based in the camp. There was nothing. Timofey Simonov believed it brought ignominy on the heads of Russians and Czechs.

He went once a month, the brigadier driving, and they would wind through the crumbling internal roads looking for old buildings where they had served. He would stand beside the runway, flanked by the hangars, and seem to hear the sounds of . . . It was appropriate that a deal with his friend, Ralph Exton, should be closed there. It was where he had served with pride. He loved it. He lifted the uniform out of the wardrobe.

A mirror covered the inside of the wardrobe door. He wasn't handsome and had no woman to look after him. He could have made a serious effort to attract one but he had held back: divorce settlements were crippling. He had balked at a marriage that might lead to paying off a woman. There had been girls in Moscow, Ostend, Bulgaria, and a few when he had arrived in Karlovy Vary. Now, he had no need for a woman. He slept alone and had the company of his dogs. He laid the uniform on the bed and closed the wardrobe door. The boots were already on the rug beside it.

He yearned for respect. It had been denied him by the British officer in the seminar on nuclear weapons in Berlin. He never forgot lack of respect: it was always punished. He chased respect and believed he had it from the senior officials at the embassy, who fêted him, and from the men at the Kremlin, who gave him the 'roof' and offered well-paid work. The old camouflage uniform no longer fitted. The uniform on the bed was from a theatrical costumier in Ostrava: it had been used in films and on the stage. The boots were his own, no longer waterproof but still wearable.

He would feel fulfilled tomorrow when he went to Milovice and did business for his oldest friend, Ralph Exton. Perhaps a quieter life beckoned in which respect would play a lesser role.

He would miss it. It was because of the respect he had gained that he had been approached for a sub-contract to the south-west of London, but he had heard nothing of an execution by rifle fire. He felt frustrated.

'It was the dog that done him, Guv.'

'Bronco's a bit headstrong. I'm not surprised our chum shut up shop.'

Six of the Surrey force had been up on the bank when the dog had been sent in for the gunman. Their chum's forearm had ended up locked between the German Shepherd's teeth. The sergeant and a constable had taken off most of their armour-plated protection and their weapons had been made safe. The dog's track had provided them with a clear view of the gardens of the house below. Word was that a Russian national was being hosted there by a spook team. He would have been under the kitchen table while the arrest was made, but since the handcuffs had gone on, he had been heaved into the back of a transport and shipped out. Lucky lad.

'It's hardly going to be a coincidence, our chum in place.'

'You saw the rifle.'

'I rather liked it, Guv. A Rangemaster, .338 calibre, more bang than he needed, but it's as good as they come. No coincidence. It was in the hands of a professional.'

'He's not said anything.'

'Wouldn't, would he? Slav, I reckon. Co-operative, but he would be with Bronco hanging onto his arm.'

Armed suspects in custody were always a source of fascination. Some were pliant, others weepy and a few wanted to break the bar on the handcuffs. This one had been strangely calm. The constable had done time in the UN's Civilian Police programme in Banja Luka, part of Bosnia. He'd tried a couple of words in that language but the man hadn't answered.

'Did you hear where the tip came from?'

'A woman phoned in to tell us what her six-year-old child had said he'd seen him. A couple of guys were sent out, the kiddie gave them the briefing and they scrambled on it.'

'It's a hell of a call, picking up something like that.'

'And political. The shit's going to be flying off the fan. We're well out of it, Guv.'

They laughed. They'd be the last of the armed-response team to leave and the footpath would be in the care of uniforms awaiting Forensics.

Outside the community centre, Bridie Riordan waited in her car. She had come to collect Oisin from the Irish-dancing club. She was ambushed. They came from behind and she was startled by the rap on the closed window. She knew Kevin's mother better than she knew Pearse's. She stared out of the filthy window into the half-light at the edge of the pool thrown down by the big spotlight that covered part of the parking area. She wound it down. There was rain in the air and it flickered on their faces. Their eyes were red but their cheeks were dry, which told her that the weeping was private.

She was civil, calm, wished them a good evening, then expressed her sympathies. Some on the mountain would have gushed but that was not Bridie Riordan's way. Pearse's mother said they had been to see the priest and talk to him. Kevin's mother told her that they'd discussed the funerals with him.

'Of course.'

She saw her boy emerge from the hall. A woman led him.

'Because we don't want any political shite,' Kevin's mother hissed.

'The shite that killed them, berets, gloves,' Pearse's mother added.

'That's nothing to do with me.'

In unison: 'We'll have no guns over the coffins, no shooting. No speeches on the glory of Ireland. Do you hear?'

'I'm sorry for your loss.'

She flashed the headlights and the woman who had Oisin led her boy to her.

'And where's your husband?' Pearse's mother asked.

'Around is he, or not?' That was Kevin's mother.

She hesitated, then reached across, opened the door for her child, then turned back to her window. 'He's away on work.'

'Is it important work, Mrs Riordan, that keeps him away when there's killing to be done on his say-so, and wee boys are sent out in his place?'

'That's a brave man you have, Mrs Riordan, that gives the orders and fills my son's head with shite and then is not here when he's blown to his Maker.'

'I'll not take it further.' The child was in, and she helped with his belt.

'Your husband, Mrs Riordan, might as well have killed our boys with his own hand. He's had death in his family, but should have known better than to send out our lads.'

'Can you sleep with the knowledge of what your husband did? If he's back from his work on the day of the funerals, tell him to keep away.'

'Your husband and Brennie Murphy are not welcome, Mrs Riordan. You know what they're saying? We heard it off the funeral directors and they'd heard the police talking about it in the field where it happened. You want to know what's said? I'm telling you what—'

Bridie Riordan slammed the car into gear. Gravel and water from the puddles spattered the two women. The small boy cried out in protest. She didn't know where her husband was or what he was doing. There was blackness on the mountain and few lights showed. She and Oisin were alone, isolated. Bridie Riordan knew nothing and hadn't wanted to know. She drove back to the farm.

He was irritable. Timofey Simonov shouted down the stairs, 'Denisov, where's my fucking shirt?'

An answer from far below: did he expect to sleep in an ironed shirt? What did he need it for?

Another yell from the top of the stairs: 'When is your wife due?'

She would arrive at the same time as the brigadier had told his boss when he had last asked. Nothing had changed. His wife would care for the dogs overnight, as she always did.

And the cause of the irritability: 'Denisov, is the TV on the news station?'

The volume must have been tweaked. It was a rolling news station broadcasting from London. On the traversing bar at the bottom of the screen there was no mention of a fatal shooting south-west of London.

'What do you think I'm going to do?'

Frankie and Malachy had walked to his hotel along low-lit streets past small hotels and bars. She had been cold and wet, hanging on to his arm. He'd seemed barely to notice her.

They were at the door. It looked like a rubbish place. If it had been in the back end of Dublin she would have rated it as a hookers' hang-out. There were weeds in the pavement cracks, broken glass in the gutter and the paint was peeling on the door. Inside the light was dim but she could see the rack behind the desk with a few keys hanging from it.

He seemed to block her at the door, and there was pain in his face. His hand came across her to grip the door jamb. He didn't speak. She didn't know whether he was a big drinker or not. She had bought six cans of strong lager, and he had drunk five, then taken hers and finished it. She knew why she had stayed with him. Frankie McKinney had not sat on a bench in the rain for the sake of her health or his peace of mind. Two kids had been blown up by their own bomb in County Tyrone. Not her problem. What was Frankie McKinney's problem? That his arm was across the door, blocking her. She pushed it.

'What's the matter with you? Are you some sort of priest?'

He dropped his arm. She saw herself in the mirror behind the desk. She was sodden. The clerk ogled her – she wondered if he stood outside the rooms and listened. He held the key, arm outstretched. She took it, pushed past Malachy Riordan and went on up. She heard his steps behind her and left a trail of wet on the thin carpet.

And afterwards?

Her mother had once referred to the glory of discovering a formerly unseen part of 'life's rich tapestry', but would never have known that glory. Frankie McKinney chased it, and went steadily up the stairs. It would be a joy to take off her wet clothes. And afterwards? She would search and find – she was confident. Already she had her coat off and was loosening her belt. He followed.

He was alone, keeping vigil. The policeman had brought beakers of coffee and sandwiches. In the calm and detached way of a professional, Karol Pilar had gone through what would be in place. He had talked, he said, with a London liaison, a woman he identified as Jocelyn. He had remarked that her telephone voice marked her as 'formidable'. He had caught her at her desk, late, and had imagined a solitary light burning and an empty corridor, beyond her door. Danny had grinned ruefully and muttered about doing 'stag with a bloody poet', but the drink had warmed him. It was good to be on the vigil, watching and waiting. Karol Pilar had forced his coat on him. He had taken off his own, unbuttoned his shirt, and used a handkerchief to dry his skin, then had done up the shirt and put Pilar's coat over it. The Czech knew what Gaby Davies had and had not been told. He had pursed his lips and chuckled. They were in a doorway that smelt of old urine. The windows beside it were boarded up and weeds sprouted from the masonry. He talked about three men from the special-weapons squad, where they would be and the plan for the next day. What would happen to him? Pilar had shrugged: depended on whether or not they won, whether it was clean or messy. If they succeeded, he would be back in Bartolomejska, at his desk, on Monday morning, writing a report distinguished by bland misinformation and submitting expenses. And if they did not succeed? No answer was required. They carried a weighty burden. Pilar said he was sorry he couldn't walk Danny into Vinohrady, take him up to the attic studio, pour him some wine and have Jana cook a meal. Did he have a girl? Danny had ground his teeth into his lower lip, gazing up at the one lit window and the high dormer. He had eaten the sandwiches, drunk the coffee and pushed Karol Pilar away. The Czech had reached inside his coat and taken out the greaseproof-wrapped cake – supposed to be for Jana's mother at the weekend. Better for him to eat a slice. Pilar, detective in a specialist squad, was probably the only one among his colleagues who was more than half human, almost sane.

A quick movement from a trouser belt to Danny Curnow's hand. Cold, hard. He was told the make and the capacity of the magazine, and slid it from sight. The Czech slipped away, moved to the other pavement each time a streetlight threatened to identify him.

It was reassuring to have the pistol. He hadn't held a weapon since he had checked the Browning back into the armoury at Gough.

The rain eased and he felt warmer. A rake-thin cat sidled close and befriended him, then saw a rat two doors down and left him.

Gaby came.

The Czech would have called her.

She would have been in his room at the hotel across Wenceslas Square, rifled in the drawers and found enough of the few clothes he had brought with him. He stripped. Fresh underwear, dry trousers and shirt, warm socks. He thanked her.

He knew where she had been and what she had done. He could read it in her. She gathered his discarded clothes and bagged them. They would likely be binned. She settled down beside him and must have felt the outline of the pistol because she eased away and pointed down. He took it from his belt and showed it to her. Her face – what he could see of it – clouded. She'd be told what was planned when she needed to know, not before.

The night slipped on.

16

A gutter dripped and Danny Curnow woke. He didn't thrash around, swing his legs and wonder where he was, why and with whom. Clarity came.

He felt the hardness under his shoulder. Answers tripped along in his mind. *Who* was easy: his head was resting on the chest of Gaby Davies, and the hardness under his shoulder was her arm. The next was harder: *why*. It was always difficult to cobble together an answer that was half satisfactory. For a moment he struggled, then gave up. Later there might be an explanation. The next was simpler. *Where*: he was in a doorway opposite the pension. A couple had come out, bent under heavy rucksacks, and lurched away. They might have been looking for a bus to the railway station or the airport. The concrete of the step ate into his buttocks and his sole warmth came from her body. The light was still on in the room high in the building, the only one that had not been switched off during the night.

She gave a sharp kick.

A dog backed away, edging towards the gutter, showing its teeth and snarling. Something for Danny Curnow to savour: her kick at the dog had not been gentle. If the animal had been close enough, and her aim accurate, her foot might have propelled it across the pavement and into the road. He didn't care to burrow in his mind for an answer as to *why* he was there but he thought she was hardening and had done so on each phase of the trip.

'Did I wake you?'

'Probably not. I apologise.' Danny grimaced.

'What for?' She seemed indifferent.

'Using you as a cushion. I don't usually crash out.'

There was little light, but he thought a smile might have clipped her mouth. She had brought him dry clothes to increase his effectiveness, not from sympathy. She said, 'You might not have crashed out years ago when you were working, but now you're old.'

He disentangled himself and sat up. She rubbed vigorously at her arm and played another trump. Gaby Davies was hunched forward, arms round her knees. Her voice was quiet – as if she believed in her authority over him. She told him that she had been to the back of the hotel, had looked for exits but there were none. Her impression was that the fire-escape door was padlocked and the targets were still inside. She was at a better angle for him to observe her. He could always tell – easier with a woman than a man. He didn't need to hear footsteps on the landing or the whine of springs when Dusty went in after Christine. There was nothing in Dusty's manner at breakfast but Christine always jutted her chin and her cheeks were flushed. It was not for Danny Curnow to pass judgement if a handler shagged an agent. She could do worse or better. He was not an expert on relationships.

He said, 'Not my business who you sleep with.'

She flushed. Her eyes blazed. 'No.'

'But in the old days it would have been a hanging offence.'

'I didn't ask for your opinion.'

'And the Joe you slept with had you wrapped round his little finger, told you what he wanted you to know and was economical with the rest.'

'Wrong. He's given me every detail of his relationship with Malachy Riordan.'

He said quietly, 'You'll get a text this afternoon or this evening, something from Matthew Bentinick. I'm not adding anything except that it was necessary to bully some truths from Exton.'

If she was happy to be bedded by the Joe, good luck to her. Would it last? He didn't imagine so, but what did he know? Nothing. He felt an ache of loneliness, and couldn't stifle it. It was good to feel the pistol in his waistband. It was five in the morning and a church clock chimed at the end of the street. It was the start of a day that would begin slowly. The pace would quicken, and he fancied it would end in stampede. He thought her a good kid, but personal happiness was low on the agenda.

He thanked her for his dry clothes. A dustcart came down the street. He thanked her, again, for letting him sleep, and wondered whether his head had shared a place with Ralph Exton.

A traveller's pocket alarm, one sold in an airport lounge, bleeped thinly. It had woken him in the Armagh hotel when he had needed to drive off into the fog for the meeting with the men on the mountain, beyond the reach of back-up. It had sounded in the kitchen at home and had sent him to the airport for a flight to Prague. Ralph Exton groped across the bed. She wasn't there.

The other half of the bed was cold. She had not come back with him. Quite brusque. He had been chucked out. He found the alarm, killed it, sagged, and swore.

His first image of the day was not the rose garden at home, the pub in the village where they served him steak or the sight of two hands – one of them his – clasped together in a handshake, deal done. And it was not the sweet mouth of Gaby Davies, poised over his. What he saw in the moment of waking was the face of the man he knew as 'Danny'. He feared him. The nightmare: he walked streets in darkness, heard footfalls behind him, then the drill. He felt damp concrete on his ankles and shins.

A clock struck. There were churches all around Stepanska. One started, others joined in. A chorus played for him. It was past six.

What could Ralph Exton hope for? Another deal, another shipment of antique furniture from last week's factory line, or computers in a container from Vietnam that looked good but were short on memory space. Money in small envelopes: no drills, no concrete. He had been threatened and believed the threat. Danny had dead eyes and was to be believed. Danny would kill him.

The horn blasted loudly enough to reach the dormer window.

The three magazines Karol Pilar had loaded for his issue pistol were on the kitchen table and his vest was hooked on a chair. He wolfed the sandwich. She watched from the bedroom door, in her nightdress. His Jana would not have suggested that he might 'take care', and hadn't asked what he'd be doing today. She said she'd make another cake for her mother and was glad it had been appreciated.

As if it were an afterthought, he kissed her cheek.

He ran down the flights of stairs, the camera bouncing on the lanyard around his neck. The cuts on his face had scabbed and now they itched. All would be done as Mr Bentinick had requested.

He went out through the building's front door. In the park, high above the side-street, he was observed by the stern-featured statue of Svatopluk Čech – dead more than a century. The writer and poet might not have considered Karol Pilar a suitable neighbour. He ran as the horn sounded again from an unmarked black Transit-style van. He had twice been beaten and his injuries, old and new, were important to him. They steeled his determination. That morning he would cross a line. There would be little future, he thought, in the Prague detective offices for a young officer determined to stand against the flow. He would risk his job. He would not be congratulated. Karol Pilar, among many talents, could play the devious bastard in the face of his office colleagues.

The back door opened for him. They were all in black. Their weapons were on racks. They drove away. It was past seven. They went west, as they had to.

A fly crawled on his face. He struggled not to open his eyes. Malachy Riordan had long tracked the fly. It had started on his arm, where the scratches and bite marks were, trekked up and over the bulges of his muscles. It had been round his neck and gone past his mouth. It had crossed his cheeks and been near to his ear. It was the tickling at his nose that broke him. The fuckin' thing was going into his nostril. He snorted and slapped himself.

The fly had gone. His fingertips were on his right cheek. The scratches were dry because the blood had been staunched.

He had been awake long enough, sharing the bed with her. He had stared at the ceiling and had noted each crack in the plaster around the light fitting. Then he had slept. The boys had been killed and it might as well have been at his hand. He opened his eyes and tilted his head. He saw her.

His fingers lay against the scratches on his cheek that her nails had made. It had been done in the last spasms, with her final strength. The tips of her fingers were bloodied, her nails stuffed with his flesh. He was on the bed beside her. He wore his vest, and his underpants were at his knees. She had lowered them before his hands had flailed at her face. She had undressed for both of them. He had not known how to stop her. Her voice had been a murmur in his ear, supposed to soothe him, and her hands gone where only Bridie's went. He had felt himself growing, had known the shame and struck her.

'What's the matter with you? Can't you do it? I won't hurt you. Doesn't your wife do this with you? Are you frightened of me, Malachy?' One blow, hard enough to loosen teeth. He'd seen the scream well in her and had grabbed her throat. The scratch on his cheek was deep and hurt. He squeezed tighter, her writhing on the bed, attempting to dislodge him and biting his forearms. He had gone on squeezing, long after the chance of her screaming had been eliminated. He had not stopped until she was still. He had lain there. He had not touched her, looked at her or covered her with the sheet.

A long time afterwards, tears wetting his face, he had drifted into sleep.

Now he saw the death pallor of her cheeks and the blue of her lips. Her tongue was out and twisted clear of her teeth, which had his blood on them. The bruises shocked him. Her throat was mottled with blue, yellow and purple welts. She had her pants on, nothing else. She had not removed them when he had tried to push her away. The fly moved on her: it flew from her chin to her chest, then circled a nipple and went on down.

He choked.

Malachy Riordan would be pushed into a cell and the door would slam. It had happened in the Antrim crime suite, and in the barracks at Dungannon, but then his head had been high and he had been confident that they couldn't hold him. He had been, then, a great man, Brennie Murphy's disciple. There would have been police in Dungannon and Armagh who dreaded the thought of a late-night call-out and the risks of a 'come-on' bomb – probably terrified by the thought of him, what he could do. His name was strong on the mountain and his wife had the respect of the community. He had not betrayed what others had died for. There would be no respect from the villagers on either side of the Dungannon to Pomeroy road for the killer of a girl, whose red hair was tangled across her face, whose green eyes were staring, and whose mouth, which had been pretty . . . She lay beside him.

He swung himself off the bed. At the window he parted the curtains and looked down. A vagrant occupied a doorway, a woman with him. He wondered if this was the day when the boys would be buried, or if the police would continue to hold the bodies. He dressed in what warm clothes he had left and bundled the wet garments into a torn laundry bag from the bottom of the wardrobe. He added her clothing to the bundle. Then he saw the small pink package on the floor that held a condom. It went into the bag too. Her handbag was on the chair. He went through it. Makeup, a purse, a passport and the notebook. He read the pages: where they should go and where they would be picked up, dictated to her by the arsehole Russian from the bank. He tore out those pages and looked again at the rest – flight times, bank numbers and expenses incurred. Her handbag went with the laundry.

At the door, he lifted the Do Not Disturb sign off the handle, opened it, hung it on the outside, closed the door and locked it.

It was past eight, from the chimes of the clock on the church tower at the top of the street. Far below him, the vagrant and the woman still occupied the doorway of a derelict building. Behind him, muffled, he heard footsteps on the stairs and voices. He sat in a chair and faced the window. The curtain stayed drawn. He couldn't see her.

It was a habit, and it amused Timofey Simonov to indulge it. He enjoyed playing the great man, employer and master, when the brigadier's wife came from Prague. When she arrived by taxi – the amount charged always queried – Simonov would nag and belittle his man. The brigadier would not walk out on him – he could have bet his life on it.

Nikolai Denisov and his wife, Elena, had looked over the edge of a cliff and felt the vertigo of standing above an abyss. They had known terror when they thought of their prospects and the future.

He had been on the phone and on his laptop. He had been speaking with bankers and investment managers in Zürich, Nassau and São Paolo, punctuating the calls with shouted questions down the stairs. Dutiful answers had returned to him.

Denisov would not leave because he and Elena remembered how it had been in Milovice when the empire had collapsed. While Timofey had organised tankers to drain the underground storage tanks and bring fuel to the wire where queues of Czechs extended each night, reports had arrived that the families of military officers had been thrown out on the street. The wives were reduced to prostitution and worked each night in brothels. The husbands would fight for the right to drive a taxi from a popular rank. Their children were sent out each night to scavenge. Fear reigned. He could remember clearly how he had flown back to Ostend in the limping Antonov. He had shown the brigadier the cloth bag with a drawstring, and had tipped out the contents. They had taken the train to Amsterdam and had traded. He had given generously to his man, the former commanding officer, and Nikolai Denisov had kissed his hand. They would not leave him: they owed him the clothes on their backs and the food in their bellies. He would enjoy tomorrow's dinner. She would have returned to Prague and Denisov would sit outside in the Mercedes and wait for him. In the meantime he would go to the old camp.

He did not have to go – his man could have done the business – but he never shirked detail. It was oxygen to him. He went into his dressing room.

Something was gnawing at him. He began to undress, then pulled on the uniform. The television played in the background. It was tuned to a satellite news channel and carried nothing about a killing. His reputation, which was precious to him – it brought work, advantage and reward – was based on his total reliability and every-time success. The newscasts told him nothing and it was past nine. He looked good in the uniform, but anxiety spoiled the moment.

He often walked. It was freedom for Matthew Bentinick to take a late commuter train to Waterloo, then stride along Lambeth Palace Road, past the Archbishop's palace and over the bridge. Usually he would collect a coffee from the café in Horseferry Road and would go into Thames House through the side door. Past ten, and acceptable. The freedom came with the escape from his home. He was ashamed of the sense of liberation he felt when he closed the front door behind him and headed for the station. How Rosie survived was beyond his comprehension. That morning he had broken ranks with Service disciplines – disgraceful – and had said to her: 'This isn't for quoting but we're looking at a sort of closure for Mary, a body in the cage. The vile little tradesman who did the shipments to that place is in our sights and we're closing on him. I've a good man there – I'm confident he can do what's needed. I'll be late tonight because it'll be developing. What's to happen to the wretch? What I told George will suffice for you, my dear. We'll nail him to the floor. Don't wait up.' A kiss on the cheek and he'd left her in the empty house. He had a spring in his stride that morning and the security men in the foyer would have recognised something about him that was almost jaunty. He might as well have shouted that a 'good one' was about to happen. The men and women on the bottom rung of the ladder were often the first to know when the Two Imposters that were Triumph or Disaster stalked the corridors. They possessed all the qualities needed to interpret body language. He went in, and wouldn't leave until it was over. She was a sweet girl and deserved his best efforts. He took the lift.

'Is he in?'

'At his desk.'

It was an aside. She had a phone at her ear and flicked the hold switch. The director general was a perennial sniffer: he liked to come down from the sunlit uplands whenever an operation was close to fulfilment. It was as if he'd have preferred a hot line to the various armouries used by the agencies that did back-up when an arrest was imminent. Had he ever fired a Glock, been on a range, worn the ear baffles and let rip at a target? Jocelyn doubted it. But he had done time on Counter Terrorism, Islamist, and would have known the long nights leading towards the dawn hits when the rams battered down housing-association doors, or batons broke through the front windows of Victorian terrace homes.

'Going smoothly?'

'Well oiled.'

She flicked the button and went back to her call. It was loose-ends time and the need to get them knitted, to anticipate confusions and set in place the secondary plans that would circumvent chaos: a custody area, a flight with route permissions, the legality of a charge sheet and an issued warrant, deniability and a fog of secrecy on the ground. He backed away. He might or might not call in on Matthew Bentinick. People of any rank in the building rarely pitched up at that door in the corridor and expected to chew the fat and drink coffee. She thought Bentinick had lost his early cheer. Last time she had briefed him, fifteen minutes ago, he had seemed preoccupied, quiet. If it went sour he might not survive the deceit and illegality. Both could be excused by success but condemned, utterly, in failure. And if it went sour then George might be heading out of the front door, ID shredded, never to return.

She wondered if George knew the man that Matthew Bentinick had dragged out of self-enforced retirement, whether it burdened him . . . and whether the scale of the catch excited him. She had the target on her screen. An interesting face, caution ever present in the eyes. Not a pushover, but the worthwhile ones never were.

He rocked on his feet. Timofey Simonov had been at the front door, had shrugged on a loose coat to cover his best-dress Soviet-era tunic and had been called back. The bar at the bottom of the TV screen in the kitchen told him that a man was in police custody in south-west London. An assassination attempt had been blocked. Unconfirmed reports indicated a foiled murder threat on a Russian citizen whose application for political asylum was under consideration. Sources said a high-powered sniper rifle had been recovered. The sum of it was catastrophe.

He felt the sweat break on his neck. There was nothing Timofey Simonov could do. He turned to his butt for quips and insults, the man he abused. The brigadier looked away. He felt as though a rug had been pulled from under him. He was silent.

The brigadier said that Elena had made borscht and showed Timofey the flask. There were salami sandwiches and vodka to celebrate the conclusion of the business. Timofey saw the pistol in the shoulder holster when the brigadier's coat flapped open. Was he losing control? His throat was dry, his mind churned and his legs shook.

He said they should go. If he was losing control new enemies would circle. He went down the steps to the car. How to recognise an enemy edging closer?

Daniel Curnow was the name she wrote and, under it, the number and the address. It was a big package, awkward to handle, but the counter staff were helpful. On the back of the parcel she wrote her name and address in Honfleur. She had done this because the strange-mannered but devoted little man called Dusty had diverted a tourist bus to find her among the dunes. It was the painting she had made from that view overlooking the bay of the Somme. It might have been better to keep it for another two or three weeks, and work at it more, but she had not delayed.

With a certain recklessness she paid for a superior delivery service and was guaranteed that it would be there by noon the next day, Saturday. She could not say whether the investment was good or bad. She hoped it would be worth the effort. There was a saying in the Lofoten islands, passed down generations: *Rather suffer for truth than be rewarded for lies*. She believed it appropriate. The truth was that he must forsake battlefields and graves; he would lie that he had scaled back his commitment to them. She thought it one of her better pictures. She waited for the return of her card and remembered the few times they had been together, him almost frightened of her, him worshipping her but failing to take the last step and desert the graves. She remembered how it had been – not easy. Far from it. She left the post office, on cours Albert-Manuel, and walked home to the loneliness. Dusty had not known where he had gone or why, but she had sensed his fear. She walked fast and the sun threw her shadow ahead of her, deep and dark, without love and threatening.

Dusty was parked outside the bar. The guide was inside with the visitors. A break had been called. His phone bleeped: *Picture sent to you for delivery tomorrow, dunes and coast, sort of peace-offering for Danny and an opening of negotiations. Hanne xxx*

He reflected. Others had been damaged, not just Desperate. Yorkie had sat in a room all night, no lights, cradling a Browning. No one had known till past dawn, but he'd gone that day to Aldergrove airport, the military wing. Gary had put in a request for a transfer to Germany and told the captain that if he didn't get it he'd go AWOL. Phil had broken up a bar in central Armagh and been taken to the cells by the Red Caps. It had all seemed to wash over Dusty Miller, and he might have been the least stressed guy at Gough where they lived, worked, did the business with the informers, paid them, crossed them off the lists when they were left in a ditch and recruited more. Always plenty, never a shortage, and the money was crap. Dusty didn't lose sleep, and he'd never heard that Captain Bentinick did. He wouldn't leave. If Desperate headed off with the girl to those islands where they lived off dried cod, where winter froze your balls and in summer the sun never set – well, Dusty would hang on in Caen. There was Christine to keep him warm at night, and Lisette to cook: he would drive a minibus. It might be the only offer Danny Curnow would get. Be a shame to turn it down.

It was a pretty little village and the group's discipline was fracturing. He fancied many had had their fill of graveyards, battlefields and the casualty statistics of war. The place offered no sense of danger. He didn't think the guide did it that well. Danny would have livened it up, but he wasn't there.

* * *

The guide would try to breathe the stench of war – burned bodies, brewed tanks – into them.

The British had arrived, infantry and mostly armour. They were purloining wine, scrounging food, peeing and catching up on sleep. Five weeks after the invasion, they had moved just twenty miles closer to the village.

The guide needed to play a big card if he was to regain control. He returned them to the previous evening, the German cemetery at La Cambe, and the grave of a young SS panzer officer.

Michael Wittman already wore the Knight's Cross ranking of the Iron Cross and had been credited with 138 tank kills. He was in a Tiger Mark 6, with two crewmen. He came in his Tiger over the horizon and up the only street, and fought a brigade for a quarter of an hour. When he reversed away – tank ammunition exhausted – he had destroyed fourteen British tanks, fifteen personnel carriers and two anti-tank guns. It was a defeat for the British on a grand scale. On his side, Wittman was known as the Black Baron. He was ordered back to Berlin, heaped with more decorations and posted as an instructor. He slipped away to rejoin his crew.

Wittman was bagged by Joe Ekins, a gunner in a Firefly, who found him in the open, hit his Tiger at a half-mile range and lived to tell the tale, modestly, until his death at eighty-eight.

The story of Wittman's end always cheered the visitors to Villers-Bocage. They muttered among themselves, confused, and wondered how a man who had such a pivotal moment in military history, Ekins, could have led a normal life afterwards. They moved on and were promised no more cemeteries, no more defeats.

'I think he told the truth,' Gaby Davies said.

'You tickled his privates. I put a rod across his back. Same answer.' Danny Curnow's head was down.

'He doesn't know. He's been told it's the Milovice complex, not where it is.'

'I have to believe him. The consequences of a lie are clear in his mind.'

They had moved: they were four doorways down the hill from

where they had spent the night, and this building was in a worse state. The cat that had befriended him was hunting behind the door and twice they had heard rat squeals. Brutal sounds, but calming to Danny – something from Vagabond days: stalking, death, then on the move again. The sun was up but little of it reached the street. Some of its brightness hit the upper window of the hotel where a light still burned and the curtains were half drawn.

'He's a good man, but out of his depth.'

'Heroes tend to be thin on the ground.' He reflected. How many had he known who could have had that label pinned to their chest, gone to the Palace, then posed outside with the little thing dangling from a ribbon? None, really. Not those men. There had been some and he'd met them in car parks, at forestry picnic sites, by the shores of Lough Neagh and in corners of the library. All lived with the fear. It was partly greed that brought them to each meeting, the transfer of the envelope, and was partly love of the adrenalin surge that came from a double life. It was also bare-bollock bravery. Desperate had Dusty behind him with the H&K, watching his back like a hawk. The real hero lived with the fall of a shadow behind him, the slowing of a car coming towards him when he was blinded by the headlights, the knock at the door when he was changing a baby's nappy: he got no medals but had won the war. The Joes had done it via infiltration. Danny Curnow had bought their treachery.

'He isn't a hero and wouldn't want to be,' Gaby said. 'He's being taken.'

'They know where to go, Riordan and the girl, and we'll follow.'

'Because we need evidence that'll stand up in court.'

'Something like that.'

He saw a face at that window, fleeting, and the curtain fluttered. He ducked his head again and played the vagabond in a doorway, but he pinched the material of Gaby Davies's trousers, alerted her.

Malachy Riordan looked up the street and down it. A woman pushed a buggy, a dog checked lamp-posts. Water was swilled on the pavement outside a café, up near the church at the top. Riordan waited his moment, checked again, then pushed open the window. It groaned with his effort and dirt flaked out from behind the woodwork. He opened it wide.

Then he took a last look round the room. What little he had brought on the flight to Nürnberg was in the rucksack, dry and wet, and her handbag. What she had taken off, displaying herself for him, was in the plastic bag. He expected her to wake, raise an eyebrow, tease or taunt, but she didn't. She had broken him. He moved the sheet a last time, raised it so that the bruising and the dark lines at her throat were better hidden. Then Malachy Riordan bent over the bed and kissed her forehead. His eyes raked across the room.

At the window he checked up and checked down, then lifted the rucksack and pitched it out. He watched it land hard on the paving. He pulled the window shut.

The key in his hand, he went out, closed the door, made sure that the Do Not Disturb sign had not fallen off the handle. He took the stairs two at a time. In the hall, he tossed the key to the man behind the desk. He was in the street.

He snatched up the rucksack, and a young guy pulled a face at him – doing a runner – and raised his hand towards Malachy. A high-five was called for, and executed. He walked fast along the street, knew where he had to go. Never before had he felt guilt, but now it chased him. An invalided policeman lived in a converted house on an estate outside Dungannon with ramps at the front and back for his wheelchair. The injuries had come from a bomb planted by Malachy Riordan: no guilt. On the far side there was a rubbish bin, contents bulging from the top, and he danced through traffic, paused long enough to ram in the plastic bag with her clothing, push it down, far from sight, then broke into a run.

'He's fucking killed her,' Gaby had said.

The tram lines had been angry on Riordan's face. He had gone past them, had been the width of the street from them, but the scratches had been clear. Danny had seen his eyes: bagged underneath, dull, haunted.

'If he hasn't killed her he's left her in a bad state.'

'Not your problem or mine.'

They were on their feet and Danny Curnow might have been slow because she reached down, locked her hand round his wrist and tugged him upright. They had seen him dump the bag in the bin. What astonished Danny was the lack of care Malachy showed. He seemed not to use counter-surveillance procedures. The man's head was down and the rucksack bounced on his shoulders. Twice, he crossed the road without warning. Horns sounded and tyres screamed. She had a catch in her voice, and might have run to get level with him.

'Just her clothes, wet – what she was wearing in the rain – and a handbag. She'd have been an idiot, the girl – a trophy shag.'

He thought they were in a tough area. The gentrification that came hand in hand with corruption and backhanders wasn't in evidence. It was a good place for Malachy Riordan to have holed up. Where she was, a conference hotel, showed poor tradecraft. But he didn't understand why the man pushed on and didn't use the tactics he'd have been weaned on. She said, in his ear, that the district was Žižkov: there had been a battle in 1420, and a rebel general, Jan Žižka, had been fighting the Holy Roman Empire. He had been a military genius and the first in Europe to use mobile artillery – pulled around on carts. She said he was a national figure to these people and his statue was on the hill above. It faced them. The target would have been a hundred yards ahead sometimes, and more often a hundred and fifty. Still the surprise that he wasn't using evasion tactics.

'I think he had bite marks. And his lip was split.'

'Could be.'

She flared at him, 'She's probably dead, murdered after fighting for her life. Aren't you angry?'

Danny said, 'She's a dissident Republican on a mission to buy weapons that will kill security forces and civilians. If I'd needed to I would've shot her, dropped her with a double tap – hopefully head shots. I would have felt nothing. I do my job.'

He grimaced. The tunnel was ahead. Its opening gaped. The target had not needed to practise the procedures. It was perfect for him. Far ahead, over Riordan's shoulder, the passageway was brilliantly lit, reflecting off white tiles. He glanced at Gaby Davies. He hadn't seen her stripped down to her knickers and a T-shirt and didn't know how strong her muscles were, but he'd recognised a bloody-minded obstinacy in her. No discussion. He used his palm to whack her arse.

He'd had to. He couldn't have done it himself. She spun on him, nearly tripped and—

He said, 'I can't. Get up there,' he gestured, 'over and then down. Do it while he's in the tunnel where I can't follow close. If I don't follow him, I'll lose him. Might not have another chance. Do it.'

He pushed her, as one would a recalcitrant teenager. She went. He could see the target in the tunnel as she sprinted towards the zigzag path to the top. He dropped his pace. The tunnel seemed straight, for ever. A couple were coming towards him, seemed pygmy small. Malachy's use of the tunnel won Danny Curnow's respect. He saw her, among the trees, gaining on the high slopes, going well.

There were men and women at Thames House who seemed to live in Lycra and to be off each lunchbreak for a run on Horseferry Road, Millbank and along the Embankment. They were obsessive: they talked diet and kit, and she knew of a woman who ran in each day from Wimbledon, around twelve klicks, and home, another twelve klicks. It seemed more important to her to achieve her distance norm than to crack a conspiracy of Islamists. Gaby did not run on the London streets, couldn't afford gym time and never seemed to get round to the exercise bikes in the building.

At the start, Gaby Davies had let rip and gone fast on the shale path that climbed the slope. The breathing problem had cut in. Prague might have been a thousand feet above sea level but was not Mexico City, Johannesburg or La Paz. Before she reached the top, where the great mound levelled out, her lungs were empty and her thighs ached. It crossed her mind that she could blow him away with a human-resources investigation into inappropriate behaviour and sexual harassment. She struggled on and she was there. She had eaten nothing all through those hours, and Ralph Exton hadn't fed her, other than a few peanuts from his mini-bar. She crowned the crest, kept running and knew from the guidebook that this place was revered. There was a huge mausoleum where the grave of the Unknown Soldier was sited, a national monument. A massive statue of a warhorse and Jan Žižka guarded it. She could have been accused – with justification – of lacking respect. She ran past two children, terrifying them, and screwed up a picture set up by a couple with a timer camera on a tripod. It flashed as she hugged the lens.

It was not only fear of failure but fear of failure with him alongside her. Humiliation.

She crossed the marble paving of the plateau, her Himalayan peak, and went for the path heading down. She was conscious of time slipping away, and ran faster. The sun had climbed and the night's rain had been pushed away. There were puffy clouds around her, and below lay the historic panorama of the city: the castle, the great churches, the squares where the statues of martyrs stood.

She remembered how, in her mind, she had denigrated him. She'd thought of him as the lonely little man who eked out days without purpose, who was almost sad and who bullied Ralph Exton for the sake of inflicting pain. Who seemed to have lost sight of the mission to gather together the evidence that would put Malachy Riordan into gaol until his hair whitened and the armed struggle withered. He had told her to run.

Who else could have said that to her?

Not the director general, not Matthew Bentinick, and she would have told Hugo Woolmer to go shaft himself if he had suggested it. No one. She could no longer feel the place on her buttock that he had smacked. Strange thing was that she wanted to feel it. She careered down the slope, sometimes on the path and sometimes the short-cuts between the shrubs. She lost her footing once, tumbling, then rolling. A stranger thing: when she badmouthed Danny Curnow – the dinosaur and torturer – she had won no applause from Ralph Exton. She regained eyeball.

The target was out of the tunnel and on a pavement. There were new office buildings around him and at the far end of the street a metro station – she saw the sign for it. She had made good time, achieved the given task. She expected no praise, and that certainty flushed out more of her anger. She came onto the street. Her hair would have been a mess, her clothing sweat-streaked, and there was dirt on her face, and her knees and elbows. And something else was even stranger: his head on her shoulder when he'd slept and she hadn't turfed him off. She had eyeball and she followed the target. Danny Curnow had not caught up.

He came out of the tunnel. It had been a great echoing journey for him. It would have been impossible to push close to Malachy Riordan. There was no cover and the fierce ceiling lights burned down. It was an excellent place for a man to go if he was concerned that a tail was on him. Danny Curnow had stayed back, and didn't know whether Gaby Davies had scaled the hill, then come down it . . .

It was as if the tunnel had spat him out. The street was straight and empty ahead of him.

He went on down it. He couldn't see the target, or Gaby Davies. His breath came faster. He couldn't run. For a surveillance tail to break out of the ordinary pace of life and hurry was an abomination. A man or woman who ran drew attention. He didn't know where either of them was, and the pistol seemed to bounce in his belt. He wondered if, by now, his usefulness was exhausted. It beat a message in his head: he had no role left. Hunger and exhaustion struck, as he shambled along a smarter street than there had been on the other side of the hill. He had barely slept and was chilled to the bone. He had no role. He was an agent handler, and the job of the agent was done. The agent was now a passenger. All of Danny Curnow's skills were in the manipulation of informers, who betrayed their supposed friends. It had gone on, moved up the track, and he might have screwed up – big-time.

It was the nightmare of any man in the tail business: a street that gave no eyeball. The metro station was off to the right. He veered towards it. It was laid down that the mobiles should be used only as last resort, that voice footprints should be minimal. So he was alone. He should have been at the Falaise Gap, on from Villers-Bocage, with the image of the cemeteries clear in his mind – where he belonged. He felt the tiredness in his legs, heard the rasp of his breath and came into the station hall.

His legs lost traction.

He was tripped.

His hands went out, reflex, in front of him. The flooring, still wet from the overnight rain, lurched up at him and the faces of commuters blurred past his eyes.

Danny Curnow braced himself for the shock of the impact.

A fist gripped the collar of his coat. He clenched his fist, was about to swing and hit—

Her voice: 'Took your bloody time.'

He didn't hit her. He could have flattened her windpipe if he had hit her. She heaved him upright. He swayed and she freed him. Her hand went from his collar to her ankle.

'You're a weight, nearly broke my leg. What kept you?'

He saw the triumph in her face. He wrenched his collar forward. She handed him a ticket. He had nothing to say but heaved, blew, no longer knew why he was there – and didn't think she did. She gestured with her head, and the arrows took them to the B line, going back towards the city's centre.

'You're lucky,' she said. 'He just missed one. You were close to fucking up. How would you have handled that?'

She led, he followed. She held back at the entrance to the platform. The target was at the far end, slumped on a bench. They heard the rumble of an approaching train. They let him board, then took the carriage behind. Danny Curnow did not know how to praise her so stayed silent. If they had lost their target then the mission would have failed. All for nothing.

'He's killed her, hasn't he – in the hotel room – and left her?'

'She didn't matter, never did. She was a bit-part player, just had a walk-on. You'll get your text.'

At the next station, following Malachy Riordan, they changed and took the C line of the metro. How would he have handled 'fucking up'? Not well.

17

It was a slow train that rattled, bumped and shook on the tracks out of the city. The hill with the statue and the mausoleum was visible through a grimy window, then blocks of housing and abandoned factories. They had left behind the tower blocks of the modern capital and the relics of the imperial Austrian-sponsored empire. The sights to either side were from the collapsed Communist era. Danny saw factories that had once been a centre of excellence for the manufacture of pig iron, or crushing concrete, or where – under a five-year plan – workers' overalls were manufactured. Their part of the carriage was half full and a woman sat across the aisle from him, reading a newspaper.

'Pretty drab and flat. So ordinary.'

He thought nerves made her talk. He always did well with silence. He sat beside the aisle and could look forward. The target was a dozen rows ahead, facing away. Danny had eyeball on the shoulders and back of the head, except when it ducked lower. The man had killed before and would do it again if he had the chance. Perhaps if Gaby Davies had spent more time in ditches, her stomach pressed to Dusty's hips, she would have learned the joy of silence. Might come to her in later life. He remembered the silence in the hide under the hedgerow.

She said, 'Almost as if it's a let-down, but it's the way of the job, no emotion at the end. Sorry, flapping tongue.'

Good of her to understand. Nerves burrowed into most people. Special forces, élite reconnaissance troopers or grizzled sergeants who ran platoons and companies: there came a time before they hit a firefight when they needed to talk or smoke. He could drift into a field of memories.

'I expect it'd figure in my line manager's assessment.'

He was in the ditch, the fire not yet lit in the farmhouse, the wind soundlessly flapping the washing put out the night before, the dog quiet, the cattle not yet restless, and the dawn chorus still to begin. The silence was like a blanket. Then the distant sound, muffled, of the explosion. A barely noted break in the silence. It had been the child scream of anguish that had fractured the silence. Now he saw that 'kid's' head, the hair uncombed, leathery skin at the back of the neck. It rose, then dropped.

'You could say, "a bright kid, but talks too much".'

It never bothered Danny Curnow that apprehension might knot the guts of those he worked with. Even Captain Matthew Bentinick might have succumbed. There were war stories about Bentinick and a sniper rifle, when the opposition had a marksman a few paces across the border and the South was squeamish about knocking him over. The magnificence that was the British military was cautious of laying down fire and zapping the bastard in a foreign field, taking out a farmer's pigs or heifers while they were about it. There had been a shot at a quarter of a mile and an enemy buried without ceremony. It had not been corroborated but was believed by many at Gough. Clever man, Bentinick: he did nothing without purpose.

'It's when you don't know what's going to happen, and don't know how you'll be.'

A ticket inspector came into the carriage and worked towards their eyeball. They had already stopped three times. At each halt, Danny had felt Gaby stiffen and ready herself, half out of her seat, then subside when the train moved on. He had not moved. He understood why Bentinick had taken him to the church of St Cyril and St Methodius . . . Two or three boys would have set off that morning on bicycles and gone into extreme danger, and would not have been able to promise they'd succeed in their mission. They had hit Heydrich and had gone to the crypt in the church. They would not have grasped how they would feel when news filtered through that – because of their actions – Lidice had been destroyed, the men, women and children massacred or put into cattle wagons. They had worked to orders, as he did. He had seen their faces on the busts in the soft light of the crypt. They had killed an enemy and triggered the death sentence of thousands. Betrayed by treachery. Danny blamed no man or woman for babbling when fear caught them.

The inspector had come to them, and Gaby had shown him the tickets. He had nodded politely, and might have wondered why three foreigners, same carriage but sitting apart, had tickets to Milovice.

They were away from Prague's suburbs and passed wide fields from which the maize had been harvested. He stood up, looked back and came out into the aisle between the seats. He started to move towards them.

There was purpose in the step and the eyes shone with determination. Gaby was rigid and Danny's hand had gone to his waist. His fingers locked on the butt of the weapon, and the index was against the safety, but there was no bullet in the breach. What to do? The man came towards him. Danny had a clear view of the bites, the split lip and the scratches where the girl's nails had gone deep. The eyes seemed dull. He stepped over a suitcase that was in the aisle, and a man moved a shopping bag. Back in the garden at Vyšehrad, Danny had had an 'argument' with Gaby. Malachy Riordan and Frankie McKinney had done the oldest trick on the counter-surveillance lecture course: the quick grab, boy and girl, the kiss with the chance to gaze over a shoulder. Danny was conscious of the marks on his own face, scrapes that would mark him out – he should be seen but not noticed, the instructors had said, but the wounds made him conscious. He was flush in his seat and Riordan came towards them.

Gaby reacted. He felt a sharp jab in his ribcage and she was pointing out of the window, gesturing at something he should see. Big decision. He followed her lead. His hand on the pistol butt was tight and his finger hard against the safety lever. When he looked to where she pointed, he had to twist so his back was to Malachy Riordan, who was coming down the aisle. The footsteps came closer. What was he looking at? A combine harvester. He peered at it as if it had the same significance as a space shuttle and lost sight of it. Then he looked at a trailer with a grain pyramid in it. Fascinating.

Riordan passed them. Danny watched a stand of pine trees. He could smell Riordan: no toothpaste, no shaving lotion and no deodorant – stale sweat, dirty socks and damp clothing. It was not to be expected that a man would kill a girl in a cheap hotel room, then stay close to her for most of a night and the next morning, than remember to change his socks. He had smelt beer on the man's breath too. Riordan was gone.

He drew a deep breath. He felt the stress in his shoulders where the muscles were tight.

She was looking between the backs of the two seats. 'Fancy that! He's gone for a pee – he's in the toilet.'

Too bloody old. He felt it – and knew it.

'You all right, Danny?'

He was as fine as he'd ever be but too old. It was kids' work. He was fine, and she had done well. He braced himself, listened against the rumble of the wheels for the returning feet.

Malachy Riordan didn't see the views from the train's windows. He lurched back to his seat as the brakes were applied and the train slowed. A woman read a newspaper. He must have cannoned into her shoulder, tearing the pages down the centre. He was moving on – it was only a newspaper – when his arm was tugged. No one pulled Malachy Riordan's arm, and hadn't since he was a child. The priest wouldn't have done so, or any teacher, and the police had hesitated each time they had clipped the handcuffs on his wrists. She jabbered at him. He didn't understand what she was saying. She appealed to the carriage for support and behind him to where a couple sat.

He ignored her. He had not been able, when Frankie had taken off her clothes, to hold back. She had come close to him and his hands had found her throat and— The woman bleated in his ear, then at his back. He went to his seat. Malachy Riordan had the paper he had taken from her notebook. On it were directions that had to be followed.

The train pulled away. One more stop. He tried hard to put her from his mind, to think of weapons and the power they brought.

* * *

'They won't take my call.'

Timofey Simonov had called the embassy before they had come close to the district in Prague where it stood. He had called it again when they had been in the Bubenec part of the city beside the walls that sheltered it from sight. He had rung a third time when Denisov had driven him almost to the front gates, and once more when they'd gone over the road bridge north of the Charles Bridge.

Each time the same.

He asked for the contact he had with Military Intelligence, then with Overseas Intelligence, then with Internal Intelligence. Last he requested to be put through to the ambassador. At any other time he would have heard the bastard at the other end, the central switchboard that dealt with priority numbers, saying, 'Of course, Mr Simonov, straight away, Mr Simonov, just tracing him for you, Mr Simonov. Apologies for the delay, Mr Simonov.' Regrettably, the competent official from Military, Overseas or Internal was unavailable. And the ambassador? His Excellency was out for the afternoon and was not expected back that evening. There was no need to leave a message with his staff as he had stipulated that he would be unavailable. Bastards, all of them.

He sat in the back of the Mercedes. Around him the air was filled with the camphor scent of his wardrobe. His skin itched where it was in contact with the material of the uniform. Denisov drove carefully.

It was the old way, the Soviet way. The talk in every office that had access to the matter – in Prague, London, Moscow – would have prioritised the issue of a marksman held in the British capital with a sniper rifle. He had been in a location that overlooked a house where British Special Services guarded a traitor. The contract was worth good money but, more importantly, it guaranteed his access to important and influential levels of the *siloviki*. It was how the state existed. It worked from the top, down and sideways, and any functionary with ambition must be assured he possessed the protection of a personality of repute; a *krysha* was obligatory or abject failure stared. The military were always respectful. Overseas had provided the weapon and Internal had produced the marksman. His Excellency's office had handled the shipments of cash and their transfer through the banking systems. Without a roof he was a tree with its bark stripped. He would die. That was beyond doubt.

'What do I do?'

They skirted the Stare Mesto and were close to the river. Denisov shrugged. 'You will not listen. Why ask me?'

'What should I do?'

'Forget tonight's business of no importance. Dump that clothing. Take the plane this evening to Moscow. Sort out what has happened there. Here you are isolated.'

'I gave my word,' he said loftily. Would the brigadier snigger?

'You ask for advice. I give it.'

'I cannot go against my word.'

They turned off the road beside the river and swept up the hill towards the rendezvous. The man was waiting. Timofey saw him over the brigadier's shoulder. They might not meet again. This might be the last occasion on which a favour was called for, the last payment of a long-existing debt. They edged towards him. The Mercedes was in a long, slow-moving traffic queue. His friend Ralph Exton spun on a heel and waved with exuberance. The man was engaged in the illicit purchase of weapons of war and wore the look of one going for an evening in the country with a picnic and cocktails. They were alongside him. He reached over and opened the door. Ralph Exton sat beside him and secured his belt. A smile wreathed his face, 'Bloody hell, Timofey, what is that outfit?'

They clung to each other, helpless with laughter. It was so strong, their friendship.

There was a black van behind them, which Timofey failed to notice. The brigadier had seen it first on the road by the river that led out from Karlovy Vary. He had seen a black van on the road near to the airport, but it had tinted glass so he couldn't identify the driver, and hadn't memorised the registration. It was a common enough vehicle. He said nothing.

* * *

In the van, Alpha drove, with Charlie beside him. Bravo was in the back, with the kit bags and Karol Pilar. It was reported that Ralph Exton was now in the Mercedes and that the direction was as expected. He had told them little. Perhaps all that they needed to know. It probably wasn't necessary for them to know more. He thought them enthusiastic, like dogs wanting a chase in a forest where there would be the scents of boar and deer to track, with the possibility of a kill.

The sun had tipped and the light edged behind the high trees. The station had two lines, which were polished from use. It would once have been a major junction and a freight destination. Not now. Buddleia and birch saplings grew between old sleepers and the chipstone bedding had a covering of weed. Danny Curnow thought it a place where empire had ended, and there would be similar time-ruins around Basra, such as Bastion, and more in Northern Ireland. He went out of a forward door, Gaby Davies in front of him.

The target stopped and looked around, but the woman who'd had the newspaper did a good job on Danny Curnow's behalf. She and Malachy must have made eye contact, because she gave him another volley of abuse and waved the torn paper at him. It was good to have her on their side, Danny thought. Malachy Riordan went out of the station, Danny and Gaby following. It was the time when it might all go down. He could have screamed for contact from Karol Pilar but phone silence was the order of the day. The shadows had started to spread.

She said, 'That pistol, have you ever fired one for real?'

'No.'

'Done plenty on the range?'

'Yes.'

'And me,' she said. 'I got good marks. Then the instructor said that any amount of practice didn't equate to real shooting when you're trying to kill. I wasn't told we'd need to be armed.'

'Of course we're armed. It's not a bloody cake walk up the pier.'

He thought of the young men in the landing craft on a storm-tossed morning and the bright spits of flame from the muzzles of the machine-guns, then of the cemeteries where they lay. They wouldn't have known how they would be – brave or rigid with fear. Some would have made a name that would last after their deaths. Others would have remained anonymous on that day and in the hereafter. Officers, sergeants and the guys alongside them would have cursed a few as 'useless bastards and cowards'. No one knew how they would be when combat came. He didn't know, at what stage as it played out, she would take the text message from Bentinick, or how she would react, and didn't much care.

She stared ahead. He thought now that she rivalled him and had lost respect for him.

They went out of the station, and saw Malachy Riordan's back disappear round a bend.

'Where is she?'

The brigadier held open the door for him. He strode in and Ralph Exton followed. He barked the question. 'The pretty one, not you. Where is she?'

Timofey Simonov gazed around him. It was a roadhouse. He was familiar with it and trusted the owners. He always came here when he visited the old garrison area. There was a moth-eaten bear's head on the wall, a boar's with good tusks, and antlers from the deer that were shot in the fields. At the door, the brigadier had pointed to the table where the man sat. It was obvious that he was alone. He had a plate in front of him and an empty mug, but there was no crockery opposite, no handbag on the table and no coat hooked over a chair.

'Where is she?'

The brigadier had said she was pretty, and his friend, Ralph Exton, had confirmed it. The man turned. Timofey saw his face.

It did not matter to him that the man peering at him was a guerrilla fighter. It had not concerned Timofey when the fighters were North African, from the deserts, or waging their armed struggle in Africa, close to the equator. This man was from Ireland. Timofey knew – as he would say – 'sweet fuck all of nothing' about Ireland. He had learned the phrase from Ralph Exton and gloried in it. He could justify selling weapons wherever they could be paid for

– and wherever the 'roof' allowed it. On this occasion he had been brief with factual explanations. One Saturday afternoon three weeks ago, during an audience at the private residence of the ambassador, a message with an appropriate entry code had been shown him, fresh from cryptology in the signals unit. The detail had concerned the target living under guard in a discreetly placed villa to the south-west of London and the fee that was on offer. He had not queried the money that would be paid to him, and in accepting the contract he had slipped in a reference to a representative from the Irish campaign, a go-between, and a request for some trifles of armaments. It had been a good day to ease that matter into the communications net because, again, the British government had complained at the killing, many years before, of the traitor to the regime who had ingested Polonium 210. The British, in the view of many in the seat of power, were considered to have overstepped the limits of their impoverished influence. They were arrogant and displayed insufficient respect for the government of Russia. It was a strong face, a fighter's. It was the face of one of those senior sergeants in the Vityaz force for special operations. It had strength and injuries.

A split in a swollen lip. Scratches on the cheeks. A bite on the left side of the chin. The man stared at him, said nothing. He had deep eyes, dark: Timofey prided himself that he could read a man by his eyes, a skill taught him at the knee of Mr Vik. The brigadier had said that the girl had stepped forward at the bank and negotiated while the man had hung back and was overruled on whether or not the money should be transferred before the purchased items were verified. He laughed. 'Is the girl not coming? Did you exhaust her?' Good enough English, but there was no answer. He turned to the brigadier, spoke in Russian, 'Perhaps she didn't like the look of him with his clothes off. Perhaps she turned him down.'

Ralph Exton stood a little behind him, but was visible from the corner of an eye. His friend was the 'middle man' and would take a cut from the deal. Exton should have greeted the Irish man and had not. Neither did he ask about the girl or joke at her absence. The light was failing. The Irishman gazed at Timofey's uniform, seemed to say with his eyes that only a buffoon wore such clothing. The brigadier put money on the table. They left. The girl was not there and the man's face had been scratched, bitten and punched. For precious minutes he had forgotten the news in the bar on the screen, and the refusal of officials at the embassy to take his call. They went out into the last of the sunlight.

The brigadier took a call, then murmured in his ear where they would meet the driver who had brought the gear. Timofey knew all of the old camp ground: he was always emotional when he came here.

The van had come. The headlights had flashed. They were loaded through the back door. Black-gloved hands shook theirs. They heard names: Alpha, Bravo and Charlie.

There was a brief hug from Karol Pilar, arms around Danny Curnow, but he made no gesture towards Gaby Davies. The van lurched forward.

Danny was told that the targets were at a café, by a garage, then had left. They drove fast at first, then slowed when the Mercedes was in sight ahead.

She must still have had the nerves because she needed to talk. 'Finishes tonight. We'll see him into custody with the local crowd, then brief the embassy people on extradition to Belfast. We'll do a run to the airport, get the witness statements and file the photography in the office during the afternoon and evening. Sunday is chill-out and do the washing. What's your week looking like, Danny? Any plans for Monday morning?'

He said he had a group coming in at the start of the new week. After an early lunch he would have them on the beach at Dunkirk, then do the cemetery. In the evening there would be a talk from the guide travelling with them. That was his Monday.

'Is it always difficult when you come down off a big operation? Flat and low key?'

He said he felt waves of exhaustion, and that Monday was too far into any future to think about now.

'And you don't even have to be here.'

He didn't argue or take offence. There was indeed no need for him to be squatting on the floor of a van driven by Czech police, their weapons alongside him, a pistol of theirs stuck into his belt. He had no more business there.

'I would have coped,' she emphasised. 'I wouldn't have needed the verbal equivalent of a rubber truncheon. You could have stayed at home, gone round the cemeteries and battlefields. Do you talk to them about heroes? The world's left you behind, Danny. Well, Monday morning for me will be a whole new scene. I'll be turning my back on this place and you. I might bring a picnic and sit in the gardens behind the office, then go in and find out what they've given me. People like Matt Bentinick feed off poor lost souls like you. They're bloody leeches, and they're comfortable because you're so thankful to be asked that you'll do as you're told with no fuss. And you always want to come back. You were scarred, and managed to quit, but never lost the habit. You had to have a last fix. The fingers flicked and you came running. It won't happen to me. I thought, at one stage, that I might get to like you. How wrong I was. Damn you, have you nothing to say?'

They followed the Mercedes. He didn't give her the satisfaction of a riposte. He turned away, tapped out his text in the near darkness of the van, then hit send. He had agreed with most of what she had said. She was quiet now. He was something of a passenger, 'along for the ride', and she had the authority of Thames House behind her. The warrant would be in her name. Karol Pilar had the muscle of three heavily armed specialists, and an agent no longer needed handling. He could have pulled out, for all his usefulness that morning, and might have been lucky with a flight to Paris, then a fast TGV out of Gare Saint-Lazare, four stops to Caen. He might have caught the closing of the Falaise Gap and had dinner at the restaurant across from the marina where all the tours went on their last night.

'God, Danny, did I say that?'

'You didn't hear me argue.'

'I'm so sorry. I want to say—'

'Someone said once, "Rather than love, than money, than fame, give me truth." Don't apologise.'

Danny Curnow closed his eyes. The night gathered.

He sniffed. Jocelyn expected it: it was George's style. The man wanted to talk.

'Coffee, George?'

'I don't want to interrupt . . .'

'It's the cappuccino capsule, yes?'

He nodded, and slid into her cubicle. It was not a comfortable chair that he sank onto, but she seldom encouraged visitors and few troubled her. In the corridor she went to the machine, pressed the buttons and studied the noticeboard that had the usual clutter of Pilates sessions, salsa dancing, Farsi conversation evenings and the hockey team's fixtures. She allowed few into her room but he had the right to be there, and she sympathised. She had been sorting the matter of the air strip and its location.

She brought the mug back and settled at her desk.

He had the right to know. If it failed he was 'dead in the water'. He might linger briefly but then he would be out on his ear. If there was blood on foreign soil, traceable, it would be the equivalent for the dear man of having both legs amputated at the knee. Some in Thames House would be sorry to see him go, but more would regard him as dispensable. Their relationship was much dissected by juniors but without conclusions. It was likely, she thought, to be based on trust, but few in the building knew the meaning of the word, or gave a toss about it. It was mid-afternoon. She did a little grin – sparked some mischief – opened a drawer and withdrew a hip flask. It had been a present from her father who perennially regretted that she was not male and didn't handle a Purdey well. She sloshed Scotch into his mug, then told him what was in place, what was planned, and explained the feed that linked the field position of the team to the Six station at the Prague embassy. If it succeeded, he would be toasted with fine wines, in a few remote corners of government, and praise would cascade over him. She told him what was left to be confirmed, and an approximation of a timetable, then let him talk.

He said, 'With their influence over the Czechs, Magyars, Poles, Slovaks, Slovenians and Austrians, you've done well. They're under the thumb. We're not going to have Red Army tanks rolling up the high street, but we'll have bloody cold winters if the Gazprom taps on the pipelines are closed off. It has to be Germany.'

She favoured a flying club near Chemnitz.

'They'll go ape-shit. Forgive the vulgarity. The old Soviets are back running the show. They don't reckon the clock ever nudged forward. And we have their whistleblower's assassin tucked into a cell, but that's minor in comparison with what we can achieve tonight. They use our country as a lavatory, piss in our streets and think nothing of it. We'll send a message, a discreet one, and they'll be throwing their ghastly crockery across the banqueting halls and chipping the gold-leaf paint they love off the ceilings. It'll let them know we're still breathing.'

If there was 'blood on the ground', he would be out, and the telegrams from the foreign ministry in Prague would be deluging Foreign and Commonwealth by morning. The politicians would be queuing in disorderly lines to claim his body parts, and the Americans would be chortling at the screw-up. He'd be gone, exorcised from the Service's history. Much was at stake.

She said, 'There's a fair bit riding, George, on the man we have in there – the freelance who was, and is, Vagabond. Experienced, but no spring chicken.'

'If he's good enough for Matthew Bentinick he'll have to do. Matthew didn't offer me coffee – said he was too busy. In a rather bloodythirsty mood but perky enough.'

'We have to hope he has cause to be.'

He shook his head, declined a top-up from her flask, grimaced and left. She would have bet he'd be back later and that the Spartan single bed would be in use adjacent to his office that night. She had been there at the start and would be there at the end. There were always two bottles of a cheap French bubbly in her floor fridge, likely to be long past a drinkable date, but they lived in hope. An agent doing routine deals with Irish dissidents had been propositioned to broker a weapons deal. He had thrown up a name and bells had rung. The formidable persuasive powers of Matthew Bentinick – God knew he had reason to hate – had fashioned the mission with the care of a sculptor working with clay, and had dragged a man from obscurity. It would not only be George who took early retirement if it ended in disaster: Matthew Bentinick would follow him out through the door, and so would she. A life without Thames House, for Jocelyn, was not worth contemplating. They were all in Vagabond's hands.

Young Gaby Davies might go in an avalanche of recrimination, if there was blood on the ground. She didn't even know the target at issue. Jocelyn knew, and her future would rise or plummet on that knowledge. She swigged from the flask and spluttered. Many remained in blissful ignorance.

A meeting was in progress, one of those at which the following month's diary was explored. The operations area at Palace Barracks' Five compound seemed deserted. He'd been with a detective from the police service. The old stager, his boss, was in his corner, screen on, low light, nibbling a sandwich. It was the end of a bizarre week. It had started with him escorting a stranger on an expedition to a hedgerow and an exercise in nostalgia for past methods, and seemed to be ending in a confusion that he hesitated to understand. He did not particularly care to. He said, 'I just heard—'

A soft voice: 'What?'

'About the boys who died in the explosion on the mountain.'

'The "own goal". You heard what?'

'A cop told me – from Serious Crime. He has a brother working from Dungannon. He told me that the command wire was cut.'

'Really?'

'When the kids tried to fire it, the device was certain to malfunction.'

'Nothing certain in this world.'

'The threat to the target never existed.'

'I'm wrong. The only certainties are death and taxes.'

'May I correct you, boss?'

'Feel free, Sebastian.'

'Advance knowledge of a command cable laid, then cut. The only certainties are death, taxation *and* a tout on the mountain.'

'Nothing is as it seems – be dull if it was.'

Sebastian could have added more, but did not. He left the older man to finish his sandwich and went to his own desk. Life returned to the operations area as his colleagues spilled in from their briefing. He could have said he'd had word of the absence from the community of Malachy Riordan, kingpin of the high ground, whom he had seen last Monday from a ditch. Perhaps it was known at a different level from his own. He muttered, 'They also serve who only stand and wait.' He assumed that, abroad, an arrest operation was in preparation, evidence gathered and a smoking gun for provenance. The man who had been in the ditch with him would be at the heart of it. He would be outside the loop and the broadsheet crossword would claim his attention. He was not new to the Province and the Palace complex yet had accepted that he knew little. Soon after the transfer of all Five personnel to the purpose-built fortress in the barracks, a wag had typed the truism: 'Anyone who believes they know the answer to Northern Ireland's problems is ill-informed.' Another had typed: 'Every time we find the answer to NI's problems, they change the question.' They'd both been on the wall for twenty-four hours, then were deemed 'inappropriate' and had been removed. He knew so little of the way the bloody place ticked. A secretary of state had demanded after a first visit: 'For God's sake get me a large Scotch. What a bloody awful country.' Maybe, but he knew too little to judge, except that death, the Revenue and touts were abroad on the mountain.

She was coming from Dungannon and had the boy with her. Bridie Riordan would not have wished to take Oisin to the doctor's surgery but had no option. It was hard at the best of times to find someone she trusted, or liked, who would take her child for an afternoon or early evening. A litany of excuses, but most involved the hackneyed 'My Dermot/Sean/Fergus has the flu, and I'd not be wanting it given to your Oisin. Another time.'

Headlights from an oncoming car picked them up. Attracta Donnelly was the widow of a proud patriot of the mountain, now resting in the village's Republican plot. Siobhan Nugent was the widow of a tout who had been rightly executed for the betrayal of the community's finest fighter. He was in the same cemetery as Jon Jo Donnelly, but Mossie Nugent's grave was against a wall. Bridie Riordan saw the two women walking from the shop. She knew where they lived. They were walking towards the Nugent house, and the arm of Attracta Donnelly was in the elbow of Siobhan Nugent. She drove past them. They were in conversation, like old friends. She swerved and the boy squealed. She told him to shut up and he started to cry. She slapped his leg and braked.

Brennie Murphy's hand was shielding his eyes from her lights. He knew her car well, and came forward. How was she doing?

She was fine, but no thanks to the Donnelly and Nugent women, close and confiding. She felt a great weariness. Was Brennie going to the funeral in the morning?

'Have to be there, but not prominent.'

She would go too.

'I can't not be there, but there's hostility towards us – directed at Malachy. God knows they were grown boys and not coerced. Are you asking me whether this is over, missus? Not while there's blood in our veins and breath in our lungs. We won't bend the knee. We're not for compromising our principles. Not Malachy, not you, missus, and not me. We go on.'

Could there be touts again on the mountain? Had touts killed the boys?

'If there are, I'll find them. If there are, they'll wish they'd never been born. I think not. Safe back to your home, and I think he'll be back with us by another evening.'

She wound up her window and drove home.

Dusty had parked on the main road and allowed the group, with their guide, to go past an old farmhouse, where smoke billowed from a chimney, to what had been a charnel house. He enjoyed a cigarette, and a wide grin spread across his face, accentuating the gap between his front teeth. He laughed. He had his phone out and read the text for the fourth or fifth time. He did a little jig. He was in his fifty-ninth year and thought he might have achieved a bit of matchmaking. He started to tap in the reply. His fingers were big and could be clumsy on the small keys. It took him as long to compose the message as it did to smoke the cigarette. He read back his message: *Dear Miss Hanne, With respect, not before time, and I promise I will give Danny Curnow a good kicking to make sure he gets to H'fleur to thank you in person for your kind gift. Sincerely, Dusty Miller.*

He'd miss him. He'd miss the taciturn quiet, the far-away look, the silences when his mood darkened. He deserved some happiness, did Desperate. They wouldn't stay, of course not. Too much baggage on the Atlantic coast of Normandy for them. Maybe they'd go to those islands way up off Norway in the Arctic Circle. She'd fill canvases for idiots to buy and he could do odd jobs, lose the chill in his body and the memories. Fuck it all: no one now bothered to raise a glass to what they had done – sort of written out of history, weren't they? He'd stay, but he'd miss him.

Dusty sent it. Might be the last trip he did, now that the big anniversary was past and the folks were getting older. The world might move on – might.

The river was almost the last stop in the tour. After the slaughter at Villers-Bocage, the tide seemed irreversible and the issue was the closing of the Gap. Falaise was a historic town with good churches, a fine medieval castle and a statue of William the Conqueror in front of the mairie. *The Gap had been closed, which ensured a significant victory for Montgomery. It was a decent way to round off the trip.*

The guide would have talked about tensions between British and American commanders, the Americans saying their allies went too slowly and without commitment, the British sneering about PYBs – Pushy Yankee Bitches. A visitor might have asked, 'But weren't they all allies?'

One or two would have raised the vexed issue of collaboration, and the impromptu firing squads greeting those who chose the wrong horse to put a shirt on, or plain women having their heads shaved. The guide would have responded quietly that we as a people were indeed fortunate to escape occupation and the temptation to find love, or food, wherever it came from. They would have been through the village of St Lambert-sur-Dives and stood where Major David Currie, of the South Alberta Regiment, blocked the road, pushed aside the fleeing German remnants and won the Victoria Cross. Such a pleasant place and so desirable for a summer holiday cottage.

They would have gone on along what the guide called the 'Corridor of Death'. They were by a river. The guide sat on one side of the slow-flowing shallow water, where cattle came in the evening to drink, and they would have been opposite him on a farm track. He would have talked of the greatest German defeat since Stalingrad. Little of it made sense to the visitors, and they wondered now why they were there. Memories of the cemeteries were consigned to their cameras, and perhaps they had begun to talk of dinner – their final meal together.

The guide would have attempted to interest them in the statistics of the closing of the Gap, twenty thousand prisoners taken and many thousands killed and wounded in the incessant air attacks at the choke point before the 1st Polish Armoured snapped it shut. It had been a killing zone.

On the way back towards the hotel in Caen the minibus would have stopped beside a Tiger tank, freshly painted, on a concrete base. The visitors would have piled out and had their photographs taken by the gun barrel. It was the same model as Wittman used at Villers-Bocage, and the fittest would have scrambled up beside the turret and sat astride the 88mm gun. Time for glad rags and a last supper.

Matthew Bentinick stood at Jocelyn's door. He chuckled.

'All the players are moving into place. You know any of the old Afghan sayings? I don't suppose you do. Try this one. "A pashtun can wait his entire life for his revenge, then curse himself for his impatience." Good, isn't it? Apposite. It'll come for him out of a clear blue sky – or, rather, come from the moon's beams. All up to speed?'

She said that the last reports on the link had put them at the edge of the base, about to enter old territory. She told him what had been readied in anticipation of a conclusion, and where, and that unequivocal directions should soon reach Gabrielle Davies.

'It's as clear as mother's ruin. She can't dispute it. We just have to wait and hope. Wait, hope and trust that the unexpected doesn't shove its oar in. It never applied to me, but my mother used to say that men in Maternity were a nuisance and best in the pub, out of sight and mind. You might try it.'

A maid wanted to replace the towels. There was a smell. A master key was used. The body was found. The police were called.

Karol Pilar said, 'We're about to enter the perimeter line of the camp. Go back three decades. There were continuous fences with tumbler wires for alarms and razor wire at the top. It made a continuous encirclement of the whole complex. It would have been patrolled by armed troops and dogs. And the area close to it, where we are now, was a closed zone. Local people could be arrested and shot for entering it. It was the central command headquarters for the Soviet forces: they numbered fifty-five thousand. It was a place of huge significance in the Cold War and would have been a prized intelligence target to your agencies, the Americans or the Germans. The principal operations room is deep underground, with reinforced concrete roofing and walls. From there the start or end of the Third World War would have been directed. There were squadrons of tanks here, artillery experts and the Soviet Union's finest attack aircraft. Tactical nukes were stored here. The equipment was first class and for European battle conditions it was at least as good as that of the Americans, maybe better. It came at a price. The civilian population, at home in the Motherland, was left in penury while resources went to the military. There was a joke, a Russian one. "In 2020 we're going to put a man on the moon. In 2050 we'll put a man on Mars. In 2100, we'll provide boots for everyone." The cost buckled the regime. They went home, took what they could carry and left the rest to be looted by my people. Inside and on the walls of a building, there's a slogan, "The Soviet Union for ever, and it will never be Different." I don't laugh. My mother liked poetry, and in particular that of the British nineteenth century. She used to read to me, and I remember everything.

'"My name is Ozymandias, king of kings:
Look on my works, ye Mighty, and despair!"
Nothing beside remains. Round the decay
Of that colossal wreck, boundless and bare,
The lone and level sands stretch far away.'

'I did it well, yes? For Ozymandias you can name Brezhnev and Andropov, Chernenko and Gorbachev, and all of those defence ministers who had medals on their chests. Their work mocks them. Finished, gone, now a wilderness. Except that a new Soviet Union has arisen. The president and his *siloviki* asset-strip the country and protect themselves with repression. They have new gulags for opponents and use the taps on the gas pipelines to do the work of armoured divisions. That is the new world, and this is the old version of it. Today Timofey Simonov wears a uniform. It is pressed and clean, and I saw it when he came out of his villa. The new Russian has a love for the old days. I don't laugh. It is no joke to me. I think he comes here often, remembers the noises and marches with ghosts and feels he is part of a great power. He yearns for it again. He is a good target, the best. It will give me sublime pleasure to take him – at whatever cost to myself. He struts and recalls the might of long ago. He is a target of high value and—'

'The high-value target is not the Russian creep. He's in second place—' She broke off and groped in her coat pocket.

She pulled out her phone. The screen threw light on her face, which showed her growing disbelief. Danny Curnow watched. When he stretched up he could see past Karol Pilar and over Bravo's shoulder. The road stretched to a short horizon. The headlights were off and the driver, Alpha, had the van's sidelights to guide him. He was hunched forward and when he went into the potholes he swore. There were lights ahead. Too many bends for Danny to see the tail of the Mercedes, but the lights would have bounced high enough to catch the tops of trees. The last of the three in the black overalls, Charlie, had been working on the weapons as Pilar had talked, seemed satisfied that all were armed and made safe. He had checked the spare magazines, and seemed to have the little cans ready – gas or flash-and-bang. There was a medical box too, and a camera. Everything was checked and cleared.

She must have read her screen three times. He waited, not long.

'I don't believe it.'

What did she not believe? He stayed quiet.

'This is ridiculous, beyond belief.'

He stayed silent.

'Look at this.'

Her phone was shoved under his face. She gave him time to read and scrolled down. The target was designated as Timofey Simonov. She had the job of gold commander. She had no concern for the arrest of Malachy Riordan but evidence linking him to further weapons sales was to be recorded. The Czech, Pilar, had details of the exfiltration procedure. She was wished luck. The authorisation for the taking of Timofey Simonov was from Matthew Bentinick. The sender was Jocelyn. She rounded on him. 'Did you know this?'

He saw no reason to lie. He nodded.

'You let me make an idiot of myself. What am I supposed to do?'

Danny Curnow said, 'It's the end of an operation. We have webs that lead us to the spider and we must follow them. One element was Malachy Riordan, and he took us part of the way. A stronger line came from Ralph Exton. He took us another hike forward. The spider, the bad bastard, is Timofey in his fancy dress. He's the target the big people have chosen. I just try to do my job and not think too much.'

'Ours not to reason why?'

'Do the job as best you can – without getting damaged.'

Her hand went onto Danny's. Warm, gentle. Karol Pilar said they were going now into the base. The van slipped off the road and began to crawl forward. Her hand had gone. He had no place there, and knew nowhere else to be.

18

It was the entry to a labyrinth.

He had been in the great camps at Tidworth or Larkhill, at Catterick, and knew the maze of side roads that led between the office blocks, the administration areas, the training teams' locations, the armouries and arsenals. This one was the size of all of them put together. No signposts, little that was recognisable because of the height that the trees had grown to in more than twenty years. If they had not had the glow of the lights to follow, in the top branches of the trees, they would have had no chance of doing the tail. There were guard posts where the barbed-wire barriers, rusted and sagging, had been dragged aside, and buildings where the windows were broken and the doors hung askew.

Beyond the guard posts, set back among the new forests, there were single-storey offices. Once the tarmac would have been lined with whitewashed stones to prevent wayward drivers going onto mown grass. All gone. He wondered if Nature was a wrecker or whether it laughed at the pygmy efforts of man to create an artificial grooming. He saw the squat entrances to air-raid shelters. Little was clear.

The lights of the Mercedes were far ahead, and he thought the driver travelled slowly to preserve its tyres and chassis. Their own transport was typical of a vehicle pool – army or police – and would have had basic maintenance only, not what he and Dusty gave the minibus. In low gear it coughed and spat. An extraordinary place.

Karol Pilar gave them brief facts: 'The activity here is for the people who come from abroad and want to drive a tank. A company offers that chance. Men come, get drunk in the Old City in Prague, then the next morning are here to drive a tank . . .

'For eighty euros you may buy fifteen minutes as a passenger in a BMP personnel carrier. To be at the controls you have to pay three hundred. To be in a T-55 main battle tank you pay two hundred euros for a ten-minute ride. To drive the T-55 you pay even more . . .

'They have built a camp, away to the west of the site, and it is a replica of a fire base for the Americans in Vietnam. You can pay and be dressed like the Viet Cong, black pyjamas, or in American fatigues, and you fight with bullets of soft plastic.

'In the Communist days, the Czechoslovak Army had three and a half thousand tanks of its own. Now, the new Czech Republic has thirty-five tanks of its own. At Milovice, the entrepreneur has five tanks that belong to him and an MI-24 attack helicopter, but without an engine. There are other collectors. Together they have more tanks than our government. Crazy . . .

'Why do people get satisfaction from travelling in a war machine, and pretending to fight? Why not go to Afghanistan and fight for a day, a week or a month? I do not understand. Would it be a good financial venture to buy a bank building and have people pay to pretend to rob it? Do you think—'

He stopped short. The driver had braked hard and doused the side-lights. The Mercedes had shown them a control tower with the skeleton shape of window frames on the roof where the observers would have managed air movements. They had passed great reinforced hangars where the aircraft had been protected behind huge steel doors, and there had been the open space of the runway, the taxi strip and the aprons. There was a moon but it was not full. The Mercedes had killed its headlights. Ahead was an open space, four or five hundred metres across. Gaby was close to him and stretching to see for herself. The engine ticked over. They would have been against the background of the tree-line but couldn't follow.

They couldn't go forward, and had no light ahead to guide them.

There was a gusting wind that blistered off the van's roof. No one spoke. Danny thought, kept it to himself, that they were short-handed. It was cheap-skate. They might have had a dozen men and four vehicles, but they would still have been under-resourced for tracking a target in such a location. Not his call.

Alpha was beside the driver and had a monocular with night-vision capability. It was passed from Alpha to Charlie, from Charlie to Bravo, from Bravo to Karol Pilar. The sounds were of the wind, the rattle of tree branches and the squeak of movements on the metal flooring. Pilar passed it to Danny, but Gaby intercepted it. It was her call, not Danny's, and she had the right to look through the thing before him. He was just a passenger, making up the numbers and knowing his place. The hard man required to whip an informer into shape – gain necessary co-operation – was redundant. She elbowed him. He reached out in the darkness and her fingers found his hand. A moment of calm amid the chaos? Dream on, Danny. The monocular was in his grip. It was a poor view. He would have had the worst eyes of all of them, clapped-out vision.

The Mercedes, a blurred shape, was in the middle of the far runway. Beyond it there was a line of hangars, great doors pushed shut and grass growing over the curved roofs. The Mercedes waited, blacked out. They must have lights to guide them. If the Mercedes pulled away, didn't use head- or side-lights, and they had only the rear lights to guide them, they'd lose it at the first bend. He couldn't know whether they had shown out or if this was merely a sensible precaution against a tail.

And if the blame game kicked in, and they had shown out, he wondered who would field it. Himself? Just tell them to get lost. Gaby Davies? She could say, with justification, that she had been excluded from the planning stages, and would walk away. Karol Pilar? He would say he had done nothing beyond the instructions given him by a superior officer. Alpha, Bravo and Charlie? They had done as they were told. He scratched in his memory. He seemed to recall an avalanche of missed meetings, lost tails, the frustration of getting back late to Gough, faces of thunder, and the sharpness of colleagues who had not fouled up.

It went forward. Pilar had the night-sight gear. Danny Curnow saw nothing, but the whisper was that the Mercedes had eased away and come off the far side of the runway onto an old concrete apron, then into the tree line. No lights.

Danny Curnow said, 'We depend on you, Karol. Your judgement. How far and how close? Your call.'

If Gaby had interrupted him, made an issue of command and control, he might have slapped her. She didn't. They started off across the width of the runway and were without cover. They had to cross it. He asked Pilar if there was any sign of it having been a piss-stop for the Mercedes. He was answered briskly: no one had emerged from the vehicle. It had been a precaution, professional procedure.

He said, 'An old boss of mine used to say, "If life were easy it wouldn't be worth doing." Sort of about perspective.'

His arm was hit, hard, by Karol Pilar's closed fist. They nudged across the concrete. With no lights to follow, they might already have lost the target.

They had driven a hundred yards, Ralph Exton estimated, had taken a left, then another, and a right. Denisov had switched on the headlights and they went faster. Buildings loomed out of the trees, and a fox crossed the track. It broke its stride, stopped to stare balefully at them, then scooted. He liked foxes. They fitted well with Ralph Exton's image of himself: hunted, persecuted, a survivor, relying on his wits to see the next dawn. He shared the back seat with the Irishman. They hadn't spoken.

It would have been difficult. They could have talked about the smell of burning skin or the danger of cigarette smoking to health, or the amazing performance of the modern cordless drill. They could have discussed the weather on that mountain and whether it was usually blanketed by fog. He had nothing to say to the man. He smelt rank. He had seen little of Malachy Riordan's face, only glimpsed the scratches on his cheek. He had seen the lip, though, and there were small indents near the chin that he assumed were from a bite. He was practised at 'not my business' and avoiding involvement. He was happy trafficking cigarettes to the North of

Ireland and was not burdened with thoughts as to where the money raised from the sales went and what it did.

The big question was about the procurement of weapons: a business opportunity. He saw pictures of funerals on TV. If they were from Ireland no one in the pub turned to the screen. If they were from Iraq or Afghanistan, the room went quiet and there were the usual meaningless statements about 'heroes one and all'. Ralph Exton did not relate the deals from which he took a good cut to the Irish hearses. He wore blinkers. Ralph Exton was well versed in concentrating on what mattered to him. He ignored what did not. He understood about the lights. He wondered where Gaby Davies was, how far back, and assumed she was with the handler, a cold bastard who had read him like the proverbial open book. There was something lovely about her, something rough, honest and vulnerable. She wasn't worldly. A deliberation faced him, but not that evening. Home to the little woman who sometimes shared his bed, his local pub and dodgy contacts book, or off with the officer? God alone knew where it would lead and whether she'd nag the rough edges off him. Gaby Davies would be behind him, with the handler, and they'd probably have back-up. There would be hoods with dungarees, balaclavas and high-velocity firepower.

They came into a clearing and the headlights caught a closed truck. A man stood close to it, dragged on a cigarette and swore at them because the light was in his eyes. Timofey Simonov was out first.

He was told, 'Over there, Ralph. That building – you see it? There is an iron door in the end of the wall. I used to go through it to work each morning. It was the command bunker. Thirty-six steps down and proof against even tactical nuclear strikes. My desk was there. And Brigadier Denisov was my senior officer. It is our place, our territory, and a disgrace that it is treated as a rubbish dump. It is where we have the weapons and where your business associate can shoot. It is good, Ralph?'

Good or bad, it was where they were. He climbed out. The wind whipped him, ruffling his hair and bugging at his coat. An owl hooted in the darkness. He stayed back, looking longingly for shadows and cover.

'It is a pity your friend did not come.'

Malachy Riordan said nothing. He allowed himself to have his arm held, as if he was from Spain or Italy where men touched, and was taken to the back of the truck. A finger was flicked: an impatient instruction.

The cigarette was thrown down, the butt stamped on, and the flap lowered. It clattered, metal on metal, and he flinched at the noise. There was laughter at his reaction. He was told by Timofey Simonov that there would be no ears, eyes or mouth to report anything within five kilometres of where they stood. The boxes were lifted out. The man who had brought them helped the brigadier. The headlights of the truck and the Mercedes lit the open space and the track up which they had come, probing further back into the darkness and making more shadows. He heard an owl. Malachy Riordan knew about owls. He was a night creature, seldom out on the business of war in daylight. He knew owls because they valued the quiet of the mountain.

The boxes were piled up, light chains and padlocks round each. Malachy was invited forward. He felt in his hands the hardness of her throat. First she had taunted him, then he had hit her and gone for her neck. The moment before she had realised he would end her life she had started to struggle. She had split his lip, bitten him and scratched his face.

He was given a small hand torch and a sheet of paper on which were written the items purchased, the quantities and the prices.

Businesslike but not taken from a computer, where it would have left a trace. He shut her from his mind.

He was shown on the list what he had purchased, and the items were checked against the paper. There were rifles, assault and the Dragunov sniper version. He saw rocket-propelled grenade launchers, and the larger boxes that would contain the broken-down pieces of the DSkH heavy machine-gun and the lighter PK7.62mm. There were grenades, and some boxes contained ammunition. The torch was aimed towards a last box and he was told that it held the new Semtex stocks. It was what men in the armed struggle dreamed of: not the quantities that had come from Libya thirty-five years back – so great an amount that it could not be hidden satisfactorily or used because too few men were trained for it – but sufficient to set alight East Tyrone and the Mid-Ulster area. Enough to bring off their arses the men who had said they would fight 'one day but not today'. The boxes were laid out in a line, like coffins when the aftermath of an atrocity was on the television and the dead were waiting to be buried: Syria or Lebanon.

The little man in the uniform said in his ear, 'My friend, for goodwill may I add to this collection a present from myself. Would a tank suit? A T-62, combat weight thirty-six tonnes, maximum speed fifty kilometres per hour, main armament range of four thousand eight hundred metres with fragmentation-high explosive shells. Would you take it?'

'No, sir. We have no ability to use a battle tank. I applaud your generosity but—'

The little man in the uniform was doubled up in laughter. A joke. Only for a moment did he imagine coming down the Pomeroy road, lurching into Irish Street and heading for the police barracks in a tank. He laughed too, but feebly. There were sufficient weapons here to make a difference in the war, and volunteers would flood to him. He would choose only the best, and a new world beckoned. He had woken and she had been cold beside him. The fly had flown from his face to her chin, then had skipped across the bruised line, where his fingers and thumbs had pressed, to her chest. He retched and was sick.

They stood back, gave him space. He had eaten nothing through the night, and just a small cake in the café before his pick-up. The laughter was stifled. Was he all right? Yes. He was regarded curiously. The money, he realised, was trivial to them but not to his own people. The funds paid to the families of prisoners had been slashed because of the sum allocated to him. That would change when the firepower was back on the mountain, the old songs were sung again in bars and buckets rattled. A key opened a padlock at the end of the line.

'I say again, it is a pity your friend did not come.'

She had brought his car. As Karol had told her to, Jana parked in the station forecourt. She had done exactly as directed, and had cleared out the boot – it had contained a mess of supermarket bags, old newspapers and the bag in which he kept a change of clothing. There was a blanket on the seat behind her. As she had been told to, she had filled the tank to the screw cap. She loved Karol, loved the honesty that ran in him, which, she thought, was bred from naïveté, was sometimes stupid and at others heroic. He had promised her a future. She locked the car, put the keys into her bag, went to the machine and bought a ticket for the next train from Milovice to Prague. She would go home and cook herself something, then make another cake for her mother.

The boxes were open. The headlights from the Mercedes and the Azerbaijani's van lit them and reflected off the weapons and ammunition.

He had the pages he had torn out of her notebook and had to crouch near the bonnets of the vehicles to read her writing – which was educated. Malachy Riordan shivered and the owl was still shouting, like it knew. His clothing was still damp. He had her list of the weaponry.

There were priorities: they'd have recognised them. At the top was the deal that had been agreed: money transferred, the purchased items in the boxes with the protection of greaseproof paper and masking tape. At the bottom was what he had done. They knew – they weren't idiots. He would have whacked the face of a slapper in any Russian city or kicked the arse of a whore. But she had been neither a slapper nor a whore. She had had education and style. She had been sent to hold his hand because the leaders of the Organisation would have thought him too crude to negotiate his way round a foreign city. These men knew, and it didn't matter to them. They stood back and watched him, showing no impatience.

He lifted out each weapon and laid it on the grass. Their voices were low and they exchanged cigarettes. It made him feel a little better, that they put the business of the weapons ahead of the girl. He had the inventory she had written: he started to examine the firing mechanisms and to count.

Danny Curnow watched. They were approaching the moment of intervention, but it would not be his call. Beside him Karol Pilar had the camera.

The headlights threw a rectangle of light. It would have been forty-five to fifty metres long, less in width. It lay across open ground, then petered out in the mass of birches and pines. The Czech would decide. Alpha, Bravo and Charlie, who carried the hitting power and were trained in close-quarters assault, belonged to him. Gaby Davies was crouched on the other side of him, and he doubted she had ever before been low to the ground, one knee in wet mud, watching targets who had with them enough weapons to start a small-scale war, low-intensity combat. Would she scream if the firing started and break cover? God alone knew.

He had never believed in taking passengers. A few times, more senior men – ranking officers in Intelligence – had wanted to accompany him and Dusty to meetings with touts but he'd refused them. He'd told it straight: 'No, you will not be with us. You're not trained for it, or privy to the location. You would be an impediment to my safety and to Corporal Miller's. You'll get a full brief when I return.' They were to the side of the rectangle of light. Whether he wanted her there or not was of minimal importance. She was there because she now outranked him.

The Czech understood the change of leadership. Without reference to Danny, he had passed the night-sight monocular to her. She would be aiming through the gaps in the trees, and there was bracken, which was bloody noisy if it was disturbed. She had eyeball and had hooked a microphone into her watch-strap. A cable led up her sleeve to the recorder and she whispered her commentary. This was the evidence log. Karol Pilar had the camera to back it. Twice, Denisov walked in front of Malachy Riordan. Then the Czech eased away from Danny and looked for another gap. Pilar had his own machine pistol and microphone. Away in the blackness beyond the lights the three gunmen would move on the call.

A murmur from Danny Curnow: 'What do you need?'

'Russia and Ireland together in the lens and a weapon held up. I am instructed to gain evidence, not intelligence. It will happen. Patience.'

On the other side of him, warm breath close to his ear: 'You all right?'

'Fine – why should I not be?'

He watched. They would shoot. That would be the moment of opportunity for the camera. Straight after the image was taken the arrests would take place. Easy. A walk in the park. The cold caught him.

It might have been the cold that caused him to shiver. The weapons were being counted. He watched the tout. Ralph Exton played no part. He was like Danny Curnow. He thought it the last time he would be called back to arms.

Jocelyn knew where to look and she saw him.

It was a young people's wine bar, which did good business on a Friday evening. The kids would have abandoned their desks and screens and emerged from the warrens of civil-service buildings. They were the public servants who believed themselves hard done by, underestimated, put upon, that they deserved a binge as the weekend loomed. Matthew Bentinick was the cuckoo among them. He was alone in a corner.

She grimaced when their eyes caught, then headed through the throng. The crowd was three deep at the bar and the staff looked harassed. She hadn't the energy to fight her way through to demand a single clean glass. They'd share. A Sauvignon Blanc bottle stood in front of him. Knowing him, it would be the house brand. The cork was out and the glass in front of him was empty. She pushed, did a Red Sea parting of a group from the Home

Office that had merged with another from Environment, Food and Rural Affairs, and burst through.

Jocelyn did not think that she had ever seen the mercurial Matthew Bentinick so exhausted. A tired smile cracked his face as she squeezed close to him, hip to hip. He held a pipe in his hand, not lit but reeking of stale tobacco. The Friday-night talk battered them. Where would the crowds decamp to for a late meal? Who had tickets to which game the next afternoon? Whose line manager was a bastard? She filled the glass and tapped it, showing which side was his and which hers, then told him she wasn't incubating any virus she knew of. He sipped, she swigged.

'Always the worst?'

'Always.'

'Nowhere to go but sit and wait?'

'Right.'

'Because it's personal?'

'Personal and more.'

'This shower round us, having their end-of-week moan, they have no idea what you carry, Matthew. I don't mean at home. What you carry each day at work and what you take back on the train each evening. Our family used to talk about it at ghastly reunions, which suddenly turned wonderful when you took one of the ancients out into the garden. No one else they met gave a toss. Special Operations Executive, dark nights, agents swinging under parachutes, half of them compromised and going into the cage within an hour of landing. And next morning there would be another gang of recruits needing a transfusion of confidence. They were left behind and ducked into corners in pubs to hug beers and shots of gin, and felt true cowards. They'd seem bemused that I was interested and almost grateful that I'd hear them out.'

He gulped some wine and gripped the stem of his pipe. He pushed the glass to her. 'Easy to imagine, Jocelyn, that we're the ones with the short straws, eking out the waiting time and chorusing how much easier it is to be there, part of the fun and games, not side-lined. Sorry, my dear, but's that's crap.'

The glass went back towards him and she had the bottle by the neck. The fine wine slopped from her mouth as she drank. Then she topped up the glass.

'"Them", the ones who are there?'

'Because we're in their hands.'

'We rise and fall on their successes and failures. I don't know a better man than my Vagabond. He's the best because you can aim him at a target and he'll go through fire to get to it. He won't call Health and Safety, or argue an overtime rate. He does the job. The job owns him and has his loyalty. He would have risen from his deathbed when I told him the *job* needed him. He would have left a bride at the altar if I'd stood in the church door and flicked my fingers. Did I have the right to call him back? That's the burden.'

'And the girl, and the agent.'

'She's not Vagabond. She can look after herself. Fierce little thing and she's competent. She'll come through and climb – but won't go the extra mile. That never held back any individual with ambition. The agent? A liar and deceiver, as they all are. They make their beds and can lie on them. I can justify the needs of a strategic policy that disrupts the flow of arms to revolutionary groupings – Ireland, north Africa, Middle East, Yemen and Somalia – and snipping the trade at source, with the safety and prosperity of our informant. Sink or swim? His problem. Gaby will look after herself. She won't push herself into ultimate danger.'

'But Vagabond called back?'

'I often talk about him. I sit in our daughter's room and tell her about him in a conversational way, as if she might be interested, but I'm speaking to an empty bed with a teddy bear on it – bought twenty-eight years ago from Hamleys – and I get no answer. I tell everyone who needs to know about Vagabond, who will go to the end of the road, if asked, and a bit beyond.'

She passed him a handkerchief. 'Is there long to wait, Matthew?'

'Don't know.'

'Long enough for another bottle.'

She poured the dregs into the glass and stood up, then was lost in the throng. There were protests and curses from Home Office and Defra as she headed for the counter. She barely knew Vagabond, but had begun to care.

The feet, clear of the bed, turned slowly. The toes were against the wall, then the heels. His legs were short, stubby and tanned from the summer sunshine of his Balkan home. One leg of his trousers was around his neck and the other was inserted in the space behind a window fastening. His lips were blue and his eyes bulged. His hands showed no sign of having scrabbled in his last moments to free himself from the self-tied noose. An alarm bell shrilled, boots pounded the corridor outside and an interrogator screamed in frustration.

Dusty Miller reckoned he deserved it. He was astride the stool that was usually Desperate's. The Dickens Bar was open late on a Friday, a concession to the end of the week, and the *patron* had asked where Daniel was. Dusty could say only that he was away but would be home soon. Every Friday. Desperate was in the Dickens Bar on the rue Basse, and every Saturday, but earlier, and every Sunday lunchtime before he left to rendezvous with the next batch of tourists at Dunkirk. It had been a busy and useful summer and the work had been continuous, the routine set in concrete, from before the anniversary and right through the day, 6 June, the celebration of the D Day landings seven decades before. Interest had held up over the next three months: they were now into September and there was no slackening.

There would be a new broom. He didn't know whether he would be driving out of Caen on the coming Sunday or if Desperate would be back. He thought it likely he would. He was not supposed to call him. He'd been tempted, but had not. He knew that Desperate had his mobile with him. Well, he might call tomorrow about arrangements for Sunday. He would break a rule, risk a curse, call the next morning. He had to know. But it wouldn't be for much longer that Desperate headed off to Dunkirk on a Sunday and did his stalk through Honfleur, following the woman with the ash-blonde hair and sea-blue eyes, the strong walk and the perpetual sadness in her face. There would be the new broom because the painting, a coast-scape, was on its way and had been, almost, commissioned by Dusty, his little bit of match-making.

For what he had done, he deserved a few beers in the Dickens. He'd had his supper – the women looked after him well and would continue after Desperate had gone. Gone where? To the north, where it was bloody cold and where cod was on the menu most nights. They'd look after him. He deserved his beers, and could suppose that he might just have brought a cup of happiness to two lonely souls. There was no hurry on the Saturday morning to get the group back on the minibus to Calais, and he'd be able to stay long enough in Caen to see the picture, her work from the dunes, arrive safely. He could, and did, congratulate himself.

Another beer, yes, and for the *patron* too.

The visitors were at their dinner, across the bassin Saint-Pierre from the hotel. It was too cool to be outside and serenaded by the shrill rattle of metal masts in the marina. The guide would be with them and would have relaxed, having stepped down from the plinth of knowledge. He was now 'one of the gang'. The talk flowed and, with it, the wine.

'Glad I've done it. Sort of puts it on the back burner. It was something I'd meant to do for years. Not a bundle of laughs, though.'

'I'd say it's about respect for those lads on the sands – whether at Dunkirk, hoping to be lifted off before the tide came in and drowned them, or Dieppe or on Sword and Omaha. It's a gesture of respect.'

'We've been here, Dorothy and I, to learn about sacrifice. A hard lesson, but this is the classroom for it.'

'What confuses me is how those young lads came through it, the survivors. We didn't hear anything about "stress" and "trauma", not like after Afghanistan and Iraq. I suppose people then just had to get on with it. It's what made them special.'

'I thought it might all get technical and end up repetitive and rather boring. How wrong I was. We have to come here because it's telling the dead that they're not forgotten. We're here to remember them.'

A place at the table in the restaurant was empty. Usually it would have been filled by the minibus driver. On this occasion, the guide had said that the usual man had been called away and his stand-in had declined the invitation to join them. The meal slipped down, the inhibitions of strangers loosened, and the spare place was cleared away by a waiter to give them more room to spread themselves.

'Don't know about the rest of you, but I don't think I'd consider coming again. The place might get under your skin, into your blood. All those great empty beaches, and the quiet of the cemeteries. It's hard to break away from them.'

'Any more in that bottle down there?'

The text reached Matthew Bentinick. Jocelyn craned forward to read it. The second bottle was well started.

He said, 'He'll have heard of the arrest and will – forgive the vulgarity – have shat his pants. Then he'll learn of the suicide. He'll believe that a merciful God has silenced a possible accuser and that he's safe. And he'll be wrong, which will make it all the sweeter.'

She said, 'It'll be countdown time – wherever they bloody are.'

Quiet and darkness had fallen on the mountain and the flat lands.

Few cars were in the lanes to break the stillness, and the darkness was disturbed only by small pockets of light marking the communities. It would be the start of a hard day when dawn disturbed the quiet and the dark. Emotions would be scratched raw.

Bridie Riordan sat in front of a fire that she had allowed to burn out. She toyed with her accounts book for the haulage and heard the hacking cough of her son above her.

Attracta Donnelly and Siobhan Nugent drank coffee in the tout's widow's kitchen and talked softly of lives gone by, what might have been.

Pearse's mother had sent her family to bed, stayed downstairs and ironed her black dress for the next day. The television was blaring but she didn't know what programme was on.

Kevin's mother was alone because her men were in the bar up the road and wouldn't be back until later. She had washed her hair because she wanted to look her best for the service, and couldn't have said why that was important.

Others pondered the day ahead, and more dismissed it as irrelevant.

Brennie Murphy played chess in his kitchen against himself, plotted attack and defence, and could congratulate himself: never a loser and always a winner.

It would be a slow night on the mountain and the flat lands the far side of the Pomeroy road.

'I want to shoot.'

The brigadier answered, 'Of course, but first it is for business. Then you may shoot.'

A restraining hand lay on his arm. He sulked. The grip was firm. There could be no argument. He could, of course, have shrugged it off and kicked the man's shin, might have demanded the opportunity to fire first. He did not. The marksman was never far from his mind. Nothing could eradicate the disaster of the man's failure. He sat in a cell block. Investigators would be queuing to interrogate him. He could stay silent and gaze at the ceiling or spill the dates of planned meetings and the name of his client. Would the 'roof' cover him if he was named? The matter gnawed at him.

He had shot here, at Milovice, on the small-arms range and been congratulated by the sergeant in charge. He had fired once in Africa – the last time they had flown in weapons' crates. The village had been flattened, the civilians gone – except some women or girls who had been kept for comfort and kitchen work. A petrol drum had been near to the strip. He had emptied a whole magazine at it and been told that fewer than ten of the thirty-six bullets had struck the target. He had heard squeals of laughter, a cacophony.

If his name was in the newspapers and he were subject to a warrant, the 'roof' would not cover him. He would fight, he always did, but it nagged.

'When do I shoot?'

'When he has.' The brigadier jerked a thumb towards the man who crouched over the boxes. 'When he is satisfied.'

It was done with care: each weapon was lifted from the box, unwrapped and tested for safety. Barrel into the air, cocked, breech cleared. The man was what Timofey Simonov had never been: a fighter. Where was Ralph Exton, his friend? He looked for him – then saw him. His friend hung back in the shadows, his cigarette flaring as he dragged on it. He didn't think that Ralph Exton would want to shoot. The darkness was total beyond the light thrown by the vehicles.

A mobile bleeped.

Behind him, the brigadier's coat rustled as his hands went into his pockets. The brightness of a screen flashed. The phone was snapped shut. Denisov was at his shoulder. 'He did the decent thing. The Serb hanged himself. He's dead. Relax, and wait your turn to fire.'

He took his man in his arms and hugged him. He would have done the same to Ralph Exton but his friend was too far away.

A rifle was lifted, a magazine loaded. Timofey Simonov did a little jig of relief. He turned towards the brigadier, but couldn't see him.

Danny Curnow was crouched, weight on one knee, clear of the light.

The weapons were counted, the ammunition checked. He saw the gestures. Satisfactory. He wondered what the route would be. A container shipped into Cork docks? A freighter drifting along the coast off Kerry, met by a couple of launches at night? A trawler coming from the Atlantic waters off the northern coast of Spain and making landfall off the west of Ireland where the coves were? It was none of his business.

His job had been to stiffen the agent, who was now 'surplus to requirements', as was Danny Curnow. He might as well have been with the tourists on a last night in Caen, then going home to read emails about the following week's timetable. He watched.

Gaby Davies was behind him, close to Karol Pilar, and they

spoke in whispers. The Czech had the camera. He needed to catch them together, same frame, Malachy Riordan, Timofey Simonov and the weapons. He didn't know where Alpha, Bravo and Charlie were. He was a passenger now. A baton had been passed.

His tongue moved slowly across his lips. They were dry, as they always were in a moment of crisis. He had seen it once and Nikolai Denisov did not expect to see it again. A warning given once was as good as a warning given many times. For a second or two, he had seen the glint of polished glass. It might have been from a camera or a night-sight image intensifier. One or two seconds was enough. He stood very still and listened. An owl hooted and a dog fox barked; a light wind was in the trees, and there was the whine of an old door, with corroded hinges.

He heard everything. He had used an old trick, taught at the training colleges for middle-ranking officers of the GRU back in Soviet times. He kept the Siemens hearing-aid in a felt pouch in his pocket, had it with him more often than a firearm. The quality was good and the price was steep – he had paid 800 euros for it. He could hear whispering too. He couldn't make out what was said, or in what language, but his straining ear picked up the voices. GRU instructors had advised the use of hearing-aids after they had been employed for covert patrols in the murderous wasteland of Chechnya.

Which of them was responsible? The Irishman who was likely to have killed the girl he had travelled with? Or Timofey Simonov's 'friend'? He favoured the friend. He would have liked to seek out the man, and put a knee hard into his groin, then catch the chin with a swinging right fist.

He went to Timofey Simonov and told him to shoot the rocket-propelled grenade launcher, with armour-piercing capability. As its back-blast would endanger the Mercedes, he would move the car first.

'I can fire the RPG, yes?'

'Why not?'

He went to the Mercedes, eased himself into the driver's seat, slipped the hearing-aid from his ear, took the pistol from his waist and laid it on his lap. Then he waited.

Malachy fired. He knew no feeling like it. He felt the impact against his shoulder, smelt the whiff of cordine and heard the crack. He was invincible and fearless.

He imagined men in uniform falling in front of him. He aimed shots at tree-trunks that the headlights caught. He fired well. He saw the mountain again as a place where they wouldn't dare to come unless they were in armoured vehicles with helicopters overhead. He thought of the best boys he could recruit, and how men from as far as Magherafelt and Omagh, Lurgan and Newry would beg to be taken as volunteers. He fired and hit. Each time. He saw gobbets of wood fly from the tree he aimed at. He was supreme. Frankie McKinney was forgotten. So were the boys, his wife and son, even old Brennie Murphy. The weapon was sleek in his hands, and he heard jabbering in his ear.

'I want to shoot. Before you finish.'

He handed over the rifle reluctantly, and stepped back.

'I screwed the focus.'

Gaby hissed at him, 'You have to be ready with it. They were together. I waited for the shutter sound.'

'The target's behind the Irishman.'

'For God's sake, just do it and—'

The bickering between Gaby Davies and Karol Pilar was cut short. Timofey Simonov had the rifle at his shoulder and aimed half-heartedly with a shaky hand. He had pulled the trigger, not squeezed it, and nothing happened. A jam. He prevented the Irishman from taking it back, and the dealer who had brought the weapons came forward. Danny Curnow, on his knee, saw it all. He knew how to react to a jam . . . and so did Malachy Riordan.

The Mercedes had eased back during the shooting and doused its lights. It seemed to float away, in low gear at snail's pace among the trees. It was hard for Danny to follow it.

Riordan took charge. There might have been dirt in the

chamber, a damaged bullet in its casing or faulty chemicals. Danny Curnow thought it good rifle discipline. He reckoned a range instructor would not have done Immediate Action better – Riordan had the magazine off, then went into the cock–hook–look routine. With 'cock', the bolt was dragged back and a round flew out. The headlights caught the dulled old gold of the casing. The 'hook' was the activating of the safety gear. A glance inside must have satisfied Riordan when he did the 'look'. The last round ejected was picked up and pored over. Danny Curnow saw Riordan's grimace: problem identified. Magazine back on. Safety off.

The rifle was snatched. A shot was fired. The rifle recoiled into the Russian's stomach. He swore. And there was a shout of pain, then a howl of anger. He didn't know whether Alpha, Bravo or Charlie had been hit. Chaos erupted.

Gaby Davies's moment. A Secret Serviceman was reported to have shouted, as his principal was lying mortally hurt on the pavement slabs, 'Christ, it's actually happening.' It was. She had good response.

'Go! Go for him.' Her shout.

She had a fist in the Czech's collar. The man looked to Danny Curnow for an order, and didn't get it. Gaby used her knee, firmly into his arse, and shifted him.

It was the start of the charge – and half baked.

Danny Curnow was behind the Czech policeman who ran abreast of Gaby Davies. The girl matched his pace and they went across open ground, tufted grass and the foundations of an old concrete base. Two of the boys were coming out of the side, to the left. They were shouting. So were Pilar and Gaby. Why would she yell? Danny had no idea. Noise and pandemonium. The light failed.

The big van had brought the weapons and the man from it was short and wore nondescript clothing, greys and darker colours, with a baseball cap that celebrated an American college football team. He would have been smart – he sold weapons, old Warsaw Pact stocks and the detritus lying around in the Balkans. There were said to be four million unregistered, unlisted firearms in Serbia, Kosovo, Albania and Montenegro. It was a tough market, and only the smart should apply. He was straight into the cab, straight on with the engine, straight off with the lights.

Danny Curnow had a glimpse of Riordan and the Russian. One fast wrestling movement and the assault rifle was in Riordan's hands. He ran and Timofey Simonov clung to the tail of his coat and wouldn't let go. The rifle butt was swung at him and would have hit him but he had the grip and wouldn't give up on it. The boys with the firepower had torches on the weapons that threw out thin light cones. One caught the tail of the vehicle and sent random shots at it but likely missed. Another torch beam, and he saw Ralph Exton.

A gutless creature, but sensible. Ralph Exton was lying on his side and had his hands over his ears. Thoughts jangled in Danny Curnow's mind as he ran, guided by the rakish light of the torches. He wondered how long Ralph Exton, paid betrayer, could survive once the cavalry had moved on and the dawn had come: two big enemies lined up and furious in their shouts for vengeance. Obvious who had betrayed them: Russians coming after him, Irish hunting for him, a price on his life – men would queue for the chance to put a bullet into Ralph Exton's brain. Danny careered past him.

He followed the torches, listened to the shouts and moved. He was out of the cleared area, past the neat row of boxes in which the weapons had been brought and among the trees. Murphy's Law never failed to give value. They blundered among the undergrowth and searched. Sometimes old buildings loomed up, and there were ventilation shafts with rusted metal caps, air-raid and blast-shelter entrances.

He thought he was part of a loose cordon line, and heard Gaby Davies's voice, increasingly shrill because the chance of a foul-up was high. The cold seemed to catch him. The owl and the fox had gone quiet. He heard the blundering advance of the searchers – and was part of it.

19

If there had been good fieldcraft – and there was not – the line should, as one, have stopped. They should have rooted themselves, stayed still and quiet, should have listened. The exhilaration of the chase won. Danny Curnow heard only the blundering pace of the charge.

The boys with the torches went quickest, the narrow beams pushing ahead of them and bouncing back off trees, bracken, tangles of brambles and the shells of buildings. All three were in the ragged line. Simple enough for Danny Curnow to put in place the scenario: a bullet had come close, hit the vest or the webbing at the waist and there might have been blood. Shock, trauma and a yell had done the job for Murphy the law-maker. They were in front. He knew that Gaby Davies, her big night, was with Karol Pilar away to the left. Danny was to the right, and had no torch. He knew the futility of what he was doing and had drawn the pistol – why? Why indeed? Might have been Dusty a pace behind him: *Don't mind me asking, Desperate, but why have you got the shooter out? We're not here to slot anyone.* Dusty always asked the sensible bloody questions and those that had no answer. He slowed.

The moon was above him but had little strength on the ground. Most of its light fell on the trees' canopy.

He was cocooned in the darkness, the voices faded and the torch beams had filtered out. He had once been in a sangar, well sited with good camouflage, and they had watched a crossroads where the tout had said that two cars would meet and that the heavy stuff – an American-made Barrett rifle, model 82A1, with a 50-calibre round – would be transferred. The Green Slimes didn't know where it was coming from, what car would be used, where it would be taken to: only a crossroads had been identified. There had been chaos. The South Tyrone Hunt had come through and the crossroads had been filled to bursting with baying hounds and horses of all sizes with their riders. He could have broken cover, shouted to the master and pointed in the direction the fox had taken. It had been a good one, with a fine brush, and had headed away at not much more than a brisk trot, which meant it was confident. Chuckles from him and Dusty in the wet and the dirt of the sangar. A war was being fought, and a marksman's rifle was about to be transferred to a man who would kill with it. An operation, planned with the precision of the military, had been screwed because the locals were chasing a fox. The cars never came that day. The quiet had returned and they had watched and listened. Always best.

He stopped.

Sometimes he could see the torches and sometimes he could hear voices. More often there was the noise of movement. They needed a dog or, better, a pack. He was against a tree.

A deer came past him, young, fast and bounding. It would have been no more than four paces from him and didn't swerve. Good that it showed no sign of identifying him. He was against the tree, masked by it. The deer went on. Darkness had never unnerved Danny Curnow.

So much to hear.

The wind made the most of it: it made the trees scrape bark on bark, twigs against branches, and seemed to sing. He heard the voices.

Danny Curnow held tight to the butt of the pistol.

One was whining and against it there was a deeper, angry voice.

He looked for the source, and tried to cut out the other sounds around him. He no longer saw the torches or heard the cordon.

Close to and below him. He was still . . . He concentrated and the voices were clearer. He saw the shape of a low wall a little to his left, the pit beyond it and the one step that was visible.

'It is because of you. I do a stupid deal, unnecessary – for a friend. It is catastrophe.' The whine of Timofey Simonov.

Then Malachy Riordan: 'You dress like a carnival queen, and you have no security. We're blown away.'

'The leak will be on your side.'

'No way – and we'll be wanting the money back – all of it.'

It was dark. Timofey Simonov's feet were in deep water. It sloshed at the ankles of his boots and smelt dank. He was against the wall. There had been a table there and a small hard chair with it. He had been awarded – because of his importance in Military Intelligence – a computer, which was on the table for his personal use. He had been valued.

His voice quavered: 'I was paid to arrange the elimination of a man. He was an enemy of the state, had betrayed it and fled to London. I was well paid. It said on the television news before I left my home that the man I'd bought had been taken by the British police and was held. If he had confessed his involvement and given my name I would have faced a calamitous fall. I live here quietly, but I must earn protection. To gain further protection I accepted the contract from the state. What did I hear this evening? Maybe you do not care, but I finish. What did I hear? The man hanged himself. I am free of involvement and I come here. I could have danced with you. A burden off my shoulder. You understand?'

'To have a burden on the shoulder, yes – and being unable to shake it off.'

'I am happy. I am helping Ralph Exton, who is my friend. For not many hours, for a few minutes, I am free of the anxiety. Then the rifle fires and they come from the trees. You are a ship and you think you are safe from the reef, but there is another rock, and more dangerous. Irishman, are you honest?'

The voice was quiet, the anger faded. 'I'm honest. I don't lie or cheat.'

'A fighter in a guerrilla war, and you do not lie or cheat? But you kill?'

'You accuse me?'

'Not for killing your enemy. Your face. The scrape on your face, her nails. How was she your enemy?'

'I don't cheat.'

'Your wife . . . You do not cheat on your wife.'

'No.'

'And the girl is dead?'

Timofey Simonov strained to hear the answer.

'Yes.'

A screech owl called.

'My fighter for freedom, be honest. Could it have been you who was tailed, compromised by the British agencies? Could it be you? Honest.'

'No. What do you know of intelligence?'

The owl called again. The sound came down the steps and into the bunker.

Then the call, sharp as always from the screech owl, was lost because Timofey moved along the wall and the water there slurped. His boots had begun to leak.

'I was GRU. It is Military Intelligence. I was here. My desk was here and we were in this bunker for Alert Status situations. If it had been war we would have used a bunker that is deeper and nuclear proof, but this was for simulation of attack and defence. The general, he commanded Central Forces, was behind you, and my brigadier was to the side, but I was the general's favourite. He would question me, test my answers, try to ridicule me, but he followed what I said. I know about intelligence.'

'I came very carefully. I stayed in a back-street, did cut-outs to see a tail . . . I know about surveillance – human, cameras and audio – and I saw nothing. It was not me.'

'And not me. There was a woman's voice. She is of a British agency. My driver is cleared. Who else is left?'

'The bastard.'

'My friend is left.'

'He set it up. He did the middle work.'

'He is my friend. When I had nothing, he lifted me. Today it was all to help him. I make nothing on this deal, nothing. For my friend, to help him.'

'I saw him in Ireland and showed him a drill. I switched the drill on. I lit cigarettes and held them close to him. Asked him why he sold weapons for use against his own people. I got a quick enough answer. I can tell you each fuckin' word of it. "There's a recession on where I live, and I've a family to keep, and you pay me. Good enough? I need the money." It's what he said.'

'Get me away from here and I'll do you more weapons.'

'Your friend was a lie.'

'He is walking but he is dead.' Timofey's voice had risen, anger in it. He felt a hand on his arm below the epaulette. It squeezed hard.

'Dead, but not yet dead. Your driver didn't wait around.'

'I think he stays for me, a little away, at the old transport-pool depot. He might wait there. My driver is loyal to me, is nothing without me.'

'He might stay. We'll give it a bit longer, then get clear.'

'I am in your hands. It hurts when your friend betrays you. I have people indebted to me in responsible positions, with authority. What is there for you, my freedom fighter?'

'I go home, back where I came from. Say nothing, deny. Answer no questions. Hope to confuse . . . but certain to be convicted. Photographs, prints, DNA, and what's on these clothes. The door closes for life – that's twenty years. I don't see the mountain, don't hear it, don't smell it. I don't see my wife or my son, except through glass. He was your friend, but I checked him.'

'We give it more time.'

It had been a dilemma but only briefly. The screech owl's call was the best. It pierced the evening air, and he could do it well enough for it to pass. And the bunker helped Danny Curnow – underground, the call would be muffled.

They had come out of the trees. One of the boys was first. All of the torches were off. The monocular would have guided them. He would have stood out, a white shape against the tree, then Gaby and last Karol Pilar. His hand had been across his mouth. They had all stood a few metres from the bunker entrance and listened. She knew the order from London – she'd read the text. She might argue and bitch but she was a company girl and when push went beyond shove she'd knuckle down and do as instructed. The fling with the agent wouldn't survive the homecoming, but Danny was no expert in relationships. He could have done a master's in failed ones.

He supposed it was because he was a 'little man,' comfortable inside a laager. He needed to belong – he had done in the army, which was a brotherhood, then in Caen and with the visitors, living with the cemeteries. It was not that he had felt vindictive towards Timofey Simonov, to whom he had never spoken. The man had done nothing to him . . . And Malachy Riordan, who kept alive the embers of an old war, was not in the equation. Neither of them mattered to Danny Curnow, but it was as if he had taken the shilling and therefore was obligated, not that money had been discussed. He hadn't contemplated turning his back when the call to return had been spoken in his ear, against the ripple of the waves on the beach. It was almost over. He would be home in the morning, back with Lisette and Christine. Dusty would bombard him with questions, and then he might contact Matthew Bentinick to talk about remuneration. He'd never been good at getting the best possible payment. It was almost, but not quite, over, and a little of the business from long ago was unfinished.

He stood back from the entrance and the boys let Gaby Davies and Karol Pilar come near to him. They all listened and the voices were plain, murmured, and English was spoken. She touched his arm as if that were an accolade for showing his worth, and the Czech gave him another punch on the shoulder. The boys had the monocular. They did the reconnaissance of the steps and peered towards the targets but couldn't see them.

Near to conclusion. It was always a massive let-down, what the trick-cyclists called 'burn-out anticlimax'. She didn't touch him now, and was bent close to Karol Pilar. She was in charge of the day and he had command of the moment. They whispered urgently to each other. Neither asked Danny for advice or an opinion. He stood back. It hardly mattered to Danny Curnow that he was ignored.

'Get them out.'

'I'm not sending boys in there. It's a hell-hole.'

'They have to be brought out, and we have a schedule.' She had control, authority – the first time in her life that it mattered – and Gaby Davies used it.

'I will not put the boys in danger ahead of myself, and I am not going in there.'

'You have stun grenades?'

'We have the M84, 180 decibels and a million candela – I already told you or Danny – with two-second delay.'

'Get the show on the road. Use them.' She pushed him away, a dismissal.

'It could have a bad effect in there. Trapped?' A last query.

'We have a schedule to keep, and their welfare is their concern. Do it.'

She was elbowed back, no ceremony, and crouched. She put her hands over her ears. Danny Curnow turned away and took a sort of shelter from the tree nearest him. He heard the rasp as the pin was pulled, then the noise of the impact as it bounced on the first step and went down.

'He'll have waited and . . .' It rattled, like a tin can dropped in a supermarket aisle.

Timofey Simonov had said he would call the driver who had brought him. He was sure his man would have waited. Unthinkable that he would abandon him.

He couldn't see it, only heard it, down three steps, leaping, and then the splash into the stagnant water. One moment he had been close to Riordan, and the next the man was gone, his movement making waves in the water. Riordan was down, almost under the water. Timofey Simonov did not understand.

He stood, was exposed.

The light burned out his eyesight and the explosion killed his hearing.

Hands gripped his waist and he was dragged towards where he thought the bunker's steps were. He tripped on the bottom one and was hit, a cuff with the heel of a hand at the nape of his neck. He had no clear thoughts. Dazed and bewildered, he was pitched forward and stumbled, then propelled upwards. Torches greeted him. The last blow caught him between the legs and he lurched higher. The lights in his face were indistinct and blurred and he saw the movement of mouths in the holes of balaclava-covered faces. He was snatched.

There was a woman, young. His arms were wrenched back to his spine, above his buttocks. The tunic was torn from his chest, buttons exploding, and fingers searched him. The handcuffs were on his wrists. He could not have walked. They had hold of his arms at the elbows and his boots trailed along, the toecaps scuffing the ground. He heard nothing and saw little. In his mind there were confused images of his dogs and his home on the hill above Karlovy Vary, the assault rifle he should have fired, and the brigadier – where was he?

Timofey Simonov shouted at the darkness and the trees: 'Denisov, where are you? Denisov, tell them who I am . . .' He couldn't hear his own voice and no answer came. The silence blistered round him. Twice his boots snagged and he would have fallen onto his face but for the hands that gripped him. He tried to shout once more: 'Denisov, explain to them who I know, who my friends are.'

Trees loomed past him, and there were guns close to him. It was time to despair because he grasped with sharp clarity – that they knew who he was and who his friends were. He was dragged away and tears welled in his damaged eyes. The silence clung to him.

They ran. Gaby Davies kept up easily with the boys. They moved their prisoner as if he weighed nothing. The third, she thought it was Bravo, was behind them. If the prisoner slowed he kicked the back of the shin as encouragement to keep going. She felt almost ecstatic. The pity of it: she was far from the bar in Pimlico, at the end of Horseferry Road where they would be gathering that night – those inside the circle of knowledge – drinking. Perhaps the director himself would have prowled down from his eyrie on the upper floor to hand out personal congratulations, like confetti. But she wouldn't be there. Gaby had been with the Service long enough to know how the zephyr of excitement came into the building: it had a force of its own and ignored the strictures of need-to-know. It celebrated any coup they pulled. Triumph, no details and no names, always seeped through doors, then up and down lift shafts. The prisoner bleated. Did she resent that so much had been kept from her? Not at all. He was a high-value target, and she had taken him down.

'Where's Danny?' It was the Czech.

'What? What did you say?'

A shout. 'Where's Danny? I don't have him.'

'Somewhere behind us.'

'I haven't seen him. None of us have.'

'Well, he's a big boy, isn't he? We have a schedule.'

'Are we leaving him?'

What else to do? Darkness governed the timetable, the cover of night, and the absence of senior officials at their desks, playing with their bloody screens, keyboards and Blackberrys. By daylight the hopes for success would wane. They were on the edge of illegality and needed the cover of darkness to be gone and finished by dawn, the erasure of evidence and the completion of a mission. She was unlikely to be sympathetic to a suggestion that they call a halt and wait for him to show.

She called back: 'He can look after himself.'

She fell, and swore. Bravo heaved her up. She wore trainers, lightweight, good enough for a jog in a London park. She'd bought them for a hike round Kielder Water, in the Northumberland National Park; at home they thought she was a clerk with the Revenue. The shoes were not good enough for running and weaving, sliding and slipping in a forest in near darkness. She'd tripped on a concrete block.

'Is that what we do?'

'We leave him, of course we do. He'll find his own way. It was never expected he'd go with us out of here.'

'Did you hurt yourself?'

'No.' She said it too fast, confirming the lie. The shoes had been useless at Kielder Water and had given her a blister. She'd not gone far before settling at a viewpoint and smoking a quarter-pack of cigarettes. They looked stylish, and were useful in London, but not here – and she'd lost one in a mud pool. She was handed it – Karol Pilar had found it for her. 'I didn't hurt myself.'

'And what about Ralph Exton?'

'I'm not a nanny either. I can't hang about.'

'We leave Exton too?'

'Is this a school trip? Do I have to round them up? They can come out together.'

She had been to bed with him twice. She had been lonely and stressed out. She had marginally enjoyed the experience and had thought of a future of sorts for them, but that was when she had been running in the wake of Danny Curnow. It was her call now. What she would do, when she was home, was take the clothes out of her case, separate the underwear – everything that he, with not especially nimble fingers, had touched – find a plastic bag, stuff it in, take it down the street to the first rubbish bin and dump it.

'You leave Danny Curnow – good guy – and you leave Ralph Exton, who was the most important voice in the affair? It's what Mr Bentinick told me.'

'They can walk, tell each other war stories. Can't get my fucking shoe on.'

But she did. The old blister had come back. They reached the van. The Russian was bundled inside, Alpha with him, then Gaby. Karol Pilar, Bravo and Charlie, who drove, were squashed into the front. They went out fast, over potholes, and as she rocked on the hard surface, she realised she had not thought of the other player in the game: Malachy Riordan. Her instructions, without equivocation, had been to ignore him. Bravo found a rock station, from Bratislava, and they went for the main road.

'Can you hear me, Malachy?'

It was fifteen minutes since they had left. Danny Curnow had leaned against a tree, let it take his weight. He was near to the entrance of the bunker.

'I stayed because I owe you, Malachy.'

There were times when all the proven lessons went out with the bath water. There was no good reason for Danny Curnow to have stayed in the forest around the desolate buildings of the former base. And less of a good reason for him to go to the bunker's entrance, stand on the top step and silhouette himself against whatever light the moon gave. It seemed the right place and the right time. Maybe he'd waited too long.

'The occasion and the opportunity came together, Malachy.'

There was no answer from the blackness, and he assumed the man was still huddled at the far side of the bunker. He knew he was alive. If he had been dead, well, the Russian wouldn't have made it up the steps. It was clear that he'd been pushed up and was too dazed to negotiate them on his own – and two voices had alerted Danny. He assumed he had delivered a body blow. Malachy Riordan had spent a quarter of an hour in hiding, hearing nothing but the wind in the trees and the occasional night bird's call. Knowing that the Russian was gone – having heard the footfalls blundering away at speed – he had been steeling himself to emerge and slide away, hoping to find obscurity.

'I used to see you as a kid, Malachy. I did surveillance on the farmhouse. Your father was the target, and I was often tasked there. I used to see you go to school and come back, and in the holidays and at weekends you'd be with your father out at the back or working on the lorries. I watched you, Malachy.'

He listened and heard nothing. He might have been talking to himself – he often did, sitting in the cemeteries or at the back of the beaches by the closed ice-cream outlets. He might have been speaking to the headstones in their precise lines or to the men who had sheltered in the shallow pits of shifting sand in the dunes when the aircraft had swooped on them. Sometimes in his room he talked quietly to the pictures on the walls.

'I was there when the priest came and told your mother that your father had died in the ambush. You came out of the door. What were you? Eight or nine? You screamed, Malachy, and I heard you. I knew then that you'd be a fighter and that you'd not be caged. I killed your father. I ran the agent who touted him. They said I was the best and I ran many agents so I killed many men. It's a burden. I'm wondering if you feel the same weight because of men you've killed. They say it's better when you talk about it. I've tried to find somebody, anybody, who'll hear me out but don't seem to know how to go about it.'

It was colder and the wind had freshened. It gusted through the tunnels the trees made and past the buildings. He aimed his voice at the abyss beyond the steps, but heard no movement. The man would be like a rat in a corner, considering his best chances and failing to find any. He persisted and felt as if he'd come across a soul-mate. He'd never talked to Dusty like this.

'I shouldn't think your burden would be any policeman you'd shot – have you killed any, or just hurt them, damaged a leg or an eye? I'm not up to speed on the statistics of your war. They brought me back to run the agent here. Malachy, two things about you surprise me. You're a big man, a hard man, an intelligent man, a fighter, who has the respect of the crowd up at Palace Barracks. They want to bang you up, shut the door on you, but they admire your professionalism. It's always a plus for them – good tactics and strong commitment. But you must be carrying a burden – you are, aren't you? Because of the girl.'

He sat down on the top step. His knees were against his chest. He held the pistol loosely, not as if he believed himself threatened.

'I'm a part of your life, just as you are of mine. I killed your father and I've destroyed you. That's the way it is. I'm not taking you in. I don't have cuffs, or an arrest warrant, and I don't have an army out there behind me. I just wanted to talk. Funny thing about you, Malachy, I don't reckon you as a theorist. Some can spout every hour and every date of an 'atrocity', always the victim, never to blame. You're not one of them, I'm told. You're a soldier. The first thing that confuses me is how you didn't smell the tail and the deceit. It kind of lets you down in my image of you.'

He was answered by the quiet.

'What else bothers me about you, Malachy, is that you killed the girl. Nice-looking kid, smart and bright. We'd the impression she was here for kicks – know what I mean? She wasn't one of the ideologues who recite doctrine for twenty-four hours a day. She wouldn't have lasted, would have been out the door in a year and holed up with a banker or a broker in Zürich or Hamburg, like the struggle was a rite of passage for her. Some kids backpack round Australia but she wanted something with more muzzle velocity. Did you have to kill her? Why?'

He scratched his nose and realised, then, that he was at the heart of it.

'It's the burden, and it never goes. "The cliff I'm going to climb gets steeper, and the rock I'm going to carry to the top gets heavier." That's what the burden's like, and I couldn't think of anyone other than you to talk to about it. But you won't answer me and we'll sit here a while longer. You've shoved that scumbag Russian into their arms, bought yourself time. He was what they wanted, not you. You were just the route in, otherwise insignificant. You have a little time. And I'm in no hurry.'

With a last juddering heave, the wheels of the van cleared a pothole on the track and they lurched onto a decent surface. They were on a public road, lights glowing in the sky above the trees, within touching distance of a sort of civilisation, and had shed the old world of great armies and traditions in their backpacks. Charlie put his foot down.

Alpha worked round her, not gently or with compassion. He did his job. He wrapped a strip of plaster over Timofey Simonov's face, then trussed his legs. He took off the handcuffs and taped the man's wrists. The handcuffs went into a deep pouch pocket in his trousers. She recognised that the symbols of evidence were being removed. The man was supine and might have thought himself already dead: he had received, as yet, no explanation, and Gaby Davies felt no need to supply one. They came into the town.

It was quiet. There were high apartment blocks. Some had lights on and open curtains, but the majority were dark. The village of Milovice, which had been a closed community, boasted no night life. They faced deserted streets, a closed-down railway station and a small parked car.

They spilled out. Alpha and Bravo took the arms of the prisoner, then dragged him, boots scraping along the ground, towards the car. It was well away from light, well placed. Karol Pilar had the keys and opened the back hatch. A bigger man would not have fitted into the boot but Timofey Simonov went in, his knees pressed to his stomach. That was how it was done, she reflected. She was not in any police service. He had not been informed of the charges laid against him, or of any rights. He was a turkey travelling to a Christmas table. She was hugged – the boys took it in turns. Alpha and Charlie were enthusiastic, and Bravo was apologetic – he couldn't squeeze her tightly because of the flesh wound in his arm near where the bullet had ricocheted, but he kissed her cheeks. Then they were gone in the van, job done.

The satnav was plugged in.

Karol Pilar drove.

She said to him that he should do it. Premature? She didn't think so. He kept his feet on the pedals and she took the wheel, leaning across him, while he tapped out the message that would go to the secure offices of the station chief in Prague.

He showed her. *Pick-up. On schedule for delivery.* She nodded. It was sent. She heard a muffled groan. The route would be the D8 highway, then the E55 and on to Teplice, then the border.

Tiredness came over her in waves. She let her head drop and her eyes close. She declined to confront the questionable legality of taking the prisoner, and had a suspicion of a smile on her face.

She was imagining the response back in London, a building beside the river, the pleasure and satisfaction. But there was a border to negotiate before she could expect praise. It didn't cross her mind that she should wonder where Danny Curnow was, what move Ralph Exton had made to extricate himself and the Irishman. It was a matter of priorities.

They walked arm in arm. She might have stayed, done battle with another bottle, but Matthew Bentinick had helped her up and led her from the bar. It had been a shaky passage out – elbows had been bruised and drinks slopped, but they'd absorbed the protests. The cool outside was sobering.

He was taller than her and she needed to skip from time to time to match his pace. They came to a stop at a small building site off Horseferry, where a wall had been exposed and there was a tap. It hadn't been disconnected. She went first. Jocelyn, keeper of secrets for the Security Service, known to her peers as a resolutely private woman, crouched beside the tap and turned it on. When water gushed to the pavement she cupped her hands, splashed her face, rinsed her mouth and spat. Matthew Bentinick was dressed for the formality he practised in Thames House – as if a degree of dandyish eccentricity enhanced his standing. She held his jacket and he pulled up his cufflinked shirt sleeves. His tie was safe inside his waistcoat. Water dribbled from his hands, cheeks and chin. When he had turned off the tap, he produced a large handkerchief from his trouser pocket and offered it to her for her face and hands. He was easing into his jacket when the phone warbled. He took it out.

He read. He passed it.

She said quietly, close to his ear, 'Well done.'

They were again the servants of the state. Their arms were no longer linked and their stride was brisk because work needed to be done from offices on the fourth floor. There was no celebration that any man or woman on the pavement would have noticed. Each in their own way had focused on the priority of the hour: a small man with a protruding stomach, thinning dark hair and bright but suspicious eyes, as seen in the surveillance photographs. Neither Matthew Bentinick nor Jocelyn allowed any other person entry to that space.

'Nobody tells you about the burden when you start out. Your people wouldn't, and mine didn't.'

Danny Curnow talked as if to himself but had an audience.

'It's not accepted by your godfathers or mine that we'll carry the weight of it through our lives. Accept it and they have to take the guilt, so they don't. Big people reckon they're above guilt or blame. They'll tell you to get a grip and move on. They don't care. They use you, bleed you and walk away. Same for you and me.'

There had been movement in the darkness, a lapping of water against a lower step and, once, a stifled cough. He believed that the fighter would have been experienced enough to protect his ears and eyes when the grenade was thrown. It would be cold down in the bunker. His purpose was to break the man, and he thought he was on course for success. Nothing personal, but Danny Curnow intended to walk away a winner.

'It's no secret, Malachy, that you weren't the principal Tango – sorry, I'm using our old jargon. I was Vagabond then and came out of Gough, and "Tango" was our shorthand for a man like your father, Padraig Riordan. No one would ever have said we should *kill* your father – we didn't use language like that. We'd have said something like "How far do we go to remove this man from our area of responsibility?" Simple enough question, and there was a simple enough answer. "As far as is necessary." It was a no-brainer. You with me, Malachy?'

He paused to let it sink in. Danny Curnow had always been well practised in allowing silence to hang.

'You aren't seen as the equal of your father so, today, you weren't the main Tango. The Russian was, and you were just a way of getting to him. We wanted him, and you don't need to know why. You got us where we wanted to go. This wasn't about arresting you. What they did in Lithuania was different – take down the buyer and bang him up in a shit gaol in Vilnius. It's not what they've got in mind for you . . . You want to come up out of there or are you happy?'

It was the turning of a screw. Always good to be patient. The business of destroying a man should be done slowly: blurt out the big lines too fast and the man can shrug them off. He felt confident. He had nothing left to contribute to the mission but was manacled to the job – Matthew Bentinick had called him back because he did it well. He'd done it so well that it had nearly broken him.

'You can come out of there, walk into the village and get a train into town, then the bus out to the airport. I won't be on the same flight, because I don't go to the UK or the Republic. You won't be stopped at the desk but will be allowed to board. It's all arranged, Malachy. You have free passage and can use whatever passport suits you. You'll not face arrest for conspiracy to purchase weapons, or for previous attacks on security-force personnel, or for killing that girl. You'll get to Ireland and you'll have the number for the driver who'll take you back up to the mountain, and you'll say where you want dropping – maybe near the place where you threatened the dealer, the chancer you trusted, with the drill. Tomorrow afternoon, if you shift yourself, you'll be safely back with your wife and son. From the moment you go through the back door, though, you'll have the weight of the burden. It'll be heavy on your back . . . For God's sake, come up out of the cold and all that shit down there, dry out and have a fag while I tell you about the weight you'll be carrying.'

He was wrapped in a cloak of his own making, and his sense of reality had drifted away. It was a challenge Danny Curnow faced, and challenges were for health and exertion, and satisfaction . . . at home, in Caen, no challenges existed, and nothing awaited him.

'You'll be allowed to go back to your own ground, but the burden will crush you. You went on a journey with the hopes of your organisation ringing in your ears, but you'll return with nothing. No assault rifles, no machine-guns, no sniper gear or mortars, no military explosive. You'll have nothing to show for the trip – and nothing to show for the money. They cleaned out the coffers so you could buy the hardware you claimed you needed. A star kid went with you, a looker, and now she's dead. Last, you gave men's work to two kids who died while you were far away and safe. I'm getting there.'

He heard the coughing and the sloshing of water. He knew that, very soon, the man would emerge, close to breaking.

'Every move you made was failure, Malachy, and that will be the rumour spread on the mountain. We can do that effectively, past masters at it. Slip the gossip in, stir the dirt. Who was the tout who gave the tip? Why was a high-profile fighter, hands-on with the weapons, allowed back, and what deal had he done? Where was the money? Why was it paid over before the weapons had been delivered and who has the numbered account where it's banked? What happened to a girl, with an education, who's found in a flea pit in a red-light district of Prague? How did Riordan, the strong family man, get the scratches on his face – and what split his lip? It comes down to this, Malachy. Who's going to believe you? Why were you not arrested? Where's the money? What's the situation with the girl? Tongues flapping. Cold-shouldered, backs turned, earth still high on the graves of the kids who died when you weren't there. Who will believe you? I'm telling you. No one. Were you yourself the tout? We can feed that into the community. You'll be ignored, discredited, then investigated, and when you're isolated they'll kill you – sentence of death for betrayal. Talk your way back to trust? I don't think so. The burden's already there, but we'll hike it. If it helps, this wasn't on our original game plan, but I was stuck with my boss at a bus stop, after a bit of history tourism, and it seemed a good way to screw you. Nothing personal.'

He played the big card. That was his way, proven in old times. The weapon would not have protected him, and he would not have used it. He had never taken a life and only fired on a range. He had seen Riordan with the rifle in the moment after Simonov had snatched at it and expected him still to have it. He would make his gesture, it would be answered, and the battle would be won. He had no doubt of it. He savoured, for a moment, the feel of the pistol in his hand. Squat and compact, comfortable, offering reassurance . . .

He was Danny Curnow, who had been Vagabond, and did not need reassurance. He threw it forward. The pistol cannoned into the sloping roof of the steps going down into the bunker, then splashed into the water. The sound echoed up at him.

He used a voice that was casual and confident: 'I've no quarrel with you, Malachy, and the proof is that I've thrown down to you the personal weapon I was issued with. I don't have another. You're safe to come out, and the circus has moved on, just you and me left. Come on up, Malachy.'

Danny Curnow wanted him snapped like a brittle twig. Not gunned down in an ambush and facing the tributes of martyrdom – the part of the graveyard reserved for heroes, where the fresh flowers were. He wanted him isolated, fearful, held in a meld of contempt and mistrust. It was the way it would end. Even the men on the mountain, the faithful followers and the kids, would find the war impossible to prosecute further.

'I'm waiting, Malachy. We're two of a kind, both fucked and no future. Let's talk.'

There was a surge of movement below. Vindicated. He had shown, he reckoned, all of the skills that the man who had the Vagabond call-sign would have known, and it would be appreciated: terse praise from Matthew Bentinick, and a glass down at the Dickens Bar when he got home. He heard the squelching approach from the bottom steps and the heavy splash of water. Then he was hit.

It was a blow to his chest.

A shape pushed past him, a shadow. It stopped over him. There was the swing of a weapon and his chin was hit, gratuitous, and the shadow was gone. Still numb. In shock. Not in the plan. Not suggested by him or agreed by Bentinick . . . A great weakness enveloped Danny Curnow and was across his body. He tried to feel where the blow had struck but couldn't find it, only the wet. The blunder of running boots became quieter and peace settled on him.

Ralph Exton heard the shot. He knew the sound of a rifle. In the fields, at winter, round the 'royal' village, they used shotguns to bring down pheasants that were barely old enough to get airborne. In the woodlands, surrounded by the *Private* and *Keep Out* signs, men culled deer at dawn with rifles. He cringed, and the cold clawed at him. He had no light and his arms were tight around him. *Fuck me . . . Just another day in the office . . . Fuck me.* He might have been near to moving. He had gained enough courage to think about getting up, groping round him, heading anywhere that might get him clear, but there had been the shot.

He hugged himself, hoped for comfort but failed to find it. He didn't dare to move.

They slept well. Many had drunk a good quantity of the house red, and the bags were packed. The world of shock and horror, courage under fire and of 'doing the job right' seemed of small relevance. A return to normality awaited them.

The house below Dusty was quiet. If Christine were to visit him it would be later. Lisette was already asleep, and snoring gently. He was sitting on Desperate's bed. He wouldn't have been there in the old days at Gough when each of the senior NCOs had had a cubbyhole to call their own where privacy was fiercely preserved. If he had, he would have been out on his ear. There were no photographs of her on the bedside table, but she was all around. Barely a space on the wall for the new picture to hang. Which almost settled the matter. He thought it was the end of the road for their friendship: he would wave his man off, wishing him well, and might see the flash of blonde hair streaming from her ponytail. He'd wave as they drove away, the pictures to be delivered to them at a later date – miles away, if either of them had a pinch of common sense. He should phone, shouldn't he? He should ring Desperate. Well, he would but not yet. For the moment, in the room with the paintings, he sat on the bed and remembered their times together, deaths, and hardships, stretched nerves and peace of a sort: fine times, but harsh. His mobile was in his hand. He'd talk about the new work coming early in the morning and how Desperate should get himself to Honfleur and . . .

* * *

He should have lain still.

When his radio call-sign was Vagabond, and when he was Desperate with Dusty behind him, the drills were fixed in his mind. The darkness clawed round him and the numbness had given way to pain. The weakness was more easily reckoned, and old rules were forgotten. About the only thing he remembered from the clinical courses run by the medics was the Golden Hour. And, more vaguely, the Platinum Ten. None of it, blurred and hard to hold onto, seemed relevant. There was no one behind him and the enemy was long gone. Platinum Ten was about the emergency first aid that could be provided by the battlefield medical team, who would sweep in by Black Hawk or Chinook, an Apache riding gunship above them to suppress the bad guys' fire. The Golden Hour was the crucial time – so the lecturers said – between injury and receiving expert attention. It would not come in ten minutes or an hour. The forest around him was quiet again, except for the wind and the owl that mounted a vigil over him. The bird was close, on a low branch: he couldn't see it but its call was persistent – he was an intruder on its territory, he thought, and it wanted him gone. He should have lain still and waited for help, but hadn't believed it would come. He had crawled a little way from the steps, then came to a birch tree that blocked him. He had used his strength, the little he had, to bypass it, and had begun to crawl again. There was no hope of help.

He was as isolated as they would have been on the dunes, the shingle and the wide sands. No medics there. He had a better understanding of their situation than ever before. He crawled, an animal's instinct. He moved, didn't know where to.

20

He had come to a halt. Hadn't the strength to go further. He'd gone some 150 paces from the entry steps to the bunker. There was a low wall that might once have been the edge of a parking compound, and he rested against it. He managed to get his back upright, then sagged.

He was far beyond Platinum Ten and probably the Golden Hour. He had done what he could. But he couldn't stop the bleeding in his chest.

What he had achieved was a poor response to the 'sucking' of the chest wound. That had been the instructor's word, and the same science would have been employed to save lives on the battle coasts seven decades before, with few medics on hand. It was an open wound that sucked in air as his lungs heaved; he carried no occlusive dressing, no steriliser and no sanitised paper smeared with petroleum jelly. He'd heard once, from the battlefield surgeon who'd talked to them, that a driving licence would do the job. There had been a hesitant chuckle from that audience of experienced military men who were doing time in the Province – they were never alone, always had back-up close.

A driving licence could be wedged across an entry wound and the sucking of the cavity *might* hold it in place. It was bloody hard in darkness, with exhaustion setting in. He scrabbled his wallet from a zipped-up pocket. It fell clear; so did his phone. He had to scuffle to find the wallet, then pulled out the card. He clamped it on to the wound, and had his hand over it.

More of the briefing came back to him, but it slid. He was so tired . . . Five critical features to be checked and they were the first five letters of the alphabet. A was for Airway, and it was mostly clear, but blood was coming from his mouth and coughing hurt. B was Breathing, which was ragged and there were bubbling sounds from his lungs. C was Circulation, and the bleeding was internal. D was Disability/Deformity, which would have been a broken spine but the bullet hadn't hit bone or ligament. And E was for Exposure. A carer would have looked for the exit wound, treated it and tried to maintain a degree of cleanliness, but it was behind him, far down his back, and he couldn't reach it. The list of letters was about all he knew and, living in Caen, he had little call to know more – but the boys on the beaches wouldn't have known that much, and the medics wouldn't have reached them. Some would have had sand in their wounds, and more would have drowned when the tide came in later that day.

There was something he should do, but coherence slipped and he lost the thread.

Danny Curnow barely swam. He hung on but the water was around him and soon it would lap over him, covering his mouth, nose and eyes. Then he would see nothing but the darkness that was now around him. A few people were watching him, he was sure. Matthew Bentinick was there, and didn't encourage Vagabond to keep fighting. No: Bentinick stood tall and austere in his office clothes, watched him and took time off only to load more tobacco into his pipe. There was no criticism and no praise. Near to Bentinick, Gaby Davies had the posture of a young woman who had achieved a position of authority and was not prepared to let it slide: loose-fitting jeans, old trainers, feet apart, hands on hips, back straight in a shapeless anorak. The wind whipped her short dark hair but her eyes pierced him and would not be deflected. She was power. Dusty Miller was there – funny, that. Dusty didn't seem to recognise him. He was near to Bentinick and Gaby but wasn't focusing on his Vagabond. Danny heard himself call, 'Hey, Dusty, Desperate here, right in front of you, need a heave up. Not in a very good state . . .' But he didn't come. Neither did Karol Pilar, nor Malachy Riordan . . . And he saw fair hair, tugged by the wind off the sea, and heard a voice with a soft, guttural accent talk about 'commitment'.

Nobody came into the water and nobody took his wrist. He was sinking. More faces watched him, from the crypt of the church of St Cyril and St Methodius. They were surrounded and condemned, gazing at him.

Danny Curnow might have slept – but the ringing was too loud. He cursed it: he couldn't sleep if a bell rang so close to his face. He grappled for it. It persisted. The phone was what he had forgotten after the blow to his chest. He scrabbled among leaves and saw its dull light but couldn't reach it. It rang, teasing him.

Dusty stood by the window, his curtains wide. He could see across the yacht basin towards the old buildings of Caen. Christine slept a little noisily behind him, and he felt good. He actually felt blessed, as he always did when Christine came to him. She'd stay till nearly dawn, then would slip on her robe and tiptoe away. Of course her mother knew, but it was the ritual of the house. It might have been the same long ago when a young German officer had visited a back bedroom – perhaps with a view of the cliffs he would die defending – and shagged the teenage daughter. Because he felt blessed he had the phone to his ear.

He liked the girl, Hanne. He might get his privates chewed off, but the phone would be on vibration mode. He liked and admired her. One day, he might win a cuff on the shoulder from his friend and gruff thanks, rather than a chewing. He wanted to tell him what he'd done. The cool of the small hours was on his naked skin, and few cars moved below him. The masts rattled sharply and a few gulls screamed: truth was, and at his age it was unlikely, he felt a sort of softness he'd hardly admit to. He might get torn off a strip when the phone was answered – wherever Desperate was – and might not. It was worth the chance.

He listened, heard it ring out.

Very still, then relaxing. Listening. Gaining confidence. Ralph Exton moved. The call of the phone was a beacon for him. At first he was on his hands and knees, then on his feet but crouching. He tried to go slowly and make no noise but he scuffed leaves, crunched broken glass and broke twigs. He had been too long on his own and was cold, hungry, thirsty, and had been too long in fear. He went towards the phone.

Ralph Exton was not a man easily annoyed and seldom lost his temper. They had left him, and that angered him. He was used to Fliss winding him up – not many men he knew would have found the condom wrapping under the marital bed, then binned it. She was on the Pill so a condom meant a comparative stranger and the potential risk of HIV, so it had been a precaution against sexually transmitted disease. He remembered pausing beside the green and black bins behind the house and wondering if it was for recycling or landfill. He'd turned the cheek when she'd come back, late and flushed – she would have been with the dentist. His temper had held over breakfast when they'd had to send Toria to school – aged fourteen – with a love-bite on her throat. And he'd kept his temper when the cat had messed on the expensive carpet he'd brought back from Armenia. And when the village shop had indicated that credit was a thing of the past.

They had left him. The handler, the bully, wasn't there. The woman, happy enough to have a fling with him, had ditched him.

They had taken Timofey, his old mate. A devious bastard, but favours done had been returned, and his 7.5 per cent commission, plus expenses, on the deal was already banked. The driver had done an early runner, as had the guy from the Caucasus who had brought the gear. They weren't his problem.

Neither was Malachy Riordan, a hard fighter by reputation, but so obviously out of his depth and far from what was familiar, nor the girl who had gone missing. No problem with them.

Gaby Davies had responsibility for him and should have looked for him. Danny, who had never had another name, ought to have made bloody certain that Ralph Exton had a lift out of this place.

Then he had heard a voice, couldn't put a face to it, doing a monologue – it had gone unanswered, and he had stayed still. A shot had been fired, likely to have been from an AK assault rifle, and he had heard the noise of flight, then the phone. Didn't Gaby and Danny have a duty of care to him? He was quite close to where the phone was when it cut out.

No light, only the moon, and there was a vague silver mist above the ground, which insinuated itself between the trees. He saw the shapes of buildings. He was bent low as he walked. He stepped on the phone, which broke under his foot. He tripped on an inert shape and heard the wheeze, then the faint oath.

He steadied himself and the body winced. He peered down, squinted, could make out what might have been a driving licence or credit card and the fingers that held it in place. Danny. He remembered the voice – not the whispered curse, the bubble in it, or the wheeze. The voice he recalled had been crisp, quiet, could do it line by line and word by word: . . . *the ingratitude, or arrogance – unsure which – that leads to a paid informer, a betrayer of trust, forgetting who pays him . . . It's those horrible, big bloody computers and resources that are limitless. We can find you any time and any place . . . You would be at the mercy of a telephone call . . . a call to Russia or a call to Ireland, and an address given . . . Fuck about with me, Ralph – with me, not with Miss Davies – and we'd let you run awhile and the tension would near kill you and the fear of shadows and when you were on your knees and swearing suicide we'd make the call . . . Nasty old world.* No room for misunderstanding. That had been Thursday. This was the start of Saturday. It had been a long week – and a long one always left him tired, not thinking as clearly as he would have liked. He saw the man on the ground, the stain on the shirt and bare skin. He could have kicked him, could have walked on past him and gone into what was left of the night. Or he could have knelt, and did so.

He asked the obvious: 'Is it hurting much?'

'Still shock, but pain keeps coming.'

A stutter in the voice and the bubbling was back, with some froth. Ralph pushed his head forward so that his ear was against the mouth. 'It's a bit of a hole.'

'Two, actually. One at the back . . . Don't think of moving me. Best to leave alone. I don't suppose you're trained.'

'No. Never thought about it.'

'Well, it's not the sort of evening class they do in the village hall. Not the same as coronaries and blackouts and fractured hips.'

It had been a long sentence and seemed to tire him more. Ralph now had an arm under the guy's neck and held him steady. The eyes were wide and looked hard at him. They had been deep, dark and bright when he'd threatened, but had dulled. He thought it was how men would have been when a colleague was down on a battlefield . . . *How are the mighty fallen, And the weapons of war perished.*

He didn't know what to do.

'What were you shot with?

'The rifle he had for target work.'

'Bloody hell. Miserable beggar showed me a drill, power up, held it close, but I fooled him. Bad luck he was that close to you.'

'I taunted him, tried to break him. First step was to loose his cool, then walk on him.'

'What you did with me.'

More spittle was at the lips. He rummaged in his trouser pocket. A nurse would have bawled at him. Not a clean handkerchief, but what he had. He wiped Danny's lips and cursed that he had no water with him – and no knowledge.

'More success with you. Do you know where we are?'

'No idea.'

'Would anyone find us?'

'Wouldn't have thought so – we drove a hell of a way. I haven't a clue where we are, and I left my phone at the hotel. It's on charge. Sorry, but . . .'

'But? Sorry for what?'

'I stepped on yours, banjaxed it.' He did it with what he hoped was the lightness of casual conversation. Out of communication. Ralph didn't think he had the strength to dump the man, go off into the night and wave down a vehicle if he ever made it to a public road. He couldn't have left him.

'You've reason to hate me.'

'Never was good at that, hating people.'

'And reason to walk away.'

'Not in the mood. I'm all right where I am.' He used the handkerchief on the forehead where sweat was building.

'You ever had the feeling that a blind is about to be drawn on you? With the drill?'

'Not then. It was a bit bloody when they took me up the mountain in a van, no windows and hooded. But the face garb shifted and I saw what I was sharing the back with: bin liners they'd have used for contaminated clothing – blood or cordite – plenty of heavy tape for wrists and legs, and a spade for digging a hole. That wasn't great. Want to know what's been the worst eye to eye with a sticky end?'

'Want to know.'

'It was what you said to me, Danny. The burden, the fear, the over-your-shoulder stuff, folks hunting for me. That was as bad as anything.'

'Not much to say.'

'Don't fucking apologise. My wife, having a fling with a tooth-puller, tried to come clean and I shut her up. It puts you in the wrong when someone apologises. Anyway, what you did was in the name of the state.'

'I'm what they use, the justification.' So faint.

'And I'm what they do business with.' He spoke with a bogus cheerfulness, as if the confessional had little relevance and would be forgotten the next morning. They'd be right as rain, both of them.

'Puts us together.'

'Frogs in the same bucket. We're at the bottom and can't climb out until they decide we might be of no further use. If they're feeling good, they'll tip us into a pond. If they're not, well . . .'

'I'm not proud of what I did.'

'They didn't ask you to be proud, or wait in line for a medal. Did anyone ever stand on the pavement and watch you march by, full uniform, clap and thank you, show some gratitude? Can I tell you something, Danny?'

'Tell me.'

'You don't take it with you. You don't take the good or the bad. It's like the slate is wiped clean. No pockets in a shroud. Do you have a girl, Danny, who'll get you up and running?'

'Used to, should have.'

'Go after her, Danny. I might do the same myself. Danny, I think it'll be better when the light comes, not too long. Then they'll be out looking for us. Why not get a bit of sleep?'

'I might.'

'There's no hate, Danny.' His eyes welled.

'Thanks.'

The tears ran down his cheeks. He fought to keep the quaver out of his voice. 'Get a bit of sleep, and you'll feel better for it. Pity there isn't a cup of tea.'

An Austrian long-distance haulier, en-route to Berlin, picked up a man he believed to be a Briton from the side of the road. He was glad of the company and would drop his hitch-hiker on the outskirts of Prague. He shared his sausage with him and his coffee.

A van waited for them at a lay-by on the road that ran from the Czech town of Teplice to the German community at Altenberg. The frontier was a kilometre ahead.

The detective had talked incessantly and she had listened reluctantly. 'Russian organised crime groups have broken our nation's faith in the country's institutions. They have infiltrated them and targeted the political élite. Godfathers are linked to the judiciary, *mafiosi* to elected representatives.'

Two men lifted the trussed figure and he was carried from the boot of the car to the van's rear doors. One checked a pulse and nodded. They shook hands. Gabrielle Davies believed a degree of formality was appropriate and Karol Pilar made no attempt to kiss her cheek.

'It is the equivalent of every inhabitant of the Czech Republic paying thirty pounds a month because of the theft by the Mafia. They have stolen our country. We don't know now who owns us, which faceless thieves. They have penetrated all that we value. Elections are a theatrical sideshow. Corruption is an assault on the principle that everyone is equal before the law.'

Good work achieved, a task well done, and both would have

reckoned themselves central to the success. She was driven forward, ignored a *Nicht Rauchen* sign on the dash and accepted the offer of a Marlboro Lite. She didn't look into the mirror to see the disappearing tail-lights of the Czech's little car.

He had said, 'I tell you, Miss Davies, that the Solntsevo organisation from Moscow and the Tombovskaya group from St Petersburg have made huge investments, billions of Czech *koruna* in Prague and Karlovy Vary. They safeguard their most important routes for trafficking prostitutes, weapons and narcotics. Our territory is a highway to them.'

Less than fifty kilometres to the strip, around a half-hour drive.

He had continued, 'You have won a fist-fight – and I am pleased for you, Miss Davies – but not a war. And, please, do not think your own country, Great Britain, is safe against this infiltration. Nowhere is safe. Do not be complacent. It was good to work with you, and a pleasure to be with Danny. Give him my good wishes.'

Now she texted again.

He was asleep. Jocelyn observed Matthew Bentinick, head on his arms, the upper body moving as he breathed. The message was already with the director general. She had accepted congratulations.

She woke him, a gentle hand on his arm. There might have been something, once, if things had been different. He started, for a moment was uncertain of his bearings, then regained his composure. He straightened his tie, smoothed his hair. She showed him the printout of the text received and a smile – short, wintry – slipped across his face. He thanked her. She said that a car was waiting at the side door on Horseferry Road, that she'd call him when the aircraft lifted. He was out of his chair, shook himself, cleared his throat, then was gone down the corridor, leaving the echo behind him of his shoes. Jocelyn turned off the lights and locked up after him.

She would be another hour in her room and expected George to drift down and take a small glass with her: he usually did when an operation went so flawlessly.

* * *

An aircraft flew from Germany into the Netherlands as a prisoner was brought to the jurisdiction of a court. The man sat hunched, aware of his surroundings and their implications. He was handcuffed, unable to smoke and could drink only water. He would be disowned by the morning and his territory would be scrapped over by predators. They were in turbulence, an autumn storm tossing them. He felt fear, and could remember as a child seeing that same fear on the features of new men brought to Perm 35.

He was surprised at how considerably Henry Carter had aged. But still, so many years after his formal retirement, he was reputed to be 'an officer of thorough integrity'. The man stooped but had a pleasant smile. Must have been at least eighty. The good thing about Henry Carter, an archivist of quality used on both sides of the river, was that he had long before lost sight of the personalities of the day. He wrote reports. They were without bias because he was unaffected by factions on the rise and those losing influence, and seemed to have retained the ability to cut to the quick. He professed to admire birds more than people, and could be feisty but usually held it in check. A good man, useful, but seemed frail in his suit. His eyebrows needed a trim.

The hand the director general shook was thin, the veins prominent and the skin discoloured, but the grip was firm. From a briefcase, scuffed but with the old EIIR symbol still visible below the lock, a folder was taken and handed over. Carter was a veteran, had done time on that ghastly fence dividing the Germanys and had run an agent across, waiting through the night for him. He understood the work in the building, regardless of the passage of time and changed operating procedures. The director general took the folder. He would read typed pages because Carter still eschewed the keyboard and screen. He glanced discreetly at his watch. He was due to lunch at the American embassy – their man was up for rotation and would be happy to get the hell out of London in the grip of November. He thanked Carter and escorted him to the outer office; a probationer would take him down to the canteen for a sandwich.

He went back into his office and buzzed his PA: he didn't want to be disturbed before the car came to ferry him to Grosvenor Square.

The folder was titled 'Vagabond'. The director general imagined he would enjoy reading it: the operation had engendered satisfaction. He lingered on the word. *Vagabond.* He opened the file. There was a précis on top, then the full version below. He took the briefer one. There were to be contributions by principal players, then Carter's remarks, and there was space in the margins for him to add his comments.

Quiet settled in the room, and he read the first page.

Statement of Gabrielle Davies, Security Service Officer

It was a good operation throughout and I was able to maintain positive levels of control at all times. My team worked well under my leadership. The 'rendition' of Timofey Simonov, listed as a Target of Value (our sole priority), met no obstructions at the Czech/German frontier, where the new personnel awaited us and we dropped the Czech policeman. The flight was uneventful and I have no record of any significant remark by TS. On the ground, TS was read his rights by local officials and they signed for his custody. I then returned to London. It has been put to me that it was 'poor procedure' to leave Daniel Curnow (increment) and Ralph Exton (covert human intelligence source) on site at the former military base of Milovice. They should have kept close to me, followed my instructions, and not permitted themselves to be separated. I accept no blame for their being split from the main party of us at a time of some confusion as we engaged ruthless and experienced criminals. Digitalised images of TS and Malachy Riordan with weapons have now been transferred to local prosecutors, and will augment earlier images of TS at his residence with the CHIS. My conclusion: the recruitment of the 'increment' was an unnecessary expense and he added little to the outcome of the operation.

Ambitious, able, but lacking verve or imagination and unlikely to think outside the loop. I believe she has a good future in the Service and will go far.

Promote her, let her rip, then find her level behind a desk. Watch her and look to advance her career.

Statement of Karol Pilar, detective UOOZ team, Prague
Following the transfer of the accused to a foreign jurisdiction I drove across country to Karlovy Vary and gained a vantage-point looking at the villa on Krale Jiriho, residence of Timofey Simonov. The prized dogs were left in the yard for the night – the king is dead, long live the king – and Brigadier (ret'd) Nikolai Denisov slept with his wife in the main first-floor front bedroom (formerly occupied by TS). I was not present the following evening but Denisov and wife used TS's invitation to attend a charity gala at Hotel Pupp. (Relevant or not relevant?) My seniors dictate no further action will be taken against this Russian national and believe dust should be permitted to settle. It was a pleasure, and good experience, to work alongside Daniel Curnow. I was privileged.

A good officer whose modesty should not be allowed to mask his talents and input into the success of the operation. He should be cultivated and used where appropriate . . . I fear his hatred of organised crime groups (Russian ethnic origin) will stunt his promotion prospects in Prague.

An important catch, and worth serious remuneration. Buy him and own him.

Statement of Jocelyn Ferguson, Security Service
A good operation, well performed at all stages by Five staff. I think, already, a significant message has been sent. My latest information is that the prosecutors in the criminal case against Simonov (Timofey), to be brought to trial early next year, are very confident that allegations of illegal weapons transfers, using transport based in Belgium, will be proven. The evidence submitted will cause, hopefully, maximum embarrassment in Moscow's siloviki *circles. Without the drive of Matthew Bentinick, nothing would have been achieved.*

A formidable administrator, lacking in morality, with a compulsion for hard work, and a devotion to MB that is not entirely appropriate.

Should be separated in the building. Right for the jihadist teams.

Statement of DS Conor Williams, MPS Special Branch.
The arrest of an unidentified marksman in south-west London when staking a safe-house where a Russian national lived under our protection will have severely unsettled FSB operatives at the Kensington Palace Gardens embassy. The subsequent suicide is not important: the damage is done to them and they will sweat on it.

An excellent result. Where would we be without the help of dog walkers and mums on the way to and from the school gate? The best eyes and ears we have.

Letter of thanks, oil the cogs, to commissioner, Metropolitan Police Service.

Statement of Matthew Bentinick, Security Service officer
I led a dedicated team and am delighted to report success in all areas of the operation. It was a job well done. I was particularly pleased with the efforts of Gabrielle Davies. I congratulate her and am happy to say she exceeded my expectations in leadership and performance. I pay tribute to those in less substantial roles, including former sergeant, Intelligence Corps, Daniel Curnow, Vagabond from days of old, but regret that in the final stages his actions fell outside his immediate brief. We hurt our opponents and cannot ask for much more. There may be some who suggest my rigour in pursuing this case is governed by a personal situation – quite untrue and an unworthy accusation. I regret what happened to Curnow but we are in a grown-up world – as he well knew. He would have accepted that only the breaking of eggs leads to the making of an omelette.

A warrior from a bygone age, finding it difficult, I assume, to conjure up sufficient worthwhile enemies. To resurrect something of Cold War times and to have linkage with the present stuttering campaign of the Republican 'left-behinds' in the Province would have brought a rare opportunity for his talents to be showcased. Amusing, likeable and utterly vulnerable, he is idiosyncratic in taste and style but remains a welcome and refreshing breath of air from the 'by-numbers' box-tickers that I occasionally feel have taken ownership of the twin Services. However, his treatment of Curnow is unsatisfactory by current risk assessment and duty of care requirements. Does the end justify the means? Others must decide whether this 'end' was worth the high price paid.

Devious beggar, but effective, and who among us can appreciate the torment of his daughter's situation? Sometimes crass, but utterly incisive in decision-taking. Ruthless, but should not more personnel in the Service demonstrate that trait?

Statement of Ralph Exton, covert human intelligence source
I did what I could, thought I did it quite well. I make my own bed and I lie in it, so, I left myself open to pressure from your lot and have only myself to blame. As I always say when life gets fruity, 'Fuck me . . . Another day at the office . . . Fuck me', and usually the sentiment tides me over. Everyone I dealt with from Thames House was an utter shit, with neither manners nor concern for me, like I was some mid-European slapper brought in to scrub the toilets. I wouldn't give them, again, the time of day. An exception? There's always one. Danny. Hold a bloke in your arms – when all the others have buggered off to collect their medals and herograms – while he's slipping and bleeding, and when you've been abandoned, and you get kind of fond of him. He'd been tough on me. No question. But he was honest. Never dealt with anyone else who had that honesty, real truthfulness, told it like it was. Brilliant guy. The whole history of what happened is in the safe-deposit box of a solicitor who practises human rights, state abuses, all that

crap, so don't come after me and expect me not to scratch your bloody eyes out.

And me? Not too bad, thank you. My wife found out, painfully, that her dentist friend was putting himself around and had done a bunk, sharpish, because the husband turned up with a weighty wrench. We had a chat, her and me. We go back a long way, good times and awful ones. We're selling up in the leafy lanes, and think we're getting a good price. We're looking at an opening for an antiques business on the coast at Torbay. Our daughter's coming with us. I hate all of you, which is rare for me, and despise you, too. I'm quite sorry about poor old Timofey S: pompous but not altogether bad, and probably not deserving the twenty years' gaol he'll get. The exception? I can't and won't ever hate Danny Curnow, a first-class guy. You'd have been bare-arsed without him.

A lovely man, and great fun to be with. Deprecating about his personal courage but as brave as a lion. The story about the drill, not making a drama from a crisis, is apposite. He made me laugh. Torbay is a good choice: all those trawlers floating about and reeling in fish and so much else that's been dropped off in the high seas – many opportunities for scratching a living. Antiques, brand new or recently new, should be right for his entrepreneurial skills. I think he'll come through well, and has the resilience. I hope the Service will take responsibility for his and his family's safety. In the forest, before that hung-over stag group showed up to drive a tank, alone with Curnow, he displayed great tenderness when others had bolted. The Service should take the responsibility seriously.

What am I supposed to do? He's a tout, inherently dishonest, untrustworthy. Shouldn't be permitted airs and graces, and if he's above himself then a tax inspector may pay a visit. (A judge in chambers to place a gagging order.) I'll not be blackmailed. Should be cut off and left to swim, or to sink.

Statement of Sebastian James, Security Service officer, Palace Barracks, NI

Acting on London instructions I visited the hide behind the Riordan farm on that Saturday evening. I was in place when a taxi dropped Malachy Riordan at the end of the farm lane. I have no psychiatric training but he looked to me a devastated and insecure man. He came home and was greeted by his family, who were back from the double funeral of the bomb casualties. He sat outside his door, with his dog, through the evening and late into the night. I stayed (had PSNI back-up) and when the dawn came he was out again. Strange: he seemed to know that someone was watching, but did nothing. He looked up often enough, as if searching for me, and I was ready to bug out fast if he came. He didn't. Every other time I've seen him he was a character of presence, importance and authority, but that's gone, like a snake's shed skin.

Two women came. I identified them as Attracta Donnelly, widow of a prominent PIRA fighter, KIA 1991, and Siobhan Nugent, also a widow but her husband was murdered as an informer in the same year: now close friends. I could not hear the words used but the body language showed he was under fierce criticism and could not rebut it. This is the mountain of the legendary Shane Bearnagh, the 'rapparee' or guerrilla fighter of centuries ago, and these are fiercely independent and resourceful opponents. Whatever happened, Riordan was a man destroyed and seemed to ride their punches, verbal, like a fighter waiting for the towel to come into the ring. Extraordinary. What happened when he was away is outside my remit.

Subsequent intelligence indicates Malachy Riordan is a spent force, ignored and humiliated. Something else that first day. From my POV, and with my binoculars, I could see a deserted barn, 1500 yards due east of the Riordan farm. In my work area there is an old stager, a former major in a Fusiliers unit. He runs the CHIS, Antelope. He met that morning, I had decent eyeball, with Brendan (Brennie) Murphy: local strategist and motivator. I assume Antelope and Murphy are one and the same. They should not meet again in that location. Anyway, Riordan is now – my opinion – history, a busted flush. I do not expect him to survive.

Concerning lines 6 to 1 from bottom: should be redacted. I understand that Riordan was a secondary target, but the result stands up well in comparison to the main objective. A dangerous man removed from a combat zone. He obviously murdered Frances McKinney, but I fancy that an additional confrontation took place at Milovice before he shot Daniel Curnow: I cannot speculate, except that Curnow damaged him irreparably. Interesting. Riordan is walking dead. He seems to know and fear it.

A silly young man, Sebastian James, imagining himself clever. A vacancy might arise, with swift expedition, for the teaching of intelligence-gathering to local forces – Baghdad or Kabul?

Statement of Hector Mackay, consul, FCO, Calais
I was at the funeral, as HMG representative, of Daniel Curnow, UK citizen but resident in Caen, France. The interment was in the British military cemetery at 49 rue de Fumes, Dunkirk. The Commonwealth War Graves commission, under pressure from a nameless London-based agency, had agreed to find a grave site within the confines, at the extreme north-east corner near the canal. It will carry his name, and the logo 'Vagabond'. It was a small occasion, a padre from a base in Germany, a Mr Dusty Miller, who claimed to be a life-long friend, a blonde woman, who declined to identify herself to me – she asked the gravedigger to place a picture in the gap between the coffin and the earth but I did not see what it showed – and two French females from the house in Caen where Mr Curnow had lived. Also, a representative of a battlefield-tour company. There were medals on the coffin, quite a few. It was short and no refreshments were served afterwards. We all went our various ways.

Poor that the Service, amid such enthusiastic self-congratulation, was not present: a stain on its reputation. I wish I had known him, not that it would have been easy. He would have been a man I respected. He did his duty, but few thought it necessary to offer gratitude. A different world, thankfully not mine. Yes, I would have liked to know him, and walk with him on those beaches.

I'll not take lecturing from Carter. An old man doing an Icarus imitation. Wax can get burned and it's a long way down. We did well and behaved with discretion. I'm aware of necessary etiquette.

Conclusion of Carter, Henry
In brief: a successful operation but insufficient regard paid to the costs it would incur. Some might feel shame for that; others might not.

We will not indulge in Stalinist or Cuban self-flagellation. At the end of the day, among all the cock-ups and cut-backs, we did something that was professionally satisfying. A downside with Vagabond but not nearly outweighing the good. Remember Matthew's damn omelette.

He closed it. Tomorrow was another day, and a cabal of northern Islamists was due to have its front doors stoved in during the hour before dawn. It was unlikely that he would ever find time to read the full version, but his chief of staff, a young man with prospects, would annotate and put in place his margin notes. The PA was at the door, holding his coat, hat and gloves, and told him the car was waiting.

It was a cold afternoon and that bitter wind was coming down the coast off the Dutch and Belgian shores, seeming to sweep the dunes. Wide sands had been left by a retreating tide and Dusty, by now, was capable of imagining the long lines of patient men who had waited there, hoping for a lift out. The guide had the tourists and they were on a concrete slipway, but Dusty was left to himself and could imagine. God, he missed Desperate. The sand was in his face, his shoes and his hair. There were runners on the beach, down by the water line, and a couple of heavy-tonnage bulk carriers far out, on the way south from Rotterdam. He missed him so much that his soul ached.

The whistle came. The clouds were low, scudded, and there might be a frost or at least some sleet. Always, at this time of year, with the full force of winter beckoning, the guide had to marshal the visitors and keep up the time discipline. They wouldn't wish to be at the cemetery when the dark made it impossible to read the names, units and ages. He caught the movement back towards the minibus and scurried to be there before them. The most important moment of his week was Monday evening when the visitors were at Dunkirk to learn of the evacuation and see the place. Most were crushed by it. The cemetery always upset them too. It upset Dusty.

The second most important moment was the Sunday night when he'd drive up from Caen and buy some flowers at a petrol station. He could lean over the wall of the graveyard, which was locked, and drop them on the one plot that was aside from the others.

On the Monday he could go there, stand at the right end, close to where Desperate's feet would be. So calm in that place. The girl had left Honfleur, and the tour-company people never laid a posy. Only Dusty came.

He had a clear idea of what Desperate would have said, that first evening after he was put in there and the place was shut up for the night. 'Sorry if I've disturbed you, boys. Thanks for finding space for an old 'un. I'm Vagabond, no fixed abode – well, not till now. Anyway, better late than never.'

He went to the minibus, leaving the greyness of the sea behind him. He would drive to the cemetery, and the guide would keep the visitors on the move. They'd be the last out before the clang of the gate. It was always difficult, saying farewell to an old friend. He turned his back on the sea, and the sand, and drove. He could never get the face of his friend out of his mind, but didn't want to. He'd say it to himself often enough, silent but with his lips moving: 'You know why they brought you back, why they did it? Because they knew of no one better to get than the call-sign Vagabond. Never was anyone better.'